I0738056

APRIL AND THE GARDENER

APRIL AND THE GARDENER

DOUGLAS GRANT MINE

STACKED
STONE

APRIL AND THE GARDENER
Published by Stacked Stone Books
Copyright © Douglas Grant Mine 2022
ISBN 978-0-578-36441-4

Cover design by Nicoletta Spendolini
Cover painting by Arnoldo López Campos

per Nicoletta
la fonte di tutto

TABLE OF CONTENTS

Part 1: 1995 Agua, Fuego, Acatenango 1

Part 2: 1985-86 Hey Joe, Where You Goin' With that Gun in Your Hand? 153

Part 3: 1995 Friends, Enemies and Family 255

Part One
1995
Agua, Fuego, Acatenango

CHAPTER 1: A HANDSOME MAN

April Tashima stepped out of the rain into the San Francisco church where the old dry crumbled bones of Hermano Pedro lay entombed. Shifting the shoulder strap of the big Betacam SP, she made her way down the dim left-side aisle to the sepulcher. Taped-up notes scrawled in humble hands adorned the walls of the white marble crypt. Replete with spelling errors, they thanked this man the people of Guatemala believed to be a saint for his intervention in curing the affliction of the suppliant or the petitioner's mother or child or wife or husband. Better-off pilgrims had left tin or brass plates in the shape of a foot, or lungs like twin eggplants, an ear, a glaring eye, depending on what body part had been restored to soundness.

No wang and balls though, April noted. Propriety apparently outweighed gratitude among the formerly infertile or limp. Either that or celibate Brother Pete rejected lascivious entreaties out of hand. Studying the tributes, savoring respite from the morning's steady drizzle, she thought: How out of their fucking gourds were these holy men and women of old? Francesco, namesake of this church and her own California hometown, traipsing through Umbrian meadows nattering with the birds. And delirious Jeanne, the mortally confused cross-dressing maid of Orléans. Then there was Friar Pedro Betancur, who died in 1667 after a few decades of whipping himself raw and drinking vinegar and licking the suppurating wounds of mendicants and writing letters in his own blood to María madre de Dios. He spent so much time crawling, burdened, past the Stations of the Cross leading to Calvario Church on Antigua's eastern edge that when he finally succumbed to self-imposed or divinely imposed rigors, monks cut the calluses off his knees and sliced them up as relics.

Back out on the cobbled streets, her purposeful wandering resumed, April paused in the doorway of *la Casa de los Gigantes*. Two huge gaudy wooden mannequins stared out from mammoth chairs. Turning to continue on her way, she noticed a man sitting on the sidewalk a half-block ahead.

She approached him. He was long and lanky and passed out on alcohol. He sat with his back against the sky-blue wall of the house whose façade defined the edge of the sidewalk. His legs were bent in wickets, with the soles of his feet flat against the cracked cement walkway so that his body was out of the rain, protected by the roof's overhang.

April and the Gardener

April stood there looking at him. The street was deserted. A narrow muddy stream meandered down the middle of it. A mutt the color of wet bread observed her from his refuge beneath the eaves of the house on the opposite side.

She might have stepped around the man and continued on, to Tony's for a coffee or a mug of chocolate at Caffé Opera where she could chat with the Italian twins, if it hadn't been for his feet. For his beat-up black rubber boots and the way the legs of his pants had hiked above their tops. He wasn't wearing socks.

The man's stature and posture, the degree of the bend of his stony knees, had determined that his bare brown shins intersected the beaded curtain of raindrops stringing from the roof tiles just before they hit the sidewalk. The angle of his legs had left the boot-tops stretched outward, away from the shin, so that the footwear was transformed into receptacles like pitchers. They had filled up with rainwater and were overflowing, spilling gently like a spring.

She reached back and drew a tripod from a quiver-like sheath, then stepped down off the high sidewalk to the rounded stones and extended its tubular legs. She screwed them locked so that the apex was just above her waist, then slid the plastic-sheathed camera onto the base plate and clamped it. Hunched over her instrument in the rain, April peered through the viewfinder and zoomed in on the tops of the boots, in case he should pick this of all moments to shift or rouse himself. She zoomed out slightly so that both boots were entirely in the picture, the legs from just below the knee traversing the frame diagonally, dividing a patch of wet gray sidewalk from a triangle of azure wall. The only movement was drops hitting the surface of the oblong pools, and rivulets running down from the boots' rain-dimpled brims.

She held the shot for about 10 seconds. Then she panned slowly to the left a half-meter down the sidewalk to a pair of empty four-ounce bottles of pharmaceutical ethyl alcohol, white crosses emblazoned on red circles on the frosted plastic. Raindrops pattered around the bottles. One hit one and shifted the cylinder a half-turn. She drifted slowly back to the right and upward along the angle of shin until she came to the man's face.

His head hung forward and to one side, resting on the collarbone. He wore a dirty pale green sweatshirt emblazoned with the seal of Georgetown University. Clear mucus seeped from both nostrils down to cracked lips the color of plums. The sienna tone of his complexion had acquired a tinge of purple, the work of the emancipating poison in his blood. His mouth was slightly open.

There was a faint sigh and whistle from his dreamless peaceful breathing. He looked to be about 30, April's age. Sparse black whiskers stubbled his upper lip and chin but the jaw line was *lampiño* silken smooth. Tiny beads of water like diamonds, dew left by the drunk-fairy, sparkled in his long black eyelashes.

Overall, thought Professor Tashima of UC Berkeley, Except for the snot, he's a very handsome man. And that's with his eyes closed.

She stopped filming and picked up her camera, tripod and all, and went several paces back up the sidewalk, where she made a brief wider shot of the man and the street. Then she disassembled the equipment. When she was draped again with tripod and camera, she dug into the pocket of her jeans and pulled out a crumpled 50 quetzal note, a little less than ten dollars. She bent over and stuffed it into the pocket of his pants.

He didn't stir.

She walked away immensely pleased. There's the opening shot, she told herself, and the rest starts rushing once you've found a good beginning.

CHAPTER 2: PEELED WHOLE TOMATOES

(The Gardener, Take 3)

It was over a white guy, of all things.

It turned out later he wasn't white-white. But he sure looked it the first time I saw him. Green eyes a color I'd never seen except maybe in a dream, in the face of an animal, some kind of cat. Hair like wheat, curly blond tangled with light brown. Big square movie-star jaw. All he was doing was buying a hot-dog and a soda in the 7-Eleven two blocks from my house in L.A. He was up front at the counter and I was about halfway down the aisle, deciding between brands of canned tomatoes. Just plain peeled tomatoes, because my mother was going to make a big spaghetti dinner that night, with *abuela* and my aunt and uncle and cousin, *toda la mara*. She liked to cook up her own sauce, with little cubes of bacon, onions and garlic, a big carrot and a celery stick, rather than buy ready-made. It was a celebration, see. I'd received a letter of acceptance from Stanford. And they were giving me a scholarship that covered everything. Tuition, room and board, backscratcher, cough drops. Every damn thing. Back in those days I wanted to be a veterinarian. Which now could seem like an unlikely aspiration for a person like myself. And may have been a little strange even then, me being a city boy and all. We never even had a dog. It wasn't dogs and cats I wanted to treat, though. Or even cows and horses. My big idea was to be a vet at a zoo. Deliver baby rhinos, set a tiger's broken leg, that sort of thing. It sounds extravagant, I know. But I was used to everybody–teachers and guidance counselors and coaches–telling me I could be anything I wanted to be. And that was on top of my Moms, who was always very high on me and my capabilities. A very encouraging mother, one of the single variety. So something out of the ordinary was not out of the question. Not at all. It was perfectly normal. Anyway, I liked biology and had an aptitude for hard science. Another thing that was a possibility in the back of my mind was research. I figured maybe if I liked the academic life enough to stick with it through a PhD, I might become a research biologist, instead of a vet. Work at a university. Decode genetics. Wear the white coat, run the lab. Play on the faculty softball team. Marry a sexy literature or cinema studies professor. So on this day I'm talking about I was in the store to get canned tomatoes when this guy who looked out of place–

because you don't see that many pale dudes outside their cars in that part of the city–he walks up to the counter and asks the girl for a chili-dog and a Sprite. She'd just given him the drink when four Mexican kids came in. Two of them wore long baggy shorts and wife-beater t-shirts. They had homeboy tats they'd given each other, I guess, when they were all glued up or wired or drunk or in juvenile detention; *Perdóname, Virgencita,* that kind of *mojado* shit. Their girlfriend's name scratched into skin stretched over the kind of stringy muscles that somehow develop and get strong despite a bad diet of tortillas and Kool-Aid. The other two were pachucos in chinos and, despite the heat outside, long-sleeved plaid shirts buttoned at the collar but open down the front over a white tee. Gangsters. *Pendejos.* One had on a hair-net even though his head was buzzed almost bald. The lead Mex says to the girl, a black teenager: "Gimmee a large grape Slurpee." "Soon as I finish with this customer," says the girl, spooning beans onto the wiener with her back to the counter. She was Jamaican or something. Had an islands accent. For no reason *el masucho* looks the white guy up and down in an exaggerated way. Punk clown cholo jerk-off with his hands on his hips and this crazy *mueca* on his face. But *el rubio* just stood there waiting for his hot-dog, not paying these guys any attention. He didn't even turn his head. Then the Mex, who talked like a black dude with a Spanish accent, says to the girl: "Make it snappy now little Rasta posse ho. We ain't got all day." The other Mexicans laughed. One of them, the one with the net and a pocked-up face, had this wind-sucking high-pitched cackle like a hyena. The girl turned around and looked at the main man. She had this look of disbelief and sophisticated West Indian indignation, standing there with a cardboard dog-boat in one hand and a spoon in the other. It was cool in the store. Outside the parking lot asphalt was melting under a huge blinding chrome ball in the sky. A solo guitar riff, George Benson, something smooth like that, was sliding out of hidden speakers. And this girl says something like: "How dare you come in here and speak to me like that?" It didn't even register on the Mex. "An' gimme that *pinche* chili-dog, too," he says. The blond kid, who was about the same age as the Mexes, early 20s, a coupla years older than me it looked like, now he speaks up. And now that you looked at him, he was a fuckin' tree-trunk of a kid. Thick neck and keg chest and big hands, like a fuckin' bear. "What's your problem?" he says, in English, fixing the Mexican with those green eyes. Only three words. He said them in a low voice and pronounced them well enough. But I thought I caught a slight accent. A familiar one. "Maybe I don' have no problem, *guero,* if it ain't you pussy-lip face. Maybe is you got a problem," says the top *carnal.* And he pulls a switchblade from the pocket of his shorts. It snapped open real loud. Louder than any mechanism you'd think would belong to such a small piece of equipment. But if the Mexican's intention was to intimidate, *pa'que el guero quedara quieto en el molde,* he failed completely. The white guy just fuckin' smiled, if you can believe that. He set his can of Sprite on the counter and the smile turned to a grimace-like thing. It was a fearsome face, maybe more so because it remained somehow slightly amused. The Mexican might as well have been pointing a finger at him, and not a five-inch blade. *Y el rubio hijo de la chingada* takes two measured steps toward the kid and when he steps into striking range the Mex feints a jab at his belly then whips his arm out and up to bring it down in a slash like he wanted to cut this guy's entire white face off in one swoop. I don't know. The blond kid was invulnerable. Like he was standing at a point of cosmic confluence, in some kind of protective shaft. Or maybe it was just agility and experience combined with a total absence of fear. Whatever it was, he made a kind of dip and step to the side and caught the other kid's forearm in both big hands, one at the elbow and one at the wrist. Now he'd practically evened the odds. I mean it was already a partial victory. But without pausing to appreciate this or re-appraise the situation, he brought the arm like an ear of corn to his face, his mouth wide open, big *pinche* horses' teeth gleaming. And he chomps through skin and muscle and tendon, right down to the bone. It was like watching a wild animal. He grunts and gnaws for a second and shakes his head and pulls away a chunk of meat. This he spits in the Mexican's face, which by this time is also pretty pale, kinda light gray, and contorted. The knife fell to the floor. One of the pachucos took a step backward, toward me but with his back to me, and pulled a gun from the waist of his pants at the small of his back. He pointed the gun at the guero, holding it in his right arm stuck out straight at shoulder level but with a twist in the wrist, the gun horizontal on its side. *"Sueltalo!"* he screams. He musta thought he was the macho in this movie. But his yell was all hysterical and girlish. The guero lets go of the whimpering Mex's arm and turns his attention to the other one. Now, I've come to believe, from seeing it with my own eyes on several occasions during the war and experiencing it *en carne propia* maybe twice in combat, that there's something inherent in a state of mind that is indifferent to survival, when for one reason or another at a given moment you don't give a shit at all if you live or die, that tends to place a person beyond harm. I say tends to, because it doesn't work all the time. *Y este chele*, who it turned out was of Basque descent with maybe one Mestizo great-grandparent and whose name was Pedro Garay, had the previous night been sent by his girlfriend to the fifth stage of hell. Told to get lost. The only problem was that he was crazy about this girl. And he'd been contemplating, while waiting for his chili-dog, driving up the California coast a ways in his shiny new silver Audi and flying it off a cliff into the sea. So when he looked at the second Mexican and at the hole in the barrel of the revolver aimed at his chest, he was undaunted. Maybe he was even hoping the sensation of a bullet puncturing him would blot out the pain. I saw something like that in his eyes. Like resignation. Even if it was at the same time a murderous resignation. He took his eyes off the gun and looked right at me, eight or nine paces down the aisle. And I saw him start to smile again. But only the initial movement of his bloody mouth. Because the next thing I knew my focus was on the back of Pachuco's head. I let fly with a play-at-the-plate heave a 20-ounce can of Kern's *tomates enteros pelados en su jugo.* Well. Yeah. I always had a good arm. I was the 1st Team All-L.A. County centerfielder, for Christ's sake. The can sailed true. It rotated a bit so it was a lip-edge that made first contact with scalp and skull. The guy dropped like I'd pulled the lever of a gallows trap. Pedro pounced like a fucking jaguar over to the crumpled Mexican. He squatted and picked up the gun and pointed it at the other members of the defeated little tribe. None of them moved except for the one with the bitten arm. He had the wound, which was dripping, clamped with his good hand and was moaning and making a rapid bowing motion like a Japanese diplomat on bad crank. Pedro picks up the can with his other hand. He looks at the label and says, in Central American Spanish: *"Puta madre. Estos son Chapines como yo."* "These are Guatemalan like me." He looks up at me.

"Vos venís conmigo. No te podés quedar aquí con estos cerotes."

TRANSCRIBER'S NOTE: Don't think I didn't ask myself *What's the use?* before I decided to do this. This listening and typing. After all, no one besides April can see it. Nobody can be permitted to read it with Juan's name attached to it and there's no way calling him by an alias would hide who he is and what he's done and prevent him from being arrested and prosecuted and, probably, eventually, strapped to a gurney and infused slowly, under bright lights before witnesses, into oblivion.

Yeah, this is hazardous material. Dangerous not only to Juan, but to me and April, too, as aiders and abettors. But I decided that abetting Juan and aiding April is a good use of my time.

So during a long winter in a frigid part of the United States, I'm spending a few evenings a week transcribing the audio from five 90-minute videotapes. I load a tape into a Betacam VTR borrowed from the anthropology department and sit on the worn green leather sofa in my off-campus apartment with laptop on lap and the remote between me and my lazy curly-haired dog and dedicate a couple hours to tapping out the words of Juan Cano.

Most of the tapes show Juan talking to the camera. There's a tape in here with me talking, too, but I haven't gotten to that one. For much of his time on-screen, Juan is seated in a wooden chair before a wall adorned with a swatch of coarse cotton fabric–red, brown and purple–woven on a Maya back-strap loom. Sometimes he's outside in a tropical courtyard, next to a tree or a flowering bush. The camera is motionless for the most part.

Juan is telling the story of his life. But he talks, too, about the flora of those benevolent climes.

During this frozen season I've also been working on a piece about Gonzalo Guerrero for submission to a quarterly journal.

Guerrero was a would-be conquistador from Palos, Spain, a shipwrecked soldier-sailor who washed up blistered and parched nearly to death on the shores of the Yucatan peninsula near Tulúm in 1516. He survived and, incredibly, thrived. He became a hero of storied deeds until, as a grandfather and still a warrior, he was killed by an erstwhile countryman with a blunderbuss and fell from his Maya war canoe into the clear waters off the coast of what today is Honduras.

April and the Gardener

Nothing keeps me from writing as much as I know or am able to infer about the man I sometimes think of as "Gonzo" Guerrero. Given the fantastic scope of the Spaniard's life, I fear doing him little justice. But I plug away in the conviction that, from the skeleton provided, the reader will fill the gaps and add the guts and construct an imagined man worthy of the real one who sweated and slaved and loved and sired and fought and, not least in my estimation, learned well a new and difficult language.

About the other man, the contemporary one whose name is Juan Cano (but who goes these days by another), I can set down in digital files everything that individual says. I figure it will take a month or two, this task that is partly a favor to April but something, too, of a tribute to Juan. At the same time it's a connection to a part of my own life–half a year in the hills of El Salvador a decade ago–that I'm finally willing to examine. The fact of having been wounded right at the end of that adventuresome stretch had previously put me in a frame of mind ascribing it all to foolishness. For a long time, it was something I didn't want to think about.

These years later, though, after a second turn in that part of the world, I feel differently. Knowing Juan, having been alongside him way back then and now more recently, and listening to the rest and typing Juan's story have combined to cultivate the desire–the need, really–to reflect on my own deeds. "To ponder it well," as it says on the wall of my campus office in the words of the old bootlegger Don Elías Tun of the Cuchumatán Highlands.

Also, I have fresh in my mind an idea about Juan Cano's life in relation to that of Gonzalo Guerrero.

It's about parallels. Their charm and utility, but also their pitfalls. I believe deep congruities mark the lives of *los señores* Guerrero and Cano, though they lived nearly 500 years apart. Maybe that idea alone would not have been enough to get me going. The clinching element is my perception of a second parallel, one between the scholarly Jerónimo de Aguilar, the only other survivor of the 1516 shipwreck, and myself.

Juan's story and mine are strands of a long glossy black braid like that of a Central American Indian girl. The third strand is the story of April. I cannot provide that part, though I hope that, someday, she will.

CHAPTER 3: THE SQUASH FARMER

Juan Cano sat on a three-legged stool on the veranda. He wore only gray underpants; not boxers but the type with legs tight around the thighs like cycling shorts. A fountain occupied the center of a courtyard that contained a domesticated jungle, one tamed by Juan's hand. The vegetation exhaled a mossy, not unpleasant hint of decay beside a stronger scent of jasmine. Juan watched the water's flow and fall.

The highest point of the three-tiered fountain was a stone fish. It stood on a folded tail and spouted water toward a sky paved with slate. The vertical stream rose about a foot and at its apex formed an imperfect sphere like the head of a fetus he'd seen in a in-utero photograph. The ball of water, suspended where the pump's power ended and gravity held sway, retained its shape while being incessantly renewed. The water fell back on itself and splashed on the fish and trickled off the sculpted scales into the topmost shallow plane. From that platter it dropped through drains in four cardinal-point streams into a broader basin that was always full. From there the water overflowed as strings of sequins into a clear calf-deep stone pool.

Dusk was taking over. It crawled into the Panchoy Valley from the south and west between the Agua and Fuego volcanoes and around the southern flank of Acatenango.

Juan closed his eyes and tried to discern in the sound of the water the spout, the trickle and the overflow. The planes of water were heaven and purgatory and hell. It was right that the middle one should be overflowing. They were also the stages of life: boyhood, manhood and the post-prime succession of years when you become *un anciano* and nobody cares how you spend your mornings and afternoons.

Flagstone paths traversed the courtyard. The trees, some sturdy and some slender, were surrounded by bushes and flowers and fronds. The house had been built in the 1720s and for several decades had been home to the province's viceroys, the captains of *la Capitanía de Goathemala y la muy Noble Cuidad de Santiago de los Caballeros.*

It had been restored several times, after earthquakes, then abandoned for nearly a century along with the rest of the city by inhabitants weary of building back up what was only to be knocked down again.

The villa belonged to a wealthy business associate of a Guatemalan friend of Juan. It retained its original layout occupying the fourth part of a city block and was enclosed by a stone-and-brick wall draped for at least the past hundred years with purple and lilac bougainvillea and white jasmine. The dwelling itself was squared around the big patio. Another less elaborate *jardín* of flowers and orchid-bedecked trees was at the rear, beyond the kitchen. Despite its age, the house was now a thoroughly modern abode with every amenity and appointment.

Where Juan was sitting was neither inside nor out. Or both inside and outside. His bare feet rested on cool *baldosas de barro* paving a broad, tile-roofed corridor that defined the courtyard. This part of the house was where Juan had spent most of the previous five weeks, since taking up residence. Sometimes he lay in a hammock for hours, drinking coffee or rum or reading or listening to a Walkman.

After a while he got up from his stool. He looked up at Agua, the tallest of the three mountains rising black against the rosy gray southwestern sky. A cloud blowing over it was thick on the side where it pressed against the peak but stretched to wisps across the rounded cone like the strands a vain balding man hopes will conceal his pate.

Juan, known as Miguel to the few who had made his acquaintance here, stepped down from the veranda and walked along a stone path through damp grass to the base of a jacaranda where he'd spread a shovelful of ash from one of the house's four fireplaces. He squatted and took a handful and began to rub himself, the tops of his feet and his shins and calves and his forearms and hands and lastly, lightly his face.

He was not applying it to alter his color, which was that of mahogany and close in hue to that of most of the people who lived in and around Antigua. He was making himself dirty, providing a fine coat of what might have blown on and stuck during a day in the cornfield. He did this so that people outside, in the street into which he infrequently ventured, might not look at him too closely. Because if they did, they would see that his feet, despite the crude *caite* sandals, were not the horny splayed feet of a campesino and his fingers were not callused and tipped with rippled nails and scarred, the hands of a man who uses even in his dreams a stone-wasted machete like the one in a pale rawhide sheath resting against the trunk of the tree.

When he'd besmirched himself, he picked up the machete and walked past a man-sized wooden sculpture of the archangel Gabriel to the courtyard's southeastern corner. There, against the stone pedestal of one of a dozen wooden columns supporting the veranda's roof, sat his sandals and a pair of patched and worn calf-length canvas pants and a frayed shirt of coarse cotton. A big rope-net sack holding about 40 pounds of hard-shelled green-and-yellow *huicoy* squash rested beside the clothing. Perched on the bundle was a straw sombrero. A stuffed manila envelope was inside the hat.

Juan Cano, the man born and raised as Juan Cano, dressed in the clothing and reached for the hat. With it in one hand he stooped and pressed the purse's straw strap across the top of his forehead and rose, hefting the *huicoys* so they rested against the small of his back. Then, adjusting the envelope inside the crown, he put on the hat, which smelled of wood smoke and vinegar. Hunched forward, his hands hooked over the straps stretched tight behind his ears, he went along the corridor singing in a low voice:

> *"Camptown races sing that song,*
> *Doo-dah, doo-dah.*
> *Camptown racetrack five miles long,*
> *Oh, doo-dah day."*

He went past the kitchen into the garage that once had been a carriage house and opened the old wooden door studded with broad-headed verdigris brass nails. Hands hooked on the taut straps, Juan, now silent, stepped into the street. He turned and walked along Calle del Arco. The load of squash pressed against the cords of muscle flanking his spine. His sight was fixed on the cobblestones a step ahead of his step. Oil residue from the exhaust of cars had made purple and blue and yellow swirls on the dun and gray stones.

Every several steps he looked up. It was the dinner hour. The sidewalk was crowded with tourists, European and Japanese and North American, looking for a place to eat, and with Antigueños on their way home from work or from errands. They stepped around seated Kakchikel women from surrounding pueblos or the shores of Lake Atitlán, blue-headdressed women from Santa Catarina Palopó selling *huipiles* and placemats as they tended dirty children, cajoling them in their own clipped throaty language or reprimanding them in Spanish, addressing them as *Usted,* plugging the eager mouth of the smallest with a brown breast.

Juan walked to the end of the street and turned left and went another half block before crossing into the plaza of La Merced. He stopped at a stone bench beside a green garbage can donated, according to the stenciled message, by the Rotary Club of East Salem, Oregon. He let slip his load and sat down.

Directly in front of him was a cross of cement cylinders set atop a cement sphere. The church, with its faded ocher Baroque facade of climbing grapevines and flitting birds and falling grape leaves, stood to his right. Built by men determined to make something that would not fold and break when the earth bucked, its walls were seven feet thick and shored by squat buttresses, each the dimension of a castle keep.

A gaggle of boys played soccer between the little square's fountain and the church. Some wore shorts. Others were still in school uniforms of blue pants and white shirts. Thumps of the ball and tireless feet slapping the paving stones punctuated their cries and jolly curses.

An old woman between the boys and Juan was doing a steady business at a brazier. She turned ears of yellow corn and white corn with a wrinkled dark hand, searing them golden in the undulant blur above the embers. The delicious smell reached Juan. It reminded him of his grandmother.

He took off his hat and looked at the envelope. It held seven thousand U.S. dollars in 100-dollar bills. He put the hat with the envelope in it back on his head.

When he looked up again he saw a man approaching the church from Sexta Avenida, from the direction of Jocotenango. He wore a gray felt cowboy hat. His clothes were clean and pressed; green twill pants cinched tightly with a broad black belt around a compact waist into which was tucked a long-sleeved faded blue work shirt. He wore thick-soled black oxfords, recently polished, and carried in his left hand a plastic bag holding a rectangular soft-cornered bundle that might have been a folded poncho or a few yards of fabric out of which his wife would make a dress. The man was short and trim. His legs were so bowed a pair of fighting dogs could pass between them.

It wasn't always easy to know which men were Indians. With women it was simple. They wore *corte y huipil*. But their husbands and sons, except in the remote countryside, had given up their wool skirts or knee-length cotton trousers for the garb of the men who long ago had taken their land and women and gold and destroyed their gods and given them in exchange sugar, the garrote, *aguardiente*, the Virgin Mary and the Spanish language.

As he entered the temple, the small man took off his hat with his left hand and crossed himself with his right. He was beak-nosed and beardless and his skin was the color of teak. That did not mean he was not Ladino. Whether you were Indio or Ladino, by now, had little to do with your blood. It had more to do with what you thought you were. With what language you learned first and which one you preferred now. Sometimes it had to do, simply with where you lived. Even so, Juan knew somehow that this man's Spanish would be hesitant and embellished with a singing

Maya accent. He was certain that when this man reached his pew and kneeled, he would make his appeal or give his thanks in Kakchikel or Tzutuhil or, if from farther away, in Mam or Kiche or Kekchi.

Juan left his sack by the bench and walked across the paving stones to the three wide worn white marble steps that took him up into the church. He removed his hat. He passed beneath the low *bovedas* and down the cavernous temple's left aisle past a 400-year-old dead black wooden Jesus in repose beneath a cloak of green velvet.

The Indian man, a good 20 years older than Juan, had chosen a spot about halfway to the altar. He was sitting toward the central aisle.

Juan sidled in at the other end of the same pew.

That bench's only occupants, they sat in the church's hollowness for a few minutes. Then the elder man kneeled.

Juan gave him time.

After a while the younger man spoke.

"Ey," he said in a church-voice, little more than a whisper.

The older man looked up from his prayer and over at Juan.

Without saying anything, Juan flicked his wrist and sent the packet sliding along the polished wood. He put his hat on and got up and walked along the shadowy aisle, back out into the lamp-lighted night and over to his net full of squash.

CHAPTER 4: HEADING BACK DOWN THERE

Joseph Guinness stood at the midpoint of the bridge over the gorge that is the southeastern boundary of the Cornell University campus. He looked down at the white water coursing 200 feet below. A student had killed himself yesterday–the second of the spring semester–by jumping off this bridge.

The railing was cold and Joe gripped it tightly against a sudden feeling of precariousness. It passed, but not before it provided a thread of connection to these most recent suicides, the boy and a girl. He wondered if they had come determined or if they were uncertain up to the final instant, if they had vaulted the rail at a lope or if they had climbed carefully over and stood on the narrow ledge, looking down.

How long had they paused? Were they in unrequited love or humiliated or drunk or just very, very sad? How in the world had they come to believe their lives were worth nothing?

A freshman who was struggling in his Archeology 101 section had shown up at his office that afternoon to explain his circumstances and beg indulgence. The boy's mother was drying out in pampered stir and his father had just written him that he'd had it with her, he was getting a divorce. The kid–Frank or Fred–said his eczema was flaring up and he hadn't been able to sleep because the itch was driving him crazy, and that these various things had made it impossible for him to study. He'd started bawling.

"Hey, hey," Joe said. "Take it easy. Your grade from me doesn't matter. It's a fuckin' college course, is all. Don't sweat it. There's another month left. Try to get what you can out of it. Some of the reading is pretty interesting. But don't worry about it. You'll pass."

The kid looked up. He was wearing an oversize flannel shirt and he raised the shirt-tail to his face and dried his reddened eyes and wiped his nose.

"Thanks, teach," he said. "I don't wanna blow it off. Really. I was even thinking about majoring in archeology. Or, like, anthropology."

F. stood up and extended his hand and they shook. He looked at Joe with dejected hound's eyes, and it was then that Joe figured he might have just been conned. The kid left and the professor sat back down, feeling neither generous nor compassionate.

The evening air was damp. Halos of hazy light encircled the streetlamps at both ends of the bridge. Joe stared down at the water and asked himself if giving a kid–an unstable or depressed kid with other problems–a failing grade could be a final straw that might make a three-second plunge and unimaginable thump an option more palatable than perseverance. How would he feel if he rebuffed a student who came crying to him about his grade and then the kid went and jumped off the bridge?

He hawked and spat and watched the gob fall. A foamy bead, curving. Gone.

He continued on his way. A Counting Crows song about Mr. Jones and a flamenco dancer blared from the open door of a fraternity house–the Dekes or Dorks or

Geeks or Sci-Fi's, Joe didn't know which–on the hillside across the street. It had been those cut-stone manors of the Hellenic brotherhoods that had given the bar he was approaching its name, The Chapter House. The pub was the first building past the bridge, into the realm of "off-campus." It hunkered like a toll station marking passage from academia into the real world of hedge-trimming and the PTA, home-refinancing and sidewalk-salting.

Despite its name, the joint for years had been avoided by the Greek crowd. That's why it appealed to Joe, who had never banished the idea, formed as a 1970s undergraduate, of fraternities as the domain of dimwittedness and barfing.

As soon as he pushed open the door, he knew Chepe was already there. Linda Ronstadt was singing *"Lo Siento mi Vida"* on the jukebox, the flip-side of her "Tracks of my Tears" cover. Chepe usually played both songs at least once during an hour of conversation, a fairly regular bull-session between the two *compinches* in which Chepe would seldom fail to state that, although he did not find Ms. Ronstadt all that pretty, he would not hesitate to marry her if only she would sing to him every night.

"Porque tu sabes, carnal, she's half Mexican."

"Ey, cabrón!" Chepe shouted when he saw Joe enter. "Over here!"

Though he and Joe spoke Spanish together, Chepe did the second part of hailing his friend in English. It was Chepe's policy "to not let the Gringos know you are a speaking-Spanish person."

Chepe thought "spic" was short for "speaking-Spanish person." His English was correct but encumbered with a thick accent and improvised syntax that foiled his efforts to blend in. He also had a knack for spinning a commonplace.

During a faculty meeting the previous week, he had declared that the administration's refusal to upgrade the Anthropology Department's computer system "really gets under my goat." Twenty minutes later he recommended to a colleague, "As in Rome, do as the Romans."

Joe sat down. The top of the wooden table had been inscribed over the decades with pen-knife grafitti, mostly Greek letters and hearts-and-initials but with a *Fuck You* and an *Eat Me* in rough calligraphy.

"Did you hear the *pinche* radio, *carnal?*" Chepe asked his friend.

The Mexican was already high. Three small empty glasses, taller than shot glasses but not as big around, sat before him, a trace of slightly verdant liquid at the bottom of each. Joe recognized it as Hornitos Reposado.

"Que pasó?"

"Guadalajara blew up."

Chepe was from Guadalajara. He was in Ithaca as a visiting professor for a year, brought on the recommendation of professor Guinness, his erstwhile colleague and pal during Joe's year at *El Museo de Antropologia* in the D.F, where he'd worked while writing his doctoral thesis.

"Blew up?"

"Just like you heard me, man. *Los cabrones de Pemex.* There was a leak in a pipe from the refinery and the sewers filled with gasoline fumes or gaseous diesel or whatever the fuck and after a couple days started exploding, in a *pinche* chain reaction. Professional terrorists couldn't have done a better job, the sons of whores. More than 20 blocks of downtown destroyed. Like a fucking earthquake.

"I talked to *mi mamá* an hour ago. The family is OK. Nobody was at home. But the house is gone. That's what she said, *carnal: 'Se fue.' Que ya no existe.* A pile of rubble. She said she and all the neighbors were complaining of the smell since Monday. For more than two fucking days! Telling cops and firemen and calling City Hall to tell them what the problem was. Because it was so obvious, my nephew Panchito could have figured it out, and he's five *pinche* years old. Fucking fumes were coming out of the sewers!"

He took off his glasses and rubbed his eyes hard with the heels of his hands. Then he put the wire-framed specs back on, perched high on the bridge of his snake-eating eagle's beak.

"They've already recovered more than a hundred bodies, and they only started digging a few hours ago."

"*Q'hijos de puta,*" said Joe.

Joe liked Hornitos Reposado too. He caught the attention of a waitress. He thought he recognized her, but not from here. She was new at the bar.

"Two more Hornitos, please."

"Right away, prof."

She smiled, and he placed her. Slight accent and good Samaritan eyes, dark and deep like the two black ones, water and dates, the Prophet said you could live on in the desert. A Sabra. Rachel or Leah, something Old Testament.

Introduction to Archeology, a couple falls earlier. She had been an excellent student.

"Well, look at the good side, *compadre*. Thank God the family is OK," he said.

"Dios? Me cago en Dios y en la leche de su madre."

Chepe let out a ranchera wail of a laugh, a sign he was well on his way to that quetzal-feathered place where so many Americans–brick-colored pitch-eyed real Americans– are bound once they wrench the top off a bottle of booze. Then, in a more scholarly tone, Chepe asked: "What the fuck could God possibly have to do with it?"

Joe held up his hands. "Don't ask me, *carnal. Es un puto decir.*"

They drank three more tequilas apiece, tossing down the liquor and biting a salted wedge of lime after each *pijazo*. Chepe, with his headstart, got drunk. The last time he played *"Lo Siento mi Vida"* he sang along loudly, beyond caring whether the Yanquis knew he was a stranger.

Ya sé que no volverás
Ni tú, ni yo
Ya ha llegado el triste pesar
Debemos siempre separarnos.

By the time they left the bar Joe was half *borracho* himself. He had informed Chepe he was going back down to Central America–to Guatemala this time–to take over a dig for the ailing Owen, and when that had sunk in the Mexican got animated again and insisted they go back up the hill to his office, that he had something he had to show Joe.

Chepe was on a race rap for much of the ten-minute hike, inveighing against the cult of the indigenous that officially prevailed in his country. Not so much against the cult itself, but against the hypocrisy of most of those who espoused it.

"There's not a statue of Hernán Cortés in the whole *pinche* country but that *gachupín hijo de puta* is the spiritual father of the pasty-faces who still run it, all the time spouting about Tenochtitlán and Cauhutemoc and Zapata while they stuff their pockets and shit on the Indians."

The two men made their way huffing up through the suddenly chilly night to the Arts Quad. The expanse was almost deserted and, in the moonlight, out of scale. It looked smaller than it was.

"So whaddaya got for me?" Joe asked as they mounted the granite stairs to the main entrance of Tompson Hall.

"Hold your horse."

They clomped up the broad wooden stairway to the second floor. Joe had a real office there, with a tall window looking out onto the quadrangle. But Chepe had been accommodated in a cramped space formerly used for storage. His desk took up half the room and books were stacked on the floor in knee-high piles. A red and brown serape decorated the wall behind the desk. On another wall was a framed print by Rufino Tamayo of a skinny black dog baying at a black moon.

Chepe, breathing hard, sat down behind his desk. Joe sat in the captain's chair, the only other one in the room, facing him. Chepe leaned down and opened a drawer and fumbled around. He pulled out an envelope, a flimsy airmail one with blue and red dashes around its edges.

"Gonzalo Guerrero," he said, grinning.

"What?" Joe said. "He wrote you a letter?"

"No mames," he said, and took a single folded page from the envelope and opened it. He passed Joe the envelope. It had a Guatemalan stamp depicting a jaguar. It was addressed to Chepe at the Museum in Mexico City.

Chepe began to read aloud: "My esteemed Dr. Vargas." That was him, Jose Manuel Vargas Cordero, Ph.D. "I read with great interest in the November 1993 issue of *Raices* your article on the later years, following his return to Spain from Mexico, of the seminarian Jeronimo de Aguilar of Ecija. His life without doubt was marvelous, not to be believed were it presented as invention.

"I thought it would interest you to know that Aguilar's companion or, if you will, his counterpart, Gonzalo Guerrero, is rumored to have left a record of some of his perceptions of the world during the years his native country imposed itself on his adopted culture and the land of his children. I'm certain you are aware that Guerrero died in combat against the conquerors in territory that then pertained to the *capitanía de Guatemala.* Due to my age and precarious health, it has been impossible for me to pursue various leads concerning the possible existence of this document or these documents.

"Hence I am in no position to assure you categorically that they exist. But I am able to say that at least one of the versions regarding this matter is of a provenance not to be characterized as frivolous. I am increasingly infirm. In the interest of culture and whatever enlightenment such a record might provide for Guerrero's grand Mestizo progeny, among which I proudly count myself, I would gladly introduce you to one or more informants who may be able to direct you toward clarification of this mystery. That is, if the case be that you are able to dedicate some of your valuable time and efforts to the task.

"Without further ado for the moment and wishing you every success in your endeavors, I respectfully sign,

"Profesor Mario Barahona,   Universidad de San Marcos."

"*Estás mamando*," said Joe.

"*No estoy mamando, cabrón!*" He passed Joe the letter. "This is for real. The only thing is, it's a year-and-a-half old. And *el viejo* said he's not in such good shape. I don't even know if he's still alive. I wrote to him right before I came up here, but didn't hear back. Then I kind of forgot about it. Anyway, I told him about the commitment I had here and that, fascinating as his proposition sounded, I wouldn't be able to pursue it for some time.

"But hey, *carnal*. If I send a letter of introduction and recommendation down with my *compadre*, I'm sure this old gentleman will fill you in. Unless that 'proud to be Mestizo' line means he doesn't like pale dudes. *Porque, tu sabes, guey, que eres muy, pero muy, blanco.*"

Chepe reached down and opened another drawer and took out a half-full bottle of Cuervo, his private stash. He twisted off the top and held it up.

"To Gonzalo Guerrero, progenitor of the great Mestizo race." He took a big swig and passed the bottle to Joe.

"*Que viva,*" the gringo said, and sucked down a belt.

When they parted, *bien pedos,* on the vacant quad at midnight, they embraced and Chepe squeezed his friend tightly and said, "*Carajo, cabrón.*" He let go and held Joe at arm's length and looked at him with tears, not big enough to fall, in his eyes. He raised his left hand and touched the tips of his fingers to Joe's right cheek, tracing the thick web of scar tissue beneath the stubble.

"*Solo que no te peguen otro tiro, OK, cabrón?*" Just don't get fuckin' shot again, OK, cabrón?

CHAPTER 5: A POT FULL OF GOLD

(The Gardener, Take 2)

My grandfather got what he was after, but not in the way he was after it. I have his last name, which was my mother's: Cano. My father's last name, I don't even know what it was. I asked my mother once. I must have been about eight years old. She was making *pupusas.* She looked up from the grill, wiped the sweat off her forehead with the back of her hand, the one with the spatula in it, and looked at me for a second. I guess she was trying to see how much I really wanted to know. "Your father's name was written with a stick on the beach at low tide," she said. I didn't bring it up again. So I've got the name my mother got from her father. He and *abuelita* were married. Though that wasn't common, especially in those days. Most campesino couples in El Salvador don't go through the legal motions. I found out later, when I was there, that it becomes legal anyway–Common Law–after, like, seven years together. But even then the father has to recognize a child as his for the kid to get his surname. Something my father didn't do in my case. My maternal grandfather was Clemente Cano. He came up to LA once, when I was four or five. I can't say I remember him, though I have a hazy image in my head of a dark-skinned man whose lap I'm sitting on. He takes off his hat, a black felt cowboy job, and drops it on my head. It was big and covered my eyes. And me laughing and him laughing. Also his stub of a thumb. 'Cause he'd chopped off half of it with a machete. He only stayed a couple months, my Mom said, then went home. He disliked the city. Any city. My grandmother Rosario, who everybody calls Chayo or Chayito, said he even avoided going to Ahuachapan, much less San Salvador. So you can imagine what he thought of Los Angeles. He needed a plow or a hoe in his hands, or his fingers in the dirt. He was a creature of the *milpa,* the maize patch, *abuelita* said. A corn-planting, corn-raising, corn-harvesting demon. He wasn't always like that, though. The way Chayo tells it, what he was mostly known for as a kid was laziness. *Un perezoso.* They knew each other since they were little, see. From the same pueblito. More like a *caserío.* What's the word? A hamlet. She says when Clem was a *mocoso* his father had to drag him to the *milpa.* That he was a big whiner and bellyache artist. That what he most liked to do was hang out down at the river, chewing a twig. Fishing, supposedly. Then when he was about 14 he heard one of the *ancianos* talking about *las botijas*. These ceramic pots that held treasure and supposedly were buried in the hills. Apparently some people really did that in the old days. Like in the eighteen-hundreds. Campesinos, I'm talking about. The few who for whatever reason were able to accumulate over the decades some gold coins. They didn't trust banks. Or their neighbors much, or even their families, I guess. And these paranoid or prudent old-time Indians and Mestizos put their reales or dubloons or whatever the hell they were in a terracotta jug and buried it out in the sticks where only they knew where it was. Then some of these old guys who'd gotten rich or at least half-rich, they died unexpectedly. Which happened as much back then as it does now. Maybe more. So when my grandparents were kids, every once in a while some Fulano or Mengano from la Loma del Culo a few villages off would be plowing away, struggling along behind his *buey* or mule, busting through hard dirt and, thunk, the plow'd get hung up. The guy would think at first it was a pain in the ass rock. He'd get down on his knees and dig and when he got the thing free it wasn't a rock but a botija, maybe gouged now or broken, and spilling Spanish gold coins. And Clem, when he was on the threshold of manhood, heard somebody telling about somebody who'd found one. Chayo said it was like he'd been tapped by a magic wand. He was convinced that that was his destiny. During the next 15 or so years this guy who until then had been utterly lacking in motivation spent most of his waking hours behind a plow. He cleared idle land, share-cropped and persuaded Don Javier, the landholder around their village, to allow him to work bigger and bigger pieces. It didn't even seem like work. Because *el abuelito* knew that at any moment his plow was gonna knock and stick and there at his feet would be a cup overflowing with riches. Well, Clemente Cano never discovered a *botija* full of gold. But he did turn up hundreds of beautiful things with his plow. Ceramics and figurines of frogs and monkeys and owls, little okarina-type flute-jobs of bone or clay in the shape of a turtle or a parrot, arrowheads and hammer stones. On more than one occasion I heard Chayito wonder out loud about what became of that stuff. She never got around to tracking it down. Even so, it wasn't the artifacts, which I guess must have been valuable, or at least would be now, that made Clem's fortune. Not a fortune as you or I would think of it. You have to keep in mind that I'm talking about a well-off peasant, is all. See, since he'd taken the trouble to plow, he figured he might as well sow. And once he'd sown, it would have been stupid not to spread manure and weed and harvest. Even a sharecropper got his share. So over the years, without trying to do anything but stumble on a pot of gold in a furrow, he accumulated enough money to buy his own land, more and more of it, until he didn't really consider himself a campesino anymore. Abuela says he took to referring to himself as *"un pequeño productor, casi mediano."* My Mom didn't grow up in abject poverty, then. They always had enough to eat and a roof over their heads. Neither of her two siblings died in infancy. If they got an ear infection or bad diarrhea, which is what kills kids in the Central American countryside, my grandfather had enough money to buy medicine or take them to a doctor in town.

She went through sixth grade, too. Which was unheard-of for a campesino girl back then, and is still rare. That's not to say she was pampered. They didn't have electricity. She pumped water from a well. Didn't use shoes until she went to school. She and her mother ground cornmeal by hand, with one of those crank jobs. And, of course, she could *echar* tortillas in her sleep. She milked a cow and two goats every day. And get this. She knew how to whack the head off a chicken with her bare hand. When she first told me that, I didn't believe it. Even when *abuelita* backed her up. Then I saw it in a French movie, when I was in high school and, by way of my history teacher, who was my best teacher ever, getting deeply into foreign cinema. European and Asian, mostly, It's in 'Lacombe, Lucien,' by Louis Malle. The night I saw that movie, when I got home I saw the light was still on in Mom's room even though it was after 11. I eased open the door. "Whatja doin' Ma? Can't sleep?" I said. "Just thinkin' about things," she says. I didn't ask her what she was thinking about. But I told her: "Mom, I'm sorry I didn't believe you when you told me about chopping a chicken's head off with your hand." She was sitting propped up against the headboard. There wasn't much light, but she was sitting right in the slice coming through the half open door. So I could see the look on her face. She looked really pretty. I mean prettier than usual, because she was a beautiful woman. And amused. She says: "You're kind of a weird kid sometimes, Juancito. But I sure do love you. *Un montón.*" I think she said it in English except for the last part. By then she spoke pretty good English. Anyway, *mi mamita* always used to say that one of the things she liked

best about *los Estados* was that she'd never, ever have to kill or pluck another chicken. Abuelito Clemente didn't last long after he went home. The story Chayo and my mother got was that he took to the bottle. They fished him out of the river about a year after he'd come to see us, after he'd checked out life en el Norte and found it lacking. My Uncle Marcos, Chayo's youngest brother–so he'd be a great-uncle, really–when we finally met up down there, in the hills, he told me: 'Yeah, *el viejo* drowned, all right.'
But he–Marcos, who by then was commanding an FMLN front near Guazapa–said he never believed it was an accident.

CHAPTER 6: THREE AND ITS MULTIPLES

During her first couple weeks of work on *"Bolos,"* April noticed that most street drunks in Antigua wore a piece of incongruous attire. Many also had a facial wound or abrasion, a crusted scrape dirty around the edges and a little infected. She presumed most were the result of a stumble and fall, but that some, too, must have been the mark left by a tussle with a companion over a bottle's final measure.

Early one evening she found two men sitting on the steps to the ruin of the Capuchinas convent. The former nunnery, its austere cells arrayed around a circular courtyard and gardens, was one of the city's principal attractions. It was closed for the night now, but a lamp above the entrance provided enough light for her to work.

She walked up to them, holding her camera by its handle at her side. Both men were unwashed. Oily black hair adhered to their heads. The elder one had on over a shiny black polyester shirt with a big-winged collar an amply cut rust-colored coarse linen sweater with a plunging V-neck. April guessed it to be of Italian manufacture and supposed it must have cost its original owner at least 300 dollars. How then had it come to clothe a man whose principal ambition for the evening was that one or two people who'd parked along this street might give him un quetzal if he told them on their return that he'd kept an eye on their car, *"Bien cuidado!"*?

Maybe he found it on a park bench previously occupied by an absent-minded Milanese. Or a fashionable generous Canuck might have taken pity on him one chilly night and draped it over the shoulders of the passed-out bum.

The one with the sweater wore old beat-up canvas sneakers. The other's clothes were unremarkable except for their griminess. But his feet were sheathed in L.L. Bean duck-hunting boots with rubber soles and soft leather uppers.

The bridge of the younger man's nose was newly scabbed. What had been a shiner beneath his left eye had turned yellow. He regarded April with bovine indifference. Her approach, however, kindled a glimmer in the pupils of the older derelict. He showed his teeth, broken and mottled.

"Buenas tardes," she said.

"*'Tardes*," said the older man. The other grunted.

"*Como están?*"

"*No tan bien como usted, diría yo,*" said the one in the V-neck.

"If it would be no bother, I'd like to talk a bit with you gentlemen."

"I used to be a gentleman. *Hoy día soy un bolo, nomás,*" said the older one. He went on: "Well, perhaps not a gentleman as you understand the term, *chinita linda.* But a respectable citizen, if one of humble means. I once owned a motor vehicle. A Chevrolet pick-up manufactured in the Year of our Lord one-nine-six-six."

He'd risen to respond. Now he pursed his lips, by way of indication, toward his companion.

"My good friend here, on the other hand, has always been a drunk."

This elicited a response from the younger man. Animation struggled to the surface of his consciousness like a bubble through geyser mud.

"Why don't you think before opening your trap, *viejo cerote?* Could I have been a drunk at birth? Or as a little kid?"

"I stand corrected, *pues,*" said the other, bowing extravagantly. "I beg your forgiveness." Then, turning again to April: "Let's say then he's been a drunk only as long as he's had whiskers."

"That's more like it," said the younger man. He lowered his head back into fog.

"Bolos"–the Guatemalan word for destitute, street-sleeping alcoholics–was the working title of the documentary April went to Guatemala to make. Her previous film, the one that had made something of a name for her, had a one-foreign-word title, too. Foreign in a strict sense. It was English, but England's English.

That film was called "Wankers," and portrayed three men of Portland, Oregon who were chronic masturbators, their sex lives limited to self-gratification while watching pornographic movies. April had decided against calling it "Jerk-offs." And she hadn't liked "Onans" or "Chokers," titles friends had suggested. She'd entertained "Different Strokes," before opting for the British term. Which seemed, given the buzz the film caused at Sundance and its subsequent esoteric "success," to have been a good choice.

"Usted, señor," April addressed the older man. "Would you mind telling me about your life? I'd like to listen, and to film you talking, if that's all right."

"Why would a pretty young Chinawoman want to film an ugly old drunken coot like me? The story of my life is surely one of the less significant ones in the world's trove of stories."

"You may call me *'chinita,'* if you like. I don't mind. But for your information, I'm not Chinese. My grandparents were Japanese. But I'm from California, *los Estados Unidos.*"

"I stand corrected for the second time in the space of two minutes. *Al pan, pan y al vino, vino.* That's the way it should be, miss. Excuse both my presumption and my freshness."

"No tenga pena," said April. Taking his volubility to mean he had no objection, she withdrew the aluminum

tripod, extended its legs and set up the camera. The man sat down again on the step. She framed him.

"Como se llama usted?"

"José María Solorzano Paz, *a sus órdenes.*"

"How old are you, José María?"

"Call me Chema. Sixty-two years I have behind me. Born *el tres del tres del '33.* March 3rd. Three and its multiples have always been lucky for me. When I used to have a little money, before dedicating myself to the life of a bum, I would occasionally play some combination of 3 and 9 in the lottery. And I won several times over the years. Small or middling amounts. Never the big one.

"Also, I was blessed with three children."

"Sons or daughters?"

"Dos mujercitas y un varón."

"And where are they now, your children?"

"I was told one of the girls went to the States, many years ago now. I never had further news of her. She must be practically *una gringuita* like yourself by now. The other girl, she stayed here. I've seen her four times in the last ten years, walking down the street. But she did not see me, and I didn't call out her name."

"And the boy?"

"He was the last to arrive. When both my wife and I were nearly 40. He was born fine and healthy, though. Not like some babies that come late to a woman. All the same, he died young. Only two years old."

He stopped talking and looked to his right, up the street.

The other drunk, whom April had thought was oblivious, roused himself and said: *"Decile, cabrón, si tenés huevos."*

Go on and tell her, bastard, if you've got the balls.

April had been talking with the old fellow face-to-face, letting the tape roll. Now she bent to look through the viewfinder. His eyes remained averted. She saw his lips moving, but his voice seemed disembodied.

"Yes, it's true," he said. "I killed him. I thought he was inside the house with his mother. It was dusk. With the truck. I didn't see him at all. I thought it was a mutt I'd hit, though I didn't hear a yelp. No sound at all.

"I wasn't drunk, though!" He looked frantically at April, who lifted her face from the eyepiece. "I didn't drink at all back then, not a drop! I swear!"

CHAPTER 7: *COMO QUIERA USTED*

Ximena Yat was the only person Juan spoke with during his first secluded month in the big house. She thought his name was Miguel. The first thing she said to him each morning was: "Did daybreak find you well, Don Miguel?"

The third morning Juan responded: "Ximena, you don't have to call me 'Don.' My grandparents were campesinos and my mother was almost what you'd call poor. Just call me Miguel."

"Como quiera usted," she said. "As you wish." But the next day it was the same, and the day after. Juan didn't insist.

Ximena had come with the house. She'd been born in it, delivered by a Kakchikel midwife on All Saints' Day 1938, ten minutes prior to the stillbirth of a twin sister strangled by her own umbilical cord. She had never known another home.

Ximena was illiterate, and perfectly trilingual. Her parents were K'iche speakers from a village near Chichicastenango who had come to Antigua to sell the mother's weavings, and never left. The girl, of course, learned the language of her mother and father, who was gardener-handyman-watchman for the coffee *finquero* family that had owned the house until Mr. Angus MacSwan bought it in 1968. K'iche did her little good in the new province, though it served to inflate her pride, having been the language of Tecún Umán, the Maya prince who 400 years earlier had led the resistance to the gold-crazed hairy horsemen with gleaming breastplates, sallow skin and gray eyes like those of ghosts.

She naturally learned Kakchikel, too. Raised as a domestic in an Antiguan household, she could not get by without the ability to communicate and converse with the local indigenous population. Her childhood playmates had been the daughters and sons of the cook and of neighboring servants, all of whom were Kakchikel.

And of course she learned Spanish. That was what *los patrones* spoke to her, and what she heard on the radio and what she used with Ladino clerks and bus drivers and the shoeshine boys with whom she liked to trade barbs in the plaza.

The current owner of the home was Gen. Rolando García-Braun. Upon retirement from the air force in '91, he had been appointed director of GUATEL, the state telecommunications monopoly. He had run things there, lining his pockets, for three years. Garcia was at the same time an associate of Pedro Garay, who had mediated Juan's living arrangements here. García knew at least part of his new tenant's background. Upon meeting Juan to close their deal he told him: "There's a stubborn old half-crazy *Indita* looking after the place. Been there since *la conquista.* She was a maid for the old *Escocés* and his wife, and the people before them, too. I couldn't get her to leave. She even stood up to my bodyguards, told them to go ahead and shoot her, the only way she'd exit was feet first. *De todos modos,* I couldn't leave the place unoccupied.

"You decide what to do with her. You'll need at least one *domestica* anyway. A gardener too, unless you're one of those green-thumb Gringos who enjoys scratching in the dirt."

García had laughed and clapped Juan on the back. He had reason to be jovial. In his other hand he gripped a briefcase, just handed to him by Juan, containing 1,000 hundred-dollar bills; a year's rent at about twice the market value and paid in advance.

Juan smiled too. Get a load of this *chele* pig, he thought. Calling me a Gringo. The *leche*-faced Gallego-Kraut motherfucker.

Juan had immediately disliked the general and his Lexus SUV, his brace of snarling Rottweilers, tasseled Italian loafers and red-haired Argentine mistress, who during their exchange, while cooling herself with an Andalusian fan, had whined, *"Ay petiso* (García was short), *que aburrido es este pueblito. Cuando volvemos a Miami?"* But Juan was not in a position to express antipathy.

He might be obliged to continue counting on García as a padrino during his stay in Guatemala. Between the general's ties to the highest echelons of the armed forces and his recently concluded service, principally to himself, in the federal bureaucracy, he could get almost anything done, or undone. Even from Miami, where he'd just been named consul.

He had already provided Juan with a new identity, that of a certain 28-year-old Miguel Zelaya, from Zacapa. According to the conditions Juan set for leasing the home, García had given him a birth certificate, passport, *cédula* and driver's license. The papers were not forgeries, but as genuine as García's own. The general also left him a nearly new Toyota 4-Runner, on loan, and a crooked personal banker on the board of *el Banco Industrial,* in case Juan needed to move his money.

And he'd bestowed on him Ximena Yat.

It took Juan a couple weeks to learn anything of Ximena's life. Not that she was taciturn. She spent a good part of the day talking, in a muffled monologue, switching between Spanish and *lengua,* while she swept or cooked or while dousing and soaping and rinsing and wringing Juan's clothes at the big concrete double sink beside her room off the kitchen.

At first he was content to bid her good-morning and good-night and answer her queries regarding his preference for lunch or dinner. This, though they were in sight of each other or crossing paths throughout the day, what with Juan watering or pruning or weeding or otherwise tending the courtyard plants. Or lying in a hammock on the veranda or searching for a volume in the library or simply roaming, somewhat aimlessly, through the place. She must have thought her new boss a strange one; a man who by choice remained a virtual prisoner in his home.

One afternoon during Juan's second month there, Ximena paused to lean on her mop-handle a few feet from where he sat at a round wooden table on the veranda. He was sipping coffee and reading a book.

"A young man like yourself, Don Miguel," she said. "Good-looking and healthy and not without means. Do you never feel the desire to get it wet?"

It was the first question she had posed him beyond the eminently practical or necessary.

"Get what wet?"

"Your thing. You know ... A man should not keep his horse always corralled."

Juan Cano, after all he'd seen, was hard to astonish. But his face now betrayed the inability to muster a response.

Ximena lifted her apron to cover her mouth as her eyes went wide with alarm, then showed a trace of devilish amusement.

"Oh, *Madre Santisima,* No! Not with me!," she squealed. "I only wanted to advise you that there is a brothel up on Third Avenue. It's said to be pleasant and clean."

Juan regained his composure. "How would you know such things, Ximena?"

"There is little in this town that escapes me. Besides, I know a few of *las chicas* quite well, having delivered their babies."

"Es comadrona usted?"

"Sí, señor. With God's help, for more than 30 years I have been bringing little ones into the world. I used to keep a good count, but a while ago lost track of the exact number. In any case, it's 200-and-some. And though I'm getting on in years, my services are sought out still."

"Que grande, Ximena. My compliments."

"Sí. It's good work, it's true. To see them emerge and take the first breath. Of course I've had some difficult ones. Have had to pull them out backside-first, or three in one sitting. That's my record for one birth: triplets. But that same night I had another. So there was a day in this lifetime, September 14, 1982–it rained all day and all night– when I delivered four children."

She looked down at the floor, at the damp mop-cloth at her bare brown feet, then resumed swabbing. She didn't look up at Juan again, but moved off backward down the veranda, with each step broadening the gleaming arc of her wake.

CHAPTER 8: MORE STUPID THAN COWS

They were drinking *chaparro* moonshine liquor distilled by Carlos, who combined the roles of patriarch, guest of honor and host. By the time the shadows of the trees behind the houses had stretched across the courtyard, all five men were inebriated.

Only two were drunks by vocation. April interviewed Calixto and Elmer during her first month in Antigua. She talked with them on the sidewalk in their stupor or in a zinc-roofed tumbledown *comedor* near the market while they were sober and twitching, and at other exterior venues in varying degrees of lucidity between contentedness and collapse. A rapport developed between la Chinita-Gringa with the bulky camera and the two men, who practiced the buddy-system of vagrancy.

Elmer had invited April to come along this Sunday afternoon. The gathering was three kilometers outside town up the dirt road through Aldea Santa Ana to the east. Carlos was Elmer's great-uncle, and he was visiting from his home an hour's bus ride to the south. A stocky handsome campesino in his 60s, he had greeted April with amused, paternal and dignified hospitality.

Several children were playing in the bald yard bordered on two sides by adobe houses roofed with barrel tiles. A boy was dragging through the dust an antique clothes-iron, the kind heated with embers. It was tied to a length of twine. He made a "chuf-chuf" sound interspersed with an occasional high "whooouu." Two little girls toddled behind the iron, grinning. Then the girls began chasing hens and chicks from one side of the yard to the other.

Two of Carlos' grand-daughters and Elmer's mother were busy in the open-air cooking area formed by an extension of the roof at one end of the largest home. The younger women, Sandra and Maida, were in their mid-20s. One fine-ground moist cornmeal with a stone pestle on *el metate* while her sister and the older woman made tortillas. The low-volume fast clapping of hands was a soothing background soundtrack. A wood fire burned lazily on the waist-high adobe hearth.. Its smoke rose through a sheet metal chimney and spread to cense the small compound.

The women and children gathered around to examine the stranger and her cumbersome instrument. April extended her hand to the women. Each of them took it ever so lightly with the tips of their fingers.

The other two men were cutters and sellers of firewood, and the husbands of Carlos' grand-daughters. He introduced them as Pablo and El Seco. Their bony short horses, rope halters dragging and rough-hewn triangular wood-racks loosened, nibbled sparse grass beneath an avocado tree 15 yards away. Both *leñadores* wore a leather-sheathed machete on their belt. Carlos' machete, in an old engraved pale rawhide scabbard, was draped over his shoulder on a thong.

The five men sat on two split-log benches. One was up against the wall of the house and the other was nearly perpendicular to it. Each of them had a metal cup. The second bottle of clear liquid circulated, clinking against the rim of the vessels. April, after throwing back two shots at the outset, had removed herself from the group. She took a low wooden stool from beside the door, placed it toward the middle of the yard and sat down. With the camera on her shoulder, she began filming.

Elmer and Calixto piped up occasionally. But by the time they were all fairly well looped the discussion's two protagonists were the woodcutters. They were spraying spit and gesticulating and enunciating poorly. The debate concerned the relative power of life and death. The two were the youngest men present, in their early-20s.

"What the devil do you whippersnappers know about life and death?" demanded Carlos, the least drunk of those present. His word weighed heavily here. Though only visiting, he was acknowledged as the sire of this plot of land and scant collection of dwellings, having purchased the few hectares for the girls upon their nearly simultaneous marriages. The older man was bored by the course of the talk. But the same youth that made El Seco and Pablo the least-versed in the subject at hand also compelled them to stress their respective points. Or what seemed like points in the dim blur of a Sunday afternoon of *borrachera campesina.*

The trouble began with a remark by Elmer. He said that at dawn he had seen a *tecolote,* a small owl, in a tree along the road to El Calvario church.

"Trae suerte, trae muerte," said Carlos. The refrain associates owls with luck or with death.

Elmer wondered if death could ever be lucky. Carlos said he thought not; that the saying meant *el tecolote* augured one thing or the other.

"Es grande, la muerte," said El Seco. He was perhaps the drunkest.

"Pero la vida es más grande," answered Pablo.

"How can you say that?" The liquor had put an edge on El Seco's voice. "Like that fucking idiotic radio campaign against AIDS, the 'Use a rubber or remain faithful'-line. *Y el pendejo ese* saying AIDS is a condition of 100 percent mortality. No shit. Life is a condition of 100 percent mortality. Death always wins. And it lasts forever, while this shitty life is good for 50 or 60 years, if we're lucky."

"But we can create more life. That is a defeat of death," said Pablo, the father of twin two-year-old girls. His speech was almost as slurred as that of his companion. Even so, he had enough wits about him to realize he had blundered. He began to stutter a retraction.

As would be explained to April that evening, El Seco and his wife, Sandra, had been together in a house 50 yards up the road for nearly three years. But she had yet to become pregnant. Such a glaring deficiency had been the subject of malicious speculation regarding her husband's virility.

El Seco took offense. Pablo was El Seco's friend and *concuñado*, a man with whom he'd spent the previous three years traipsing six days a week, a few hours before each day's dawn, into the high forests to cut wood and carry it to market by 8.

"You'd like a shot at Sandrita yourself, wouldn't you? I've seen you admiring her. But I'm more a man than you any day, faggot. And I'm going to show you right now."

El Seco rose. Wobbling, he drew his machete.

Pablo jumped up and bared his own blade. He had no choice. He had just been called *un hueco* in the presence of not only Don Carlos but also the pretty Gringuita or whatever the hell she was. Who was sitting over there filming everything.

The blow that cut off Pablo's raised left hand sobered up El Seco.

The hand dangled from a ribbon of skin connecting it to the man who had used it all his life. The jets pumped by his strong young alcohol-soaked woodcutter's heart splashed on the peach-colored dust and speckled El Seco's horny crooked brown toes and the straps of his tire-soled sandals.

El Seco dropped his machete. It had passed so swiftly through Pablo it was unstained. El Seco stepped forward and clamped his hands around the spurting stump of his friend's arm and bent it at the elbow so it pointed upward. The font subsided, but blood continued to seep thickly from the wound and flowed down, painting a vermillion sheen on El Seco's hands.

"Cerote," Pablo spat at El Seco. Piece of shit.

Pablo still held his machete in the other hand. He raised it to strike but was restrained by Carlos. He and El Seco walked the wounded man across the yard to the bench.

Carlos untied the bandanna from around his neck and knotted it around Pablo's forearm. With a stick provided by Calixto, he twisted the fabric so tightly that only a few drops of Pablo's blood made it to the wound and to the air.

These fat-cherry beads fell at intervals and formed a paste in the dust.

April stood just outside the circle of men, her shouldered camera pointed at them.

There was no discussion as to what medical procedure should be followed. It was carried out with such assurance and dispatch that April, later, figured it must be the standard rural treatment for a severed limb. Like when she was a child, if she awoke with a scratchy throat, her mother would have her gargle with Listerine.

Carlos took up his machete, which was worn to half its original width by thousands of whets. He sliced through the flap that was the hand's last connection to Pablo. He set the hand on the bench. Pablo had begun to sob, almost silently and without tears. El Seco held the tourniquet stick and, at intervals, twisted it a quarter-turn.

When the bleeding stopped, Carlos rose from his knees and walked around the corner of the house to the kitchen. He took two rags to protect his hands and lifted from its baked clay supports above the smoldering fire a blackened ceramic platter–*el comal*.

All heads turned toward Carlos as he approached. Waves of shimmering heat from the *comal* distorted him. As Carlos knelt, Pablo turned his head away and buried his face in his opposite shoulder. El Seco extended the wounded arm. Pablo bit into his own good right arm high on the bicep. Carlos held the plate against the amputation until the wound smoked and turned black. A thin rivulet of blood emerged from the corner of Pablo's mouth.

Carlos set the plate on the ground. He took the bottle of *chaparro* from under the bench and poured some on the smoking stump. It hissed and the air smelled sweet.

Elmer's mother, Carlos' niece Ana, had been inside the house all the while. She had watched the fight and the cauterization from the doorway. She disappeared inside again, to return with a daub of lard in her palm and a piece of clean white cloth over her shoulder. She knelt before Pablo and rubbed the lard over the charred skin. Then she wrapped it in the cloth. She shook her head slowly. A single plump tear overflowed each eye and tracked down her brick-colored cheeks.

"Men are more stupid than cows," she said softly.

Carlos and she helped the swooned man inside and stretched him out on the bed, a straw-filled canvas mattress on a post-and-rope frame.

Carlos came back out. He and the other men sat down on the benches. The bottle was passed. April set her camera on the ground and brought her stool closer and accepted the bottle when it was offered. Her slightly shaking hand, holding the bottle, felt awkward. She took a small swig, passed the bottle, then clamped her hands together between her knees and looked around. The others too seemed to be trying to forget about their hands. They seemed to have been made uncomfortably aware of them. Carlos picked at a callus, then scraped dirt from beneath his nails with a splinter.

El Seco got up and walked over to the black lines of blood on the ground. He kicked dirt over them, then bent down to pick up his machete.

He had his back to the house when Pablo stumbled out and grabbed the machete Carlos had leaned against the wall.

"You cut off my hand!" he shouted. *"Te voy a matar!"*

Pablo bolted and Carlos took off after him. But the younger man was across the yard, scattering chicks, in three long steps. El Seco had turned around at Pablo's cry and was backing away as Pablo raced at him, his weapon raised and wavering. El Seco's face was stretched taut.

It looked for an instant like he would not defend himself. It looked like he was willing, as if in penance, to receive Pablo's blow. But at the last instant, grasping his machete in both hands by the handle and the blade, El Seco raised it horizontally before his face in self-defense. When it was over, they saw that he had sliced into the fingers of his own left hand in clenching the blade.

Pablo's descending overarm stroke, which would have split El Seco's skull, struck El Seco's raised blade.

But it was not metal that struck metal. In lunging, Pablo had overshot his mark. His right wrist struck El Seco's machete.

This time El Seco's blade went clear through, detaching the hand outright. Pablo's machete, still grasped by the hand, flew past El Seco's ear and struck the dusty ground.

CHAPTER 9: BODYGUARDS

(The Gardener, take 4)

So that's how Pedro and I became acquainted, through an encounter in a 7-Eleven that turned violent. We jumped into his Audi and he peeled out of the parking lot. He didn't say anything for the first couple minutes, just checking the rear-view mirror. He was calm, sliding through traffic. He cleaned the blood from the corners of his mouth with his index finger and thumb and wiped it on his jeans. He drove fast, switching lanes but using his blinker. When we pulled onto the freeway he reached down to the floor and picked up the Mexican's gun. Holding it in his right hand, hefting it, steering with his left, he looked at the gun, then the road, then the gun. "Ruger Speed 6. This is an excellent weapon," he said, in Spanish. "You tell a guy, even someone who knows about guns, that you've got a 9mm revolver and he'll probably say Must be a .38, or a .357 Mag. But these Sturm&Ruger people in Connecticut were smart. For years there's been a glut of 9mm ammo on the market. Costs a third of .38 bullets. So they made this little prick."   Then he reaches across to the glove compartment, opens it and takes out a pistol. Just leaves it there on the open shelf. The Audi's suspension was amazing. The gun barely trembled. "That's a Glock. Austrian. It holds 14 rounds. Which is why gang-bangers like those assholes back there will pay a thousand bucks for it. Beside the fact it's a well-made piece. But if I had to have only one gun, it'd be a revolver. Something like this, with a fast action. Simpler. More reliable." I told him I knew fuck all about guns. Which was true in those days. Now I'm a fucking expert. With assault rifles, at least. And he says, wise-ass but friendly: "Why would you ever need a gun? Cans of tomatoes abound." *Abundan,* the fucker says. "And they're legal and much cheaper." *Chele* Chapin joker. Because you see, Pedro, like the can of tomatoes I chucked, was Guatemalan. Back then, he was 21 years old and had been in Los Angeles less than a year. He'd had to come. Was in a sort of exile, because he had shot another kid. This is all stuff I found out later. Another *niño bien* kid, during an argument one blow-fueled Saturday night of club-hopping through la Zona Viva. The kid, who survived but lost a kidney, was a hopped-up, firearm-equipped Zone 10 boy too. White, with a rich dad. Which was what made evasion of consequences impossible. If it had been a poor kid, or an Indian, Pedro's uncle could have fixed it. Anyway, we're cruising along in the Audi and I'm asking myself where the hell we're going. I wanted to tell *el chelón este* to let me off, *ya.* Not that I thought he'd done anything wrong. But I didn't know if what we'd done could be considered illegal. Maybe someone had taken down the Audi's license plate number. And I sure didn't like being in a car with guns in it. I was wondering if the two injured *cholos* would need an ambulance. I was thinking about the one I'd knocked out. And Pedro says, "Think you mighta killed that guy?"   *"No mames,"* I say. "No fucking way."   I   put   the   gun   back   in   the compartment and closed it. But not before noticing how substantial it felt. In the same way, though much heavier, as the Rotring fountain pen, a cool burnished black metal job that traced a great line on a fresh sheet of paper, so you just wanted to keep writing, that my grandmother had given me for being valedictorian. He steps on the gas and says, in English now, "Nah. He'll probably live." Then, "Where you wanna go?" I had no way of knowing then that that incident was a watershed in my life and in some sense put me on the path that led me to where I'm sitting now, here in fucking Antigua Guatemala. I thought then that there was nothing preventing me from resuming my uncomplicated existence of sports, books, filial devotion and Stanford-in-the-fall. But all three of the Mexes besides the one whose lights I put out got a good look at me. And the mean crazy one, the one with the cannibalized arm, swore to *la Virgen de Guadalupe* that the *guero* would die. And that the other meddling fuck, who was me, was going to regret sticking his nose in. I found out about him, the stringy Chilango, in the following weeks. His name was Guillermo Gutierrez but he was known on the street as Junior, or El Loco Junior. He'd been part of a D.F. gang since he was a little kid, some kind of orphan or something, right out of Los Olvidados, and had climbed through the ranks by virtue of a constant disposition to spill blood, others' and his own. There in L.A. he was running a distribution operation of cheap brown Mexican junk. You hear things that may or may not be true. But word soon got around that they'd had to graft a plug from one of his buttcheeks into his arm. And the story went that some punk in his set, a *compinche* recently arrived from Mexico City, saunters up to Junior one afternoon not long after all this went down, brushes the still-bandaged wound on his arm with his fingertips and says: *"Te toqué el culo."*

Which is a boy's game of fooling around. "I touched your butt." A challenge, like wetting the inside of another kid's ear with spit on your thumb. And Junior–this is what I was told– grabbed a gun off a table and without saying a word shot the kid in the center of the chest. I thought about that little wiseass Mexican back then when I heard that, before I'd ever seen anybody shot to death, and about what he must have been thinking in those seconds remaining to him after being knocked backward, when he put his hands on the warm liquid bubbling from him. Probably the last thing he saw before his eyeballs started dimming was *ese cerote de El Loco* straddling him, looking down at him and telling him to go fuck his mother in Hell.   Anyway,   like El Loco Junior, Pedro Garay was an importer and distributor of narcotics. Pedro's product was Colombian-refined cocaine that passed through Central America on its way to the world's biggest dope fair. He was in the employ of his uncle, a colonel in the Guatemalan Air Force. When the unpleasant events of Zone 10 made Pedro's continued residence in Guatemala untenable, at least for a while, his father's brother installed him–a blood-bound ally despite his youth and recklessness–as lieutenant to the manager of the California end of an extremely lucrative business. The boss in Los Angeles was also a military officer, though retired and of a different nation's armed forces. Pedro never knew him by any name but "Charlie" or a variation of that: *Mr. Charles. Carlos. Chuck.* He had served for five years, in the late '70s, early '80s, in the U.S. diplomatic mission to Guatemala, ostensibly a member of the MILGROUP under the command of the military attaché, but in fact part of the

Central Intelligence Agency's main Central American station. His day job had been to advise his Guatemalan counterparts on strategy and tactics for suppression of a 30-year-old leftist insurgency. By the time of Mr. Chuck's departure, there was not all that much insurgency left to suppress. The army's victory over the rebels, who in the mid-1970s had been gaining momentum, was achieved by scorching the earth in guerrilla-friendly zones, including use of aerial bombardment and napalm. During Charlie's years there, Guatemala became the principal trans-shipment stop, or *puente,* for Colombian cocaine bound for the United States. There was a civilian government, a democratic façade, by the mid-1980s. But the armed forces, which had ruled overtly for decades, continued to set most policy. The mask of civilian rule suited the generals and colonels, as it had in El Salvador and Honduras. Central American army generals are not too fuckin' smart but not too dumb either to realize that in a shrinking world, their privileges and businesses were more lucrative if untainted by the unfashionable institution of military dictatorship. Pedro, well. On that day that now seems so long ago that it could have been another life, he didn't drive up the coast, or off it. He gave no indication that almost getting shot had shaken him. But what went down in the 7-11 seemed to make him somehow less upset about having been jilted. During the next hour or so we talked, mostly he talked, about his girlfriend Elena. He first described her as an "older" Venezuelan woman. I asked him what he meant by older. He'd put on a CD of Brazilian music. I could understand about half the lyrics, a woman crooning soothingly about the sensation of suffocation. "Twenty-five," he says. I asked him if she had a ring in his nose. *"Ojalá,"* he says. That he wished she did. He said he'd like to spend his life being led around by her. He even said he'd come to the conclusion that she was "too much woman" for him. That he was not up to her level. It wasn't a class thing. In fact Elena, who I've gotten to know over the past couple years, is from a poor background. Much more like mine than like Pedro's. What he was saying was that she was stronger than him. It seemed a little weird that he should be unburdening himself like that so soon after we'd met. If what we'd just experienced together can be called "meeting." We didn't even know each other's names yet. But what was even stranger was this feeling I had, one of regret that his romance wasn't working out. I remember thinking: Man, this Elena must be something else. If she's Too Much Woman for a guy who I just saw chomp his way through four crazy gangsters. We got off the freeway and drove up a winding road into the hills above the city. If you can believe it, I'd lived my whole life, from the time I was a baby, in Los Angeles but had never seen it from up there. There were a lot of expensive homes. Iron-gated entrances and long driveways. You caught glimpses of the houses, most of them with big decks supported by stilts driven into the hillside. Great places to look out over the city. The perfect place for a barbeque, or to sit and enjoy a beer and the breeze. But what they made me think of was the next earthquake. I imagined the posts snapping, the rich people's porches crashing into the ravine, the rich people who'd been sitting or standing there on them cart-wheeling down the mountainside. So maybe I was a little bit of a *resentido social,* a prospective revolutionary, even before all the life-changing shit came down. Pedro pulled off the road at a switchback. We got out and went to the front of the car and stood leaning against the hood. We surveyed the pretty city through light yellow and rose-colored smog. He talked more about Elena. Said she was the most beautiful combination of all the American races–Indian, African and European. I didn't know what I was doing on this hill with this fucking guy, leaning against his nice new dirty car. I was still charged with an adrenaline hum in the long bones. I wasn't worried about getting home. My moms wasn't gonna get home and start cooking for a couple more hours. Abuela had the good sense not to worry about me until I was long overdue. Then Pedro spits and says, "Little taste of blood, still." He goes to the passenger door and opens it. Reaches under the seat and pulls out a bottle. Flor de Caña, the dark stuff, aged seven years. The bottle, not cylindrical but four-sided, was about half full. He uncaps it, takes a swig and swishes it around in his mouth, then spits again. "Now we go with a clean palate," he says, raising the bottle again to his lips. He takes two big swallows, then extends the bottle to me. Remember, I was the jock-scholar. Not a big drinker. So I tell him, No thanks. And he says, his eyes gleaming from the hard gulps, "Come on, 'mano. You saved my fuckin' life. The least I can do is offer you a drink." I took the bottle. The stuff tasted great and we got half drunk, finished it over the next hour. Talking. Winding down from violence. I felt *una buena onda* with Pedro up on that hill. But when he finally dropped me off at home, well, I didn't imagine we were gonna become buddies, or anything. I said something like, "Maybe we'll see each other around." And he says, "I'm sure we will."

That was a Saturday in early May. When I went back to school on Monday, I found out I had new friends. Ones I didn't want. At the bell for the first class, a kid named Luis Mejía, a Salvatrucha gang honcho with a Sacred Heart of Jesus tattooed on one of his pecs–he was wearing a leather vest with no shirt–came up to me at my locker. *"Que ondas, Juan?"* he said. He held up his hand and I raised mine and accepted the slapping clasp and drop-shake. That was the way we Guanacos shook hands. He of course knew I was one and I knew he was too, though we didn't really have anything to do with each other. What with one of us an Honor Roll athlete and the other a drug-dealing member of the youth branch of America's Latino mafia. But it wasn't like there was *mala onda* between us, either. There was no *onda.* We stayed out of each other's way and each other's circles. But we were born in the same country. That was what made it possible for him to approach me. *"Pasandola,"* I said. Which means, Getting by. *"Y vos, que ondas?"*

"Tambien," he said. *"Vaya, me alegro,"* I said, and turned and started toward my class. *"No es nada,"* he said, and I turned to look at him. *"Solo que te manda saludos el Chele."* He was smiling, looking nothing like a menace to society. *"El Chele quien?"* Though they didn't abound in that part of the city, I'd made the acquaintance over the years of a few people–light-complexioned or sandy-haired people with blue eyes–known by that nickname. But none who knew me well enough to send me greetings through a third person.

And he says, *"El Chele Pedro, el mero-mero Chapín." "Pues, gracias,"* I said, and turned and walked away, leaving him standing there. Now I smiled, thinking how appropriate and obvious it was that Pedro should be known among Salvadorans by that name. But my amusement didn't last more than a second. Because it occurred to me that if this notoriously criminal kid Luis had some kind of connection with him–not only that but had referred to him with a term roughly equivalent to "the boss"–then Pedro Garay might produce ripples in the calm waters of my life. And at lunchtime it became clear that he already had. Though it was more like a tidal wave. A fuckin' tsunami. The commotion had been gaining force over the weekend and was about to break upon me as I sat chewing a bite of fried-egg-and-cheese sandwich in the cafeteria. The place was vibrating with the clinking buzz of a hundred adolescents stuffing their faces *y hablando paja.* I was sitting alone. Juana, who in those days I was hoping would become my girlfriend, had Monday lunch period a half-hour later, and none of my round-ball or baseball pals were there either. A skinny twerp leaned across the table into my face and says: "You know who is Junior?" I was startled. I hadn't noticed him approach, and I almost tipped the chair over backwards. But I saw in an instant that I was bigger and stronger than this little shit. "What the fuck are you talking about?" "I'ng talking about mi main carnal whose your fren el Chapin *cerote* wants to eat his arm. Now you unnerstan? *Pinche Guanaco comemierda?"* And he pushes the button on the blade he's got in his right hand. He didn't have time to stab me. From nowhere appeared Luis and one of his thugs.

This second guy, who I'd never seen around, grabbed the wrist of the Mexican kid's knife-hand and wrenched it up behind his back. The skinny dude went up on his tip-toes. His shoulder came undone with a pop, and he screamed. Luis took the knife from the kid's hand, folded it closed and put it in his pocket. The other guy wheeled the Mexican around and gave him a shove. *"Ve a lavarte el culo,"* he said. The boy stumbled toward the door, bent over, sucking wind, cradling his arm. The gangsters sat down across from me. "This is El Chucho," said Luis. The big one, *The Mutt*, didn't reach across to shake. He only nodded. *"Mucho gusto. Y gracias,"* I said. "But in the future I'd rather handle my problems myself. I got nothin' against you guys. But I don't want any part of your trip." "The future burn you up, *primo*. I talkin' 'bout the near future. Like tomorrow or the next day. 'Less you foun' a way to make youself hole-proof, you can't handle the future. Not by youself 'lone, anyways." I guess it was at that moment that it sunk in. That I was in trouble. The first real trouble I'd ever been in. Because I'd always been the Good Kid. Hell, I was more than that. I was a class-A bona fide Great Hispanic Hope. Look. If you excel at either sports or academics in an American high-school, you get a lot of praise. Whether you're black white brown yellow or maroon. You can be fuckin' striped. And if you excel at both, and go to an inner-city school and you're a member of an ethnic minority, the principal and teachers and guidance counselors, the fast-talkers on the city council, they latch on to you. Because they think, or make out like they think, that you exemplify or redeem somehow the whole *pinche* race in question. I enjoyed making my mother and my grandmother proud of me. But the rest of it, for the most part, *me pelaba la punta de la verga.* I guess I was very American–here I mean *Estadounidense*–in that regard. What I mostly cared about, besides my immediate family, was myself. Getting up in the world and out of a life of material worries. Not that I didn't want to be upstanding. I did. I imagined a life of civic participation, paying my taxes, coaching Little League, PTA, jury duty. The whole fucking deal. But the fundamental underlying goal was making my life–and my mother's life–comfortable. Affluent even. I wanted my mom and *abuelita,* who both had worked so hard for so long, to be able to kick back and take it easy once I finished college and got a good job. I was gonna take care of them, see. The way things turned out, I wasn't good enough or strong enough to provide for them or protect them. I eventually became what you'd call wealthy, yeah. And last year I bought my grandmother a house in Seattle and she lives what I guess is a good life up there with my aunt Marta. But even that I had to do *bajo las aguas,* on the sly, in cahoots with Marta and her husband Willie. Because by the time I was able to set her up, mi *abuelita linda* who'd always loved me deliriously, well, by that time, after losing my mom and not hearing from me for years, well, maybe she didn't really want to have anything to do with me anymore. She must have considered me gone, if not dead. I think she'd come around to the idea that it was partly, or even mostly, my fault, what happened to my Moms. Which, in a way, I guess, it was. So I asked Luis, "What's that mean, *pues?* You guys gonna be my bodyguards from now on, or what?" "I wouldn't put it like that, 'mano," he says. "You gonna have to watch out for youself mosta the time. But while you doin' that, jus' keep in mind you got some brothers gonna stan' wit you if you in a jam. Jus' like you done with el Chele. He don' forget when somebody help him out. An' the way he tell it, you the reason he still breathin'."

That's what this guy Luis said.

CHAPTER 10: A WEALTHY MAN

Joe Guinness sat on a rock on a knoll just west of the excavation site overlooking a field of new sugar cane. A pattern of rough circles slightly darker than the soil's light sienna stood out through the foot-high shoots of thick-stemmed sweet grass. The spots marked the places where Indian homes had stood two or three centuries earlier, where adobe blocks had crumbled, been eroded and dissolved by rain over scores of seasons. Not washed away. Only washed back, as a stain and a reminder, into the same dirt from which they had been fashioned.

He was thinking about the tenacity with which a people and its ghosts resist oblivion. That was one of the big reasons why he loved his job. Those circles seemed to him like magic passageways between present and past, like doors or tunnels cartoon characters paint in two dimensions that acquire in a crucial instant a third to provide escape from the danger at hand.

In his mind's eye he constructed the houses up out of the ground. He saw the long-ago dwellers laying mud-and-straw blocks one upon the other, lashing thatch to sapodilla rafters, until the earth-colored men and women had molded up out of the earth dwellings of the same color, homes that would absorb the searing sun's heat and store it against the night's chill and release the warmth gradually through the hours of darkness until it ran out just before the stars began to fade, so that the people would shiver a little as they got up to see the first rays breaking over the eastern hills.

"Excuse me, Doctor."

He turned to find a stocky campesino. The man held a straw hat in his hands, but the posture was in no way submissive. He spoke with confidence. "I am Carlos Roca. I was told you were asking for me in the village."

Two days earlier, Joe had first visited with a scholar from ECA (*Estudios Centroamericanos*), the Antigua-based research foundation that was collaborating with Cornell on the dig. The two men had inquired about Carlos in the hamlet, only to be told he was visiting family near Antigua, but that he would return by week's end.

Owen, convalescing back in Ithaca, had briefed Joe on the progress of the excavation and its logistics. He had nothing but praise for this man, Carlos, whom he had described as a peasant scholar, barely literate but an invaluable repository of knowledge regarding Mayan antiquity.

Carlos had worked on and off for the previous quarter century with a succession of North American, Mexican and European archeologists in the excavation of three of the country's most important sites. He had begun as one among a crew of diggers, instructed by the sojourning professors in techniques of trowel and brush and sieve, and had rapidly distinguished himself for his intuition and insight.

Carlos Roca was the patriarch of Tres Ceibas, the settlement a half-mile from the current excavation and the name by which the dig had come to be known. At 63 years old, he was a great-grandfather several times over. His eldest great-granddaughter had recently turned 15 and, if true to the pattern of village life, would not be long in swelling and adding another 'great' to Carlos' distinction.

He was born in 1932, several months after the military dictatorship had repressed a peasant uprising. Soldiers had killed several thousand campesinos, among them Carlos' father, who'd had nothing to do with the Communist Party-led rebellion but who a few weeks prior to the revolt had thrashed a coffee plantation paymaster for trying to cheat him a day's wages.

The soldiers arrived an hour after nightfall. The army squad leader kicked down the door, and the troops dragged their quarry naked from bed and the arms of Carlos' mother. They stood him against the wall, his cock by this time un-stiffening but still larger than normal and dangling majestically.

The last thing Carlos' father did, in the instant before three Garands spit flash and lead, was tell his executioners, in an unwavering voice, *"Son ustedes una manga de cabrones cobardes."*

"You're a bunch of cowardly bastards."

In peasant terms, Carlos was well off. He owned ten hectares of fertile farmland on the outskirts of Tres Ceibas. The spread comprised 15 adobe houses, 100 people–all of them related by blood or marriage to Carlos–six oxen, a dozen cows, four horses, several pigs, a pack of skinny dogs and scores of chickens, turkeys and ducks. A few years earlier, he had purchased a two hectare plot for two of his grand-daughters and their husbands outside of Antigua, where he had also built himself a small house and where he visited often, whenever he had a few days off.

Carlos' khaki pants and white button-down shirt were clean and well-mended. He wore black canvas Converse All Star basketball sneakers. Oriental-cast black eyes shone in a sparsely whiskered face the color of polished cedar. The hands that held his hat were thick. His was a powerful constitution; keg chest, smooth arms like braided rope, sloping shoulders and a broad back.

Joe shook his hard hand.

"*Mucho gusto*," Joe said. "*El professor Thomas le manda saludos.*"

"Thank you. He gave us quite a scare when he collapsed. We hold *El Doctor* in the highest esteem. *Primero Dios*, he will recover."

"He's recuperating from by-pass surgery, and hopes to return next year. He is my *padrino*."

"You don't say? *El Doctor* sends his *ahijado como suplente.*"

"I was hoping you would continue to work with me, that you would assist me as you did Owen."

"With delight. I like nothing more than digging up old things."

The two men walked down the hill to the site. A roof of corrugated zinc had been erected on wooden poles above the sole excavated dwelling to protect it from rain and to shield the diggers from the harsh sun.

It was a house of two chambers formed by adobe pillars at the four corners and what had been walls of wattle and mud *bajareque* packed between vertical poles. One of the walls had collapsed outward. The one opposite leaned in on what had been the dwelling space. The walls were punctured by holes where the poles, now decomposed, had been. The floor was of finished adobe, not blocks but poured or "puddled" adobe that had been floated, first with a long straight edge then with handled flat rectangles of wood or slate.

On the house's north side were three rows, each about 15 feet long, of plaster casts of knee-high plants. While excavating this structure in the months before his heart attack, Owen and his crew had discovered voids in the volcanic ash, spaces left after that catastrophic season's corn crop decomposed beneath layers of ash and silica expelled by the exploding earth. The excavators had filled the detailed molds with dental plaster to obtain perfect replicas of the plants.

Carlos swept his arm over the crop of stunted stone corn. "It's from this that we know the month of the volcano's eruption. Of course, we cannot say precisely which year or even decade it was because of the margin of error in carbon dating of the organic material. But we can be quite sure, from the height of the corn, that it happened in June."

Joe had spent hours studying Owen's drawings of the floor plan and diagrams of what had been found, and where, in this house. In the ECA offices in Antigua, he had already examined most of the artifacts, the pottery and obsidian scrapers and grinding stones and remnants of rafters and thatch that had collapsed under the weight of falling stone and ash and searing mud.

Owen and his diggers had removed nearly five meters of volcanic material to reach the floor of this house. Most of that had been deposited over days or weeks approximately 1400 years earlier by the Laguna Caldera eruption. One June day about 590 A.D. when the corn of what is now southern Guatemala was a foot-and-a-half tall, an underground river of basaltic magma, the molten rock that supports the crust of the world, reached the surface through a fissure about three miles north of what today is the village of Tres Ceibas. The contact of magma and shallow surface water produced a cataclysmic explosion that blasted skyward a million tons of earth, rock, ash and trapped boiling gas.

The Laguna Caldera deposits formed 12 layers. Beneath them were strata of what had been wind-carried ash from the eruption of a more distant volcano about 600 years earlier. On top of them were a few inches of ash that drizzled on the site during several days in 1658, when the Cerro Azul volcano erupted 15 miles to the west.

Of the layers of Laguna Caldera spew that entombed the prehistoric Tres Ceibas, some were formed when ash and stone fell from the sky. Others were left by "pyroclastic flows," or gales of semi-solid wind, volcanic fragments stirred into a scalding avalanche by expanding gases trapped in pulverized rock.

Owen had used the term "a Maya Pompeii" and was sure about its potential for revealing, frozen in time and sheathed in hard ash, a slice of prehistoric Mesoamerican life.

Carlos invited Joe to accompany him to the hamlet.

The newcomer followed him along a path through lush grass and around arching stands of golden and green bamboo for about 10 minutes until they emerged on the clearing that was the heart of the *caserio*.

They passed the house where Carlos lived alone, a structure of adobe block with a tile roof instead of the more common corrugated zinc. Carlos did little more than sleep there. Two of his sons and one of his daughters had households within 30 yards, as did five grown grandchildren, and he took all his meals with one or another of those families and spent most of his time, when not busy with an excavation, visiting with kin or playing with toddlers away from his own larger dwelling, the one in which many of the members of this community had been reared.

His daughter Zoila's house was one expansive bajareque-walled room furnished with two beds and several hammocks of coarse cotton hanging from the beams. Inside were a split-log bench, a rustic chest of drawers and a large wooden trunk. Most of the floor of tramped earth was bare, though several reed-woven mats were stacked along one wall. The interior was used principally for sleeping. Preparation of food, mending of clothes and other daily tasks were done beneath the broad overhang of roof that protected a table, two benches, two chairs, two more hammocks and the fired clay cooking hearth. It was there, on the patio, that the family took its meals.

Eight people lived in Zoila's house. Present now were three women, three young girls and an infant. Carlos introduced the American to the women as *"el nuevo profesor."*

"And he is the godson of *El Doctor.*"

Zoila, who had been making tortillas, wiped her hands on a pink apron and welcomed Joe with a delicate handshake. The other two women covered sheepish smiles with their hands before repeating their cousin's greeting.

The only male was a baby of about one year who obviously had taken his first unaided steps in the previous days. Carlos went inside. Joe sat sipping sweet weak chicory-flavored campesino coffee from a metal cup and watched the babe, who was called Beto, toddle about giggling among the chickens.

He had yet to master his stride and balance, and sometimes went barreling forth at a pace he could not control only to tumble to the ground. The white t-shirt that was his only garb–his little jalapeño of an uncircumcised penis bobbed before him as he ran–and which had been immaculate when pulled over his head that dawn was now smeared with dirt. In the following weeks, Joe came to consider this boy the happiest baby he had ever laid eyes on. He reveled in the incessant attention of his sisters, two or three of whom were always home and who took turns cradling and carrying and playing with their little darling.

Cayetana, who was five, picked Beto up and carried him the ten yards to the broad path that was a sort of main street through the village and set him down. The toddler laughed and headed with short rapid steps back toward the house with his sister behind him and inclined forward, surrounding her brother with her arms to catch him if he fell. She appeared to take as much delight from this as did the boy.

Zoila and one of her cousins were busy preparing food. A low table, a kind of counter made of split saplings, stood at the edge of the space protected by the roof overhang. Two *metate* grinding stones sat on it. The stones got little rest, as the fine-grinding of maize for tortillas was a task almost without end.

The corn, after being boiled with a dash of mineral lime, was first ground at a hand-cranked *molino* affixed to a table in the yard. The coarsely milled grain was gathered in a plastic basin and brought to the *metates*, where one of the women would place dampened clumps of it on the stone before her, take up the *mano* stone and press the coarse dough down and away from her against the *metate*, pulling back to take a small bite with the *mano* from the *masa* and press it against the stone until the mound was transformed into a thick smooth paste. From the edge of the *metate* Zoila scooped a handful of paste and patted it and molded it, turning the emerging shape against her vertical palm to form a rounded edge. Then she set it on the *comal* above a wood fire, where several identical circles were cooking. She touched the others to check their consistency, lifting and flipping one or another until they were firm and dappled with golden brown. She lifted them off the searing plate and stacked them on a clean cloth spread in a straw basket and covered them with the corners of the same cloth so they would stay warm.

Carlos emerged rear-end first from the house dragging a wooden trunk. Kneeling beside it, he lifted the lid and began removing and handing Joe items of pottery and stone, the most delicate of which were wrapped in cloth.

"I found these things plowing my fields. Also, when we bury someone we usually find something. And when we dig a well," he said.

A chest that Blackbeard himself might have filled with dubloons could not have thrilled the visitor more. Over the decades Carlos had collected an array of utilitarian and decorative handiwork. Most pieces were ceramic–plates, bowls and vases–and were chipped or broken. But there were also three exquisite pieces of jade, what Joe took to be an ear ornament and two large carved beads. Five pieces of pottery were intact, and three of them were handsomely painted. One was an archetypical Classic-era three-footed pot on which was depicted a stylized howler monkey, the patron of scribes in the Maya pantheon, writing on a codex.

"What beautiful pieces, Don Carlos," Joe said, turning the pot in his hands. "I can only guess at their age. Most of them appear to be Maya, but there are also some Pipil-looking designs. Several of these things are without doubt very valuable. If sold privately, they would make you a wealthy man."

Carlos laughed.

"I already am a wealthy man," he said.

Joe pored over the pieces for half an hour, then helped Carlos stow them again. The patriarch returned his trove to its place of safe-keeping, then asked the American to stay for dinner.

Two of Carlos' grandsons arrived from work in the cornfields, leaned their machetes against the wall and introductions were made. The four men sat down at the large table and ate first. The women served tortillas with mashed beans and salty hard white crumbly cheese and fried eggs. There was a cool melon beverage so delightful that Joe Guinness did not even want to imagine where the water to make it had come from and what havoc its microscopic denizens might wreak on his un-adapted gut. He drank it contentedly, and considered himself, if not quite as wealthy as Carlos, one lucky bastard all the same.

CHAPTER 11: INCOGNITO

Francisco's stroke did not appear forceful but the cue-ball blurred and slammed the four with a crack like a gunshot. The purple sphere slid, almost without rotating, to the cushion and caromed off on a track that could end in nothing but a fall. Juan and Francisco, the son of Ximena Yat and known by the nickname Paco, were at the better of the two tables in the back room of Fritz' bar. Two Gringos were playing at the other table.

They, the white guys, circled slowly, chalking and shooting and sipping their drinks. One was big, about six-two and stout. He looked athletic despite his bulk. The beige crown of his black-billed cap was rounded, contoured to his head rather than vertical and squared like a Catepillar or Feed&Grain sort of cap above a red face in Kansas. Tan muscular legs emerged from baggy khaki shorts. On his feet were Reebok hikers. The other guy was skinny, on the short side and blond.

They were talking about sex. About how certain episodes of sex had made a mess of their respective penises.

Every so often one of them would dust his palm with talc from a Johnson's container on a narrow table beside the racked cues. The big one was drinking aged amber rum from a shot glass in infrequent small sips. The lean fellow had a brown bottle of Gallo beer.

The Gringos must have presumed neither of the dark men at the other table could understand what they were saying. Both men at the better table appeared, despite their clean jeans and nice-enough shirts, to be not far removed from the *milpa,* in that the features of both of them were Indian. Though there were young billiards-playing Guatemalans who spoke English, nothing in the aspect or manner of the pair of locals indicated particular sophistication. It could have been, too, that the *cheles* simply didn't care if they were overheard.

Juan Cano, who Paco knew as Miguel, was listening to the big guy with half his attention, the other portion being concerned with the lay of the table. He and Francisco never talked much while shooting pool. With his ear pricked, Juan savored the incognito condition, the way he blended in here. No one suspected who he was, where he was from, or what he had done up until now with his life.

"She wasn't the first black chick I'd been with," said the large dude. "In Guayaquil a lot of the working girls are black. But this was the first time anything like this happened." He tasted his sweet warm nectar. "She was real pretty. Very dark. Smooth skin that was cool all the time. And it's fuckin' hot down there on the coast. We went from the bar back to her apartment. Well, we got it on pretty hot and heavy. Then after a while we fell asleep. And when we woke up a couple hours later, we did it again. After that second time, when I was startin' to shrink, I felt a kinda stinging. But not what you'd call pain. We went to sleep again and around dawn woke up half hung-over. So we got tangled up again. Maybe because it was the third time, we were at it for a while, and she was getting very worked up. And I could feel it by then. It was hurtin', the nap of her pubes rubbin' against my cock. It was a weird mixture of sensations. Because inside, on point, it felt great still. And she was so into it, I didn't see how I could stop short and say, Hey Waitaminute my pecker's gettin' abraded. So I kept churnin' and she came finally and I came and we just lay there collapsed for a while. But this time, yeah, it really hurt when I went soft. After a while I got up and went to the bathroom and it was a shock, I tell you. 'Cause my Elmo was all bloody. Down both sides, a strip of seepin' strawberry like you used to get slidin' into second base if you didn't have your sliding pads on."

The other guy groaned. Then he chuckled. He sipped his beer. He adjusted his tortoise shell-rimmed glasses and seemed to ponder the advisability of launching forth and apparently decided, What the hell.

He started off saying that the cornhole never held much appeal for him until he was past 25. Which would have been fairly recently, by the look of him. Then, when he was in Paraguay, a girl he was with suggested he give it a go.

It then became evident that at least he of the two northerners spoke Spanish very fluently. Without an accent. Juan figured he must be a Peace Corps or NGO veteran with a few years in Latin America under his belt.

It was in the way he pronounced *"clavado y cosido."* That was just about the only thing he said in Spanish, but it was enough; the sound of the "d;" the way a native speaker pronounces it with the tip of the tongue grazing the bottom of the central incisors, more like a "th" than the hard-against-the-palate "d" of English or German.

"She said, Why didn't I try the old *clavado y cosido,"* said the lean guy. Here he looked down at the floor and sniggered.

"What in hell is that?"

"Fuck if I know the translation. They're sewing-machine terms, the way a stitch goes. Ya ever watch a sewing machine work, close up? The needle goes through the cloth, then comes out and moves back a bit and goes through again. One of them strokes is the *clavado* and the other is the *cosido*."

"Yeah? And?"

The blond one leaned over the table and lined up his shot. "Damn, Jimmy. You ain't got much of a 'magination." He cut the 14 softly, a faint click, into the side pocket.

The big guy thought it over for a second. "Ya mean ya got her set up there in the canine mode, and ya give her a poke in the pussy, then a poke in the caboose? Like a leather-stitcher?" He laughed. "Those girls must have big assholes!"

"It ain't that they're big. They just got a way of relaxin' it, and are used to it, I guess. Anyway, I liked it the first coupla times. But then once I was doin' the backdoor with this Colombian girl named Zelida, in Panama. And after I unloaded, when I pulled out there was a gob a' refried beans on my dick. And that turned me off to the whole idea, for good. Since then I just put it where yer s'posed'ta."

Juan Cano alias Miguel Zelaya and Francisco Pop Yat were both drinking Gallo. They were on their third beer after about an hour of shooting. Juan had not won a single game–8-ball–of the four they'd played. From the look of the table now, Francisco was going to be sinking balls for the next few minutes. Juan might not even get a chance to shoot.

Paco was a master with wooden wands in more ways than one. He had extraordinary ability with a pool cue, but that was not as distinguishing as the touch he exercised in his principal vocation.

Francisco Pop Yat was a nationally known marimba virtuoso. A master, of course, of the folkloric and traditional, but also an innovator and explorer, alone among the instrument's premier Guatemalan practitioners in venturing into classical and jazzistic expression.

Growing up in the household of Angus MacSwan, a renowned wildlife photographer who had employed his mother for nearly 20 years, Paquito had been given piano lessons by Mrs. MacSwan, an accomplished soloist in her youth. Most of her other students were children of European or North American residents of Antigua, though some were the sons and daughters of well-off locals. Paco, the only Indian child taught by Mrs. MacSwan, was also the only one who did not pay. She had seen that he had talent, and was astounded at how quickly he learned to read music. That was when he was only six years old, before even learning to read Spanish.

But he also had a privileged ear. He was able to pick out on the keyboard a melody of a popular song, say, he had heard that day in the street and had spent the afternoon humming. This inborn sense of melody and harmony was also a matter of a certain delicacy in Paco's case, at least in the mind of Mrs. MacSwan. (The English language makes no distinction between the physical flap of skin-covered cartilage on the side of the head and the inner function of audition, while in Spanish there is a difference: one is *la oreja,* and the other is *el oido.*) Because in addition to having a splendid ear, Ximena's son had prodigious ears–large and protruding *orejas* that were the source of ridicule by his young playmates. Though he eventually became a centered and balanced individual–the hard-earned lot of the naturally superior character subjected to teasing and abuse when young–he still cringed inwardly, even as an adult, at the sound of the moniker *orejón,* or worse yet, *Dumbo.* When Paco was a child, Mrs. MacSwan had been obliged to search for alternative terms to describe her star student's natural prowess, it being inevitable that, among English-speakers who knew the boy–and all of the MacSwans' foreign acquaintances did–any report on the outstanding-ness of his "ear" would elicit a chuckle.

The boy studied piano for seven years. But, to Mrs. MacSwan's chagrin, at the age of 12 he opted to continue his musical training with a local *marimbero,* whose band he eventually joined as a diminutive phenom.

By the time he was a man, Francisco was not only a maestro of the instrument but also a crafter of exquisite marimbas. His home in Quetzaltenango was attached to a large workshop that for the previous decade had almost never been without a work in progress.

He and Juan (both, coincidentally, 28 years old) had met two months after Juan moved into the big house. Francisco visited his mother frequently from Quetzaltenango, where his Conjunto Xela, among Guatemala's best ensembles, was based. Upon arriving late and unannounced on his first visit after Juan had taken up residence in the house, Francisco spent the night on a straw mat on the floor of Ximena's room. Juan had found him in the kitchen with his mother early and, after the introductions were made, the two men had had breakfast together.

Ximena set a table on the veranda and brought them tortillas and fried eggs and beans and salty *queso fresco* and coffee and fresh-squeezed orange juice and sliced papaya. Juan by then had given up suggesting that Ximena sit at the table with him to eat. She had invariably responded *Gracias,* but that she'd already eaten. That first morning with Francisco, he thought perhaps her son's presence might make a difference. He invited her again to sit.

"Gracias, don, que yo ya comí," she said.

Francisco, for his part, was at ease with his mother's employer. He smiled, sometimes broadly, but in a manner never ingratiating. Juan came to believe that Francisco's composure was the natural by-product of his talents. Paco did not make any effort to transmit a sense of himself as unique or gifted or special. But after not so many hours with him, Juan arrived at the conclusion that Ximena's son would not trade places with anyone on earth.

The second time he showed up, Juan told him *Que no tuviera pena,* that he should use one of the three unoccupied bedrooms, each with a large comfortable bed. That night and during all subsequent visits, Francisco slept in what Juan had come to think of as the "Horses" bedroom, for the two sculpted wooden foxhound-sized steeds that stood at the foot of the four-poster.

Now, as Paco prepared to run the table in Swiss Fritz' bar and pool hall, Juan took the opportunity to go to the bathroom. The azure-tiled, dimly lighted space smelled of ammonia. Juan lifted the toilet seat and stood before the bowl looking down. The reflection of his face was framed perfectly in the still pool and rendered in what seemed to

Juan meticulous detail. In those seconds he saw something he had never before seen. What he saw was that he was aging, that his face was no longer seamless and smooth. There in the porcelain-bordered mirror, his visage appeared slightly worn, and despite the shimmering smooth surface on which it lay it appeared to have something of the texture of stone. He felt a sudden urgent need to make a better study of it, but a golden stream crashed into the water and obliterated his likeness.

When he returned to the table Francisco was standing with the butt of his cue on the floor and the tip before his nose.

"*A usted,*" he said.

Though each by now considered the other a friend, the two men always used *Usted* with each other.

Juan took a sip of beer and studied the table. Francisco had run four of the solids, having left the easier lie of stripes to Juan. He'd even left his companion set up to sink two balls with utmost ease and with a good chance of putting away four or five.

Juan chalked the tip of his cue and rubbed the blue cube on his left index and middle fingers and proceeded to sink the two gimmes. He then executed a stylish combo to put away the eleven, and followed that with a bank of the nine.

"*Bonito,*" said Paco. "I was waiting for you to start playing."

Juan missed the next attempt, but left Francisco without a shot. Instead of safety-ing, Francisco sent the cue-ball into the little remaining nestle of bright spheres, spreading them around and leaving the way clear for Juan to win.

CHAPTER 12: KEEP LAUGHING, PAL

April didn't know it, but the wind that came up strong with Monday's dawn in the last week of October told los Antigueños the rains were over.

The school year had ended a few days earlier and children were on vacation. These were the days when their parents bought them kites of colored paper and sticks.

April went into a tienda on Santa Lucia boulevard near the post office. A dozen kites were hanging from a beam. Because they were pretty, she asked for two.

She had left her camera behind in the closet of the room she'd rented with the Nuñez family on Seventh Street. Unencumbered, enjoying not only the lightness of her step but also the break from the self-imposed obligation to record sights instead of simply seeing, she had wandered to the area behind the market. Here firewood was sold, resinous *gravilea* that caught quickly and flamed, and live-oak dense and heavy that burned hot for hours. Two grassless soccer fields took up the space stretching to *la Calle de los Recolectos*, which marked the southern edge of town.

The expanse was occupied by dozens of children flying kites. Streaming tails fluttered as the multi-colored diamonds and hexagons danced and jerked and fought to rise higher against a patchwork sky of white and gray and blue.

Not ten minutes passed before April had given away both her kites.

There was something about the light, not just here behind the market but throughout this spectacular valley. The floodtide of greenery over walls and the hills and *jardines* and outlying streets exuded an element that suffused colors to their fifth essence. It was not that the colors were especially brilliant. They were more deep than bright, wet-looking even when dry.

The walls of most of the homes were painted with *pintura de cal* made with quicklime and water and, in colonial times, partially refined sugar (though these days that ingredient was replaced with white glue.) Powdered pigments provided hue; gradations of ochre and sienna and cornflower-blue and pink. About a third of the houses were white, simply *encaladas*. The rest were pastels, with white or otherwise contrasting trim.

Even the gray of the clouds was remarkable; a pearly, luminous silver-edged gray. The light and colors and abundance of ruined colonial architecture made the city a favorite of painters. April saw a few almost every day, working mostly in *aquarela*, seated or standing behind an easel set up on the sidewalk. Many faced south, so that the Agua volcano loomed in the background of their compositions.

On her way from the soccer fields to *el parque* she paused behind an *aquarelista* at work. An older man, he wore a broad straw sombrero, a smock and canvas sneakers. His subject was the facade of San Jose el Viejo church and a half-block of outer walls of adjacent homes, purple bougainvillea and orange *collar de reina* spilling over. The pencil drawing was complete and almost all of the church's façade had been colored, in bone and dun and amber and ash.

The painter was set up directly across from the entrance to the local branch of the BAM, el Banco Agricola Mercantil. The sound of a car door slamming made April turn her attention from the canvas to the other side of the street, where a man had just gotten out of a blue Mitsubishi Mirage. He was locking the door when the bank guard called to him.

"Yes?" replied the man, pocketing his keys.

This institution, like the half-dozen other bank branches in town, employed private security agents. On the threshold of each, as well as at the entrance to jewelers or jade-sellers, there was a uniformed man or two men standing with a shotgun held ready across the chest or dangling beside the leg. They accompanied soft-drink delivery trucks too, these men with *escopetas* and poorly tailored uniforms. And beer trucks and even vans delivering bread. The idea was that they protected the businesses from robbers and the trucks from hijackers. It was obvious, though, that against a determined criminal, one prepared to kill, they were useless. They did not even use bullet-proof vests. Someone sufficiently ruthless could simply walk up and shoot them and proceed with his robbery, as happened sometimes.

The criminals had nothing to worry about from the real police. Agents of la *Policía Nacional* did not usually stray more than a block or so from headquarters on the south side of *el parque.* Those on duty could be found standing around or sitting around in groups of three or four beneath the portico, scratching their chin or combing their hair or struggling word-by-word through the sports pages or the classified ads of the previous day's newspaper or one from a week ago. If they patrolled at all away from the main square it was to fulfill their principal mission, the smiling, understated extortion of bribes from shop owners, restaurateurs or motorists.

So bottling companies and breweries and big bakeries like Pan Bimbo hired private guards to ride with their cargo, and the banks hired them to stand out front. Maybe the guards had a few years of military service as something more than a conscript. Most were poor souls trying to make a living for their families. But some of them, now that they had a stripe on their pants and had been given a peaked cap and a weapon, began believing they were invested with genuine authority.

"Are you a client of the bank?" the BAM guard asked the motorist.

"What?" replied the man, who was taller and fairer than the average Chapín, but not an eminently out-of- place Viking type. His car had Guatemalan plates and was not a rental. Apparently he resided here.

"Do you have business with the bank? Are you coming in?"

"No. I'm going to Guatel to make a phone call." He indicated the state telecommunications office a half-block away at the corner.

"Then I'll have to ask you to move your vehicle. This space is reserved for the bank and its clients."

The car-owner muttered something April could not make out, though she could hear that he'd muttered in Spanish. Maybe he was South American, an Argentine or Chilean, she thought. What she'd heard him say up to now seemed to her a native-speaker's Spanish.

He took out the key and put it back in the lock and opened the door.

"Why didn't you tell me before I got out?" His tone was disgusted.

"I thought you were coming into the bank," said the guard.

The man got back behind the wheel and pulled the car up ten meters, just past the edge of the bank's facade. He got out and again locked the car and took a couple steps toward the corner. Then he stopped and turned and walked back to the guard. The guard was holding his shotgun in one hand, pointed at the ground.

"I moved the car, alright," said the man, speaking loud enough for April and the painter, who by now was also following the scene, to hear. "But I'll have you know that this street is a public thoroughfare and is not anyone's private property. Not the bank's, or anybody else's. If the bank wants a private parking area, then it should build one on its own property."

"One must respect the rules," the guard responded.

"What rules!?" The man raised his voice. "The ones you make up as you go along?"

"I don't make them up. I have an order."

"From whom?"

"From the director of the bank."

"The director of the bank does not own the street."

The guard perceived something in the man's accent. "You're not Guatemalan, are you?"

He used Usted, the polite form of address.

The man's face turned red. He brought it closer to the brown face of the guard. "What the fuck difference does that make? But for your information, I am not, Thank God. If I'd been unfortunate enough to be born *en este país pendejo,* I'd do everything in my power to emigrate."

The guard laughed. It was a laugh intended to sound superior. But it came out sounding defensive.

"Keep laughing, pal. It only makes you look more like a clown." The foreigner wheeled and started again toward the corner.

"Te cuidas," the guard called after him. An everyday sort of leave-taking. But here it could only be perceived as a jibe, maybe implicitly menacing, even, because of the switch from Usted to Tu.

The owner of the car spun around and marched back to the guard.

"And who might I have to take care against?" He was shouting now. "Armed asshole bellhops? Just because they dress you up and loan you a gun, that doesn't make you a man."

He turned on his heels and started again toward the corner.

The guard was not looking at the man. He had turned his face away in the middle of the other's rant and was staring off into the distance, blank-eyed.

He stood like that, looking at nothing, or at a hilltop outside town. Or at his future dissolving into mist. Then his jaw clenched and he flipped *la escopeta* up from alongside his leg and pumped a shell into the chamber as he took a long step after the taller man. He held the gun straight out in one hand like a huge pistol and fired into the center of the man's back.

CHAPTER 13: BLOWN UP BEFORE HE WAS BORN

(The Gardener, Take 1)

I never knew an Asian person before I met April. There was a Peruvian Chinese kid, Robi Wong, in my high-school. But he was two years younger and didn't play basketball or baseball. So we didn't hardly cross paths. Anyway, if you would have asked me, I'd have said he was South American, rather than Asian. Why do I think of April as Japanese as much as Gringa, then? Who knows? She was born and raised in the States and so were her parents and I think even her grandparents. Wait. There was one kid I knew. Billy Ngô. Billy was like me, in that he had his mother's last name. That's pretty much where the similarity ends. Except for the fact we were both basketball players.

His mother was Vietnamese and his father was a black GI. I guess they never were husband and wife. Maybe she'd been a prostitute over there, I don't know. In any case her kid, at least when he was young, *era un hijo de puta.* Or who the hell knows? Maybe she was completely upstanding, from a good Buddhist family, and she was Billy's father's one true love and he would have married her, and everything. In any case, Billy didn't know much about his old man. He said he got blown up before he was even born. I guess this isn't much to the point. When she sat me down here, April said to talk about my life, and here I am slandering old skinny Bill. But I wanted to tell about this thing that happened just a few weeks before I left the States, when I ran into him. It happened the morning of the same day I met Pedro. Which makes it appropriate as a beginning, seeing how that was the day things started to change for me. Billy looked Asian. He had a kinda flat face and squinty eyes. But he was also tall and dark. He could speak Vietnamese, but made out like he didn't. It was like he rejected that part of his background. He only hung out with black kids and went out with black girls and thought of himself as black. If you asked him, he would have said he was black. He acted blacker than the black dudes, even. The way he talked and dressed and walked. It's not like there was a crowd of Vietnamese kids he could have hung around with, anyway, not where we lived. Not back then. This is south LA I'm talking about, in and around Lynwood. There weren't even any Chinese there, besides Robi Wong. This is a part of Los Angeles where over the 20 years or so before this time I'm talking about there was a kind of a seepage of Latinos–sounds like a *pinche* disease or something, "seeping Latinos"–mostly Chicanos and Mexicans but Salvatruchas too, into what used to be pretty much black neighborhoods. That's where I grew up. And there was Billy, who'd been in the 'hood from at least Middle School on. Maybe earlier. Nobody knew at first how to pronounce his last name. The absence of a vowel either before or between the N and the G had everybody stumped. If somebody asked him how to pronounce it, a new teacher, say, Billy would look her in the eye like the menace he was, like he had a chip on his shoulder, which he did, and say real slow: 'Nih-guh.' But that's not how you really pronounce it. I mean, I don't guess I say it like a Vietnamese person would. But it's more like 'No' than 'Nig,' despite what everybody called him, and what he called himself. Which was 'Billy the Nig.' He was an exceptional hoopster. He could have been a star if he'd gone out for the school team. But he had an attitude problem. He was always in trouble. He got kicked out of school a couple times a year for fighting. Then he quit for good when he was 17. Once, before he dropped out, I tried to talk to him about playing on the school team. That conversation didn't last too long. Billy said the coach was an asshole. Then he says, lookin' me right in the eye, 'Anyway, playing with a ref is for pussies.' I didn't pursue it. He wanted me to take it as an insult. And if I would have been in a bad mood I might have taken it that way. The kind of mood, say, where I felt like getting the shit beat out of me. See, I used to play, too. Played for the school, Lynwood High. My main sport was baseball, but I was a pretty good round-baller, too. I started on the varsity. But I wasn't as good as Billy. I played guard, because I'm only five-ten. Well, five-nine-and-a-half, really. But I usually say five-ten. Billy was completely undisciplined, but in terms of talent, he was better than all three of our forwards. I swear, he could have been in contention for the All-Metro team. Which in LA is pretty fucking good. Could jump like a fuckin' puma. He lived with his mother a few blocks from us. I hadn't seen him for six or seven months after he quit school. Then we ran into each other not long before I split for what's turned into this long exile, if you want to call it that. It was a Saturday morning, early. I was goin' down to the playground to shoot some baskets. Just fool around a little. I didn't expect anybody to be there. It was only about 8 o'clock. I turned the corner and even from a block away I could see it was Billy. I remember thinking: Fuck. Because he really was a bad-news kid. A vicious fighter. A few years earlier, on the same night but in different fights, he'd maimed two kids. One was black and the other was Chicano, and one lost an eye and the other got half his ear bit off. I don't remember which was which. Billy spent 10 months in reform school for that night. Reform school rather than jail, because this was when he was 14. And to make things worse, I mean worse for me and my state of mind the morning I found him there at the playground, the last time we'd seen each other we'd talked some shit. During a pick-up game around Thanksgiving. A Latin-black challenge. I remember it not only because of the altercation with Billy, but because it was the only Latin-black challenge where we didn't get blown away. Our team was mostly Mexes. There are a lot of good

Chicano basketball players these days in big cities out west. You get your odd tall Mexican, especially since they get all their shots and vitamins growing up in the States, and everything. Sam Sanchez was there that day. He's a good six-four and strong. So we had at least one good forward to crash the boards. Where we were usually hurting was at center. But this game was right after this guy Pepe moved to LA from the Dominican Republic. After we got to know him better everybody called him Chico. Because that's what he called everybody else. It was always 'Oye, chico'-this and 'Oye, chico'-that with him. Anyway, he was a damn good round-baller. And at least six-six. He was black, too, is the funny thing. In fact he was one of those very deep black-violet African kind of blacks. He knew about seven words of English, and of course the first friends he made were Latin. So he played on our team, at center. He made the difference and kept us in the game that day. We'd been playing for a while. An hour at least, I'd say, and the score must have been about a hundred to a hundred or somethin' like that, although we just kept it as 'up 2' or 'up 4.' It stayed real close. The lead was going back and forth. I don't think there were ever more than eight points difference. Well, you know. Just because there's no ref doesn't mean there are no rules. Everybody knows them and, for the most part, most of the guys are pretty good about admitting it if they foul you or travel or step out of bounds. You know when you do it, most of the time. There are disagreements, yeah. And in the course of any pick-up game you have some lip and gesticulation. That's part of the game. Maybe because this game was close, *el cerote de* Billy was parking himself in the key to go up for offensive rebounds, in flagrant violation of the three-second rule. After about the tenth time, I called him on it. 'You count too fuckin' fast, *tamale,'* he says. "Least I know how to count, Saigon,' I say back to him. I was hot and into the game and pissed. Sometimes when I'm like that, I just let fly without thinking. If you're composed enough to have in mind your own well-being, you don't diss Billy Ngô like that, by calling him, basically, a gook. Which is his sore spot. Because he's capable of killing you. The other players kept us apart and calmed us down. We ended up losing. Even after they gave us a chance to win. Not on purpose, or anything. Because they were all aware that losing to us, you know, would have been a hard thing to live down in school the next week. What I'm saying is, we had the opportunity to win. But we blew it. We were all tired-assed after about an hour and a half. The score was tied and Jess Cleary, who was my teammate on the school team and their center, says, 'How 'bout next basket wins?' And Billy says, 'But they get the fuckin' ball out!' Even so, the other guys on his team were confident. I remember it very clearly. I took the ball downcourt and whipped a no-look pass to Sam right under the basket and he went up for what should have been our victory. But he got rejected, in-your-Spic-face stuffed by Billy, who not only cleanly blocked the shot but wrenched the ball away from him. About 20 seconds later, Jess slammed the winner. That was the last time I'd seen Billy before this Saturday morning, only a few weeks before I headed for the border. He was shooting at the basket with no net. The level one. The hoop at the other end of the court had the attraction of a chain net, but was an inch or two off level. So basically, it sucked. But rather than mosey down to where Billy was, I pulled up there, dribbling high and slow. Because it wasn't like we were buddies or anything and I wanted to just stroll over to where he was loping around flicking up jumpers and tossing hooks and say, 'Hey, Bill. What's up? Wanna continue where we left off?' I didn't remember this basket hanging down like it was. And I thought, he probably did it. That was his kind of trip. Wreck one thing, then move on to the next. He of course could dunk, and sometimes he'd hang on the rim after jammin'. That was the kind of jivey shit he liked to do, like talk with his hands held up in front of him, fingers sticking out all over the place. I was at the other basket shooting, for about five minutes maybe. I was minding my own business. I wasn't even looking down toward Billy, though I couldn't help but glance that way, you know, sort of peripherally, once in a while. But I wasn't concerned about him. So it caught me by surprise, I might have looked a little spooked, even, when he says out of the blue from only a few feet away: 'Hey, Juan.' He'd come down without dribbling. And he must have been putting his feet down real soft. 'Hey, Billy,' I said. Then I said: 'Haven't seen you around much.' And he goes: 'Nah. Been gone a while. Out to Missouri. Got an aunt there. Little cousins, everything.' This was news to me. I thought his mother was the only family he had. He sounded different. Almost friendly. So I asked him, 'How ya doin'?' 'I'm doin' fine. Doin' real good,' he said. Then he comes out with: 'I don' know if you want to play a little one-on-one. It don' matter really. But anyways I jus' wanted you to know I got no hard feelings against you, Juan. And that if I ever said anything nasty or 'fensive to you, well, I hope you'll forgive me.' I thought at first he was shitting me. I said: 'Are you shittin' me, Billy?' 'Nope, I ain't,' he said. He bounced his red and black ball once, hard, and tucked it back under his arm. He was smiling in a way that looked almost embarrassed. 'I ain't the same person I useta be,' he says. 'I just wanted you to know that.' 'You don't look no different,' I said. And he said: 'Maybe not. But I ain't mean no more, see?' 'What are ya? On parole?' I go, like a smart-ass. 'Nuthin' like that,' said Billy. And he gives a little laugh. Then he thought about it for a second. 'Well, yeah. Maybe it is somethin' like that. 'Cuz it's true I gotta answer to somebody all the time now, somebody who always wit' me. An' I know you gonna be surprised, Juan, 'cuz you ain't got a high 'pinion a me. An' I unnerstan' why that so. But I walk with the Lord Jesus Christ nowadays. Done let him inta my heart. Feel real good about it, too.' Now I started dribbling a little, slow. 'I guess that's good, Billy. Guess that'll help keep you outa trouble. Put a damper on your sex life, though, I bet.' 'Don' matter,' he said. 'Tain't poontang and dope what make a person happy deep down.' And I go, again like a dumbass wiseass: 'I seen you lookin' pretty happy once or twice with a handful a' one and a handful a' the other.' He smiled. But nothing like his old 'Get-ready-to-get-stabbed' smile. 'That was the old me,' he said. 'When I was lost. Now I'm found.' I stopped bouncing my ball. 'Well,' I say, 'Jesus Christ got nuthin' against one-on-one hoops, right?' 'Nothin' ay-tall,' says old Billy, with a grin. 'In fack, Jesus love one-on-one. He a puny little Jewish dude, but he the one-on-one champion years runnin' a the Jordan River Valley League.'"

CHAPTER 14: THE THRILL OF COPROLITHS

Pablo Toscano's right wrist was cauterized just as the left had been twenty minutes earlier, and he survived. He even came to discover a vocation–something that might never have happened had he not been butchered–and he helped Joe Guinness and Carlos a great deal with the work at Tres Ceibas. Along with Elmer, who turned to evangelical Christianity, Pablo quit drinking as a result of that Sunday's carnage. El Seco, for his part, became a full-time, dedicated *bolo*. He abandoned Sandra and was struck by a bus and killed in the capital a few months after the machete fight.

Sandra ended up getting together with Elmer, despite their being second-cousins, and she got pregnant right away. Pablo was depressed during the first couple months of his convalescence, but Carlos's grand-daughters and Maida helped him through his darkest times. Pablo was a lean man. His forearms before the amputations were wiry, and afterward they got even leaner, atrophied for the lack of anything at the end of those muscles to exercise them. Some of the locals started calling him *Pinzas* (Tweezers), because of the way he was obliged to pick things up, by pressing the object between the tips of his skinny forearms, crimped and sheathed in shiny scar tissue.

It wasn't that they were making fun of him. When christening someone with a nickname, Guatemalan campesinos, and city folk also for that matter, tended to appraise a salient trait, even if it was an inadequacy or a disability, and describe it with candor but without malice. It had been like that in El Salvador, too. When Joe had been down there, at the museum and then in the hills, he knew a simian-faced guy known to his friends as *Miquillo* or Little Monkey, a long-lashed and full-lipped individual who wasn't effeminate but who was hailed unabashedly by one and all as *Cara de Puta* (Whoreface) and a stutterer called *Helicoptero* for the way the start-up of his speech resembled the "wha-wha-wha" of a chopper's rotor.

Carlos, a whittler, took pity on his grandson-in-law and came up with the idea of fashioning for him some prosthetics. By the time El Seco met with his unfortunate fate, Pablo had been practicing for nearly a month with the devices. When the rains stopped in late October and it was time to get back to work in earnest at the dig, he had the hang of them and was in better spirits.

Joe, who had been at Tres Ceibas for nearly four months, marveled at Pablo's transformation. He considered it heroic, an extraordinary example of the sort of quotidian valor that marks so much of peasant life in poor countries. This man was demonstrating day in and out that, as a tree can be improved–saved even–by the trimming of its limbs, a human being likewise pruned can become a better human being.

"Since I was a kid, as long ago as I can remember, I have been ready to fight," Pablo told Joe one day at the dig.

"Measuring all men as rivals with the fists or the machete. No need to do that any longer."

They were working in Structure 2, a 1,400-year-old house. The abode, after removal of tons of dirt and compacted ash, sat in a ten-foot-deep hole. Pablo was squatting in the corner where the hearth had been, uncovering a pot. His pick and horsehair broom attachments were strapped on his arms and he had been working hunched over the piece for two hours, delicately chiseling away the hard pack around it.

Carlos Roca had carved from cedar five different implements to be affixed with a belt around the forearm. Six weeks after the machete fight, Pablo had tried them on for the first time. They fit snugly over leather scabbards that shielded the still tender tissue. There were two tools for the left arm and three for the right.

The broom was for the left hand, as was a device of Carlos' design on which a wad of paper could be affixed and which was used exclusively for the cleaning of Pablo's ass. That had been the invalid's first request, made even before the scabs had fallen away, because he was mortified at the prospect of requiring help in the latrine for the rest of his life.

For the right hand were a spoon, which Pablo used to feed himself, and another implement attesting to the cleverness of its maker. It was like a crab's claw. The outside flange was curved and stationary, while the inside one, slightly bowed, was attached to a leather hinge making it opposable to the other. By means of a tug with his teeth on a knotted thong emerging from the wood near his elbow,

Pablo could clamp a broad range of objects and hold them fast.

Finally there was the pick, a simple tapered digit. Pablo used this to scrape compacted ash from around artifacts or other items of interest, such as fossilized feces of people or animals.

Pablo got excited whenever he found a coprolith, an important discovery because its microscopic analysis provides a wealth of information on diet, local flora and parasites.

"Encontré un cerote!" (I found a turd!) he would shout. "Maybe it's the early morning dump of my great-grandfather's great-grandfather."

Pablo's enthusiasm pleased and amused Joe. Sometimes the professor found himself savoring his contribution to instilling in Pablo and some of the other diggers an idea of the significance of history.

But most of the time he was aware that these people, Carlos and Pablo and the other men he hired for the excavation and instructed in its techniques, as well as their wives and sisters and daughters whose cooking he ate almost every day and whose kids he played with and whose company and jokes he enjoyed, repaid him many-fold for whatever slight education or skill he may have helped to impart. They all called him either *Doctor* or *Profesor.* But it was he who felt like their student; an apprentice again, as he had been in the Salvadoran boondocks, in the ways of hard and simple life.

CHAPTER 15: A CHILD'S CHEEK, SO SOFT

Juan Cano and Pedro Garay sat drinking espresso at a table by the window in Tony's coffee house. It was late afternoon on a Monday and they were the only customers. Diego, Pedro's three-year-old son, stood before a pedestal fan, punching buttons to change the rotor's speed. Tony, who was busy at the roaster, called out in English: "Hey kid, try not to chop off your fingers."

Pedro set down his demitasse and leaned toward his friend. "So. What are you doing with your money?"

"Nothing. It's in a bank in the Bahamas."

"Fuck, man. There it's not even earning interest! Don't you want to make some investments? Assure an income for the future?"

"There's nearly a million dollars," said Juan. "I couldn't spend that in the rest of my life, even if I tried."

Pedro leaned back, his palms flat on the table. "Maybe. You'd just as soon drive a Ford as a Porsche. Wait 'till you get hooked up with somebody, though. Then you'll know what expenses are."

A tangle of jasmine from the house next door hung over the wall along the sidewalk so that a spray of white blossoms filled one corner of the roasting-shop's window. As Juan watched Dieguito, who'd tired of the fan and was now checking out Tony's boom-box, a hummingbird arrived at the flowers.

"*Mira!*" exclaimed Pedro in a whisper. "*Un colibrí!*"

Juan called softly to his godchild, and the boy came clambering into his lap. The bird's emerald and copper body and tiny bright eye stood out in precise relief against the elliptical blur of the wings. More than fly, it slid abruptly from station to station, sideways and up and down, to poke its narrow beak into the blooms.

After less than a minute, it darted off.

Diego jumped down and went to stand in the doorway.

"You should be doing like that bird, dipping into chapina nectar, flitting from flower to flower," said Pedro.

Juan said nothing.

After a moment, Pedro said: "You mean to tell me you haven't met any girls here?"

"I don't get out much."

"Why not?"

"Just don't have the urge. Been doing a lot of reading. Taking care of the garden. There are a couple big cookbooks in the library. I'm becoming quite the chef."

"Nada de mujeres? Zero?"

"Poco. Every couple weeks I drive up to Guate, near el Trebol, a place called Las Flores. There's a Guanaca there I like. Caterina. She's funny."

"Man, I know that place. It was great even when I was a kid. We used to go there in high school. But what do you need whores for? You could be sailing through the cream of Guatemalan society. *Aquellas niñas bien de la capital* are wild, bro'. You pick them up in a nice car, give 'em a little single-malt and a couple lines of blow, take 'em out dancing, they're in heaven. I can give you the numbers of a couple trapeze artists."

"Nah, that's OK. I'm cool."

They sipped their coffee and looked out the window, watching people pass by on the opposite sidewalk. Pedro and Diego had come up from Venezuela because Enrique Garay, Pedro's father, was dying of cancer. His ordeal had ended three days earlier, and most of the week prior to that, Pedro had spent at his bedside in an expensive private clinic in the capital.

"They had him on junk for most of the last month," said Pedro. "I pulled an easy chair from the corner to the side of the bed, where I could see his face and hold his hand. They brought in a cot, and I slept there at night."

"Y Dieguito?"

"My brother Rafa picked us up at the airport and we went right to the clinic. That was a good day for Papi. He was awake when we walked in and had more of his wits about him. He was especially glad to see Diego. Elena had some reservations about the boy making the trip. Anyway, Dad had Rafa crank up the bed a little so he was more sitting than lying down.

"You know, it's a lot for a little kid. Though I tell you, he was very calm, and called him 'abuelito' and asked him where it hurt and said the Colita de Rana bit and everything. But after a while I asked Rafael to take him down to the finca, where he could play with his cousins, get to know them. He was down there until Friday, when they all came up for the wake."

After a while Juan said: "Now you're an orphan like me."

"Yeah."

Pedro sat there thinking. "Did you go to catechism? The whole *primera comunion* thing?"

"Yeah. When I was ten. It was a big deal for my grandmother."

"Remember that stuff about the Holy Trinity? How it's so mysterious that nobody can understand it and you shouldn't even try?"

"What else could they say? It's supposed to be monotheism, but it doesn't look like it. So they tell you to take their word for it, not to sweat it."

"Something happened the morning after my first night there with Papi. I woke up early. Light was just starting to come through the window. He was sleeping, or knocked out on morphine. He wasn't horizontal. The bed was still cranked up a little. It was warm in the room and he had only a sheet covering him, pulled up to his chest. He had on a gray t-shirt and his arms were very thin, stretched out along his sides on top of the sheet. They were as white as the sheet, with a design of blue veins on them.

"The chemotherapy gave him an extra two years of life. We would talk on the phone and he would say, yeah, he was ill but he felt good. Strong, even. Kept playing tennis and walking the golf course, everything. Kept diddling *las cuarentonas, tambien*. Every couple months he'd have a few days or a week of chemicals, depending on what his numbers were. And the cancer didn't progress.

"But it's like it learns eventually how to work around whatever they throw at it. And then it's downhill fast. The last three months they kept filling him with stronger and stronger poison and bombarding him with radiation.

During the final stage, it was as much the treatment killing him as it was the disease.

"He was skinny and bald and the radiation burned patches of scalp and the tips of his ears. And that first morning when I was alone with him and he was asleep, seeing him like that, all I wanted to do was to lean down and kiss his cheek and leave my lips pressed there against his cheek for a second.

"So that's what I did. And that's when this weird thing happened. When I kissed him, even though his head was scabby and his cheek rough with stubble, in that moment, with my eyes closed and my lips touching his face, he became Dieguito of, like, a year ago, when he was two. A very young child's cheek . So smooth and soft, and I felt the same feeling I get sometimes when I kiss Diego while he's asleep. And later, though it's not the same thing or anything, I got to thinking about that Trinity rap. How ridiculous it seemed in those days to think that the son and the father were one, that the son didn't come after the father but was there from the beginning with him. But then this thing happened, that when I kissed my father he turned into my son. So it was like my son and my father were really the same person. Well, not the same. I know they're not, that Diego is his own self and, *carajo*, I sure as hell don't want him to turn out like *el viejo*."

The breeze picked up and rustled the ball of long fronds like the burst of a 4th of July rocket at the top of a tall palm in the garden of a house across the way. A truck stopped at the corner, its brakes screeching.

"I hadn't felt like a kid in a long time," said Pedro. "But these days there with Papi, I swear, it made me feel like a little boy again. All I wanted to do was rest my head on his chest. You know, the way a kid falls asleep sometimes in his father's arms. I just wanted to listen to his heart beat, and feel his chest rise and fall."

"Hola, guapito," came a woman's voice from the doorway. April stood in the threshold, her hand resting on Diego's head.

"Hola," said the boy.

She came in and went to the counter and stood before four glass-sided bins holding coffee beans roasted to varying degrees of darkness.

"Hi, Tony," she said. She spoke to him, a fellow American, in English.

"Oh, April," responded the proprietor, looking up from his work at the grinder. "How ya doin'?"

"OK. A little shaky still. I saw a guy get killed this morning."

"No."

"Yeah. A bank guard blew him away with a shotgun."

Tony switched off the machine and came to the counter. "A bank robbery?"

"Nope. Just an argument. Over a fucking parking space. Can you believe it? The guy called the rent-a-cop an asshole or a faggot or something, and the fuckin' guy killed him."

"Holy Christ. Did the police come?"

"Eventually. Took 'em 20 minutes. And it happened two blocks from headquarters."

April lifted the lid from one on the bins and leaned over it and closed her eyes and inhaled. Then she replaced it and said: "Wouldn't 'a made any difference, though. The guy lasted about one minute. Less maybe. I don't know how long it was. I was kneeling over him. He'd fallen forward, face down. And I ran across the street to where he was. When I rolled him over he was still alive. It musta been like 30 seconds after he got shot. And I swear, he had this surprised expression, like he was flabbergasted. Then he gurgled up blood and couldn't breathe and he just closed his eyes and coughed, once, and died. He sprayed blood on me with his last breath."

"Holy Christ," repeated Tony. Then after a few seconds, "What about the guard?"

"He split. Dropped the shotgun and ran off. A woman was screaming and this guy who'd been painting–'cause I was watching him paint when all this came down–he was yelling, 'Stop him!' But the few people who'd seen it happen, it was like they were frozen, and the guy turned the corner. I guess he got away."

Tony made her an espresso without her asking for it. He set it on the counter.

"Wanna shot a' rum in that?."

"Me vendría bien," said April.

Tony reached under the counter and produced a bottle of Botrán Anejo. He filled the small cup nearly to the brim. "That'll steady ya," he said.

"Thanks," she said, and took the saucer and cup to the table next to the one where Juan and Pedro sat.

"Was it the first time?" Pedro asked.

April looked puzzled. "First time?"

"The first violent death you've witnessed."

"Yes. And I hope it's the last." She sipped her coffee. "The only other dead person I've ever seen was my father, and that was in a coffin."

Dieguito came to the table by the window and pushed a chair behind that of Juan. He climbed up on it and from there onto Juan's shoulders. He grabbed Juan's hair with his left hand and with his right made as if switching a flank behind him.

"Arre, yegua," he commanded. Giddyap, mare.

"Who are you calling a *yegua?* Want me to buck you up to the ceiling?"

April addressed Juan for the first time. "He looks more like you than like his father."

Pedro laughed. "That would take the cake. Made a cuckold by my best friend. No, it's just that the boy looks like his mother."

"How do you know I'm not his father?" asked Juan.

"'Cause I know he is," she said, indicating Pedro with a lift of her chin. Then, looking at Pedro: "I saw you two kicking the ball in *el parque* yesterday, and he was calling you 'Papi.' He's the kind of boy you notice. You want to just sit and watch him."

The tables were close together. April was relieved to make small talk, about the weather, and where was a good place to eat. It pushed from her mind the face of the dying man.

"So. You're Chapines, then?"

"Sí," said Juan. "Well, we two," indicating himself and Pedro. *"Este pequeñito* is more Venezuelan than anything. That's where his mom is from, and where he was born."

"And do you live here in Antigua?" She looked from one to the other.

"I do," said Juan.

"Not me," said Pedro. "We live in Caracas. The boy and I are just visiting. We're going home tomorrow."

April looked at Juan. "And what is it you do here? If you don't mind my asking."

"Yo?" said Juan.

He thought it over for a moment.

"I'm a gardener."

***

Two days after they had met at Tony's, Juan tapped the iron-ring knocker on the door of the house of the Nuñez family on Eighth Street, where April was living in a rented a room. An elderly woman wearing a black shawl over a gray dress answered the door. Her left eye was clouded with cataract. She sized up Juan with the right, and made no effort to conceal her disapproval.

"Who shall I say wants her?"

"Miguel Zelaya," he said. Then added, "From the coffee shop."

April came to the door a minute later in shorts, a sweatshirt and moccasin slippers. She did not immediately recognize the man standing there, and Juan thought for a second he'd been a fool to come. Then she placed him.

She smiled, her eyes onyx hyphens. "Nothing to do in the garden today?"

"A couple hours this morning, *no más.*"

"Y tu amigo, y el niño?"

"Ya se fueron."

"They left you *solito.*"

"I guess so."

After a moment she said: "I can't invite you in. This isn't my house."

"That's OK. I was just wondering if you'd like to see the orchid show, at the old University. What's now el Museo de la Cuidad. By the park. A friend of mine and his group are providing the music."

"Ahorita?"

"Sí."

She looked at Juan for several seconds. Though she was only a few weeks shy of her 30th birthday, she looked at this moment, in her too-large shirt and slippers and momentary indecision, like an adolescent.

"Yeah, what the hell," she said, in English. Then, *"Como no. Si me esperas un momento, ya vengo."*

"Te espero."

She closed the door. Juan leaned against the wall of the house. He saw the stocky old man in the Stetson making slow progress up the opposite sidewalk. He'd seen him a couple times before. Today the old man used a single cane, though on other days he gripped one in each hand, progressing by tiny steps. His eyes remained on the ground a short distance ahead of his feet. When he reached the point directly across from Juan he stopped to rest and lifted his chin to scout the block ahead. After a few seconds he continued on. He made extremely slow progress now up the street, toward the row of big *piletas* where Indian women were doing laundry.

April reappeared, in the same sweatshirt but in jeans and Nike hikers. They walked the five blocks to *la Universidad*. Founded in the 1500s, it was the first university on the American mainland, even older than the ones in Mexico City and Lima. The building's foremost courtyard was filled with milling admirers of thousands of orchids arrayed on waist-high tables and stands, or on branches and logs and crusts of bark laid out on the paving stones. April and Juan meandered slowly along the pathways bordered by the delicate plants, their petals violet on white, purple on yellow and yellow on pink.

Halting to admire a cluster of a russet and saffron variety called Little Tiger, April asked, "I wonder how they do it."

"Do what?"

"Live on only air."

Juan was about to tell her that was not the case. That the tendrils fixed nutrients from rainwater and dew. But he liked the idea of living on air. So he didn't say anything.

CHAPTER 16: EARLOBES PLUGGED WITH JADE

It was only intuition with a dash of deduction, little more than a gut feeling, but Joe believed that one of the reasons

Gonzalo Guerrero stayed on in the New World and threw himself, however unwittingly, into becoming a principal progenitor of the Iberian-Amerindian people was that he delighted in magic mushroom juice up the ass.

He could not publish this thesis, even couched in more scholarly terms, as a theoretical sort of finding in a quarterly. Still, Professor Guinness was a widely acknowledged authority on Mesoamerican antiquity, and the idea about use of hallucinogenic fungi by the long-gone archetypical "foreigner" seemed to him a valid inference. It would have been secondary or tertiary to those more compelling reasons Guerrero himself provided Jeronimo de Aguilar–that he had beautiful children he was intent on helping to raise with his Maya wife, and that he could not very well go back to Spain and walk around Palos with his body and face adorned with dark swirls and his earlobes plugged with jade.

Joe, who had been ruminating on Gonzalo Guerrero of late, saw in those very tattoos and piercings evidence of a psychedelic bent in the make-up of the Spanish adventurer. He thought Guerrero's capacity to transform himself so radically was likely enhanced by having stepped across a threshold dividing one kind of reality from another. And while shaving his tanned face this warm morning at his Antigua apartment, to which he repaired for a few days a month from the dig, he was thinking about arranging somehow to try for himself a psilocybin enema. Maybe he'd do it with a narrow-necked gourd like the ones depicted in that employ on the walls at Bonampak, the site in Chiapas where members of one group of Maya, a people who had long been characterized by academes as generally bucolic farmers and traders, are shown ripping the fingernails out of their prisoners of war prior to chopping off their heads with obsidian hatchets. That flight of fancy brought to mind something he had read about John Cheever and what the author had said, in his still-drinking days, about what he wanted his epitaph to be. It comprised two lines; that here lies John C., who never left a woman wanting or never passed up the chance with a lovely maid or matron–something to that effect, Joe couldn't recall the exact words of the first line. But the second line was: "And who never took it up the ass."

Which, it turned out, apparently wasn't true.

It was inevitable in turn that that musing led to the old Salvadoran saw: *"Sos un macho comprobado?"* Are you a proven macho?

Joe, when they'd asked him that for the first time, among the guerrillas in the hills of Cabañas in 1985, thought it meant, Have you fathered a child? And although he had not, two of his partners over the years had become pregnant–one of them twice–and had had abortions. So he knew for sure he was fertile, that he'd demonstrated his studly bonafides, and that was what he supposed was the gist of the inquiry.

"Sí, más de una vez," he had answered. Yes, more than once.

Which elicited from those present cackles and guffaws, it being the most self-ridiculing response possible. Because *un macho comprobado* is he who has experienced a stiff one up the wazoo and decided he didn't like it–*comprobado,*

here, meaning "put to the empirical test." The right answer –
one known by all Guanaco males over 12–is, *"No. Soy culero
en potencia."* I'm a prospective faggot.

The Maya took their mind-altering concoction by way
of the lower terminus of the digestive tract for the fast effect
and to avoid the nausea that can precede the trip if the
potion goes through the stomach. Joe knew about that,
having eaten mushrooms in Venezuela and in Colombia,
riding around *el Parque Arqueologico San Augustín* on
hyperkinetic horses. It was the only time he had ever been
on a rented horse that loved to flat-out run, and maybe it
was because of those exuberant *caballitos* and the
remoteness of the place–a ten-hour bus ride over bad roads
from Popayán–and the abandon with which his friend and
traveling companion Alfredo and he could ingest those
things without concern for responsibilities, of which at the
age of 23 they had none, that he recalled that time as one of
unbounded freedom.

Alfredo was Venezuelan and Joe's former college
roommate. At Cornell, the same august and lovely
university that now employed him. After they'd finished
their undergraduate studies–Alfredo was an architect–Joe
went down to Venezuela to visit. Alfredo took him to a little
Andean town near Mérida where Venezuelan and
Colombian hippies devoted to mushrooms had set up
communes. They had their own greeting, like the flashed
peaceful V of U.S. hippies. The shroomheads' salute was
one hand cupped palm down over the vertical other in
representation of the object of their affection. Alfredo and
his friend Joaquin and Joe had picked some with the locals,

plucked them right out of platters of dried cow dung. They put the little golden-beige sorcerer sombreros in a satchel then hiked along a stream into a deserted valley, where they sat on a big rock and ate the mushrooms, Alfredo garnishing his with a dollop of canned condensed milk to help it down the gullet, while Joe just gobbled his plain.

The day grew warm and after a while, though the rushing water was freezing, Alfredo and Joe stripped and jumped into the crystalline pool beside the rock. They held on to boulders at the edge of the pool to keep from being pulled away downstream. At one point Joe jumped out and, with his Nikon F, took a photograph of Alfredo stretched out and sheathed in the glistening torrent. His back was arched, head and face under a frothy cascade from the rock above and behind him. An ice sculpture of a wiry sprite.

It's true, the mushrooms make you feel a bit sick to your stomach for a half hour or so before you get off. Joaquin did not seem to be enjoying the drug's effect. He said he was cold. The clothes that Alfredo and Joe shed, a sweatshirt and sweater and a pair of pants each, Joaquin put on over his clothes and he lay bundled and curled up on the slope of a large slab, absorbing the sun's rays.

Alfredo and Joe walked off down the bank of the stream. They strolled along naked, their balls tight and *pijas* shrunken from the dip–Joe's *con el caño recortado* and Alfredo's *directo de la fabrica,* unmodified–for about a kilometer. Then again, who knew how far, since time and distance were the most unimportant of variables in the suddenly non-Newtonian world. They stopped at a tree and climbed it and sat up in the tree talking some but not much and looking around the valley at the mountains and studying the leaves and the bark and any beetle or small lizard crawling around on the branches. They were in the Garden of Eden.

"What would somebody say if they came along and found us here?" Alfredo asked after a while.

Joe thought for a moment. "They'd look up and say, 'What the fuck are you naked *pendejos* doing up in that tree?'"

They both had laughed long and loudly, sitting each on his limb. And it was still funny to Joe these many years later. As he recalled all this, he smiled and rubbed the remaining daubs of shaving cream into his neck and made a couple final upward strokes against the skin that just in this past year had begun to sag.

The photograph of Alfredo encased in shimmering water hung framed on the wall in Joe's office up in Ithaca, next to the window looking out over the Arts Quad. Next to the picture, also mounted on a mat and framed, was a piece of paper with something written on it. It can only be read from up close.

It is signed Elias Tun. Not actually signed, because Don Elias couldn't write. But that is who it is attributed to. Attributed by Joe. He knew the man and, on a break from his work in at the Museo de Antropologia in el D.F., had spent a week with him in the Cuchumatanes north of Huehuetenango in Guatemala. Sr. Tun was a peasant farmer and a bootlegger and was by his own reckoning, back then in 1981, just shy of 100 years old.

Elias Tun told Joe Guinness a lot about that part of the world and its people, how they had come to be there and what they believed were the powers a man had and the basic mistakes a man could and usually did make. Don Elias, when he would finish relating a history he would pause and say the words Joe had typed on the framed page:

"I do not know if that is how it really happened. I only know that is how my fathers told it to me and their fathers to them.

"But if you ponder it well, you will see that it must be true."

CHAPTER 17: THE NAME OF A ROSE

April and Juan hit it off. In the days following the orchid fair they shared a few meals at Antigua eateries, took evening walks around town, and sat in the plaza and talked.

The second time they were together at his house, after undressing and play-wrestling and rolling around on each other, exploring, Juan spoke to April for the first time in English. He spoke it like her. Like an American.

"My name's not Miguel," he said.

April's head and shoulders made a slight jerk backward, almost as if she'd been struck. She'd been nude for an hour, but suddenly felt naked. She sat up and pulled the sheet over her.

After a few seconds she said: "What is it, then?"

"I was raised in L.A."

Her first thought was: This fucking guy is a fucking spy. I've just fucked a motherfucking agent of the CIA.

"You're American?"

"Yeah. Salvadoran, too. I was born in El Salvador. My mother took me to L.A. when I was a baby."

"OK," she said. She reached to the night-table and tapped a cigarette from her pack of Lucky Strikes.

"What's the diff?" he said. "A rose by another name ... all that jazz." He cupped her breast but she knocked his hand away.

"Yeah, yeah. But I've got to call you something. How about 'Dick'?

"Call me Juan, then," he said. "That's my name."

She leaned back against the headboard and smoked, every couple drags tipping the ash onto her partially bared, tusk-colored belly. When she got down near the filter she pinched the butt and with that hand swept the little mound of ashes off her into her other hand and deposited them in an empty glass on the night-table.

"Well then, Juan Baby. Good old Juancito. What's with you? I mean, what's your real-life true story?"

He smiled. Without condescension, but without mirth either.

"That would be kinda long."

"No problem. I've got the afternoon free. I'll be around another couple months at least. It's not longer than a couple months, is it? Your story, I mean."

"Who knows? I never told it."

"Well give it a try."

Juan's sirloin-hued penis, recumbent during the previous minutes, twitched and roused and began to stand. April leaned forward and gave the head a hard sharp flick with the nail of her middle finger. *"Cálmate, bestia,"* she said, reverting to the language they'd spoken during the previous week.

"Ow!"

"The beginning is important," she switched back to English. "It has to be good, to get your listener interested." Her back was hunched and her forearms rested on the inside of toffee thighs.

Juan pulled the sheet over his legs and loins. He put his hands behind his head and stared at the ceiling.

She fired up another Lucky.

"Well, the story you might want to hear started with my throwing arm, I'd have to say. With the fact that I have a good arm and good aim."

Then Juan Cano started talking truthfully.

***

"Why jerk-offs and drunks?" Juan asked late that same evening as he poured April a fourth glass of Chilean red. "Is it post-modern anthropology? A study of alienation?" They were sitting on his veranda and had just polished off a big tureen of pepian chicken stew and rice.

"Something like that, I guess. The study of Mankind. That's broad enough to cover it. But I don't like the 'study' bit. It's not a fuckin' treatise, and it doesn't mean to be didactic. It's an observation and a reflection and a piece of craft and a combination of portraits, but no more than that."

"Yeah. But to have some broader meaning, doesn't it have to be about a group that's identifiable ethnically or culturally, or in some other way? With a shared history?"

"Here, with the bolos, it's shared behavior. I've talked with Indian drunks and mestizo drunks and white drunks. They have as much or more in common with each other than any of them has, in his day-to-day existence, with the mainstream of his ethnic group or class."

"And from bolos and dolphin-floggers you can extrapolate or deconstruct or whatever it is intellectuals do, and gain insight into the general human condition?"

"I'm not after 'insight into the general human condition.' To me that's like asking, 'What's the flavor of salt?' I'm just saying; Here are some people who act like this, they do things that separate them from the norm, which considers them weird or pathological. And I let these people who do these things talk. Then, whoever watches it and listens to them gets to decide if it was worth their 50 minutes, or if they just wasted their time on a bunch of sots and fist-fuckers."

"What I wonder," said Juan a few minutes later as, the wine gone, he poured good Xela hills chaparro, brought by Francisco on his last visit, into narrow ceramic shot glasses, "is how you go about finding whack-offs to make a film about. It's not the kind of thing I'd imagine most people, if they're really into it, would want to publicize. I mean here with the bolos, you walk around and introduce yourself and ask them if they want to talk. But it's not like guys are hanging around on the sidewalk choking their chicken, waiting for somebody to interview them."

"That's what you'd think. But you'd be amazed." She lifted her shot and sniffed the clear elixer. "When you start down one of the lesser-trod pathways of society, it's astonishing what you find." She threw the shot back and gulped.

"Whew!" She shook her head, but was unfazed. "All kinds of people out there. And most everybody wants to talk. For 'Wankers' I put an ad in the paper, in the Chronicle. 'Wanted for project: interview subjects whose sexual gratification results exclusively from masturbating while viewing pornography.' I got my first call the next day. A guy I ended up never talking to face-to-face. I answer the phone and he says, 'Is this the graduate student?'

"Filmmaker," I say.

"And he says, 'You're a girl.' Surprised like. Then, 'Porno films?'

"No."

"'Well, about your ad.'

"'Yes?' I say.

And he goes: "'Are you in a position to pay your subjects?' And I tell him, politely, that No, I'm not, and he says something like, 'Not even minimally?' and I tell him I think money changing hands denaturalizes this sort of thing, makes it dishonest, and he goes, Hmmm, and I say, Does that mean you' re not interested? and he's quiet for a few seconds then says, 'Well, I don't know. If I were willing to talk to you,'—and note, he used the subjunctive, so that rules out a low-life–'do you think you might at least blow me? Or show me your asshole, or something?'"

April laughed now, though she had not laughed when the guy said that. "And I tell him, No, that's out of the question, and he says, Well why should I talk to you then? and I say, I can't give you a reason. You'll do it only if you have your own reasons, like maybe that sometimes a person can learn something about himself or herself talking about the most intimate parts of their lives with a stranger. And he says, 'Like to a shrink?'

"Anyway, he never called back."

Juan poured her another shot.

"What was it like at Sundance? Meet any stars?"

"You know, it tries to be very hip, all uncorrupted and egalitarian bohemian. But the documentary nominees are seated kind of at the rear and off to the side. They're not very glamorous, even in a nerdy-is-cool sort of way. The most interesting person I met that night was the guy who won my category, a young guy from Philadelphia who'd been a photo-journalist in the Caribbean, mostly in Haiti, and made a film about a Dominican guy he'd become friends with. About how this guy, who he lived with for a few weeks in Santo Domingo–they went to this car wash where you got your cock sucked as part of the carwash price, right in your car while it was getting sudsed and rinsed–wanted to go to the States but was denied a visa so he made the very risky trip in an overloaded skiff across the strait between the Dominican Republic and Puerto Rico, a really dangerous passage because of the currents and sharks. And this guy, David is his name, went with *el*

Domincano, filming the whole thing, including some fucking big scary hammerheads circling the boat. And after they get to Puerto Rico he followed the guy around, who was pretending to be Puerto Rican, going to various offices to get a birth certificate et cetera, and flying with him up to New Jersey, because you know, Puerto Ricans are U.S. citizens and once this guy got his papers in San Juan he was free to go anywhere he wanted in the U.S. and stay and work. And how he got a job at a Wendy's in Newark but was wounded his first week on the job when the place got stuck-up–by two Dominican kids, it turned out, and had to have half his right hand amputated, or not exactly amputated, but lost it because basically it was shot off, 'cause one of the kids had a .45. And the guy, Dave, was filming the Dominican guy, whose name was Fernando, at work when all this happened and got the whole robbery and violence on film. The dumbass robbers didn't even realize there was a guy in the place with a mini-cam filming the whole big cluster fuck."

CHAPTER 18: FLOWER FREAKS

Juan set up April's camera in the courtyard just outside the canopy of a flowering tree. He pointed it up a little, turned it on and went to stand near the trunk.

The tree was about 18 feet tall. Its thick branches bore broad, leathery leaves. Juan reached up and pulled down a low branch, along which were several flowers. The gaping pods were brown on the outside and russet-orange inside. Out of them radiated long narrow yellow petals, five each off a stem that broadened at the tip like a bone.

"Here in Guatemala this tree is called Mano de Leon. Lion's Paw. But to me, as it did to the Aztecs, the flower looks more like a human hand. They called it 'macpalxochiquahuitl,' which is a mouthful. But it's just the running-together of 'macpal,' which means hand, 'xochitl,' flower, and 'quahuitl,' tree. So this, in Nahuatl, the language of the Aztecs, is the 'handflowertree.' The Aztec language is like German in that way, with a lot of long fucking words.

"The Aztecs had a sophisticated system of plant classification. Of course they didn't use the same criteria used in European botany. But their system was objective and rigorous.

"It was natural that they should dedicate a lot of time and energy to that kind of observation. They were flower freaks. That was one of their principal traits, besides being fascinated with bloodletting. Actually, they combined the two things; flowers and violence. Of a warrior slain in battle, they said he experienced 'a flowery death.' Flowers were the fifth essence of nature's beauty. And death in battle, like death on the sacrificial altar, was the most essentially beautiful way to die. The bloodier, the more beautiful.

"This tree, you find it a little higher in the wild than where I'm standing now. They're quite common above 2,000 meters on Agua and Acatenango. It blooms most of the year.

"Sometimes in high milpas you'll find a solitary one the farmer left when he cleared the rest, so it stands there bedecked with flowers, spreading over a circle of cornstalks shorter than the rest of the patch. Some anthropologists think it was revered for centuries before the conquest. The Mexican botanist Maximino Martinez wrote that for many years a single anomalous specimen stood outside Toluca and that it was venerated by the Indians, who maintained that that particular tree was the only one of its kind in the world and that the gods had willed that none other should exist anywhere, ever.

"For modern botanists, this species is related to California's Fremontodendron californicum, named after the explorer John. C. Fremont. Up there it's better known as the flannel bush."

Juan went to the camera and turned it off. He unlatched it from the tripod and put it on his shoulder. Then he stepped closer to the tree and took close-up footage of the flowers.

CHAPTER 19: AN OWL IN HIS MOUTH

Though Carlos Roca, who quickly came to be Joe's right-hand man on the Tres Ceibas dig, had made her acquaintance a couple months earlier–the day she filmed the double amputation–the professor from Cornell did not meet April Tashima until the morning he and his crew of diggers uncovered the tomb in the floor of Structure 2.

Burial beneath the floor of a Maya home was not uncommon in Classic times. In other such graves uncovered in Guatemala or Belize or Honduras, even some later ones from the Yucatan, the bones usually were found in a large urn buried vertically. The year Joe Guinness was at the *Museo* in Mexico City, he and his colleagues made a large display replicating an *olla funeraria,* a cut-away urn showing the deceased (a painted clay representation of the deceased) with some valuables–cacao beans and a few semi-precious stones, and food–curled up inside the pot, which was something akin to a womb from which this big, world-weary infant would be born again into another dimension.

It had been Carlos, working with Pablo, who had discovered this tomb while excavating the floor of Structure 2, which Joe and Carlos had believed to be simply a common home. Carlos at some previous point had mentioned to Joe in passing *"una Chinita de California, también ella un professor universitario, con una camera grande"* who had been there when the machete fight went down and who was making, God knew why, a documentary on drunks. She, he said, had done some interviews with Elmer, who, after he'd quit drinking, had come to Tres Ceibas to live with Sandra and to work, like Pablo, with Carlos and Joe as a digger.

Now Carlos, on a recent trip to Antigua, had invited April to come down to the site to film Elmer and Pablo at their tasks, because he supposed that she might like to show as part of her project that abject alcoholism need not always end in desolation and early death. The day she came down was the day they were going to see what was in the cavity covered by the rock slab they'd discovered in the floor of this home.

Carlos had struck a broad stone sealing some sort of chamber, and Joe had taken this to indicate it could be a more elaborate and maybe even prestigious form of burial. They spent a day chipping away adobe that had been used as mortar for the crypt and clearing dirt to completely expose and measure the slab. Carlos and Joe and all the diggers were excited about what they might find inside. It was the kind of anxiousness that was a welcome interruption of the daily tedium of a dig, and a feeling Joe relished, similar to that of a child on Christmas Eve.

That morning, as they were finishing their coffee and refried beans and tortillas at a table outside the house of Elmer and Sandra, a Toyota 4-Runner pulled up and parked near Carlos' house. The door opened and out stepped an Asian woman of medium stature in blue jeans a yellow t-shirt. Both Carlos and Elmer rose and walked across the dusty yard to greet her. They brought her over and introduced her to Joe, and she sat down and had some chicory coffee and a tortilla with salt.

Joe noted her very short fingernails and the three holes, which light came through because there were no rings or pegs in them, along the cartilage of one ear. He was impressed by the fluency of her Spanish. She spoke it almost as well as he did.

A little later, the entire eight-man crew, most of whom had begun excavating Structures 3 and 4, another residence and a bathhouse, broke from their tasks to witness the unsealing of the grave. Joseph, Carlos, Elmer and Caradelija

(Sandpaperface, for his acne-scarred complexion) were on the floor of the house with chisels and two crowbars. The rest, including April, who was filming, watched from ground level above them.

Carlos and Joe worked their tools between the slab and the stone lining the sides of the chamber, gently loosening the lid. When the slab was free and emplaced only by its weight, the four men squatted at the corners.

"Bien," Joe said, working his fingers under his corner. The others did likewise. "On three. Ready?"

They nodded.

"Uno ... dos ... tres."

None of them tried to see what was in the hole before taking three squat-shuffle duck-steps to the side and setting the heavy stone on the floor safely away. But they all heard the gasped "Aaay" from those above.

In the chamber lay a complete adult skeleton. Face up, surrounded by pottery and small statues and adorned at the wrists with solid jade bangles. Around the neck and reaching well down the thorax was a string of jade beads that gradually increased from the size of a marble to the size of a plum on the sternum. The thong had disintegrated but only a couple beads had rolled out of sequence. Smaller beads from what evidently had been ankle-bracelets lay by the foot bones. Near the head were large clamshells that must have held food for the journey to the realm of spirits.

The others deferred to the professor and Joe leaned over into the chamber, which was narrower than a twin bed and about two feet deep. On the femurs lay remnants of bark cloth the corpse had been covered with before the slab was put in place. There was a reddish outline around the skeleton. Rust-colored traces of what Joe took to be hematite, which would have been used to coat the body before burial, speckled the very pale gray bones. The jaw had lost its articulation and the mandible lay open down to the clavicle. There, in what would have been the mouth, was an alabaster carving of an owl the size of a child's thumb.

The Gringo professor slept that night beside the tomb on the floor of the house. April spent the night out at the site, in the bed in the room Carlos provided for Joe at his house. The next day, after Joe made a precise diagram and took photographs, they lifted the bones out one by one and tagged them. From the pelvic shape and structure and the robustness of the cranium, it was clear that this was a man. A cursory examination of the long bones along with what Joe could discern from the teeth and the degree of osteoarthritis of the vertebrae told him the man had been in his mid-40s, about Joe's age, when he died.

CHAPTER 20: THE RIGHT MIX OF SUN AND SHADE

Juan sat cross-legged in the grass at the base of a tree in the rear garden. April's camera was mounted on the tripod about 20 feet from him, so as to take in all or most of the good-sized tree. Juan appeared small in the frame. He was talking to the camera, gesturing to the tree behind him. It looked to be in exuberant bloom, the high part of the trunk and the bigger branches wrapped in narrow long orange flowers.

"This is a fast-growing weed of a tree, gravilea gravileus. The species was brought here from Australia 50 years ago to provide shade for coffee bushes. You may or may not know that top-quality high-altitude arabica coffees can't stand strong sun all day. Trees are planted at intervals throughout the *finca*, mostly gravileas but also paloblancos and other varieties, to form a porous canopy that, as the sun traverses the sky, provides the right mix of *sol y sombra*.

"Anyway, this tree behind me is a gravilea. And it looks beautiful, doesn't it? With all the orange flowers. But if you look closely, you'll see that the flowers are not of the tree. The gravilea blossom is much sparser and yellow, kind of feathery. These orange flowers belong to another species altogether. Here it's called 'matapalo,' which translates as 'tree-killer.' It's of the mistletoe family, a Loranthaceae.

"It reminds me of that song by Roberta Flack, 'Killing Me Softly.' My mother and my grandmother both were big fans of Roberta Flack.

"Anyway, this vine with the pretty flowers is killing the gravilea. *La muerte floreada*, like what the Aztecs called death in battle. El Matapalo is interesting in itself, and obviously pretty, but it's probably better known for the *flores de palo,* or 'woodflowers' it leaves where it's attached to the host.

"They're scars. But pretty scars. They remain when you pull away the parasite. They look like the architectural decorations called rosettes. You can cut the scarred piece of trunk or branch off, and you've got a handsome piece of natural engraving to put up on a wall or on a shelf.

"I don't know yet what I'll do with this," he signaled behind him. "I could hack off the vine and save the tree. I'd probably have to prune fairly drastically. Then again, maybe I'll just leave it. Because there's no denying, it's more beautiful like it is."

CHAPTER 21: CEREMONIAL PURIFICATION

Joe awoke before dawn. He shifted, then stretched out facing up and put his hands behind his head. He lay like that in his hammock in Carlos' house and listened to the first rooster crow. In the next few minutes, the turkeys began gobbling in the dusty spaces amid the collection of adobe-block dwellings that for the past four months had been the professor's home. As the blackness around him turned gray, he spotted a big fly, the one he had heard since opening his eyes. A bomber of an insect, it buzzed loudly this way and that, colliding with the unlit Coleman lamp on the table beside him, the crude dresser, bouncing off the roof and walls. Joe finally swung his legs out of the sack and stood. He picked up the folded map of Guatemala from the table next to his hammock and with the first swat over his head knocked the bug in a line drive against the wall. It fell to the floor, quiet.

Without waking April, who was spending a few days at Tres Ceibas and had slept on the straw-mattressed bed against the wall in the dwelling's main room, Joe left the house and walked over to the house of Sandra and Elmer, where he had weak coffee, a thick slice of papaya and two salted tortillas.

A half-hour later he was at the site, sitting on a fire-baked mud bench inside a low domed structure that had been the ancient village's bathhouse. He had brought a trowel and a bucket and had intended to finish clearing ashfall from the sauna's remaining unexcavated corner. He did not expect to find anything, as they had found no artifacts on the rest of the floor.

Instead of getting right down to work, Joe sat on the bench and looked around the chamber. Half the roof had collapsed and the early sunlight slanted in, illuminating two corners. Joe imagined three or four men of old conversing quietly in an archaic tongue about the weather or crops or some family member's illness. Perhaps one of them would splash water from a ladle onto the hot stones in the pit in the center and a hissing and plumes of steam would envelop them and their words.

"Doctor?"

April had taken to using with him that form of address, sometimes in a tone midway between facetious and flirtatious. It was an appellation that, coming from her, prompted him to think–a ridiculous, sophomoric notion for which he reproached himself–how much he would like to play doctor with her.

"In here."

She came crawling in. She straightened up to the extent she was able, slapping the dust off her jeans.

"Shall we heat up some rocks?" she asked. *"And get naked?"* was unstated but implied.

"Maybe after we finish uncovering the floor." Even as he said it, Joe marveled half disgustedly at his lack of wit and verve around her. The truth was she intimidated him. He was attracted to her and to the irreverence and rebelliousness in the kind of work she did; the making of art, though she might not call it that, out of sad and sordid aspects of human existence.

"Did they allow women in here?" She sat across from Joe on the opposite bench.

"I doubt it. This probably was for ceremonial purification. And ceremonies were pretty much a male domain. The river was for getting the dirt off."

"Maybe they purified the vestal virgins before sacrificing them."

"I don't think that was part of their canon."

"Have you ever thought about living back then?"

"I think about it a lot. In a way, that's why I got into this. Archeology involves a lot of imagination. There's so much drudgery and boring ant work, you've got so many hours to fill and for me a lot of the time they're filled by a kind of daydream of being surrounded by the activities of the time and place when the floors or the paths were being walked on."

"That's a big stretch. Across centuries and cultures, to identify with those people."

"Yeah. It is. But that's part of the big picture too. I mean, you have to be non-sectarian to spend your life doing this, digging up old shit to try to figure out how people lived. Mankind has changed little over the past 10 thousand or so years, since people started to settle down and plant crops. The concerns of the guys who sat around in here a thousand years ago steaming themselves and the women down at the river are very similar to those of most people today."

"Eating and fucking?"

Joe laughed. "That. And, you know, some singing, dancing. Getting high once in a while on some of the plants the Great Spirit saw fit to stick in there between the edible and non-edible."

It was cool and pleasant in the bathhouse, and neither Joe nor April seemed inclined to want to do anything but stay there.

"There's something about the Polish sensibility," April said. "Kieslowski, for instance, in the realm of film bowls me over. Now, you might think it's weird that I can quote this, but I learned it by heart because I liked it so much when I was doing an undergraduate paper on Joseph Conrad. He described his 'subtle but invincible conviction of solidarity that knits together the loneliness of innumerable hearts, which binds together all humanity, the dead to the living and the living to the unborn.'"

"Very well put. That was his third language, too. In conversation he preferred French to English."

"Ah, so you're a fan, too." Then: "Have you ever been married?"

"Not officially."

"Didn't want to make the commitment?"

"Oh, I made what I thought was the commitment."

"Latina?"

"Well, yeah, both of them."

"Two compañeras?"

"Not at the same time, of course. The second one, Adela, just left me a couple months before I came down here."

"How come? If you don't mind my asking."

"I hurt her. Not intentionally, but down deep. Maybe she wanted to hurt me too. We were already going downhill." He fiddled with a little mound of clay dust he'd gathered on the bench. "She'd done a series of pieces–she's a journalist, a really good one–that she was putting together into a book, on migrant farm workers following the harvest northward in the eastern United States; from Florida up to New York State; oranges to peaches to apples and everything in between. Most of the workers are Mexicans and most are Indians from the south, Oaxaca and Guerrero and Chiapas. She told me toward the end–not angrily because she didn't get angry, but she knew she had a strong card to play, and she played it–she said I cared more about dead Indians than living ones."

"And is that true?"

"I guess I should say it's not. But if you look at things objectively, it's a thesis that holds up pretty well."

CHAPTER 22: A HOLE IN THE SKY

April and Juan drove over a potted rocky dirt road down out of the high valley. They skirted the western flank of Agua to the coastal plain and passed between lush green cane fields, the giant grass topped with feathery pink tassels. After a while they turned toward the northeast and began climbing into maize country. The stalks in the *milpas* were broken and bent, the silk of the soon-to-be-harvested cobs dangling so any late rainfall would not enter the husk and rot the grain. The road, asphalt now, wound along the upward grade. At intervals, beyond the slopes bearing a patchwork of fields, April and Juan saw the black conical peak of Pacaya. It stood out in barren burned majesty from the verdure of the lower crests. A plume of pale yellow smoke rose, barely disturbed by the slightest of breezes, high against the bright azure sky.

They arrived at the village where the road ended. Juan parked beside the same house where he'd left the 4-Runner two months earlier, when Francisco had brought him to the volcano for the first time. The woman whose house it was recognized Juan and they exchanged greetings. She said the mountain had been quite active the previous week, spitting fans of red rock and ash, and that there had been a narrow flow of lava from the crater's eastern side. But for three days and nights now it had been calm, blowing only smoke and gas.

Pacaya had maintained its low level of activity for decades, slightly more or less from season to season but without a major eruption or extended periods of complete quiescence. Five years earlier, five members of a team of six scientists were killed when a minor eruption–a thunderous belch of flaming stone and gas and ash–charred them or crushed them beneath incandescent boulders launched like rockets from the mountain's core. They had been on the rim or just inside the crater measuring changes in the spewed gases and registering miniscule variations in gravitational force, part of an effort to develop means of predicting eruption.

Francisco had climbed Pacaya a dozen times since adolescence, and had become something of an autodidact volcanologist. He'd explained to Juan that when a volcano becomes distended with rising magma, its outermost shell moves a tiny distance, perhaps only several inches, from the earth's center of gravity. The movement reduces ever so slightly the strength of gravity's pull at any given point on the slope. Also, as magma rises the atmospheric pressure brought to bear on it declines and, as the pressure drops, gases escape from it like bubbles from champagne. First lighter gases predominate. An increased component of lighter gases may indicate fresh magma rising and imminent eruption. Those were the factors the Mexican and U.S. scientists were hoping to measure when, according to the one who survived–barely, with a fractured jaw, two broken legs, cracked ribs and severe burns, especially on the palms of his hands from pulling himself over glowing rocks in a slithering descent–the smoking cone rumbled for several seconds before Hell burst to the surface of the world.

Juan and April hoisted their packs and took their leave of the woman who would, as she went about her own chores, keep an eye on the car. They intended to camp on a ridge just below the crater and watch the celestial spectacle in store that night: a full lunar eclipse. Juan, who knew what to expect at the summit from his ascent with Paco, had told April to bring an extra sweater and parka in addition to her sleeping bag. He'd put a wool watch cap for her in his pack, along with a plastic bag of a dozen tortillas, a can of tuna and another of sardines, a chunk of salty *queso fresco* and four apples. Beside the canteens each of them carried, he packed two plastic liter bottles of water and a fifth of Flor de Cana.

They headed up the path. The trail rose through a forest of vine-draped ceiba and amate and avocado trees, then balsam and laurel and eucalyptus with bark shredded like a beggar's rags. They entered orchid territory, where dozens clung to the trees, purple and violet and white and perfect. The path emerged from the forest every few hundred meters to border high *milpas* and larger pastures where cattle and horses grazed on lush grass.

After two hours of hiking they came to a relatively flat stretch. Blackened trees in sparse dispersion rose from broad-bladed scrub grass like a decimated army of giants. Some were thick and dead. Others of varying heights and girths and species were scorched to an array of shades of gray but, because of the rain and sun and fertile soil, had sprouted clumps of new life, brilliant green leaves from charred trunks and limbs.

They were high enough now that the lowest of the scattered clouds approaching from the west were level with them. As they crossed the old lava plain of burned pillars, a white mist enveloped them and chilled the sweat on their faces and chests and backs. The cloud advanced over the ravaged and regenerating earth. The volcano rose ahead, the only thing clearly visible to Juan beside the stony black soil at his feet and the tiny yellow flowers sprouting from it, collecting droplets of water from the cloud.

The cloud passed. The world turned once more bright and hot. They continued on to a crest where wind coursed over them and they stopped for a break. They dropped their packs and sat on porous rocks like hard black sponges. They drank from their canteens. Both of them looked up at the smoking desolate mountaintop. April had a sudden strong sensation of being the beneficiary of great good fortune, far removed from concern. The sun and wind on her face and the dark lunar summit, its shadow inching toward them, seemed, along with this man who wanted to be her friend as well as her lover, the only salient elements of life on earth.

After a while Juan said, "What do you say?"

"*Démosle,*" she responded.

The trail descended 60 or 70 meters to follow a long ridge that led to the foot of the path up the cinder cone.

Ten minutes later they were struggling up a diagonal path etched into loose gravel and ash and scorched stone that was the stuff the volcano had brought up from inside the earth. They spent an hour making their slow way upward, huffing and sliding, striving to fix a foot or hand.

The higher they climbed the colder it became. Even so, they both were sweating profusely. Wet and tired, they reached the ridge that would take them on a level path to their destination just below and some 100 meters from the crater rim. The summit was bathed in sunlight.

Juan led the way to a roofless shelter, a half-igloo of stacked igneous rock built and rebuilt by Francisco over the years. They deposited their gear there and stripped off their t-shirts to replace them with dry ones and sweatshirts against the chilling wind.

"Let's walk a bit, see if our pants dry out some before the sun sets," said Juan.

He led April to an outcropping. There they could smell the sulfurous gas billowing from the crater in the palest shades of yellow and orange. After a while they went back to the shelter and, sitting in its lee, ate tortillas and the cans of tuna and sardines.

The moon was about halfway to its apex at shortly before 9 o'clock when the black shadow of the earth began to consume it. Juan opened the bottle of rum.

A few minutes after the eclipse began, as they passed the bottle, out of nowhere a dog appeared at their side. A scraggly mutt, its matted coat shimmered with mist from the clouds that had swept slowly one after the other across the summit since nightfall. The animal was shivering. He sidled up to Juan. Juan stroked him and asked him how the devil he had come to be stranded on this smoldering mountain. Where was his home? His master? The sad little beast looked at him and snuggled against his outstretched legs and rested his head in Juan's lap.

It took nearly an hour for the shadow to obliterate the moon. By the time it did April and Juan were half drunk, or maybe just a third drunk. When the black disc had completely covered the luminous white one, an interval was lent to the world from another dimension, a heavenly one of time out of time. The stars burned more brightly. A halo of impossibly brilliant silver defined the hole punched in the canopy of the world, a perfectly circular hatch through which some of the planet's evil and good drained into a suffocating nether space but through which virgin spirits beneficent or cruel infiltrated the atmosphere.

"Que hermoso que es," said April, resting her head on her companion's shoulder. Then, using the name she originally had known him by, she asked: *"No serás tú el angel Miguel?"*

"Far from it," he said.

The mountaintop had grown so dark that during the minutes of total eclipse they passed the bottle by tact, barely able to make out each other's form. As the shadow continued its progress and gave back what it had taken, the ridge recovered shape and detail and shadow in a dawn of platinum light.

They rose a bit unsteadily on tired stiff legs and walked along the ridgeline. The night was clear now and the lights of Escuintla, the provincial capital, glimmered to the south like strewn stars.

***

April and Juan were asleep in their bags when, at just after 2:30, they were awakened by a roar. They bolted from the sacks and, crouching at the shelter's wall, watched a fusillade of glowing red stone like thousands of tracer bullets and mortars spew from the crater. The burning rocks described a fan of arcs and trajectories according to their weight, a wild wig of tangled strands of fire. Some shot up on a near vertical path and fell within a radius of 30 or 40 meters around the rim to tumble down the upper cone, darkening as they cooled. Others sailed in soaring bridges of rose and red across the divide separating Juan and April's ridge from the volcano's mouth. Some fell in the sparsest of barrages around the shelter. They were small, for the most part, the size of a pebble or a gumball. But Juan also watched one the size of a fist land 20 meters away and roll down the hillside.

He and April peered over the top of the stone wall. The dog, which had bedded down between them, crawled under Juan's sleeping bag. Only his wet black nose peeked out.

"Did it do this when you were up here with your friend?"

"No."

"Do you think we're in danger? Should we head down?"

"I think the best place for now is right where we are. Francisco described this, said he's seen it several times."

The violent part of the show lasted about 20 minutes. For almost an hour after that, small sprays of red stone blew occasionally from the crater, though not on menacing trajectories. They remained behind the wall. The black cone's collar of rubies dimmed. Clouds of gas poured from the mountain like saffron sails. When it seemed calm enough, the two emerged from the shelter and walked to a point nearer the crater.

To their astonishment, many of the rocks around them spouted jets of blue sparks or faint cobalt flame. Juan looked at April, who was holding up her right hand and turning it slowly. At a certain angle, and only at that precise angle, tiny cyan fonts of fire issued from the tips of her extended fingers, each finger a candle and the nail a miraculous wick alight in cold harmless flame.

Juan lifted his hand and rotated it slowly. His fingertips ignited painlessly.

Then a cloud, not of gas but of moisture, enveloped them and snuffed the blue lights. April and Juan were damp and shivering.

"Vení," said Juan.

April followed him about 30 meters down the slope of the ridge. Juan, as he had been shown by Francisco, squatted and began sweeping aside with his hands the gravel and fine black ash.

"Do like me."

April squatted and watched him clear an area about two feet square. She began to do likewise, brushing away with her hands an inch-deep layer. As she did, she understood. The harder-packed ash and crushed stone beneath the loose surface was radiating wonderful heat. The deeper she scraped the hotter it got. So hot that a mere two inches down the ground was scalding.

"See?" said Juan, positioning himself on his spot so as to have a view of the gas clouds streaming from the crater.

April settled onto her own toasty parcel. She worked her feet beneath the gravel to the hard hot stratum and delighted in the warmth seeping through the thick soles of her boots. They stayed there for hours, shifting once in a while to keep their butts or thighs or backs from getting seared. Both curled up and slept for brief spells. When, later, the far-off edge of the earth turned red, they both shifted and propped their head on a crooked arm to observe the start of a new day.

The sun cleared the horizon and the wind gathered force. A thick bank of cloud advanced like a cavalry charge. They braced themselves against an onslaught that in a matter of minutes was buffeting them with the force of a gale. A thick blanket of white vapor flooded over the ridge and swirled like foam around their calves, diminishing in density up the legs but even at the waist whipped around them in visible streams. Mist coated them. The wet wind chilled them to the marrow. Even so they were thrilled by the fury and whooshing racket. Shouting above it, they made their way back to the shelter.

The sleeping bags, now drenched, were blown flat against the wall. The dog sat there trembling. Juan and April quickly gathered their gear and stuffed it haphazardly into the packs. Juan struck off and April made to follow but balked at leaving the dog. She shouted for it to come. She could hardly hear herself above the wind. The dog looked at her miserably and didn't move. April ran back and picked him up. She hurried after Juan, who'd turned to wait for her.

The tempest's ferocity decreased with each long sliding stride down the flank of the cone. It was like running down a dune. In 15 minutes they were back on the ridge bordered by the charred forest. Here the early morning was calm and bright. April put the dog on the ground. The animal scampered off downhill along the path. They took off their wet jackets and flapped them and rolled them and stuffed them in the packs. Their jeans were wet and black.

April, following Juan by a few paces, had a strong urge about half the way to the hamlet to tackle him from behind and roll him over. To sit on his chest and pin his arms and laugh down at him and threaten, laughing, to let fall a gob of saliva dangling from pursed lips only to be sucked back, like she used to do to her little brother Ben when they were kids.

CHAPTER 23: *HASTA LA VICTORIA SIEMPRE*

April Tashima, documentarian, was the unwitting artifice of the reunion between the former comrades-in-arms Joseph Guinness and Juan Cano. She had been to the dig at Tres Ceibas three times, the first two to talk, on tape, with the ex-*bolos* Elmer and Pablo as part of her film about street drunks, but the third time more because of the American archeologist with a scar on his cheek, whom she had come to like over the course of a few pleasant conversations. For some reason, perhaps to do with shared nationality but also because she knew both the professor and her boyfriend took obvious pleasure in talking about movies, she wanted Joe and Juan to meet. So she invited the archeologist to dinner in Antigua at the big house, where she had moved in with Juan not long after he told her who he really was.

Joe was in Antigua for a few days that week, at the apartment Owen had rented on Sexta Calle Poniente. The professor arrived on foot at the faded-sienna villa at dusk. He knocked at the main door, one with a heavy brass ring, and was admitted by Ximena into a cool foyer. The space was paved with flagstones bearing shallow ruts, the effect of thousands of entries, during the 1700s and 1800s, of horse-drawn carriages.

Ximena was turning to announce the arrival of a visitor when April came walking across the interior courtyard. She wore a welcoming smile.

"Hi, Joe," she said, leaning forward to place a kiss on his cheek. "Come on, let's have a glass of wine. Miguel's in the kitchen basting a turkey."

April led Joe down the long veranda. She had decided to introduce Juan as Miguel, that being the name she continued to use for him around the house in order to avoid confusing Ximena and Francisco. As they entered the kitchen, Juan was just closing the oven door behind the re-inserted bird. He turned and lifted the skirt of a faded yellow apron bearing the inscription "Il Capo Cuoco" and wiped his hands. April was looking at him as she said, "Miguel, this is Joe, the archeologist," and realized that Juan's expression was a strange one, one of perplexity. She

turned to look at Joe and saw that he too was standing there frozen, with a look on his face of, "What the fuck?"
After a few seconds, the dinner guest pronounced the single, baffling syllable: "Clem?"

It had been more than nine years since they had last seen each other in the hills of Chalatenango, since Joe had hiked to the Sumpul River and crossed into Honduras, stepping into the shallow current able-bodied and intact only to emerge on the opposite bank on all fours, stunned and bleeding profusely from the mouth. But nine years are not so many, and there was no mistaking either man in the eyes of the other.

"I don't believe it," said Juan. *"El Látigo del Mayor."* (The Scourge of the Major.)

"Don't remind me," said Joe.

They each took a step and embraced and held the hug. When they separated, Juan took Joe's chin in his hand and turned his head slightly, to see the scar. "We heard about that. *Que mala leche,* to happen on the final day of your guerrilla career."

"Not much of a career," said Joe.

April finally said: "Uh, Excuse me??" but for the moment was ignored.

"Hey. The only foreigners on our front who stuck it out for the long haul were the two Mexican doctors, *la pareja,* Tito and Victoria, you remember them? And of course Iñaki el Vasquito, the bomb-maker."

The two men leaned against the kitchen counter and looked at each other. Then they hugged again. Then both of them looked at April standing there dumbfounded.

"We're old *compas*," said Juan. "Joe spent a year in the hills with us, *en Guanaxia Rebelde.*"

"More like six months," Joe corrected him. "My revolutionary semester. Post-doc in insurgency."

April looked from one to the other and shook her head slowly. "Wow," she said. She took a bottle of Chilean white wine from the refrigerator. "Let's make a toast to this reunion." She uncorked it, got three long-stemmed glasses from the cupboard, filled them and passed one to each of the men. They raised the glasses and touched them.

"Hasta la victoria siempre," said April, thrilled and amused, too by this strange encounter.

Both men laughed, the slogan ringing slightly absurd now to both, and drank the cold delicious wine.

A half hour later they were seated at the big table in the dining room and Juan was standing over the crisp-skinned, gleaming golden turkey, slicing through the joint at the thick end of the drumstick and lifting onto a platter the succulent piece. As he carved, April filled the empty glasses at each place with Argentine red, *Don Valentín lacrado.*

"Better than moldy tortillas under a tree in the rain, huh?" Juan said to his former comrade as he passed the plate stacked with turkey.

"So how the hell does an Ivy League university professor end up in the mountains with Salvadoran guerrillas?" she asked.

"Because of a simple fistfight, pretty much," said Joe. "Actually it was more wrestling than punching. Major Rick Paniagua and I got into a fight."

"The one who killed Archbishop Garcia?" said April. "The squinty-eyed sleazy fucker in the Oliver Stone flick who holds up the bullet at the coffee klatch of the skinny greasy killers club?"

"That's the guy," said Joe with a chuckle. "Only that guy as much resembled Major Rick as the rebel cavalry charge at the end of that movie was like a real guerrilla assault. The actual dude was a very engaging and charismatic guy. *Que caía bien a todo el mundo.* He was a killer, yeah. But also a great talker, easy and colloquial and funny. That's why he was the country's most popular politician, by far. It's true, people either hated him or loved him, but more loved him than hated him. He was the only guy in the country who could get into his pickup truck, drive out to the countryside and–always surrounded by goons with Uzis, of course– park it in the middle of a small town and stand in the back and call a political meeting on the spur of the moment. And the whole town would show up and almost everybody–I'm talking about in most of the country, excluding Chalate and Morazan and *zonas de control de la guerrilla*–would be cheering him on and wanting to shake his hand. Because he talked to them straight, in their own idiom, no bullshit, asking them if they wanted to continue owning their land, even if it was a small piece, and growing what they wanted and selling the crop to whoever they wanted at the price they wanted to ask for it, and drinking *guaro* on Sunday. Or if they wanted the country to become another Nicaragua or Cuba, where the bearded dudes in berets owned everything and decided everything and if you got drunk, a fucking committee of self-righteous assholes would come over to lecture you. Of course, that wasn't what the choice really boiled down to, but that's what most people in the countryside thought it did. The guy was a natural orator. That's what makes it ironic that he died of throat cancer. But look at his funeral. A line a mile long to pass by the casket."

"Mr. Fucking Congeniality," said Juan. "But that didn't keep you from beating him up."

"You beat up Ricardo Paniagua?" asked April.

"He didn't leave me much choice. I thought he was gonna shoot me. He wasn't a big guy. Wiry, about ten years older than me at the time. Smoked a lot and drank a lot and not in great shape. He starts to lift the flap on his holster and I jump him and get him in a headlock and just kind of flipped him over and sat on him and pinned him down. I had to smack his head against the ground a couple times to knock him out."

"But why would he want to shoot you?" asked April, a fork full of dangling green beans suspended before her face.

"'Because I'm a wiseass."

"And his bodyguards, while all this is going on?" April set down her fork.

"That was his mistake. *El error del mayor.* He must have figured I was harmless. He should never have taken me there alone."

"Taken you where alone?"

"To the boonies. The ones that turned out to be my next home."

Part Two
1985-86
Hey Joe, Where You Goin' With That Gun in Your Hand?

CHAPTER 24: WITHOUT INFRINGING ON
SOVEREIGNTY, OF COURSE

Professor Joe Guinness of Cornell University met Ricardo Paniagua in El Salvador in August 1985, the latter part of the rainy season, or *invierno,* that took up precisely half the year. Cornell had been involved in two major Salvadoran excavations in the 1970s, and was invited to send someone down to help a team of local archeologists clean up and reorganize the National Museum after the earthquake in May of that year. The Arts College dean asked Joe, because of his fluent Spanish and his yearlong assistant curatorship at Mexico's *Museo de Antropologia,* to go down for the summer and the fall semester–until Christmas, was the plan–and help them sort things out.

The museum was a modest institution in a relatively new building near the *Feria Internacional* on the road to Santa Tecla, near the old foreign ministry. There had been moderate damage to the structure, which was all ground-level with a few interior courtyards, and workmen were patching that up in late June, when Joe arrived. Many of the exhibits had been damaged when things fell off pedestals and stele tipped over. It was a mess. Workers and volunteer students had gathered up everything and placed the pieces in the least scathed wing, where Joe got set up in a makeshift office and threw himself into cataloging and designing new ways of showing off the pots and sculptures, the tools and the jade and the jewelry.

Joe met Paniagua's wife before he met The Man. It was at a party the U.S. ambassador threw every year on the 4th of July. The ambassador was Chuck Buchanan, a corn-fed former college wrestling champion from Iowa, and he was holding the reception at his residence in San Benito, the most affluent neighborhood of San Salvador. Joe already had met several people from the embassy, what with him being a visiting U.S. academic and the presence of such specimens exceedingly rare during the war, now in its sixth year. The professor had received a security-consciousness rap from an embassy official; how to alter routines to avoid being kidnapped by the guerrillas, that sort of thing. His invitation to the big fete was delivered by the Cultural Affairs Officer, an amicable rotund African-American guy named Eddie who, in addition to his formal duties, deejayed a weekly two-hour jazz program on the local classical music radio station.

On the day of the party, Joe rode his bike down from the museum to Buchanan's house, which was more like a fortress than a dwelling. The street in front of it had two big speed bumps like the graves of hastily buried fat guys. He locked his bike to a telephone pole right near the entrance.

If he'd had a car–he didn't have one, but the museum's Mitsubishi Montero was usually at his disposal–he would have had to park at least three blocks away. That's what kind of event this was. The vehicles lining both sides of the street denoted a crowd of the wealthy and powerful: Mercedes and BMWs and Jeep Wagoneers and Chevy Suburbans, quite a few with diplomatic plates and many obviously armor-plated against assassination or kidnapping attempts and almost all of them with tinted windows. There was a wide slot in the pavement in front of the heavy wrought-iron gate to the driveway. In the slot was a five-inch-thick steel plate that could be raised or lowered by means of controls in a turret in the stone wall surrounding the premises. A Slinky of spiraled razor wire ran along the top of the wall.

Guests were lined up outside a narrow door through the wall. Each showed his or her invitation and identification then stepped past a business-suited guard with a Mac-10 slung across his chest and through a metal detector into the green and flowering grounds.

Joe waited his turn, was admitted and made his way through the house to the rear garden, where about 150 people in suits and cocktail dresses milled about. Over them, blue-and-white striped canopies provided refuge from an oppressive sun. Three big awnings stretched over the deck along three sides of a large swimming pool. A U.S. flag made of carnations–the red and white ones natural and the blue ones dyed–floated in the middle of the pool. On a patio covered by an extension of the manor's barrel-tile roof was a long table draped with white tablecloths and laden with hams and turkeys and rib roasts, chilled jumbo shrimp, imported cheeses, salads and an ice sculpture of an eagle.

The businessmen and military officers and politicians and their wives, the cultural figures, the journalists recognizable for the license with which they, like Joe, had interpreted the "formal attire" proviso on the invitation, were all happy to have been included in this, one of the premier events on El Salvador's social calendar. Diplomats made up a good third of the crowd. Everyone stood around sweating and making conversation while trying to balance a drink and a plate of food.

Joe was standing alone at a corner tent pole sipping a glass of cold white wine and checking things out, surveying the women and whetting his appetite for an attack on the buffet, when DJ Ed brought over a sturdy blond man in a brown suit who in turn escorted a very pretty woman in a tight short-skirted dress of dark burgundy.

"Joe, I want you to meet Ambassador Buchanan," said Eddie. "He's very interested in Mesoamerican archeology."

"Pleasure to make your acquaintance," said the ambassador through a drooping pale mustache. "We think your work here is very important. I just wanted to tell you that you can count on us if there's anything we can do. And I wanted to introduce you to Roxana Benitez. She's the *directora* of the *Patrimonio Cultural.* She works closely with your colleagues at the Museum."

"Roxana Benitez de Paniagua. Nice to meet you," she said, extending her hand to the visiting professor. Her teeth were bright white and perfectly aligned.

"You two talk." The ambassador pulled Eddie away to resume mingling.

The woman touched Joe's arm lightly with a long-fingered hand. The nails were painted the same color as her dress and her bare arms were the hue of a pecan shell and just as smooth, without hair.

"If I had my life to live over again, I would become an archeologist," she said. Her English was smooth but adorned with a thick accent.

"That would be rough on those nails," he answered, in Spanish. She seemed relieved to hear him speak her language. Unburdened of preoccupation with syntax and pronunciation, her posture relaxed. That made her even more pretty.

"Oh, I would gladly forego fingernails in exchange for that. I'm talking about a heart's desire, something that comes from within. Something more important than appearances."

Joe collared a white-coated waiter for a replacement for her drink, white wine like his, and took another for himself.

Then she said his name. Very deliberately, she said: "Joseph Guinness." And it wasn't just her accent. She was saying something else, too. Joe was certain she did it on purpose, conscious of a word game. And he thought: This woman is very sharp. This feeling made their exchange more flirtatious and, to him, more appealing. But at the same time he was slightly flustered.

Because what he had heard was a question. It was in the way she enunciated those syllables. She'd said: "Joseph, *Quien es?*" As in "Who is Joseph?"

And she had. Because then she squinted and tilted her head and asked in English, "So. Who is this person called Joseph?"

"Just a Gringo digger from the ivory tower," he answered.

She smiled politely and was willing to leave it at that for the moment. But her eyes–they were almond shaped but not black, rather hazel with amber flecks toward the edge of the iris–said that was not what she had meant. Not what was his job or nationality or *estado civil* or pedigree. Rather, What was he looking for? What did he want, deep down?

"Come with me," she said and took him by the arm and led him to where three uniformed men were talking on the poolside patio. All three lit up when they saw her approach.

"*Chanita, preciosa,*" said one, using the diminutive for Roxana. He had a laurel wreath insignia on his epaulets. The other two had three stars.

She kissed the three of them in turn on the cheek, leaning forward so that her right leg lifted just off the ground, her toe pointing back and down in a way that flexed a sculpted and burnished calf. In her mid-30s (the same age as Joe), she had the body of an athlete, the kind of muscled butt that requires several hours a week of specific exertion to keep it that way. Unless she simply was blessed, supremely, by nature.

"General Vasquez, this is Joseph Guinness. He is helping to put the museum in order, and will be among us for at least the rest of the year."

Joe, who fleetingly wondered why she had said "at least," shook hands with the general, who despite his pale face and dark circles beneath his eyes did not appear fatigued or lacking in resolve. He also shook hands with the other two, a white one and a dark mestizo, who were introduced as Colonels Arce and Salazar.

"The general is the Minister of Defense and these two gentlemen are his vice-ministers, of Defense and of Public Security," Roxana explained. "In other words, this is the troika of military authority in our country."

The general laughed and said: "Oh, come off it, Chana. 'Troika' sounds so Stalinist. In any case," he turned to Joe, "we are at your service and grateful to you for coming to help preserve our heritage."

"What part of the States are you from?" asked Salazar, the bronze one, in unaccented English.

"New York State. Ithaca."

"Ah, yes. Cornell. I'm a big fan of Carl Sagan. I believe that if you understand how the universe works, you're able to better understand how the elements of the universe, including human beings, work."

Joe couldn't tell from the expressions of the general and the other colonel if they were understanding. So he continued in Spanish. He complimented Salazar on his English and asked where he learned it.

"I studied it in school, but became fluent during four years at West Point. So I know New York State quite well. Beautiful country."

"Yours too. Especially the volcanoes."

"That's one thing lacking even in New York," said Vasquez.

Joe told the men he was interested in visiting a site about 50 kilometers northwest of the capital, north of the Pan American highway near Izalco, that had been partially excavated in the late-1970s by a team including some friends of his from the University of Pennsylvania. He told them a little about it, about how with the onset of the war the work was suspended, but that he hoped to take a walk around there, to see what had become of the place. He asked them if they thought that would be safe.

Vasquez deferred to Arce, who he said had been commander until six months earlier of the Destacamento Militar No. 3. That unit, bigger than a battalion and smaller than a brigade, was about 15 kilometers from the site, and the nearest military base.

"I know the place. Las Hamacas. That area is what we call a `zone of expansion' of the terrorist delinquents," he said. "They don't maintain a permanent armed presence, but they come down from north of there once in a while and call a village meeting and harangue the campesinos and distribute leaflets. Why they hand out leaflets, who knows? The villagers cannot read. They try to persuade the young ones to join up. Sometimes they get a few recruits like that, but mostly they kidnap several outright, force them into the terrorist ranks by threats of violence against them or their families.

"But I think you have nothing to fear. It's not a combat zone. Maybe a skirmish every couple months when an army patrol runs into a squad of *terengos*. And once or twice a year the bastards sneak up on the *destacamento* with their improvised mortars and lob a few homemade bombs, propane canisters filled with explosives, over the walls. You might hear something like that far off. *Pero no es gran cosa.*" No big deal.

The conversation was interrupted by an embassy woman appealing through loudspeakers for the guests' attention. Ambassador Buchanan was going to make a brief address. He stepped to the microphone on the patio, cleared his throat and spoke for three or four minutes in stumbling, Gringo-accented Spanish about the sacred ideals of liberty enshrined in the Declaration of Independence and how his government's objective was to promote institutionalization of democracy throughout the world, without infringing on any nation's sovereignty, of course.

He wanted to make that point "pear-fecktuh-men-tay claire-oh."

Roxana told the officers she and Joe were going to get something to eat. There was another round of handshakes and salutations. The general, bidding farewell to Roxana, asked her to convey his best regards to *El Mayor.*

It was only then that Joe realized who Chanita was. He had not made the connection when she, after Buchanan had introduced her using her maiden name–the name she used in her cultural affairs work–had completed the identification by adding her married surname, saying "Roxana Benitez de Paniagua."

Her husband was retired Maj. Ricardo Paniagua, the country's best-known politician at home and abroad, probably El Salvador's best-known personage, period. His countrymen called him simply El Mayor. Gringos– diplomats and spooks, development aid functionaries and military advisors as well as congressmen and lobbyists and human rights watchdogs–called him "Major Rick."

In the weeks before coming down, Joe had been too concerned with the place's antiquity to devote much time to the particulars of the modern nation state. But he'd brushed up a little on its current affairs and, like anyone who had read newspapers during the previous five or so years, was aware of Paniagua's reputation. The U.S. press was so fond of employing a stock appositive that readers might be forgiven for presuming "alleged mastermind of rightist death squads" was an integral part of his name.

His renown derived principally from the widely held belief–a deduction that virtually no one, not even Paniagua's supporters, wasted their breath contesting–that it was he who, in 1980, had ordered the assassination of Archbishop Leonel García.

During nearly three decades of priesthood, García had been politically and socially conservative, reticent and conformist. But assumption of the primacy of the Salvadoran church at a time when the fabric of the nation was unraveling had transformed him. He became a champion of the poor. He began using the homily of the Sunday Mass in the National Cathedral to denounce army brutality and atrocities. In what proved to be his last sermon–broadcast nationwide on the church radio station– he reminded soldiers and police of their brotherhood with campesinos and workers. He exhorted them to disobey orders to torture, kidnap or murder.

"I call on you, I beg you, I command you, in the name of God: Stop the repression!"

Three days later, García was saying Mass at the chapel of a church-run hospice for cancer patients when, with chalice raised, his heart was burst by a single bullet fired from the chapel's open doorway, a rectangle of bright sunlight. Not since Thomas Becket was stabbed at the altar of Canterbury Cathedral in 1170 had a Roman Catholic archbishop been murdered while saying Mass.

Everyone knew that Paniagua, who at the time was an army intelligence major, had ordered the assassination. Proof came to light some years later. But proof did not matter in a place like El Salvador.

Roxana and Joe Guinness joined the line filing past the bountiful spread.

"Maj. Paniagua is your husband?," the American asked.

"More than my husband. He is my idol," she said.

She studied Joe's reaction. To see to what extent he had prejudged her mate. Which, for her, would be the degree to which he had prejudged her country, and herself.

Joe said nothing and kept a poker face.

"He really is an extraordinary human being," she said. "A man for history. A man who would be of interest to a historian like yourself." She spooned several big gleaming pink shrimp onto her plate, then a dollop of cocktail sauce. "He also has the finest private collection of pre-Colombian artifacts in the country. You'll have to come to dinner one of these evenings so we can show it to you."

"Sure," said Joe. *"Encantado."*

CHAPTER 25: BORN TO DIE

On the same Sunday morning in May 1985 when the earth buckled in El Salvador, destroying homes and killing 317 people and damaging the National Museum, far away to the northwest LAPD detective Chris Sudek was examining himself in the bathroom mirror, silently reiterating that he was glad to have been born blond.

He had always loved his hair, but now he was losing it fast. The previous year, only a few months after turning 30, he began to notice fine corn-silk strands clogging the shower drain. Over the next several months the thinning on top had become obvious, and it pained him. Made him, he mumbled, look like a dipshit. An office-bound dweeb.

In the Safeway near his apartment building in Playa del Rey he had found a shampoo called Nice'nThick that was supposed to beef up each strand, and he had used that for a few weeks. But it left his locks feeling dense and dirty. He tried out new styles, parting it on the opposite side, then slicked back. But it was no use. His scalp was more visible with each passing month. He considered going to a doctor, checking out the possibility of a transplant, or implant, or whatever the hell it was they did, even though he didn't really have the money for it. Some Senator had gotten one and it had been in the news. It was true, it had made him look a lot younger. You were supposed to be able to swim with it and everything, because it was real growing hair rooted in the skin. But in the end that seemed like a faggoty thing to do.

So, on this day of the minor Salvadoran earthquake and who knew how many other catastrophes large or small around the planet, Officer Sudek settled on the burrhead solution. He went out and bought a set of electric clippers and did it himself. This first time, he'd had to re-do it twice, and it took a good hour. Because the No. 4 plastic attachment, the one he started with, left the hair almost an inch long and didn't achieve the desired effect. He looked worse than ever, like a man going bald and mortified by it. He put on the No. 2 and guided the thrumming thing again back and forth, front to back over his crown, back to front, around the ears. But he still wasn't satisfied. So he went again with the bare blade, boot-camp length, and mowed away.

That looked pretty good. Tough, at least. It was time for a change anyway. All those hours wasted blow-drying over the years.

He studied himself in the mirror. Yeah, the football-hero beach-dude look was gone. And good riddance. Hey, time goes by and marches on. A man's gotta accept that. Life is change. Nobody stays young forever. He resolved, though, to put in extra time at the gym and bulk up even more. Strength equaled, or at least approximated, youth, was the way he saw it.

Sudek was a naturally heavily muscled man. All over, but especially in the legs. He had the legs of a Scandinavian shot-putter, each thigh a suckling hog. Stumpy calves barely diminished in diameter through the ankles. His pants always wore out high along the upper inseam from the friction generated by walking. This was not to say he was clumsy or un-athletic. He was a quick big man. Ungraceful but fast and very strong. He'd been a standout offensive guard on his high-school football team. Proud of his speed, the way he could pull and skirt the rest of the line a step ahead of the running back to flatten a linebacker or cornerback. He could still pound face and kick ass, and didn't mind doing so even if it cost him some knocks and bumps and bruises and scrapes. Just part of the job.

Like he might have to do soon with that fuckin' skinny pockfaced wetback, the Migra-bait new arrival in El Loco Junior's crew.

Sudek had been in Narcotics a year. They cut you a lot of slack at first, because it was the toughest beat and delicate, with its particular savvy and tricky ropes. Which nobody assumed you were going to pick up right out of the gate. Even so, it was time he made at least a small splash. He had to bring off a little coup to show he was coming along. They weren't going to promote him unless they saw he'd penetrated at street level, that he could cultivate good intelligence. That meant dealing with little shit snitches like the one they called Viruela (Smallpox), for the dents in his face.

***

It was a hundred degrees outside under a heavy gray sky taking its own lethargic measure of time. Everyone in L.A. knew it was simmering toward a point of thunderous rupture and rain. But while you waited for the downpour, the heat pressed on the back of your head and there was nothing for Junior and his homeses to do but sit around in the viscous twilight of an abandoned South Gate home on grimy old couch cushions, backs against the wall. The house, fled three months earlier by a family that had lost a 5-year-old in a drive-by, smelled of mildew and cat piss. After the second joint of Thai stick, El Sapo had broken out the badge works. He took a bottle of India ink from his daypack and went to puncturing one of the few open patches on the upper portion of Viruela's right arm. El Sapo had made the tattoo machine himself, from a Walkman. He was proud of it and of his steady hand.

Viruela watched the needle enter and withdraw. El Sapo was so stoned that when he finished the final *a* of *para*, he raised his bloodshot eyes to Viruela's and asked: *"Nacido para que putas, 'mano?"*

What the fuck were you born for, brother?

"Para Matar," said the pockmarked kid.

"That's fuckin' lame, homes," said Pelo Lindo from the corner. "Un-original." He was busy biting his nails, for a change, because they'd grown a quarter inch up from the cuticle.

"How 'bout *Morir?*," offered Viruela. "How's that sound?"

Born to Die.

"Mejor," said Pelo.

"Bitchin'," said El Sapo. He leaned in again to start the "M" when El Loco Junior spoke up.

"I hear 'bout you talkin' to that *guero* pig Sudek again I gonna hold you down and tatoo *Soplón* across you ugly face looks like they had a rodeo on."

Fear unstoned Viruela. He looked at Junior with bright wet eyes. "Hey, man, I ain't gonna deny it. The faggot grabbed me outa the line couple days ago when I was waitin' to buy tickets for the Maná concert. Drags me 'cross the street and gets in my face. But I ain't got nothin' to say to that musclehead."

"What he want from you?" asked Junior.

"He just talkin' cop garbage. Say he gonna arrest my ass, don' have to be for nothin' even, and they deport me back to Mexico, jus' like that."

"Unless what? He want you to suck his pink dick?"

"No chingues, cabrón. I don' give a fuck if you is crazy. Go ahead an' shoot me unless I fuckin' shoot you first. But don' be callin' me no cocksucker."

"Well what the fuck he want, then?"

"What them narcotics fucks always want? Information. Wanna bust somebody. Say ta give up some nigger punk, he don' give a shit. Jus' so it be a homes with a medium-size stash. Wanna get his nose up the boss's asshole, *parece."*

Junior was peeling an orange with a switchblade. The fruit was in his left hand and the knife in his right. He'd started at the top and was rotating the sphere against the stationary blade and the rind was dangling in an elongating helix. When he finished, when the spiral dropped to the floor, he held the white ball of peeled orange up in front of him. He examined it. Then he bit into it like an apple. Juice dripped off his chin onto his bare hairless chest and formed a thin rivulet across the green Sacred Heart of Jesus tattooed between his nipples. He chewed and swallowed. "I got a idea, you pit-faced motherfucker, so lissen up good. You know that Salvatrucha basketball-playin' faggot what dented Lico's skull? *Con el cerote Chapín?* I look into that fucker's backgroun' a little. *Se llama* Juan Cano and he live with his Mamá an' Granny on Hazel Street in Lynwood. You gonna give HIM up to *el pendejo de* Sudek."

"You kiddin' me, *'mano?* I know who is that *cabrón.* He fuckin' Joe College. *Nada que ver con nada.*"

"What the fuck you care? You jus' tell Sudek this Cano piece of shit in tight now with El Chapín, that he holdin' a coupla keys a' *blanca* at Mommy's house. What the fuck Sudek know? He jus' go break down the door. An' if I got that *maricón* right, once he in there, he gonna bust somebody for somethin'."

CHAPTER 26: NO RESEMBLANCE TO ANYONE

Before he went to El Salvador, Joe had never seen the body of a person who had died a violent death. The only dead man he'd seen was his paternal grandfather who, at the age of 73, still strong and lucid, with a full head of dark hair and a powerful laugh, had suffered a massive stroke while at the wake of an old friend from Newark, New Jersey. As if to accompany his pal, Grampa had died right there at the funeral home, but in not the most decorous of spots. He collapsed in the restroom while standing at a urinal, taking a piss.

Joe was an undergraduate when that happened. He'd driven down to Newark and accompanied the body in a hearse back to Ithaca for the wake and funeral. He spent long minutes contemplating the peach-powdered gray visage of Padraich Joseph Guinness, wondering where the old man was by that time, nearly two days into the netherworld. Whether he was a ghost floating around the crest of Ben Bulben or wisecracking with the faeries and leprechauns he had told Joe and his sister about when they were children.

September 15th is Independence Day in El Salvador and in the rest of Central America. Mariana Aleman, the assistant director of the Museo Nacional, and the on-loan American professor had driven out to the University of Pennsylvania site in La Libertad province by a village called Las Hamacas. They stopped in the village and asked around, and an older man named Jacinto, who had helped during the short-lived excavations there several years earlier, took them along a path through milpas and fields to the place.

It was a parcel the average person could walk past and not realize that there was anything interesting hidden there. But if you knew what to look for, as did Jacinto, Joe and Mariana–a terrace and two mounds in an otherwise flat landscape–it was a stimulating way to spend an hour, just walking around, surveying the expanse, whetting an appetite for an eventual dig, years on. Jacinto filled the visitors in on what little they had accomplished, basically a few test pits and some mapping, before they were obliged to pack up and go home and leave the place as undisturbed as it had been for the previous thousand years.

While they were strolling around these couple acres, an adolescent boy came running over to Jacinto and informed him of the discovery of a body in a ravine on a coffee plantation on a hill that rose about a kilometer to the west.

One of the *finca's* peons, a man from Las Hamacas, had seen vultures overhead and caught on the breeze a scent of rotting flesh. He'd found the body, and word had spread through the surrounding hamlets. Anyone missing a relative should go to the ravine to see if this dead person might be that person. The body, according to law, would remain at the spot where it was found until arrival of the justice of the peace from Apulo, the district's administrative capital, who for the record would note down the time and place of its discovery and particulars of the cadaver; apparent cause of death, apparent age, height, weight and any other information gleaned from a cursory examination.

Jacinto was kneeling where the Penn team had made a pit, now only a washed depression. He rose and brushed the dirt from his knees.

"Quieren venir, doctores?" he asked the visitors.

Mariana and Joe looked at each other. "Why not?" she said, and they all struck off, following the boy.

They set out westward, away from the flats, along a path that after a few hundred yards began to rise. After another quarter mile they were into coffee trees bristling with small hard green berries, fruit that in three months would be red and ready to yield to brown hands gently stripping the head-high branches, taking care not to damage the landowner's plants because the yanking of leaves or breaking of branches, if seen by the *capatáz* taskmaster, could wipe out a long day's earnings. It had rained the night before and the coffee tree leaves shone with a bright waxy finish.

Joe licked his dry lips. His heart quickened and his breathing accelerated with the ascent. He had been biking a lot around town and had taken some hillside trail excursions into the Balsamo ridge behind Santa Tecla or up the lower slopes of El Picacho volcano on the northwest edge of the capital. He was in good physical shape. The shortened breath and tracks of sweat down his ribs were due as much to nervous anticipation as to exertion.

Jacinto had used the word *escuadrón,* or "squad." As in death squad.

The corpse was down a ways in a ravine. A few campesinos stood around above it, on the edge of the slash in the hill. Two National Guard soldiers stood about five yards from the body. Both wore bandannas over their faces in a futile gesture against the stench.

Jacinto, who knew everyone from these parts, made his way down for a closer look. Joe followed him. Mariana stayed higher on the ridge, with the boy.

After a minute or so of careful descent, Jacinto and Joe reached the man. He had been hacked with a machete several times before being dispatched with a bullet to the side of the head. A gash exposed the cream-colored skull through the scalp and matted curly black hair. He looked to be about 30 years old. He wore green gym shorts and nothing else. One leg was doubled unnaturally underneath him. There was a trail of blood down the rocks along which he'd been dragged to this spot. One ear was cut off and the fingers of the left hand were attached only by skin, as if he had raised that hand to deflect a machete blow.

Dozens of flies crawled over the face, crowding the corners of dull open eyes covered with a milky film like cataracts. White mucous filled his nose and his mouth was open. The skin that in life had been light brown was tinged yellow and stretched tight and exhibited a kind of sheen like that on the coffee leaves. No one knew who he was, but that was not remarkable. This was not the first time the body of a stranger had been found in this ravine.

After climbing back up to the trail, Joe asked a middle-aged campesino if the dead man looked familiar.

"You cannot tell," the farmer replied. "Now he does not look like anybody at all, not even like the man he was during the time his life lasted."

CHAPTER 27: CRAZY

The LAPD squad that raided the pale yellow Mediterranean-style bungalow at 117 Hazel St. in the Lynwood section of Los Angeles at 11:05 p.m. on Sunday, June 9, 1985 could have posed for the department's equal-opportunity poster. The assault on the house where Soledad Cano lived with her only son Juan and her mother Rosario was led by Narcotics Detective Chris Sudek, a European-descended pale-skinned white man, and his partner Daniel Choo, whose great-grandfather had played a bit part, as a victim, more than a century earlier in transforming the name of China's biggest port into a verb. They were backed up in this search-and-seizure operation–Sudek had received a tip that a kilo or more of cocaine was on the premises–by two patrolmen with their sights set on a drug-enforcement or anti-gang unit shield: Lawrence Lawton, a short and wiry black man, and Rafael Coronado, a hulking Chicano with a fu-manchu mustache.

Sudek had surveilled the dwelling over the previous week. He'd established what seemed to be the small family's weeknight routine of a late dinner–after the high-school senior who was the target of the raid arrived home from baseball practice–followed by a couple calm hours of TV time or homework or whatever the jock, who, according to Sudek's information, had fallen in with a bad crowd, did before hitting the rack. Lights usually were out by 11.

The four men sat in a black Camaro parked along the opposite curb two houses down. Sudek, who had jacked himself up on three double espressos in the half-hour before they'd left the station house, was in the front passenger seat. He stopped jiggling his right leg long enough to extend it and reach into the pocket of his jeans for the small circular tin of smokeless tobacco he'd used since quitting cigarettes two years ago. The pinch of snuff he lodged behind his lower lip sent a tiny jolt from the nape of his neck to the pit of his stomach, then dissipated through his tense muscles to his palms and the soles of his feet.

Rafi, sitting directly behind him, coughed. He rolled down the backseat window and hawked a gob of snotty sputum onto the sidewalk.

"I hear TB is making a comeback in this country, especially among the dampened dorsal crowd," said Choo, who was doing the driving.

"Fuck that, dude. I'm fourth-generation, too. I heard about your spike-driving coolie-ass ancestor. But my grandma changed the rich folks' sheets that your grand-daddy laundered. The only one got us beat on way-back in this country is Larry, and his people made the trip wearing a shitload of iron bling. Sudek's Polacks or Hunkies or whatever the fuck they were are newcomers compared to us."

"Don't bet on it, ah-mee-go," said Sudek. "One of my ancestors died at Antietam."

That was true. A forebear on his mother's side–his Irish half–had been drafted shortly off the boat to Boston into Mr. Lincoln's army and had run up against a Minié ball in the war's bloodiest battle. But it didn't mean Coronado wasn't half right, too. Sudek's father had come over from Poland as a child with his immigrant parents.

"Aren't we just a bunch of deep-rooted American motherfuckers," mused Lawton, who was using the small blade of a Swiss Army knife to clean his fingernails. He finished his manicure, then asked: "What about these folks we're about to drop in on? Speak-a da Eenglish?"

"The kid, for sure," said Sudek. "Been here since he was a baby. And the mother, I guess so. Don't know about the granny."

He looked at his watch.

"Let's go," he said.

They stepped out and a series of four thumps from the closing doors resounded along the empty street. The four men walked quickly across it and down the sidewalk, two-by-two, with Sudek and Choo leading the way. When they reached the chain-link fence around the dwelling, Choo and Lawton split off to head around back while Sudek and Coronado, who'd drawn his weapon, approached the front door.

Sudek pounded hard on the door with the meaty part of his fist. After several seconds, he pounded again.

Within half a minute a voice came from the other side. A female voice.

"Who is it?" the voice inquired. First in English. Then it repeated, "*Quien es?*"

"Los Angeles Police Department," said Sudek. The declaration was forceful enough, but short of bellowed, and studiously un-menacing.

The words sent a shiver through Soledad. Juan's school year–and high-school career–was almost over. With the petering out of homework and studies, he had resumed that very night his job at the concession stand of the little repertoire movie house in Huntington Park where he'd worked the previous summer. A dreadful thought crossed her mind that something–a traffic accident involving the bike her son rode to work, a movie-house robbery–might have resulted in injury, or worse, to Juan and brought the cops to her door at this late hour. With a trembling hand she unbolted the door and opened it.

Sudek was exhibiting a sheet of paper.

"We have a search warrant for these premises," he said, stepping in without waiting to be invited. Coronado followed him.

"Where's Juan Cano?" he asked the woman.

"He's at work. At the Lumiere cinema, up on East Gage." Soledad followed him across the small living room and into the kitchen, where Sudek stepped across to the back door and opened it. The other two officers entered.

"Here's *abuelita*," said Coronado from the hallway after Rosario emerged from her bedroom, sleepy and confused and tying the belt of a faded maroon terrycloth bathrobe around her narrow waist. "But the kid's room is empty."

"May I ask what is going on here?" said Soledad. The kitchen was now crowded, with six people either standing in it or in the doorways on two of its sides.

"You ladies might as well take a seat and make yourselves comfortable. Have a cup of tea or something. Because we're going to be a while," said Sudek.

"A while doing what?" asked Soledad.

"Searching the house. For drugs," said Sudek.

"*La droga?!*" Chayo piped up. "*Pero eso es ridículo.*"

"I can assure you there are no drugs in this house." Soledad stood directly opposite Sudek, her legs spread slightly and her hands on her hips. She felt self-conscious for not having a bra on under her pajama top, which featured a pattern of silver-dollar-sized yellow and white daisies.

"Mom and Grandma generally aren't the first to find out that their kids are branching out into work that earns them more than handing out popcorn," said Sudek. "In any case, *señoras*, you're not goin' back to bed for a bit. What time does the kid get home?"

"Not until around 12:30. The last show is at 10."

Three of the cops–Choo leaned in the doorjamb, standing guard over the two women seated at the Formica-topped table–spent the next half-hour ransacking the home. They rummaged through all the dresser drawers, lifted the mattresses, looked behind books on the shelves, removed cushions from the furniture and squeezed them, rifled through closets and emptied kitchen cabinets. Lawton lifted the lid off the tank of the toilet in the house's single bathroom to see if a plastic-wrapped package might have been submerged there. Coronado emptied the refrigerator and the freezer.

Sudek was occupying himself with Juan's bedroom. What at first had been half-muffled sounds of shifting furniture and drawer-openings were now amplified, coming in slams and bangs as the squad leader shook spikes and sneakers from an oversized gym bag and kicked them out of the way, then flung the bag itself against the wall. He flipped the twin bed up on its side, produced a switch-blade knife from the pocket of his nylon windbreaker and began stabbing the box spring's underbelly.

When he realized there was nothing to be found there, he paused and surveyed the room from his knees. A bead of sweat dripped off the tip of his nose. His eyes fell on an aluminum baseball bat leaning against the back wall of the room's small closet.

"Those fuckin' things are hollow," he thought. "And that cylinder would be just about perfect for holding a packed key." He rose and grabbed the bat.

Sudek had never played baseball. But even he could feel that the bat was its normal weight.

"Hey, Danny. Bring the Mom in here, will ya?" he shouted.

Soledad had risen from the table and was leaning against the stove, her arms folded across her chest. She'd been observing the Chinese-American detective, then had turned her attention to her mother, who was worrying the fringed edge of an orange individual placemat woven of coarse cotton. Soledad was suddenly assailed by the strangest, out-of-nowhere question, one that never before had crossed her mind: Did I do the right thing in bringing that baby here?

She didn't dwell more than an instant on the response, only long enough for a flash of recollection of a cool adobe house and chickens crossing a packed dirt corral beyond the door. Of course I did, she thought, just as the crew-cut muscle-bound boss of this team of invaders called for her presence in Juan's room.

Choo made a jutting motion with his chin, and followed Soledad down the hall. She entered the room. Choo and Rosario, who'd risen and come along, took up the doorway.

A red-faced Sudek was sweating profusely. He stood in the middle of the room with the bat. He held it like an oversized nightstick, the right fist on the handle, tapping the barrel in a slow rhythm on his left palm.

"Señora, if you know where your son might hide something he didn't want anybody to find, you better let me know right now," said Sudek. His words were clipped and he sounded short of breath. His eyes were gleaming and open wide. "Otherwise I'm gonna start smashing these walls with your little slugger's Slugger."

"Juan has nothing to hide," answered Soledad. "Unless maybe it's a magazine with naked girls in it. But even for that, I wouldn't know where to look."

The cop closed both hands around the bat's handle and turned his back to all three of the people watching him. He extended it back and, with his right foot planted, strode with his left toward the upturned bed and the wall it leaned against. As if chasing a high fastball, he whipped the aluminum cylinder across his body and sent it crashing into, and through, the gypsum-board wall. Shifting his weight only slightly, he swept the bat back again, cocked his hands, and let fly a second time.

Chayo shrieked weakly.

"Fuckin' A," muttered Choo. His face showed a nervous sort of amusement, but also a hint of what looked like frustration. As if he'd seen such behavior before and was growing tired of it.

Sudek huffed and appraised the damage.

Soledad strode toward him, shouting a question.

"*Estás loco?*" she wailed, right before laying her hands, from behind him, on his shoulders.

He wheeled.

"Loco?! Me loco?!," he screamed. Soledad raised her hands again as if she wanted to grab his shoulders from the front and shake some sense into him. But he parried and turned her around, then brought the bat, which he now clenched horizontally at either extreme, up under her chin.

"What's loco is for a little woman to assault a police officer in the line of duty. That's fucking batshit loco," he shouted as he pulled back and up on the shaft, barely feeling the resistance it encountered at Soledad's throat. Her heels rose and her feet curved and her toes pointed like those of a ballerina.

Rosario whimpered, "Ay, ay, ay." She tried to push past Choo into the room but he shifted a half step to block her. He pivoted to subdue the elderly woman, who felt in his embrace like a child.

When Choo turned back to look at his partner, Soledad Cano's plush green slippers dangled from her feet a good six inches above the floor. She was limp and her eyes were closed.

CHAPTER 28: THE UGLINESS OF ENVY

The American archeologist did not have to wait for a dinner invitation from Roxana Benitez in order to make the acquaintance of Ricardo Paniagua. One day in late August Joe rose from the desk in his cluttered, improvised office at the museum and walked down the corridor to that of Mariana. He was going to invite her to go with him that night to see the new Scorsese flick, After Hours. When he entered the foyer where her secretary sat, an area with a sofa and a coffee table that served as a waiting room for those with appointments with Mariana, a lean man, mid 40s, in blue jeans and an open-necked khaki work shirt was sitting on the couch. He sat with one ankle resting on the other knee, a posture that exhibited one of a pair of expensive Texan boots made from reptilian leather. On his head were lightweight earphones connected to a Walkman clipped to his belt.

Joe registered this man's presence in little more than a glance. He asked Lisette, Mariana's secretary, if Mariana was busy. Lisette said she was conferring with someone from the *Patrimonio*, so Joe asked her to ask Mariana to come by his office when she finished. As he was leaving, the man on the couch removed his headphones and asked him, signaling by way of a jutted chin a point somewhere around Joe's midriff: "Navajo or Hopi?"

"Excuse me?"

The man pointed with a crooked index finger, one that looked as if it had been broken and poorly set. *"La hebilla. Es una belleza.* I was wondering if it is Navajo or Hopi."

Joe looked down at his waist. Cinching his jeans was a rawhide belt with a silver buckle inlaid with a phoenix of lapis lazuli. It was not the most typical of Indian styles of the southwestern U.S., lacking the turquoise that might have identified it to less of a connoisseur. But indeed it was of Hopi design and manufacture, and he told the man so.

"You have quite an eye. Have you lived in the southwest?"

"No. But I've spent some time there," said the man, rising."With friends. Collectors." He took a step toward Joe and extended his hand.

"Ricardo Paniagua," he said as they shook. Joe noted the hint of a smile as the man appraised his reaction. Indeed, Joe was momentarily flustered. But it seemed to him he'd experienced only a mental, and not a physical flinch. He hoped that was the case.

"Joe Guinness. From Cornell University."

"It's a pleasure to meet you, *Doctor.* We share an appreciation for this land's history and for the beauty of what our ancestors left behind."

Paniagua said, "our ancestors" without a trace of irony, though he was one of few Salvadorans, perhaps five percent of the population, of pure European ancestry, predominantly Spanish but in Paniagua's case with a French-descended mother. Though burnished by the sun, it was evident Paniagua's natural complexion was light, and his wavy hair was a sandy brown. His nickname during more than 20 years in the armed forces had been *El Chele.* Now, in speeches at rallies of the nationalist, virulently anti-communist party he'd founded and of which he was "President for life," he spat the same term - *estos Cheles hijos de puta* - in reference to U.S. and European policy-makers and journalists who, according to him and his followers, were sticking their noses into Salvadoran affairs with their squawking about human rights. He'd suggested on occasion that some or many or all of them should have those same pointy little Saxon noses punched into their pasty faces.

"I have a modest collection of pottery and small sculpture. Maya and Pipil."

"I've heard it's not so modest," said Joe.

"Es una cosa fea, la envidia." Envy is an ugly thing.

"Perhaps we'll persuade you to lend, or even donate, some pieces to the museum to improve our permanent exhibition. I'm getting the impression the best material is in private hands, either here or in the States."

"I agree that's a shame. Our heritage is the patrimony of all good Salvadorans and it would be wonderful to be able to share it with the public, have it on display for children to see here in the museum, on field trips and all that. But we are a poor country with inadequate infrastructure. This museum does not have the resources to mount an exhibition worthy of the pieces themselves, nor to provide adequate security. Because, my American friend and esteemed doctor, another of our misfortunes is that we are a lawless people, and many here are prone to violence."

It was not quite a smirk, the look Joe had noticed before and which again crossed the otherwise friendly face. It was a glimmer in his eye, and the way that sparkle combined with the gleam from a gold crown on one of his front teeth. Not a solid gold tooth, but a gold frame around the white tooth.

"I haven't found that to be the case. Your countrymen have been nothing but kind and hospitable to me."

Despite what Joe had read and heard of Paniagua as a beast, the man exuded conviviality. Without evident guile, with a ready smile and his clipped folksy accent, he established an easy confidence and rapport. He had addressed Joe from the outset as "vos," which coming from someone else could have been perceived as a breach of etiquette. From him, it sounded natural.

He took a pack of Marlboros from his shirt pocket and offered Joe one.

"No thanks. I don't smoke."

"Good for you. These fuckin' things'll kill ya." Paniagua lit up. "I'm not saying we're not kind and hospitable. Only that we have other characteristics too. Then again you've recently arrived and it would be unrealistic to imagine that you, so soon, would have acquired a reliable catalogue of our blessings and faults."

"It's my intention to get to know El Salvador and its people as well as one is capable of doing in seven months."

"That may not be sufficient. But we will do everything we can to make your time here as fruitful and enlightening as possible."

The door to Mariana's office opened and out walked Roxana with Mariana behind her.

"Oh, Joseph," said Chana. "What a pleasure. I see you and my husband have acquainted yourselves. That's marvelous. I was just passing along to Mariana the good news of a $20,000 donation, specifically given to support the museum reorganization, by Abram Hassan. You've seen their big department stores, no?"

"Yes, I have. I've even met Abram. At Primera Raqueta. I've been playing squash there. Nice guy. That's great. We certainly can use it."

Paniagua shook hands with Mariana and again with Joe. "Well, doctor. It's been a pleasure. I'm sure we'll be seeing more of each other."

Roxana gave Joe a kiss on the cheek and she and her husband left.

After several judicious seconds Mariana said: "So. You met the boogey man." Her smile was playful. "Did you check your hand? For blood?"

Joe, ridiculously, looked at his hand. It was clean.

CHAPTER 29: IN THE DREAM, HE SMOKED

It took Juan Cano, when he was 18 and that was his only name, three weeks to retrace in the opposite direction the route his mother had followed to the North, a destination that, back then, had seemed worth any sacrifice. Against the flow of other furtive waders, he forded the river near El Paso, just as she had done. He travelled by bus to Guadalajara then on to el D.F, down through Oaxaca and Chiapas and across Guatemala to the land of his birth.

His mother occupied his thoughts unrelentingly. Her irremediable absence burgeoned into an omnipresence. The huge oppressive fact of her non-existence made Juan's life meaningless, a vessel with room for little more than anguish.

The journey was a descent along an endless highway bordered by scorched dirt. His butt ached and he stank sourly. There was a stretch in Oaxaca when he suspected he'd shit his pants. His asshole burned. But the packed bus hardly ever stopped. There was nothing he could do but endure until late afternoon when, in the fetid bathroom of a *comedor*, he was able to confirm his suspicion and wash his ass with his hand and a trickle of water. He left the soiled briefs in a puddle of strangers' piss.

Sweltering rooms with greasy caved-in beds. Soft-bodied roaches and gut-sickness. It was an unraveling, the downstairs tumble of a ball of string that his mother, with courage and strength greater than his own, had wound. Back to square one. Only now, because he was a man whether he wanted to be or not, he was worse off than when he'd been a baby in this part of the world. His exhausted, anxious, unclean person was the negation, *en carne y hueso*, of Soledad's life.

In the days after her death, grief was partially eclipsed by hate and rage. Once vengeance, or what he had believed would constitute vengeance, was exacted, the energy he'd spent figuring the logistics of violence could be dedicated to nothing but remembrance and regret.

Rolling across Coahuila early in his flight, Juan had recalled another scene involving cops from his and her life together. It was the sole incident, prior to *el desastre*, in his store of memories of her that had anything to do with the police.

He must have been 10 years old. It was before she'd become a U.S. citizen, but she had her Green Card and was legal. They'd gone out to Hollywood and taken the tour of Universal Studios, watched the belly-shot cowboy stuntmen plunge from the roof, somersault in graceful slow-motion dying and land on their backs on huge cushions. Mother and son had placed their hands in the impressions left by the hands of stars. She'd told him who were the Latinos – Rita Hayworth, Anthony Quinn, Raquel Welch–though few Gringos ever suspected as much. At the end of the day they'd gone for Kentucky Fried, where his mother repeated her opinion that, although good, the Colonel's recipe was not as savory as that of Pollo Campero. Afterwards they were sitting on a bench waiting for a bus that would take them home. It was getting dark.

When they'd been there a few minutes, an LAPD patrol car cruising curbside slowed and stopped a short distance beyond them. Two officers got out and walked back to the bench.

One of the cops was Hispanic. But he wasn't the one who addressed his mother. It was the other, who was lean but with bulging muscles in his chalk-white arms.

"Could I see some identification please, Mam?"

Soledad looked up at the tall white strong cop.

"Why?" she asked.

"No reason," he answered. "Just show me some ID."

"Well, you should have a reason," said Juan's mother, who by this time spoke English well, though with the thick accent she never lost. "Because what you are doing is in some sense a search, and the Fourth Amendment to the Constitution of this fine country protects all people who reside here, citizens or not, from unreasonable search and seizure. You know the meaning of 'unreasonable'? Means without a reason."

Juan was looking at the face of the cop, an expressionless totem of Anglo-ness. Then the boy looked at the Hispanic officer, who was repressing a smile.

His mother had not immediately opened her purse. But by the end of her little discourse she was reaching in for her wallet.

The Popeye patrolman remained stone-faced another couple seconds. Then Juan saw him look down at the sidewalk, scuff at something and shake his head slowly. He exhaled a "Fuck me" sigh and waved his hand dismissively, disgusted with Juan's mother or with his job or with himself and said: "OK, OK, *señora. Olvidelo.* Forget I asked." He turned and walked back to the car.

The Latino cop looked at Juan. *"Y tú?"* he asked. *"Te lo puedes todo el Bill of Rights?"*

"No," said Juan.

"You'd be wise to learn it," he said. Then he wished them *buenas tardes* and followed his partner back to the cruiser.

***

Twenty-five days after departing the golden state of broken dreams, the adolescent Juan Cano, his knees drawn up almost to his chest, sat over the wheel well of a packed bus travelling from San Salvador to Ahuachapan, El Salvador's westernmost province. The mid-morning heat made his head ache. It pressed the passengers more tightly against one another and leeched the air of oxygen. Juan's right shoulder was hard against the wall of the bus. All the windows were down. Through the one at which he sat came a draft scented with manure and wet grass. A coffee *finca* bordered the road on both sides. The leaves of the coffee trees were brilliant and clean.

The man next to Juan stank. Or maybe it was the guy in front of him. Or the general common blended odor of toil and poverty. Juan had caught a few whiffs of himself before boarding that dawn. Not exactly Old Fucking Spice.

There was no longer an aisle down the middle of the bus. The seats meant for two people on the right side held three. The ones meant for three, on the left, had four. The last passengers able to pry themselves in had only one butt-cheek on the hard flat seat. They leaned against each other in crammed support but did not speak. A canvas knapsack rested on Juan's knees and atop that a cheap paperback edition of Salarrué short stories, *"Cuentos de Barro."* He'd read a couple between the capital and the turn-off to Sonsonate. Then the motion of the bus and the day's stupor had lulled him to sleep and it was almost as if, during that hour of repose, he weren't a fugitive and an exile all alone in his foreign native land.

He was on his way to Ahuachapan to look for his great-uncle Marcos, the youngest brother of his grandmother. Or for one of his great-aunts, or a second cousin; really, for any trace of his extended family. He figured there must still be people there named Cano or Zelaya, his grandmother's surname. His plan was simply to ask around. Find out who was left. See whether they were willing, still, to recognize him as kin.

When the bus braked abruptly he'd been awake for only a minute and was groggily reviewing the residue of a dream. In it he'd been collecting cigarette butts on a sidewalk. He had been in a state of anxiety while doing this. Because in the dream he smoked (in life he did not) and was hard up for a few drags. He was gathering what he could find, even dirty or damp stubs, with the intention of taking them apart to salvage the shreds and roll them into something smokeable.

A murmur filtered through the press of passengers. In the muttering Juan made out the word *chafas* (military men). When the driver opened the door, a soldier in camouflage fatigues with an M-16 assault rifle across his back stepped up into the bus.

"Everybody out. Bring your bags and satchels. Anything left inside will be confiscated," he said, and stepped back down to the roadside.

Another soldier opened the rear door from outside. It took a few minutes for the grumbling crowd to file out the two exits. A squad of nine soldiers awaited them. One had a radio on his back and the others, except the one who'd boarded the bus and who apparently was the lieutenant, though he wore no insignia, carried backpacks. The troops were dirty and sweaty and their faces were smudged with greasepaint. The leader wore a floppy olive-drab field hat. The others were bareheaded or wore visored olive-green caps or pirate-style headscarves bearing the Atlacatl battalion emblem, an Indian prince in loincloth and feathered head-dress brandishing a spear.

"Men and boys up against the bus," said the squad leader. "Women and small children down there. By small I mean under 12." He signaled with a pursed mouth, like a camel, to where two soldiers stood several meters away.

The men, who numbered about 30, were ordered to turn and raise their hands and spread their legs and lean against the bus. A soldier began at each end and worked toward the middle, frisking them. When that was done the leader told them to turn around.

They'd been standing in the sun for nearly a half-hour by the time the officer reached Juan. He was examining the documents of each male while a soldier searched whatever bag or bundle the passengers carried. Two young men—one looked to be about 15—had been pulled out of line and sent to stand with a trooper ten meters down the road.

"Identification," the leader demanded of Juan.

"I've got my passport," said Juan. He took from his pocket the dark blue document with the eagle seal. "I'm a U.S. citizen, down here visiting family."

The officer opened it. He looked from the photograph up again into Juan's face.

"Says here you were born in Ahuachapan."

"That's right. My mother took me to Los Angeles when I was a baby. This is the first time I've been back."

"Mala suerte, my fren'. Your mother should have kept you up there. You can be a *gringuito* when you're in California eating *un Whopper con Queso.* Down here you're another Guanaco turd, just like the rest of us."

He slid the passport into the button-flap pocket on his right leg. "Over there with those two."

CHAPTER 30: SO FRESH THEY'RE NOT YET DEAD

Ricardo Paniagua ordered two Pilseners, one for himself and one for Joe, and two dozen oysters. The waiter had been awed–nervous but honored–by the appearance of such a notable personage at his table, one of several along a veranda on the second floor of a seaside beer-and-seafood joint in the port of La Libertad.

It was mid-afternoon and most of the lunch crowd was gone. One table remained occupied by four men, middle-class guys from the city who'd taken the afternoon off to feast on fresh Pacific fare–filets of sea bass grilled or sauteed in garlic butter, whole seasoned and seared snappers, shrimp-and-fish ceviche marinated in lemon juice with onion and cilantro and strips of sweet green pepper and jalapeños, jumbo shrimp prepared any way you wanted, oysters on the half shell and *conchas*, firm-fleshed inky mollusks found only along this coast–all washed down with draughts of icy Pilsener with the ace of hearts label or green-bottled Suprema. Six or seven beers each over the course of a long afternoon of jokes and talk about *fútbol* and pussy.

The only other man in the restaurant was wearing, incongruously for this joint, a tie. A flabby mid-level executive of an air-conditioning distributorship or insurance agency, he sidled ungracefully out from behind his table behind a much younger woman. She wore a dress and stockings and was coquettishly deferential, laughing at his every comment. Joe took her to be his secretary, out for a tryst with the boss that would end up on the cool sheets, porno flick on the closed circuit, of one of the short-stay motels, the Doral or Ambassador or the Capri, that vied for young lovers and adulterers along the winding highway from the capital down to the port.

All present, the beer-drinkers and the fat man and the secretary and a family group–a grandmother, two moms, two adolescents and three young kids finishing their meal two tables away–had noted the major's arrival. The family members made hushed remarks to each other but the male clique responded gregariously, their bonhomie fueled by brew. Their calls of *"Salud, Mayor!"* and *"Dales duro, Mayor,"* were received with a wave and a smile by Paniagua. The chubby man looked around for what he imagined would be a full-blown detail of bodyguards with Uzis. But there was no squadron of henchmen. No thugs, no submachine-guns. None in evidence, in any case.

Paniagua, after calling Joe that morning and inviting him to lunch, had picked him up at the museum and driven the 25 miles to the coast in his armored bulletproof Nissan Patrol. The drive had taken precisely the time it took to play Carlos Santana's collection of dreamy instrumentals called *"El Amor Eres Tú"* on the SUV's stereo. Accompanying them in the back seat, a machine pistol across his lap, dark glasses on despite the smoked windows that prevented those outside from seeing in, sat Ramón, whom Paniagua had introduced to Joe as *"Ramón el Jamón,"* eliciting a laugh from the bodyguard. (Later Joe learned that Ramón, over the course of nearly a decade of service to the major, had earned another rhyming nickname; *"Ramón el Matón,"* or Ramon the Killer.) He, to all appearances an unremarkable customer, sat now at a table on the ground floor, foregoing the upper-level sea breeze, sipping tomato juice spiced with Tabasco Sauce on ice beside the stairway, ready to advise any late lunchers who might wish to ascend that they would have to be seated downstairs, *disculpen la molestia,* that the top section had been reserved. His Mac-10 rested, mostly hidden by the table, on the chair beside him. A Glock was tucked into his waistband beneath a sky-blue guayabera.

The major was meticulous in the preparation of his oysters, gleaming wet on their pearly shells, the rocky rough gray half-shells nestled on a bed of lettuce surrounded by wedges of lemon.

"This is the way," he said, tapping a single drop of Tabasco, then one of Worcester, onto each fat morsel. Then a pinch on each from the bowl of salt, then a squeeze of lemon that made the mollusks contract.

"See how they move? That's how you know they're fresh." He lifted one and slurped it into his mouth and Joe wondered whether these animals were still alive when they were being eaten.

But he did not wonder long or let it bother him because he had prepared his plate of a dozen in the same fashion as the major, and he savored them one after another. When he came to his last oyster, he asked, "What about cholera?"

The cholera outbreak that had swelled to epidemic proportions in Peru a year earlier had reached this part of the Central American isthmus a couple months before Joe's arrival. The government was broadcasting a radio and television campaign on hygiene and food preparation designed to reduce the incidence of the disease, which had already killed a few dozen rural folk. One of the recommendations was to abstain from raw shellfish, a prime vehicle for the spread of the bacteria.

"*Me vale verga* (I could give a shit)," said Paniagua. "One has to die of something. It might as well be something that gives you pleasure. It's like this AIDS thing, or salt. I hate wearing a rubber. That's all there is to it. I started fucking without rubbers as a kid and have fucked that way for 30 years. A case of clap once in a while I accepted as the price to be paid. No big deal. And now they tell me I have to wear a latex hood over my dick? I tried it, but it's like taking a shower with an umbrella, you know what I mean? Defeats the purpose." He took a drink of beer. "What's the point? I don't like the taste of food without salt, blood pressure be damned. So if I keel over one of these days at least I'll be well fed and well fucked and the coroner will find a smile on my face."

Paniagua was renowned for his sexual appetite. He had divorced his first wife to marry Roxana, who during the first year of their union had kept him out of the whorehouses and off the backs and bellies of his several lovers with a daily ration of her own considerable charms. He had not even wanted another woman for eight or ten months. But there was no way around it. One woman simply could not keep him satisfied. He loved the curve of this one's rump, the profile of that one's breast, the way another moaned, this one's color, that one's hair. That was how God had made him. And Chanita knew it.

Indeed, it was Maj. Paniagua's image as a macho's macho, a hard fucker and fighter and drinker and cusser, poker-playing straight-talking back-slapping giver-of-hell that had earned him the admiration of so many of his compatriots. That is what they had been taught to admire in a leader since the first in a long line of saber-rattling or pistol-packing *caudillos* took charge saying: "Here am I with my very large testicles. And we're doing it this way because I say so, *carajo.*"

"Anyway," Paniagua continued, "I'll know when it's my day to die. They have tried and come close to killing me twice, either the faggot *terengos* or the faggot *pescados*. But neither of those was my day to take leave of this earth. Every morning I wake up and ask myself, will this be the day? And every morning I am answered with the assurance: today is not the day."

Though it was not common knowledge, Paniagua during the previous five years had narrowly escaped two assassination attempts, one an ambush with assault rifles and rocket-propelled grenades on his motorcade in San Miguel province and the other a close-range attack by a single gunman who, in a restaurant parking lot, was dispatched from the realm of the quick by Ramón with a single shot through the eye the second after he pulled a revolver from the pocket of his sport coat. The major was not certain who was responsible, but it fit into his scheme of things to assign one effort to the guerrillas, and the other to the Christian Democratic Party, which with CIA funding had defeated him in the presidential election of 1984. The symbol of the Christian Democrats was a stylized fish, and adherents to that party were called simply that: *pescados.*

"Fuck it. The prospect bothers me not in the least. Death is not sad or tragic or even ugly. That would be like saying birth or eating or taking a piss was tragic or ugly. It just is."

The tide was out. Thousands of smooth gray boulders buffed by the surf, most of them the size of a grapefruit but some as large as a medicine ball, were exposed along the curving strand of light brown sand. Two hundred yards out from shore on the blue-gray sea, off a rocky outcropping up the coast, a dozen surfers straddled their boards. Some were Gringos, but most were locals who had become hooked on the sport over the years by carefree, oblivious Californians who did not let a little thing like civil war dissuade them from enjoying some of the best waves in the Western Hemisphere. It was true that La Libertad was not in one of the "conflict zones," where combat was to be expected. Even so, its environs were the scene of two or three sizeable clashes a year, just enough incursion by the rebels to oblige the government to worry about the port's defense. Even so, the Gringo surfers' only concern was the thrill of hurtling down the face of a six-foot swell. This coast had steady great waves, cheap lodgings, good beer and shrimp and fish and dozens of cool skinny little brown dudes, 14- and 15- and 16-year-olds with peroxide-streaked hair and patched-up boards who carved the hell out of set after set every day and who were nothing but friendly to the *chele "broders,"* teaching them a little Spanish and procuring for them locally grown weed and babes.

"I'd like to stop by the museum sometime, if that wouldn't be a bother," Paniagua said.

"No bother. Just gimme a call. I'll show you around."

The fish came. The two men drank beer and savored the firm white flesh charred cayenne crispy on the outside. They used their fingers to pick the snappers clean. By the time–a half hour and two more beers later–Paniagua asked for the check, the plates held nothing more than flimsy skeletons of fine white bones and seared heads, the eyes staring dully.

CHAPTER 31: THE EYES OF JUSTICE

San Salvador has little to boast of in the way of architecture. Most of what is there now was built in the 20th century under the auspices of utilitarian functionaries or the nouveau riche, and looks it. The city was not the original capital, is not even a colonial-era town. Not that the three Salvadoran cities that date from the 17th century have much to show in the way of architecture either. In those provincial capitals, all named for saints, hardly anything remains of the earliest churches or customs houses or residences of lieutenants of the viceroys, the first buildings of substance that the pink-skinned bearded men whipped the copper-skinned smooth-faced men into building for them.

Even so, the capital has two monuments that aspire to grandeur and stand in some contrast to the mediocre hodgepodge.

One of them is a statue of Jesus called *El Salvador del Mundo*, The Savior of the World. The representation of Christ is 30 feet tall and stands on a globe with blue oceans and white continents atop a 20-foot-high pedestal rising from the center of a sloping plaza of flowering trees and palms.

The earthquake that brought Joe Guinness to El Salvador toppled the Lord from his pedestal. The world came crashing down with him. Besides the death and grief it caused, the disaster made an unattractive city even less attractive. Piles of rubble and abandoned buildings marred by fissures dotted downtown when Joe arrived, and they were there when he left.

In September, three months into Joe's stay, the repaired figure of Christ and the world were restored to a place of vigilance over the city. The restoration was celebrated with a large and colorful ceremony orchestrated by the fat mayor and sanctified by the archbishop. Joe watched the event from across the street at the high end of the plaza. Hundreds of children in blue and maroon and gray uniforms from dozens of schools were arrayed across the expanse at Jesus' feet. A hundred doves had been distributed among them for release at the moment of the statue's unveiling.

After an hour's delay in the ceremony's commencement, the archbishop said a prayer and the mayor made a short speech and the children sang the national anthem then an Easter hymn that, although it was not Easter, was appropriate to hailing a resurrected Christ.

"Hallelujah!" they sang, the young and the old. The mayor tugged at a dangling rope and the tarp covering the statue fell away. Everyone cheered. The children tossed the doves, white and gleaming, toward the azure midday sky. But instead of rising and circling and sailing away inspiringly, the birds flapped and floundered wildly as if drowning in air and crashed on the flagstones and grass. Some of the spectators laughed. Others gasped. There were expressions of solemnity, even pain. The doves took a minute or so to limber their cramped wings pressed too long and hard by small anxious hands. Then, to generalized relief and mounting applause, one by one they took flight.

The city's other stab at distinctive monumental architecture had been erected only two months prior to Joe's arrival, and had withstood the temblor unscathed. It was in the center of a traffic circle not far from the home the museum had provided him in the Miralvalle neighborhood on the capital's northwestern edge, at the foot of El Picacho volcano. On a circular cement platform stood a 40-foot-tall structure of white cement. It was an eight-foot-wide monolith with a rectangular space cut from the slab making it a tall monolithic frame. A smaller slab, a platform, extended horizontally from the lower edge of the frame. The monument did not end at its apex in right angles, but was cut away in a cradle-moon crescent.

Gray flagstone paved the space around the base. The rest of the plaza, which was bordered by the circle of asphalt that was the road, was covered with thick green grass and studded with flowering shrubbery. The towering pale slab was simple and bold. On sunny days, it was like a huge sundial and was complimented by its shadow crossing the plaza. On more than one occasion, while driving by it at night, Joe wished they would have left it like that, unadorned and stark and strong. But they had not.

One night he was coming home from a long meal, up at El Bocadito in Los Planes de Renderos with Eddie, the cultural affairs guy from the embassy, when he saw that a statue had been erected on the platform extending from the slab. Framed there by the cutout and illuminated by floodlights stood a giant robust and naked woman with both arms raised. In her right hand she held a sword. In the left she held a balance. It was after midnight, and the plaza appeared deserted. Joe stopped at the curb and got out of the Montero. His arrival stirred from their rest two National Police officers sitting on cinderblocks beneath a tree across the street. They stood and cradled their G-3 assault rifles.

Prior to emplacement of the sculpture there had been no police presence at the circle, though the neighborhood, especially Joe's street rising toward El Picacho, was regularly traipsed by army troops heading up the slopes to where guerrillas sporadically pitched camps, depending on their occasional objectives on the outskirts of the city below.

"Buenas noches," Joe called out. *"Solo quería admirar la nueva obra."*

"Buenas," they replied in unison. Reassured by his greeting, and probably by the fact that he looked white and had arrived in an expensive vehicle, they sat back down.

Joe climbed the stairs to more closely examine the statue. She was evidently an incarnation of Justice, in that she carried the accessories of her classical rendering. But she was not blindfolded. Who the hell was she, then, and what was the idea or intention of a sculptor who cast Justice with the use of mundane and fallible sight? He raised his hand to shade his eyes against the spotlights. Then he stepped over to the base of the monolith, where two bronze plaques had been affixed. One was inscribed with the preamble to the Salvadoran constitution, which begins with a phrase to the effect that the essential purpose and justification of the State is the uplifting of human beings in body and spirit. Directly below that plaque was another bearing the names of the 60 individuals, 59 men and one woman, who in 1982 had formed the Constituent Assembly that wrote the above-cited document (the fourth constitution in El Salvador's century and a half of independence). The names of the framers were listed in four columns except for one, which was carved in letters larger than the rest and centered at the top of the plaque. That name was Ricardo Paniagua.

Joe shook his head and smiled. "Fuckin' A," he said. He felt a chill and he sneezed.

"*Falta de guaro*," said a man from behind him. A "lack of booze" was postulated popularly as the cause of various ailments.

Because he had not seen anyone else on the plaza nor heard anyone approach, Joe was startled.

"Don't worry, sonny. It's just a harmless drunkard." The man held in his right hand a liter bottle of Tic-Tac cane *guaro* with about a third of its contents remaining. He did not sway. He stood still and straight and his speech was un-slurred. He wore sandals, dirty pants and a long sleeved flower-patterned polyester shirt closed by a single button just above the navel. His chest was hairless but his chin was covered with sparse gray stubble. He looked to be about 50 years old.

"What do you think of this homage to our founding father?" he asked, and laughed.

"I liked it better without the statue."

"But look at the tits on her. She's got a nice ass, too," he cocked his head and tilted back the baseball cap covering it. He took the few steps separating them and extended the bottle. Joe saw the cops rise and move to the curb on the other side of the road. But they made no move to come across.

"I don't think the sculptor's intent was erotic," said Joe.

"I suppose the sculptor's intent was to immortalize Paniagua," said the bum. Here he gave the first sign of inebriation, when he said distractedly: "But man does not live by *pan y agua* alone. He needs *guaro*, too."

Joe was not in the habit of sharing liquor out of a bottle with street drunks. But for some reason, perhaps because he'd been drinking Flor de Cana with Eddie and had a buzz on, he accepted the proffered vessel and took a swig.

"*Sos pijudo,*" said the man, which meant literally that Joe had a large penis but figuratively was the drunk's way saying Joe was a good sport. They sat down on the stairs and looked up at the statue. Joe asked the man if he lived around here.

"In a shack in the ravine," he said, sweeping his arm behind him. After a minute of silence and another sip of liquor, he continued: "Since they put up this thing I've been coming up late at night to look at it because it amuses me to no end. It is really very funny."

"Funny?"

"Yeah. Except they got her in the wrong pose. I picture her how she should be, if this was to be a real monument to that son of a whore. It's right that she should be naked. But she should also be hooded, with her thumbs tied with wire behind her back and cigarette holes burned into her chest. How would that be for a monument?"

Joe looked up. It was not much of a stretch to imagine her like that.

After a moment the man said, "I know the fucker."

"You know Ricardo Paniagua?" Joe was skeptical.

"Intimately. Or rather he knows me intimately." He again seemed completely sober. "What else would you call it when someone sees inside your head?" He made a dry laugh that ended in a croak. He leaned toward Joe and placed a hand on the bill of his cap. He lifted off the hat and inclined his head so the light from the higher spots illuminated his pate.

It was not baldness, or even thinning of the hair. There was a swath down the center bare and shiny and traversed by a jagged white scar from a wound that had been crudely stitched.

"The work of Mr. Paniagua's own hand," he said, replacing the cap. "I used to be a bus driver. I was active in the union and we went on strike. In '81, because the owners were making a ton of money and we were eating shit. This," he tapped his cap, "is what the father of the constitution called a 'haircut.' One day they grabbed me as I left the terminal. Stuffed me on the floor of a Cherokee. Took me someplace I never knew where and asked me all kinds of stupid shit I didn't know what the fuck they were talking about. They tied me to a chair and that animal sliced my scalp from front to back with a pocket knife. Then he grabbed the hair on both sides and pulled on my hair. Slow. He's asking dumb fucking question and you're screaming and your eyes fill up with blood and there's so much you feel like you're gonna drown in all the blood, and you imagine your whole *pinche* scalp and then your face being pulled right off your skull, so you see yourself sitting there tied to a chair in the clothes you left your house in that morning but instead of a face you've got a skull there between your shoulders, where your face should be."

Joe's own face was a half-grimace and it seemed he'd forgotten to breathe. He sucked in some air.

"La puta madre que lo parió," he said. The whore mother who bore him. He reached for the bottle. He took a deep gulp that burned his throat and stomach and made his eyes water. He handed the nearly empty bottle back to the bum, who finished it off.

CHAPTER 32: DON'T STEP ON ME, ASSHOLE

The open-sided helicopter barreled through the air at a hundred miles an hour 3,000 feet above verdant hills and valleys and patchwork fields of corn and beans where a war was going on. It wasn't unheard of that the Gs might use either heavy caliber machine-gun fire or one of their few SAM or Redeye surface-to-air missiles to shoot down an army chopper like the one Joe Guinness was flying in with retired Maj. Ricardo Paniagua to a site of archeological interest.

It was cold up that high. The Vietnam-era Huey beat its way along and wind poured in through the gaping sides and around the professor and Paniagua and the two gunners leaning on their M-60s and looking down the barrels at the dangerous earth. It was a sunny mid-morning but it had rained almost every afternoon for the previous six months and the fields about to be harvested contrasted with darker patches of lush pasture and stands of trees, a quilt of shades of green from light lime to dark ivy.

A half-hour earlier, Mariana and Joe had been sorting pottery in the museum's main storage room when a noise that started as a background growl grew above the roof into a thunderous racket. They had quit what they were doing and went along the hall to the interior courtyard, from where, though the open side, they saw the dull gray-green chopper, a gigantic insect, settle onto the museum's grassy grounds. Out jumped Paniagua, running crouched beneath the rotors. The pilot cut the engine, the rotors slowed, drooped and stopped.

Paniagua, a big smile on his face, said: "Do you have a couple hours? I want you to see something I'm certain you will find interesting."

The aircraft's only seats were in the cockpit, for the pilot and co-pilot, and those in the doorways for the gunners. Paniagua and Joe sat on the metal floor with their backs against the bulkhead that separated the main part of the fuselage from the turboshaft engine and tail section. Paniagua gave his guest–a bit flabbergasted at first but altogether willing–a pair of plastic ear protectors like stereo headphones. The Major, the pilot and co-pilot and both gunners wore helmets with a visor and a thin-stemmed microphone sticking out from the left side to a point in front of the mouth. A cord attached to the helmet was plugged into a multiple socket hanging from the ceiling.

They took off and flew to the east for about twenty minutes before Paniagua and the pilot exchanged words. Joe saw their mouths moving, but could hear nothing over the headset-muffled roar of the engine and rotor and wind. When they finished talking, Paniagua pushed the stem of the mike down from his mouth and signaled to Joe to uncover an ear. The major leaned over so that his mouth was right next to the American's head.

"Something's come up. We're making a stop," he shouted.

Paniagua slid forward and took from beneath the co-pilot's seat a vest of green canvas. It did not button or buckle or zip but was designed to be slipped on over the head, like a poncho. Paniagua gestured. He held it up and Joe slipped into it and felt it being secured it at his sides with Velcro flaps. Then Paniagua pulled from beneath the pilot's seat two slightly curved metal plates. With both men on their knees in the middle of the floor, the major hefted one and slid it into a pouch sewn to the front of the vest. He got around behind Joe and slipped the other plate into the pouch on the back. Each of the plates was of cast iron and weighed about 20 pounds and with both of them in, Joe was almost immobilized.

"There may be some shooting," the Major yelled into his traveling companion's ear. "Not to worry. No bullet can go through this." He rapped his knuckles on the armor.

That's fucking comforting, thought Joe. What about my head and legs and arms and balls?

The professor had little time to weigh these matters. First one, then the other gunner opened fire. The pilot dived several hundred feet. Joe's back flattened against the bulkhead. He felt his organs press against each other and upward on his lungs. It was hard to breathe. The pilot banked steeply to the left, still diving. Directly below Joe now was the bright maw in the side of the aircraft and the patchy wooded and grassy terrain, but the powerful centrifugal force not only prevented him from falling through the door but would have kept him from jumping through it even if he tried to.

It was like a carnival ride. The helicopter swung, a violently rocked cradle, as the pilot banked to the right then whipped into a circular descent. For a few seconds the craft hovered a few feet above the ground, then set down. The rotor rippled the long grass like the surface of a lake in a gale. The gunner to Joe's right blasted away, though Joe could not see or even imagine what he was firing at. The weapon flashed and smoked, sucking the cartridge belt from the metal box alongside and spurting a fountain of hot cylinders that sparkled in the sunlight.

Joe turned and looked through the other door. A soldier with no pack or rifle but with a comrade draped over his shoulders like a sack of corn was running toward the chopper. When he reached it he made a slight turn, heaved the wounded man onto the floor and without even a glance or nod to anyone in the aircraft began a sprint back to where he'd come from.

The pilot revved the deafening engine. The helicopter lifted off. Now both gunners fired short bursts into the woods. No time was wasted on evasive maneuvering as the young lieutenant at the controls made straight for the clouds or some point in the void several hundred meters and several butt-clenching seconds away beyond which the guerrilla AK-47s and G-3s could not harm his ship or his crew or his passengers. The chopper flew up and away.

Joe looked at the wounded soldier. A mine or grenade had blown off his right foot halfway up the shin. His pant leg was in tatters and small wounds from shrapnel dotted the upper part of his mostly bare leg. He was shot up with morphine, conscious but glassy-eyed. Layers of quilted white fabric and gauze and tape enveloped the stump of his leg, making what was left of his calf as thick as his thigh. The dressing was soaked through, but the stain was not the color of blood. There was blood in it, but the stuff that an hour earlier had been flowing through a closed system, maroon and thick and warm, had diluted once outside its container. It stained the bandage a rosy watery red that faded toward the edge of the stain to pink then to an almost clear wetness tinged brown at the limit of where it had seeped. A stain the color of dirty water.

There wasn't much to do for him that hadn't already been done. Sticking out of his left arm was an IV needle connected to a tube leading to a bag of plasma pinned to his shoulder. Paniagua scooted over to him. He took off his windbreaker, exposing a small holstered revolver, and placed the folded jacket under the soldier's head. Then he unfastened the plasma bag and held it up so it would drip more effectively into the body.

Joe presumed this medical evacuation mission canceled the trip to wherever Paniagua had wanted to take him. He figured they would head back to the capital, to the landing pad at the Military Hospital. But ten minutes after leaving the site of the skirmish, or whatever the fuck it was, the helicopter descended over a forested hollow ringed by wooded hills. Joe edged nearer the doorway as the pilot circled. He realized they were going to land, though in a much more leisurely fashion than before. The gunners were idle and the descent was smooth, a wide easy gyre.

A few hundred feet up in the air is the perfect vantage point for the initial survey of an unexcavated archeological site. Especially one like this, which, though overgrown, obviously included monumental architecture. Two tall mounds covered with earth and brush and stubby trees rose from opposite ends of the flattest expanse. From this altitude, Joe could not tell how high the buried pyramids stood. But there was no doubt that is what they were.

As the aircraft made another circle and began its descent, he saw what looked like a portion of carved stone crest decorating the apex of one of the structures like an Andalusian lady's comb. Erosion or an earthquake, maybe the one that had caused the destruction in the capital, had exposed part of the side of this structure. The front, where buried steps would have led up to a small temple at the summit, was a slope of about 60 degrees. But this partially denuded side of the stone pyramid was steeper.

The plaza between the pyramids was too overgrown to land on. The pilot selected a clear spot in a rectangular space defined by two long banks like levees. He set down and killed the engine.

The pilot and co-pilot and Paniagua took off their helmets and got out. Joe removed his ear protectors and scooted on his backside across the floor to stow them under the pilot's seat. On his knees, he wrestled his way out of the vest.

Joe stood. The wounded soldier was staring at the ceiling. Joe imagined he was not lucid enough to be wondering what the fuck they were doing landing somewhere so soon. But the Indian-faced boy was awake and had enough wits about him to direct his attention to Professor Joseph Guinness as *el chele* made his awkward way around him.

He looked directly into Joe's eyes. *"No me pises, cerote."* Don't step on me, asshole.

The comment took Joe aback. Then, because he felt so wired, he said, *"Ni loco, primo."* He jumped down and went to where the pilots and the Major stood surveying the environs.

"What do you think this is?" Paniagua gestured toward their immediate surroundings.

"Looks like a ball court."

"That's what I thought, too." Then he turned his attention to the pilot. *"Mira, teniente.* You take our passenger there," he signaled toward the chopper with his chin "to the hospital and come back for us in three hours. Even if we didn't have him to care for, this is not a good place to leave the bird sitting on the ground."

"At your orders, *mi Mayor."* The lieutenant and the co-pilot and Paniagua went back to the aircraft. The flyers climbed into the cockpit. Paniagua jumped into the fuselage behind them and lifted the lid of a narrow locker between their seats. He pulled out a machete. As the engine roared and the rotor gained speed, the Major knelt beside the soldier, stroked his head and said something to him. Then he jumped out and jogged to where Joe stood.

When the chopper had receded enough to permit conversation, Paniagua lifted his arms to encompass the surroundings. *"Que te parece, doctor?"*

"I'm astounded. I thought all Salvadoran sites with monumental structures had been discovered and at least surveyed. What's puzzling is that it is so far east. If it's Mayan, it redraws the maps."

"It has to be Mayan," said Paniagua, sliding the machete under his belt. "What else it could be? The Lencas didn't build pyramids or ball courts. Neither did the Pipiles, though I would bet a million dollars this site dates from several centuries before the Pipil migration."

"Whatever it is, it's important," Joe said. "I can't believe it has remained a secret." He stopped looking around and looked at Paniagua. "How long have you known about it? And how many other people know about it?"

"A few months. A few others."

It was only 10:30, but already hot. Down on the ground, the air was heavy. The two men climbed up the face of one of the long levees bordering the court.

"What was the story with this game, professor? Was it the winner or the loser that got sacrificed?"

"Who knows?" said Joe. He told the major he had seen both versions represented in the literature. But he also expressed the opinion that both could be apocryphal. They sounded, he said, like a sensational angle that somehow gained currency. But even if on occasion it could have been considered an honor to have your heart yanked out and offered to the gods, he could not imagine that a player really facing that prospect would be motivated to win. So Joe personally figured it must have been the loser who went under the obsidian knife. That is, whenever the game was to be followed by human sacrifice, which probably was exceedingly rare. In most games they were just playing ball, displaying their skill and prowess and providing a spectacle for the well-off to bet on.

Paniagua started toward the taller of the two jungle-covered mounds. Where the undergrowth was thick, he used the machete to clear the way, and Joe followed him.

They pushed through the brush to the plaza between the pyramids. A shrill squawk made them look up. A pair of large green parrots flew over the top of the far mound and into the forest beyond.

Minutes later, Joe was panting and sweat-soaked, his chin close to the ground as he looked for passages like tunnels through the brambles and branches. He found handholds and footholds among the roots and grabbed vines and saplings. Some of the scrub had thorns and he was thankful for his long-sleeved shirt.

Paniagua was below the American and to his left. Joe could hear him cracking branches and swearing and huffing. The knowledge that he was a killer and that he had a machete and a sidearm occupied a spot toward the front of Joe's mind.

It took them 10 minutes of struggling to make it to the top. Joe stood up, dripping sweat from his nose and chin, about 50 feet above the forest floor. Catching his breath, he saw that he was at the base of what indeed was a crest comb. Like the rest of the structure, it was almost completely covered by leafy brush and moss and vines. A crumbling area of perhaps 30 square feet was exposed. It was of stone set with mortar and was about one quarter the breadth of the apex temple.

The comb rose about three meters. Most of the sculpted stone and stucco facing had fallen off the exposed area. But there remained part of a sculpture of a droop-nosed face in elaborate headdress. It nestled between glyphs that Joe was almost certain identified the deity as Venus, a star-god of many incarnations most often conceived of as the brother of the sun. His actions were for the most part malevolent and dangerous, especially during the phase when the planet is the morning star, as had been the case during the previous weeks.

"Hijo de la gran chingada," huffed Paniagua as he hauled himself up onto the flat summit. "My hands are cut to shit." He stood up and held them out for Joe to see. They were scratched and bleeding from superficial cuts, but in no worse shape than the American's.

The major walked to the edge of the level section. To the drop-off that afforded the most unobstructed view of the jungle.

With his back to Joe and his hands on his hips, Paniagua looked out over the buried remains of an ancient ceremonial center, beyond a hidden ball court, across swaying treetops to the northern mountains. White wreaths of cloud adorned the far peaks.

"Goddamn it, my country is beautiful, is it not?"

A crazy notion came to Joe. How easy it would be to take a step forward and give a shove. A five-story fall. Rid the world of a murderous torturer. Do his part for the *summum bonum* of mankind, a part that had fallen to him fortuitously.

But the impulse passed, leaving Joe's heart beating hard.

They stayed up there for a while, looking out. Paniagua smoked two cigarettes, then they made their way down. It was not until nearly an hour later, after they had made a tour of pretty much the entire site, that Paniagua got around to the main reason for this trip. They were back on the floor of the ball court, both leaning against the bordering rise, side by side in the shade.

"There must be great stuff inside these pyramids," said the major.

"I imagine so. If there are tombs, and the tombs were not looted in the following decades or centuries."

Paniagua told Joe that this site, potentially magnificent, was one he could help the professor bring to fruition. That Joe was the man for this job but that he would need the backing of someone here, someone like himself with the power to make it possible but also with the knowledge to appreciate its worth. Paniagua was animated. And after a couple minutes it dawned on Joe that he was outlining a proposal to go into business with him. Not only regarding what would be recovered from this site, but that he wanted Joe as a kind of private scholar to validate and promote, for sale in the United States, part of what was to be found here and part of his personal collection. What now began to gnaw at Joe was not so much the fact that this guy was a money-grubbing hypocrite in addition to being a vicious killer, a guy who spouted a lot of shit about his nation's cultural heritage but who also was determined to sell that heritage to the highest bidder. What was getting to Joe, starting to really piss him off as Paniagua continued talking, was the notion that this fucker thought he might go for it. What did Paniagua see that gave him the idea Joe was corrupt or weak?

"You got the wrong guy for that plan," he said.

"*No creo,*" said Paniagua.

The two men stood facing each other.

The calmness of Joe's voice surprised him. "If I had evidence that you were engaged in the illegal trafficking of artifacts out of this country, I would denounce you to the authorities of your country and mine, and give them the evidence, and you would go to jail."

There. He'd made his rap of honor. He felt quite good.

Paniagua regarded him for a few seconds. Then he chuckled. *"Otro gringo pendejo,"* he said, shaking his head. Another gringo dope. The charmer was still there, only slightly perturbed.

"What makes you capable of imagining I would allow you to do that? I didn't have you pegged for an imbecile. You must know that before you could do anything of the sort I would have you killed and fed to my dogs. Where the fuck do you think you are? In the fucking Berkshires?"

A long time later, after Joe had taken time to ponder it, he thought that if he'd just shut up, left it at that and not said anything more about the proposition or about Paniagua over the next few months, if he'd not been a wiseass, that might have been the end of it. The major would not have bothered himself with *el pendejo yanqui* archeologist or ever see him again. But it's true that *el pez por la boca muere.* The fish dies by way of its mouth. An ill-timed or well-timed word can ruin or exalt a man's life.

It came to Joe in a flash and without thinking, he spoke.

"But my disappearance would greatly sadden your lovely wife."

CHAPTER 33: A LITTLE LOST

Joe pushed himself off Paniagua's chest and stood panting over the unconscious man. The major's head, hair tangled with dirt and leaves from the fight, was turned to the side. Joe's sweat-soaked gray Cornell Baseball t-shirt stuck to his back and the beads on his face slipped into one another and formed rivulets down his cheeks. He licked his lips, then dropped to his knees and put his ear against Paniagua's chest. The sternum rose slowly and Joe heard a strong heartbeat and he was relieved. Now he moved quickly, reaching down to untie the laces of the man's boots. Stripping the nylon cords out through the eyelets, he pulled them free. Kneeling, he tied the two laces together then fashioned a slipless loop near the end of one, leaving a six-inch tail. He rolled Paniagua onto his stomach, took the far wrist of the major and placed it on his back. He threaded the other end through and cinched the cord around the wrist, careful not to pull so tight as to cut the circulation. He took the other limp hand and put it on top of the snared one and wound the line around the joined hands, a few turns vertically, then a few horizontally, pulling each wrap taut until he came to the end of the cord and the major's hands were joined fast behind him. Joe tied off the end to the tail he'd left on the other extreme, yanking it hard and closing with a tugged square knot. Then he rolled the major a half turn, unbuckled his narrow belt and pulled it out. He slipped the belt under the shins and threaded the strap through the buckle and cinched it tight just above the ankles. He pulled on the long end until the feet rose off the ground and the legs were bent at the knees. He slid the strap beneath the joined wrists and back around and pulled tight first one half-hitch, then another, giving a final strong tug until he was satisfied that the leather knot, though thick and cumbersome, would not slip apart even with a good amount of rolling around once Paniagua woke up.

The bowline, the square-knot and two half hitches. All you'll ever need, he thought, standing there in a clearing in a Central American jungle beside a complex of marvelous buried ruins over a lean infamous man he'd knocked out and hog-tied. Thanks, Boy Scouts. *I'm fairly well prepared.*

Sometime during the frantic, almost hallucinogenic previous quarter hour, dark clouds had covered the sky. A clap of thunder reverberated across the forest canopy. Seconds later the first thick drops began to fall, each one making a sound as it struck the ground or a leaf or Joe's boots or Paniagua's bowed back.

Joe stood there expecting a downpour, but only scattered drops fell. He looked around, then up at the sky, suddenly dreading that he might hear an approaching chopper. There was another rumble of thunder, but no drone of aircraft. All he knew was he had to go north. But with the cloud cover, he could not locate the sun. Then it came back to him. The courts were always laid out on a north-south axis. That way in the mornings or late afternoons of a thousand years ago, the players would not be blinded by a low brilliant orb.

Despite his dire circumstances, that made him imagine a young Maya ballplayer of pre-history standing in his regalia–hips girded in thick cotton padding and leather, distraught sweaty tattooed visage–telling a black-robed priest with a stone knife that, damn, he would have made that goal (and been able to continue enjoying the beating of his heart) if only the sun hadn't got in his eyes. This picture came to Joe as if it were a one-frame cartoon, like Larsen's "Far Side" strip his father had so loved, with the excuse-making ballplayer saying something like "Geez, coach!", and Joe knew there was humor in that, that if he would have thought of it an hour earlier when they first arrived he would have laughed at his own joke. But now he didn't chuckle or even smile and he wondered, not in rational interior monologue but rather in a jumble of sparks, if this was one of the effects of doing violence to another man, that you forfeit for some period the capacity to laugh.

They'd approached from the west, so it was clear that the far end pointed north. He walked through the middle of the court, pushing branches of the higher scrub out of his way, and out the other end. His only coherent thought was a wish that he would have brought a canteen.

Joe walked for two hours, mostly uphill and through moderately thick growth, before he came upon a well-trodden path. There were no fresh footprints or hoof prints on it, but he knew it must lead somewhere. The country was so small that it was difficult to walk in any part of it for more than a few hours without encountering someone. He followed the trail to the northwest.

The sun sank and Joe grew hungry and desperately thirsty. After about another hour's walk he came upon a mango tree with ripe and ripening fruit dangling from nearly all the branches. Several mangoes splotched yellow and red and orange lay on the ground. They were rotten in spots but Joe used his pocket knife to cut away the foul parts and sucked on the sweet slippery flesh. He filled up on the better part of five mangoes, then licked his sticky fingers and wiped them on his dirty jeans. As he sat beneath the tree, about 30 small green *lorito* parrots flew over him with a chorus of squawks. The flock was trailed by two straggling pairs. Mariana, on a trip out to Tazumal soon after he had arrived in El Salvador, had told him they mated for life.

Joe rested until he was bitten a few times on the neck and hands by *jenjenes*, gnat-like flies active at dawn and dusk. He had an hour left of light and struck out again on the path. As daylight faded, the sounds of birds and crickets from the woods grew louder.

He continued walking along the path, which by now had leveled. He imagined a dotted line marking his route and connecting him to Paniagua's bound form. Then he imagined, like in a satellite photograph, the contours of Central America and Mexico and North America and he thought of his parents and brothers and sister in New York State and his friends and colleagues who soon, sometime in the next day or two, would be calling each other to ask if they'd heard that Joe was missing in El Salvador, after some kind of fight he'd had with the baddest man in the land.

It grew dark, but Joe could still make out the path. He continued along it for another half-hour or so as it descended. He came to a stream, a broad one glimmering in the scant light from a bleached bone half moon and gurgling around rocks and boulders. He stepped onto a stone a meter from the bank and squatted there, dipping his hand into the flowing water at his side and lifting the cupped hand to his mouth to drink.

He leaped from that rock to another one. Then to another, a flat-topped boulder in the middle of the stream. He lay down with his hands behind his head and looked at the moon and the stars for a few minutes before closing his eyes.

He was on a dimly lit packed-dirt street walking past ramshackle wooden houses unlike dwellings of the Salvadoran countryside. The houses were like those in Caribbean ports or along the isthmus' Atlantic coast, in Limón or Bluefields. Only these structures were much taller than is common, towering over him and leaning inward slightly on both sides to create a canyon through which he walked. He went barefoot along the middle of a dirt road and he had a small hole in his foot from a parasite that had burrowed into his sole. He worried that the hole in his foot would get clogged with dirt. As he progressed into the shadow of the wooden valley, harsh white lights began to illuminate random rooms in the structures on either side. In each of the brightly lit rooms a black woman appeared in the window or, if it was at street level, in the doorway. At first they just stared at the man passing their home, but as Joe continued they began shouting at him in a guttural, raspy language. Though he could not identify the tongue, he understood what they were saying. One said: "Come to my room for a visit." And another, a few steps on: "I have something nice for you." Joe looked down, trying to keep his eyes on the dusty road, but each time he was hailed he could not resist looking up to see who had called. He heard, "Do not pass me by, handsome." His eyes found that woman standing in a threshold. She was incredibly fat and seemed to be stuck in the doorway. Her hands massaged pendulous breasts and as she regarded Joe the fat woman began to laugh. Joe wanted to escape. He looked ahead and saw nothing but the chasm made by towering precarious wooden homes. He turned and looked behind and found the same perspective, a canyon stretching forever. He turned again and began to run in his original direction only this time saw a glowing red light far ahead. That light became his destination and he tried to break into a sprint. He pushed at the ground with all the power he could muster, but he could not run. He leaned forward and pumped his arms but his legs were moving in slow motion and the buildings to each side passed at no faster a pace than when he'd been walking. And the women were still there in the windows and doors. Now they were all laughing. All except two, who Joe knew to be his mother and his sister, even though they too were black. Joe cried, "Mom! Lisa! Are you against me too?" The two women, who looked out from the same window, appeared amused by Joe's question and looked at each other with knowing smiles. Joe's mother turned to her son and said, "Joseph, come here and take refuge from your trouble." Joe stepped over the threshold into the ground-level room. Though a moment before they had been a few floors above, Lisa, in her teens, now lay on a bed in this room naked and staring at her brother with wide eyes. Joe turned his attention to his mother, who stood in a darkened corner. From the corner his mother said, "Go to her." He looked again toward the bed. His sister waited. Joe stood in the center of the room becoming excited as his eyes played over the curves of his sister's body. He took off his clothes and walked to the bed and as he climbed on top of his sister she said, "I love you, Joe." When he had finished he was very happy and had forgotten about the nightmare of howling women in the street outside. He lay beside Lisa and stroked her hair and whispered in her ear, but she did not respond. She was still now and cold. Joe knew he had killed her and he began to cry. His mother came from the corner and stood by the bed. "What's the matter, son?" Joe was grieving because of his sister's untimely death, but he said through his sobs, "I have a worm in my foot and can't get it out." "Let me see," said his mother. Joe sat on the side of the bed and lifted his foot. His mother used spit to clean the dirt from around the edge of the hole and began to squeeze. The head or tail of a white worm emerged and Joe's mother grasped it and began to pull. At first she pulled slowly, and inches of the creature came. Then she pulled an arm's length at one tug and the animal continued to issue from the opening. Joe watched horrified. Hand over hand his mother pulled the worm out of him until a resistance was felt and no more could be extracted. He felt a sharp pain in his abdomen. When she tugged again on the slimy string the pain shot through his body. The worm was wrapped around his intestine, and he told that to his mother. "In that case you will never get rid of it and I am wasting my time." She bent over and bit the worm off flush with the sole of Joe's foot. Then she said, "You had better go now." When Joe was outside, he realized he was not nearly so far away as before from the red light at the end of the road, and that the red light was a building in flames. He could run now and he flew on his feet to the blazing house. Several women leaned out of windows with flames leaping behind them. All the women were Felipa, a prostitute at the capital's Casa Gloria with whom Joe had become friends, and all were screaming and dropping bundles to the ground. Joe ran to one of the bundles and as he picked it up he saw it was a baby, a happy baby who looked up at him with gleaming eyes. Joe ran back and forth along the front of the house trying to catch all the bundles the Felipas were dropping. He caught several but could not catch them all, but it did not matter because none of the infants was injured by the fall and all were happy and smiling as he picked them up and lay them in a row away from the burning house.

In the haze between two forms of consciousness, Joe felt wetness in his pants. Half awake on the rock, he realized he'd had a wet dream. He remembered it had been with Lisa and was disgusted, more so because he recalled how much he had enjoyed it. He got up, stripped off his pants, then rinsed out his underwear in the river. He looked at his watch. It was three in the morning. He spread the briefs on the rock to dry and pulled on his jeans. Then he lay back down and, it seemed to him, slept again before it began to dawn.

Still early that morning, only a half-hour further along the path, he smelled smoke. A whiff, then it was gone. He continued walking until he came upon a cow standing on the trail facing him. She smelled like moss and seemed impossibly wide in the day's new light. Big-eyed and placid, she stood there blocking his way. He tried to shoo her into the brush, but she did not budge. He picked up a stick and tapped her on the left front leg and she finally turned around and went walking along the path the other way. Joe followed.

In a few minutes he came to a *caserío*. Thin plumes of white smoke rose from the dwellings. Rust-colored chickens strutted through the patches of short-cropped grass and across the bald earth. A few goats grazed. Two black pigs lying next to each other across the path did not stir as Joe skirted them. The first person Joe saw was a small boy, maybe four years old, running along the path toward him. When he saw the stranger, he stopped and looked back from where he'd come, then ahead to Joe, then back again.

"*Hola muchachito*," said Joe, moving toward him. The boy ran off in the other direction.

Joe followed him to his house, where several people were seated around a split-log table.

"*Buenos días,*" he said.

"*Buenos días,*" replied a few voices. The whole family regarded him.

"I'm a little lost. I'm not from these parts."

Two of the men laughed.

"You don't say," said one. "Come. Have something to eat."

They made room for him on the bench and Joe sidled in. The woman tending tortillas at the *comal* poured him water from a plastic pitcher into a metal cup. Joe drank it down and she refilled the cup.

"That's good," he said.

"Have you been walking long?" asked one of the campesinos, a middle-aged man in a straw hat with a tattered brim. He wore thick-framed black eyeglasses mended at the hinge with a green rubber band.

"Since yesterday afternoon. From the south. I slept down by the river."

Another woman put two tortillas and a ladle of beans and some crumbly white cheese on a blue plastic plate and passed it to Joe. He tore off one piece then another of the tortilla and used them to scoop up the beans and cheese.

"Where is it you're going?" asked the man with the glasses.

"I don't really know."

The answer left those at the table perplexed, but no one pressed the newcomer. After a moment Joe said, "I'm kind of in trouble."

***

Later that day, the older man with the mended glasses walked with Joe to San Jose las Flores, a three-hour hike through verdant hills, and delivered him to Padre Ignacio, who, the campesinos figured, would know what to do with him. The two men, the Spanish priest-physician and the North American professor, talked late into the night at the house that served as a makeshift rectory when Nacho was spending a few days in the town, to baptize or marry or bury or to bring his far-flung parishioners the benefit of the Eucharist and the benefit of the antibiotics in his bag and his diagnostic and remedial skills.

Nacho, who covered in both his roles much of Chalatenango province, had heard on the radio, as had everyone in the country by now, that Maj. Ricardo Paniagua had been hospitalized in the capital for a head injury inflicted, it appeared, by an archeologist from the United States. When Ignacio heard from Joe that he was that man, the Jesuit laughed and said: "*Puchica, 'mano. Te pelaste.*" Holy smoke, brother, You freaked.

Nacho informed Joe that Paniagua's injuries appeared not to be serious. Though conscious and lucid, the major had been held overnight for observation. He also said a nationwide manhunt was underway for the major's assailant.

The next morning Joe stood at a basin and splashed cold water on his face. He peeled off the sweatshirt Nacho had given him to sleep in. Beneath that was a white t-shirt, also borrowed from the priest, emblazoned with a 1960s peace sign.

"*Que tal dormiste?*" asked Nacho from behind his guest.

"*Bien.* I enjoy sleeping in a hammock. It's like the womb." Then, "What do you think my options are?"

"That's what we must talk about. With *el comandante* Raúl. He's pretty much in charge aroundd here."

After coffee and a couple tortillas with *queso fresco*, they walked across the plaza to a corner where Raúl Funes, commander of guerrilla forces in the zone, was waiting for them on the stoop of a roofless, bombed-out cinderblock house. He was smoking a cigarette. An AK-47 rested across his thighs. Ignacio made the introductions.

"*Le diste verga al Mayor?*" You kicked the major's ass? asked Raúl with a slight smile, apparently delighted at the image but wanting confirmation from the man whose very hands had done the throttling.

"*Más o menos,*" said Joe.

He and Nacho sat down on the chipped cement steps.

"Well, I don't know what you think," said the guerrilla chief. "But I had a meeting with my staff last night, and the way we see it, you can't stay around here. They're already deploying two elite battalions to the area where you left Paniagua. That guy is like God to them. That makes you Judas and the Devil all wrapped up in one. And to make things worse, *Gringo*, they've offered a $50,000 reward for information leading to your capture. So just about no one can be trusted.

"I've picked a squad of four men. You have to travel fast and light and not be visible from the air. At night, mostly. And you'll have to avoid towns, even our towns."

"OK. But to where? The border?"

"No. That's where they think you'll go. They'll seal the border in this sector. They will already have coordinated with *los Hondureños*. You know, all the *chafas* in these parts are chips off the same block. So we can't try to get you out of the country right now. Not yet. The idea is to move you to the Morazán front. Stash you with *los compañeros* del ERP, at least for a few weeks."

An hour later in a house on the plaza, Joe was outfitted for life in the hills by Lito, the leader of the squad that would take him to Morazán. He was given a government-issue backpack, U.S.-made and supplied, that probably had been taken off a dead soldier. Ignacio gave him two extra pairs of thick socks and two pairs of underwear. In addition to the sweatshirt he'd given him to sleep in, he insisted Joe take two more t-shirts and a thin but tightly woven sweater.

"It gets cold at night."

The guerrillas gave him an extra pair of pants, turned out by their seamstress collaborators in the towns, cut fatigue style with large button-flapped pockets on the thighs from a medium-weight black blend of polyester and cotton. They gave him a soldier's camouflage tunic with a corporal's stripes and an Arce battalion patch featuring a feathered spear on the shoulder. Lito put the extra clothing in a plastic bag and placed it in the bottom of the pack. Then he shoved in a nylon GI hammock and on top of everything a hooded poncho that would double as a tarp, to be draped over the hammock, when they stopped to sleep.

He looked at Joe's feet.

"Those boots will last you for a while. It would be better if they laced up higher. But we'll see how you do in them. Maybe in Morazán we can get you some better ones."

Joe had carried a backpack many times. On hikes in the Adirondacks and Poconos and in the Sierra Maestra of Mexico. But he'd never worn a military harness like the thick-strapped web-belted one Lito gave him. When he put it on it sunk in that he was embarking on something very different from a camping trip. Four canvas pouches were attached to the belt. Two held metal one-liter canteens. In another was a big metal cup with a wire handle that was the guerrilla mess-kit. The other held loaded clips for an M-16. Lito tapped that one.

"If you get into any shit and the guys need these, just pass them on."

Get into shit, thought Joe. I'd say I'm already in it.

Lito fastened the buckle and adjusted the shoulder straps. Inserted behind two strips of fabric sewn to one of the straps was a hefty tablespoon. The rebel pulled it out.

"Your silverware," he said, smiling.

CHAPTER 34: THE SWAY OF THE MOON

They were eating *sopa de patas*, spooning tripe and gelatinous stewed cartilage out of their mess-kit cups to celebrate the end of basic training. Everyone was slurping the rich broth and savoring chunks of squash and carrots. One then another rose from a rock or a log and again dipped his or her vessel into one of three five-gallon cans, erstwhile containers of powdered milk, full of the salty soup carried up from the field kitchen by the river. Assembled here were not just the recruits, but half the camp; 40 or 50 insurgent soldiers, everyone who wasn't on patrol or on guard or off on some mission to Cabañas or farther afield in liaison with another front. This was a special meal, something of a feast, in honor of the inductees into the revolutionary army.

Noé, a handsome fighter with a maroon beret and a wooden cross on a thong around his neck, turned to a kid with tangled ringlets and asked him in a manner that was at least half ball-busting: "Hey, *colocho* (curley), what's it feel like to be un *verdadero guerrillero?*"

A couple rebels stifled a laugh. Others smiled. The expression of others didn't change at all. They'd been at this for six years by now and had seen hundreds of kids go through a few weeks of running and crawling and target practice, and many of them weren't around anymore. For some of the veterans, whatever this or that cherry had to say wasn't of paramount interest. They were here for the soup.

The colocho, neither a campesino nor a city kid but a third-year high-school student and son of a cabinetmaker from a small town on the coast, said: "It feels good." It looked for a moment like that was all he was going to say. He pursed his lips and let a gob of spit fall between his boots and covered up the spit with dirt. Then he looked up and said: "It's the first time in my life I feel like I belong to something. Something bigger than me. Like, I have a brother, see, and maybe if somebody came up to me and said, 'Hey, look, we're gonna shoot either you or your brother. Which will it be?' If they said that, then maybe, at least I like to think I would say, 'Hey, well, shoot me then, shit-eater.' But I'd have to think about it first, and who knows, if I thought about it too much, what the fuck I'd say.

"But here I don't have to think about it. Not anymore. I mean, I thought about it before I came, and I've had a chance to think about it a lot in the past few weeks. Now that decision is made, and it makes me feel tranquil to know that for any one of all of you here I'd willingly give my life.

And I barely know you. Like my life is a little thing compared to this big thing we all make up."

Noé's smirk had disappeared. By the time the kid finished, almost everyone was looking down into their soup cup. Except Joe, who was looking around and whose eyes fell on Victoria, a Mexican doctor with a sweet Aztec-Galician face, the most un-Aztec things about it being freckles across the cheeks and her glistening green eyes.

Someone farted loudly and everybody laughed. Some got up and served themselves more *sopa* and others lit cigarettes and resumed talking about whatever they'd been talking about before the colocho got onto the subject of the meaning of existence.

The last guerrilla had just spooned the last piece of *huisquil* squash and sip of broth from the bottom of his cup when a loudening whistle came from the sky. It was as if the *chafas* had been waiting for them to finish partaking of this mid-day celebration, like they had waited for the newbies to get their training in so as not to take unfair advantage. Like, Let's see if their training has done those green little Commie motherfuckers any good. And then they'd opened up with the two 155mm howitzers emplaced near the dam about six miles to the south.

The round sailed overhead and exploded beyond them. It was a loud explosion and seemed to Joe close by. Some of the rebels had dropped their cups when they heard the shrill note of the shell's flight and dived for cover. Manuel, this group's *masucho*, shouted orders and everyone ran to grab their rifle, jam essential gear into backpacks. The second and third rounds landed on either side of the encampment, the right distance but off line. Those explosions flashed and reverberated through the trees. Big branches cracked and fell.

The new fighters, including Joe, who'd returned to Chalate after three weeks in Morazán, had been divided among the camp's several squads, each under the direction of a sort of lieutenant, though the rebels did not use formal ranks. Several veterans, following Manuel's shouted directives, took refuge in two bunkers only ten meters higher up the hill. The rest of the rebel force sprinted through the forest. Joe stayed close to Manuel. It seemed to him like a round was striking the mountain about every 15 seconds. Some of the explosions sounded far-off. Others were close enough to hurt his ears and send warm wind against his face. He did not know how much later it was–he only knew he had been running long enough over difficult terrain to be soaked with sweat and to feel a stitch between his ribs–when the commander stopped and threw down his rifle and slipped off his pack. He tore at a pile of rocks. Joe did not wait to be told to help, and within a minute, with the hands of others who arrived panting in twos and threes, they cleared the entrance to a tunnel.

"Vamos, vamos! Pa'dentro!" shouted the chief. Hunched-over rebels filed quickly into the dark mountainside. A few flashlights in the line played over tramped earth but did not provide enough light to prevent some from stumbling. Joe knocked down the man in front of him and fell on him.

"Perdón, perdón," he stammered. But the man beneath him, instead of damning him, burst out laughing.

"Get the fuck off me, faggot!" the tackled fighter cried, as the file backed up. He was laughing so hard that Joe had to laugh too and they untangled themselves and continued on deeper into the sheltering earth.

About 20 yards into the hillside the tunnel opened into a cavern. A few of the rebels lighted candles and set them in ceramic candlestick holders on the ground or on the lids of a row of steamer trunks against one wall. Joe looked around. The cave was not natural but carved from the mountain and shored up with timbers. Beside the trunks were four large metal water cans, their spouts covered with tin cups. Within a few minutes the shelter was filled with guerrillas. They sat with their backs against the wall or against their packs. Some smoked. Some drank from their canteens. Joe settled himself between Lalo and a stocky middle-aged woman who was not a fighter but one of the camp cooks.

The artillery rounds hitting the woods came through the earth in muffled thumps.

"Did anyone see any casualties?" asked Manuel.

No one said they had.

Joe touched Lalo's arm. "How long does it usually last?"

"A half hour or so. They're not very effective for the most part. Sometimes they get lucky. But, you know, they're a long way off. They've killed more cows and civilians with those things than *compas*. The thing is, sometimes they use the howitzers before a heli-transported mission. That's what we have to find out soon. Whether they're making some kind of incursion."

"How long can people stay in here? Does the air run out?"

"No. It's ventilated. There's another way out, too. You can stay here as long as you've got water and food. There's enough stocked for a couple days, but we would never spend that much time in here anyway. If it looks like they're coming into our zone looking to engage, we make a move. If they come in battalion strength with air support, most of our force makes a tactical retreat to the north. We leave behind a half dozen guys to lay mines where they're going to pass and to snipe and harass them. But we don't fight them on their terms whenever they decide their guns are getting rusty. A big mobilization costs money and materiel and they end up with nothing to show for it, even if they stay a month. Because they have no intention of trying to set up permanent posts here. They know they could not maintain them.

"If it looks like a smaller operation, say a couple companies, well, they're on our turf and we pretty much just harass the shit out of them for a few days until they decide they've had enough and go home."

It was cool in the shelter. Shadows cast by the candles fluttered on the walls and ceiling. Joe felt chilled in his sweaty t-shirt so he took it off and felt in his pack for his army tunic. He put it on over his bare chest. Some of the rebels fell asleep within minutes Gardener snored lightly. Those who talked did so in hushed voices. After a while the woman next to Joe unwrapped something from a handkerchief. She nudged Joe and handed him a piece of tortilla.

He thanked her.

There wasn't enough light to see her features clearly, but she had a broad nose and a thick head of hair. She and Joe each ate their half-tortilla, chewing slowly. A little while after she finished she said quietly, not really to Joe but as a simple observation: *"Hoy es Once de Luna."* Today is the Eleventh day of the Moon.

"Como dice?" asked Joe.

"Once de Luna. The best day to conceive a child."

"Why is that?"

"Children conceived on the Once de Luna turn out strong in body and spirit. I can attest to that. Four of my six were conceived on or within a day of the eleventh–it doesn't have to be exactly on the eleventh, just close–and those four were tireless and happy and gracious children. The three boys working in the milpa with their father and the girl helping me in the house. All four of them joined *los muchachos*. The girl and one of the boys fell in combat. But they, like their two brothers were exemplary *compas*. That one, Samuel, over there," she pointed across the cavern to a shape against the opposite wall, "is mine. His brother is up on the Villa Victoria front.

"The other two, the two conceived under a brand new moon–a boy and a girl–they are lazy and sickly. They live with their grandmother in Panchimalco. I love them just the same, of course. But things are as they are, there's no getting around it."

She was wearing a dress, a flower-print shift of polyester fabric that gave off a subdued sheen in the candlelight. She stretched her legs out, smoothed her skirt and slipped off her plastic sandals. She crossed one foot over the other and straightened her back against the wall.

Joe offered her a sweater but she said she was fine.

"Sometimes the authorities have a good idea," she continued. "But they are not usually good at putting it into practice. They try to do it by giving orders. That's not the way. Like in the time of my grandmother and grandfather. They were from Panchimalco. Me too, that's where I was born. Well, people from Panchimalco are very traditional. I don't know if you know that part of the country, but it is a place where even today some of the old folks speak Nahua. One of the few places in our nation that has some Indian culture still. Well, the people of that region believe the moon influences all aspects of life; the life of plants and animals and men. They believe that life was created by the moon. That the sun nourishes life once created, but does not create it. Life is from the moon. And that there's a moon for planting and a moon for harvesting. Now, prior to the Once de Luna, there are moons when our parents *nos pintan*, when they set down the first lines of our form. Like a sketch. Then comes the Once, when we are conceived.

"The authorities of those days wanted to take advantage of this natural state of affairs. They wanted the children of Panchimalco, or at least the greatest number possible, to be conceived on or about the Once de Luna. So on this famous eleventh day of the moon, the night watchmen employed by the township would circulate along the streets at about nine o'clock, sounding a drum and calling out: 'It's the engendering hour, Good Sirs!' To which upstanding citizens were supposed to reply from behind the walls: *'Estamos en eso!'*

"Relations between spouses were authorized during those three days. Outside of that period, the watchmen were supposed to remain vigilant against illicit sexual activity. The old folks say this was not all that difficult because almost everyone in Panchimalco sleeps on a *tapexco.* That is a platform made of stripped saplings. And sexual intercourse on such beds makes a racket. So it was easy for the vigilantes to determine if couples were observing or not the period of abstinence.

"The ordinance was vigorously enforced. A husband caught violating it was given 20 strokes with a branch in the atrium of the church, with the whole town looking on."

"And you, señora. When were you conceived?" Joe asked.

"Well, of course one never knows such things for certain. I only know what my mother told me. And she swears my father planted the seed of me on the very Eleventh, not a day before nor a day after."

"I don't doubt it," said Joe.

He reached down and untied the laces of his boots and stretched out, his head resting against his pack, disposed to take a nap. He wondered at what point in the lunar cycle he had been conceived. Just as he was dozing off, a guerrilla came in from outside to signal the All Clear.

CHAPTER 35: THEIR BOOTS SUCK

Every guerrilla recruit took a new name upon joining up, but Joe never did. For the locals, it was mostly a matter of security, so that fewer people knew, or could find out, who or where your family was, a way of protecting them in case you were captured and then scorched or punctured or electrocuted, and made to talk. But you adopted a nom de guerre, also, to mark a break with your previous life and to signal your dedication to the struggle. A born-again kind of deal. To Joe it seemed so evident who and what he was–the Yanqui professor who'd knocked out *El Mayor*–that if he were ever captured it would have been ridiculous to try to pretend he was Beto or Luis from Usulután or Cabañas.

So he remained just Joe. Some of the compas called him El Gringo, in an affectionate way, and some called him, El Viejo, because at 34, back then, he was a decade or more older than almost all the other "new" fighters, and already had salt sprinkled in his short black hair and beard. But most of them just called him Joe.

The Gs had an eclectic collection of audio cassette tapes which, to save on precious batteries, were not used much but broken out for festivities held a couple times a year in towns in *la zona de control,* usually on the day of the patron saint of a given municipality. Gasoline-powered generators provided electricity for the audio system and there was eating and dancing, though no drinking, which was the rule in all of guerrilla-land. For a reason Joe was never able to figure out and for which he could not obtain a cogent explanation, most of the *muchachos* and *muchachas* dug Creedence Clearwater Revival. At any big guerrilla party there would inevitably come the plaza-jamming turn of Proud Mary and Down on the Corner, a mass of young revolutionaries bobbing and stepping, many of them with an assault rifle slung across his or her back. The gang Joe was with also had a couple Hendrix tapes in its meager travelling music library. Jimi was popular there, and though the vast majority of the rebel hipsters didn't speak English, they knew parts of the lyrics. In those early weeks of his revolutionary tour, some of his new *compañeros* got a kick out of hailing him by crying out: "Eeeeyyyy, Joe! Uere ju goink wit dat gunin yuhan?" Then they would laugh. At first it made Joe chuckle, too. Until it started to bug him a little, as he began to take himself more seriously as a blossoming insurgent, a soldier in the struggle for a more just and equitable world, or at least a more equitable El Salvador.

By the time he met Juan, Joe had been in Chalatenango for two months. Maybe, even after he began entertaining the notion that he could become a genuine FMLN combatant, he wasn't deep down convinced he was going to hang around for the long haul. But the idea held out a certain amount of allure. In any case, during those first months he was in no hurry to move on or get out. He didn't think much about things back home. It seemed there was not much of importance waiting for him in the States.

One day El Chusón, a member of his front's rebel brass, and Joe were sitting on a fallen tree trunk on the outskirts of camp when three *compas* came tromping up the path with big heavy packs on their backs. One of them, a kid Joe had never before seen, walked up to Chus and the two men greeted each other, obviously friends, and exchanged a few comments about how the mission–humping medicine and medical supplies from the Honduran border–had gone. Then this guy and the other two, also young and wiry, made their way down the path into camp.

About ten minutes later, from behind him, Joe heard a voice.

"They've got all the fuckin' money in the world and the best-equipped army, but I tell you, their boots plain suck."

Joe, turning to look, had the sensation he was hallucinating. Because this person–the brown-skinned, black-haired eminently Salvadoran-looking guy who had just been talking with Chus–had made this complaint in unaccented idiomatic American English. He was sitting on a rock about 10 yards away. A new green-nylon and black-leather U.S. government-issue infantry boot was sitting half-unlaced on the shade-dappled ground in front of him. One of his legs was crossed over the other.

Whether Juan Cano, who was known here to one and all as Clemente, or Clem, had spoken in this way within earshot of him intentionally or if it was a coincidence, Joe never found out. Later, after they'd become friends, Joe noticed that even though the American kid's slangy Salvadoran Spanish was indistinguishable from that of his mates, Clemente occasionally reverted to English to swear or mumble disgruntlement or chastise himself.

"Nice fuckin' blisters," he said now, peeling a wet gray sock off his foot which, even from where Joe sat, looked red and chafed and sore.

CHAPTER 36: ISMAEL, THE AVENGER

Santos told Clemente and Joe about a boy, a fighter in his early teens, who died in his arms. The three men were digging a trench on a damp hillside to fortify their camp, the base of about 150 guerrillas of the Farabundo Martí National Liberation Front. It was early 1986, during the few days of sprinkles that can interrupt the six-month dry season. Clem had been a guerrillla for half a year, and he still missed things. Like movies. And shooting hoops, the clank of the ball off the rim, the jingle of a swish through a chain net, the thump of the grainy rubber sphere, so pleasing to the touch, off the asphalt of a schoolyard court.

Basketball was what he was thinking about while shoveling there, before Santos began telling the story of this kid, Ismael.

Central America was once, for several years after independence from Spain, one country. The guerrilla movements of the 1970s and 1980s clung to this idea of fraternity along the isthmus. In the '70s, it was not unusual to come across Salvadorans in Sandinista ranks, or during the following decade, Nicas and Chapines and the odd Tico and Honduran in the FMLN. Santos was Guatemalteco, a middle-aged guy who by this time had been 20 years a *compa,* in his homeland and in two other countries. He was a communications specialist, a wizard able to construct a radio out of Coke bottles and baling wire. He was also a jazz freak, a devotee of the late 50s, early 60s hip cats; Coltrane, Mingus, Monk and Sonny Rollins.

It was his love of that music that made him well-disposed toward Americans. Or the idea of Americans. Until recently, he had never actually met one, though he listened religiously to the jazz show hosted every week by Eddie, a cool-seeming guy from the embassy of "the empire" in San Salvador. Then, all of a sudden, this little stretch of warfront had ended up with two of those rare creatures in the flesh. The older guy even looked like one.

And it was to these two Gringo *compas* that Santos, over a moonlit eve of spadework and the sharing of a few cigarettes, told a story from the war in Guatemala. From 1979. When his ORPA–Revolutionary Organization of the People in Arms–unit had entered an Ixil Indian village two days after a squad of Kaibiles had left it. (Kaibiles: Guatemalan army commandos named for a 16th-century Maya prince never subjugated by the Spaniards. Motto: "I am a Kaibil. If I advance, Follow me. If I falter, Urge me on. If I retreat, Kill me.")

Santos's patrol, drawn by a stench, had entered the hamlet and found a single survivor. He was a boy of about 11 who, when the army troops walked in, had been up a *nance* tree on the edge of the settlement trying to shake down the tangy yellow fruit.

The rebels found the boy on the floor of his adobe house, whimpering, with his skinny ashen arm draped over the bloated naked blood-crusted body of his mother. Santos and his comrades spent all day and evening burying the 40-odd corpses, infants to *ancianos*. They took the mute and blank-eyed boy with them further north, to their regional camp, where he was coddled by *las compas* and, over the following weeks, nursed back to a semblance of physical health.

After a few days the kid, who took the name Ismael, was able to talk. He told how the Kaibiles had lined up the men, including boys his age and stooped or limping *viejos*, in the clearing at the center of the village. The males numbered about nine, or relatively few for the size of the *caserío*. Only three were fighting-age, in the prime of life. Because it was true, the boy had said–and as the Kaibiles had alleged–that several of the hamlet's men had joined the insurgents.

When the men were lined up, a soldier passed behind them and yanked each one's hands together at the base of the spine to twist a short length of wire around the joined thumbs. The squad leader, who was wearing a black beret, then made a crazed harangue. The older villagers could comprehend only about half of what the man was saying, as the officer was speaking Spanish. But even they understood the word *subversivo*, which figured prominently in the tirade.

Women and small children stood gathered at gunpoint across the dusty tramped clearing.

After delivering his speech, the lieutenant drew a knife from a sheath at his waist and approached the first man in line.

"Do you know who I am?" His saliva sprayed the Indian's face.

"No," came the answer.

"Yo soy El Tigre de Chajul, the one who carries your ear in my pack," he shouted, and sliced off a clay-colored ear.

The leader of the soldiers asked the second man the same question, and received a negative response.

"I'm the Chajul Tiger, collector of ears of shitasses!."

The third, when required to respond, sobbed, *"Usted es El Tigre de Chajul."*

"Correcto," bellowed the officer. "The one and only," he yelled as he sliced through the cartilage.

The lieutenant mutilated each of the men in the same fashion. By now the women were wailing and gasping, many of them on their knees and pressing their face in the dust.

The boy related the second part of the squad-leader's rant: That there was only one of him, a sole officer in the entire armed forces of the fatherland who availed himself of none of his privileges. That he slept in the rain under nothing but a poncho beside his men, ate their same fare, exposed himself not equally but more so to danger, and killed the enemy alongside them. That was the reason he commanded their absolute loyalty.

"I take my spoils with them too," he cried. "And in that, Yes, I go first. Not because of rank, but because I am the strongest and most willful and that is the natural order of the world. The fiercest stallion wins the mares."

He told the bleeding men, some of whom had dropped to their knees, others upright but wavering: "Now you uglies will watch as I fuck each of your women, girls to hags, so you all might have clear before you die who is *El Tigre de Chajul.*"

Other soldiers dragged the women one by one to the middle of the village clearing. There El Tigre, dirty fatigue trousers and underwear bunched around his boots, engorged penis bobbing before him, ripped off *el corte* skirt of each and rammed into her. Some he penetrated only once, defiling them perfunctorily, to withdraw and carry on with the next. Others he stabbed for a minute or more. He never came. Every so often he let a gob of spit drop from his lips to his cock and stroked himself with his fist.

The boy who one day would become Ismael was too terrified to cry. He watched from the boughs of the *nance* as his mother and two sisters—one older and one younger than he was—were violated. His father, who had wanted nothing to do with *los guerrilleros,* was among the maimed.

When the last girl had been raped, the lieutenant pulled up his pants and took from a soldier a Galil assault rifle, the Israeli-made Kalashnikov knock-off that was standard issue in the Guatemalan army. He turned it on the line of men and opened fire. When they were on the ground, some still and others writhing, he replaced the curved clip and went nearer and fired another 30 rounds from closer range into their heads and bodies.

The women by this time were silent, or almost so.

The soldiers, a dozen of them, spent an hour raping, then killed the women and girls with bayonets. They sat on them and stabbed them through the heart, or sliced across their throats.

Santos said that Ismael, over the following three years, became an impassioned little fighter, gaining renown for an intrepid ferocity. When finally he was wounded in an ambush, struck by a bullet in the abdomen, it had been Santos who picked him up and carried him like a sack of squash (weighing about the same 80 pounds) several hundred yards. When he was sufficiently away and well-enough hidden, he lay him across his lap in a stand of pine.

"*Era todavia un niño,*" Santos said. "But that was the only time I ever saw him smile."

CHAPTER 37: *LA AUTOCRITICA*

A week after an FMLN guerrilla squad led by a rebel whose nom de guerre was Lalo shot down a military helicopter, killing all eight of its occupants, a 34-year-old foreigner in the rebel army, *un arqueologo norteamericano*, lay awake in his hammock in the dark. On this pre-dawn nearly seven months into his time among the insurgents, Joe Guinness reached a decision. He kept to himself most of that day, lazing around, writing a little in his notebook. In the late afternoon he went down to the river and bathed.

Along with the kid from L.A. known as Clem, Joe's closest friend among the rebels was a man in his early 30s named Omar, from Usulután. He was a valiant and seasoned fighter. In the time Joe had been there, Omar had been included in all of the difficult missions. Now he was technically under arrest, but not confined anywhere, there being nowhere in the camp to confine him. His sanction boiled down to not having a gun and doing punitive labor digging latrines pending a "verdict" on the charge of insubordination that had been brought against him by the front's commander, Raúl.

While Joe was away on a medicine-transport detail to Arcatao on the border, Omar had refused to form part of a firing squad. A squad of two, which had been ordered to take a recidivist bootlegger to a clearing in the woods about a kilometer from the camp and shoot him. The man, *un anciano*, had been caught a third time distilling chaparro corn liquor. The first time, two years earlier, his still had been destroyed and he was given a formal warning before an assembly of villagers and guerrillas, the great majority of whom supported the prohibition on alcohol in the swaths of the country under FMLN control. The second time this man was caught, his still was again destroyed and he was banished from the region. But after a year away he had begged to be allowed to come back to the only home he had ever known. He was permitted to return to his shack up the mountainside, but warned that if he resumed the activity that he knew was illegal, he would pay the most severe of penalties.

When he was caught again, Raúl ordered his execution and designated as executioners Omar and the front's political officer, who–and this may have been why Raúl chose him, aside from not liking him and his dogmatic university Marxist rap–was nicknamed *El Chaparro*, which in addition to being the word for moonshine also meant a person of diminutive stature. Shorty.

Raúl and the pint-sized commissar had found Omar cleaning his weapon outside his lean-to, and the commander informed him of the mission.

"You do it," said Omar, looking up for only an instant at his superior.

"I'm telling you to do it," said Raúl.

"I'm not doing it," said the rebel. *"Y punto."*

So El Chaparro and one of the Basques, another of those who believed the attainment of Worldwide Social Justice sometimes demanded the sacrifice of innocents, or at least the not-all-that-guilty, took the old man up the hill and killed him and buried him. And now Raúl had Omar digging his days away with an entrenchment tool. Joe found him on the camp's perimeter.

"I just wanted to tell you, I admire what you did."

All Omar said was, "Eh."

He tossed the little shovel on the ground and sat on the edge of the hole he'd dug. Joe sat on a rock next to the hole.

"I'm no murderer, is all," Omar said.

"What're they gonna do with you?"

"Who knows? Insubordination is serious. They can't let the *compas* get the idea they can decide which orders to follow. I doubt they'll shoot me. Most likely I'll be doing shit work for another month, then I'll have to make *una autocrítica* in front of the assembled troops. You know, 'I realize I was wrong and how grave a mistake it was and what an asshole I am.'"

They were silent for a while. Cicadas trilled in the trees. A dull green lizard scampered onto the handle of the shovel and remained there. He lifted his head and extended a scarlet fan from his throat, retracted it, then darted off into the brush.

"I'm leaving," Joe said finally. "If you want to come with me... I mean, if you think there's any chance they might really shoot you..."

Omar looked at him. He thought for a minute then said: "Nah." He picked up a stick and scratched some lines on the ground.

"Where you goin'?"

"Honduras. From there back to the States."

"How you gonna get to Honduras?"

"How do you think? Call a *pinche* taxi?"

Omar scuffed out his etching with his hand and began another design.

"I've got a brother in Los Angeles. Is that where you're going?"

"No. The other side of the country. New York."

"Cold there, huh?"

"Yeah."

"Nah," he said again. "I guess I'll stay. They're not gonna shoot me. My life is here. I've put a lot into this. I want to see how it turns out. Anyway, what the fuck would I do in Honduras or in the States?"

Omar used the stick to remove packed dirt from the tread of his boots. He looked up. "When?"

"Tonight."

The guerrilla stood up and unbuttoned the flap of the square pocket on the thigh of his pant leg. He reached in and took out a small circular thing. He held it out to Joe.

"Take this," he said. "Don't fuckin' tell anybody I gave it to you. That's all I need."

Joe took it. It was a compass. A cheap one, but it worked.

"In case it's cloudy. Just go north."

"Thanks."

"You didn't tell Raúl?"

"I can't. He'd make a big deal out of it. Have to check with the higher-ups, get approval. That could take weeks. But listen. I'm not taking my gun. I'll leave it at the big ceiba by where I've been sleeping. I'm gonna leave a note for him in the barrel. Just keep an eye out, and if nobody notices it by midday, you make like you found it, and give it to him. OK?"

"*Está bien.*"

They stood up and shook hands.

"*Suerte,*" said Joe.

"*Vos tambien,*" said Omar.

"Tell Clem I said '*adios.*'"

"I will."

***

The moon was high by the time he'd gone to sleep in the woods on the second night of his hike out. He was so tired he did not even hang his hammock. Anyway, he was not planning to rest until dawn. Just catch a couple hours curled up on the damp ground in his poncho, then take advantage of the moonlight to cover more of what he imagined by now must be a narrow band of hills separating him from the river that was the border. He did not intend to spend another night in El Salvador.

He lay down under a big oak. Sometime later the roots pushed up beneath him. He was cold and shivering, but he felt warm breath on the back of his neck. He couldn't move. But he could see that a root had wrapped around his waist and that it was no longer a root but two thin white arms hugging him. Long fingers of white hands with long curled and dirty nails were laced over his abdomen. Large breasts pressed against his back and a tangle of black hair not his own fell over his face, tickling his nose and lips. The hair smelled bad, rotten-sweet like week-old cane that the juice has been crushed out of.

He knew it was *La Siguanaba,* the countryside witch he'd heard about from campesinos and the peasant Gs, and that she wanted him to fuck her. But he knew he would not be able to get it up and she would laugh at him. She didn't even give him a chance, because she too knew he was incapable and she did laugh at him, a hollow metallic cackle she let out as she undid her embrace and squatted behind his head and peed on the ground. Her piss seeped under him and Joe was surprised that it was cold. Then she ran off, leaving only a bad smell and her icy urine, and Joe went back to sleep.

He woke up later because a dog was licking his face. He was startled by the beast, which, even though Joe pawed at it and cried out, only withdrew a couple steps, tilted its head and calmly regarded the confused man.

Part Three
1995
Friends, Enemies and Family

CHAPTER 38: THE FIRST GRINGO GRUNT

(The Gardener, take 8)

It's funny. Now. Not then it wasn't. *Ni mierda.* But at this distance I can appreciate the humor in it. I'd left the United States to keep from being denied my freedom. To avoid being arrested and put in jail. And there I was, two lousy weeks in a country I thought was going to be my refuge, and all of a sudden I'm deprived of liberty, shorn of my hair and dressed in green fatigues. With a nine-fingered, hardass sergeant heavily on my case. I actually thought they couldn't do it. I thought having a U.S. passport would make it impossible for them to press-gang me into the Salvadoran army. Then again, it wasn't as if I could complain to the Embassy. They took five of us off the bus. We stood there with the soldiers as it pulled away, black smoke spewing from the tailpipe. The kid, the one who looked, and turned out to be underage, started crying. *"Pero señor, por favor,"* he whined to the l-t. "I'm on my way to see *mi mamá.* She's ill and who knows if even she will survive. *Además*, I'm only 16." "You want to walk with a pack, or without a pack?" the *masucho* asked him. "But señor!" squealed the kid. *"Dale tu mochila,"* the leader tells one of the troopers. The soldier unslung his pack and grabbed *el llorón* and guided his arms through the straps. The simple fact of 40 pounds on his back quieted the boy at least long enough to take account of his new circumstance. And *el chafa cerote* goes: "Start bellyaching again, and I'll give you another. Keep it up and you'll be humping every fuckin' pack here and proceeding by means of serial kicks in the ass." So we set out at a slow march in the direction the bus had come from, back toward San Salvador. We recruits, if you can call us that, were in the middle of a single-file column. Every once in a while the kid let slip a whimper, but not loud enough for the squad leader to hear. No one said a thing. At least during the time we were walking and the 20 minutes we stood in the back of an army truck they flagged down to give us a ride to the base. I think all of us were kind of stunned. I myself couldn't stop thinking, Holy Fucking Shit I Don't Believe This. And I bet the other guys were thinking the same thing, in translation. But you know, you eventually come around to believing it. Reality does that to you. It sinks in, pretty fast. By the time our formal induction was underway at battalion headquarters, each of us had his rap ready. There was a captain and a non-com secretary who typed about seven words a minute. The officer was short and stocky and very dark with a beak nose and closely cropped hair almost all gray, though he didn't look much over 35. He spent most of the time leaning against the beige metal desk where the secretary sat filling in forms with a big black manual typewriter as each recruit provided full name, place and date of birth, address and occupation, next of kin. At intervals the officer would push himself off the desk and lean over a metal wastebasket and let drop a big white gob of saliva into the crumpled papers.

There was the minor. Another guy said he'd already served, in such-and-such a unit under colonel so-and-so, but had lost his discharge slip when his wallet was stolen. One guy said his brother had been killed while in service and he was the only surviving male in his family, and as such was exempt. The captain stares at him a second. "So you've decided you're exempt?" says Cauhuetemoc. "Not that I decided. That's the law," said the kid. The captain glares at the boy. Then he whirls around and gives the wastebasket a tremendous boot that sends it flying against the wall, scattering litter and spit. "The first and most important thing you'll learn here," he yells, "that is, before you become 'exempt'–not for this Christmas but for the one after–is that anybody with bars or stars," he pointed to the single five-pointer on his collar, "IS THE LAW! Do not ever, EVER speak that word again as long as you're in the armed forces of the fatherland." Another kid said he was still in high-school. I said I was a citizen of another country. "That well may be," said the officer. "I see that from your pretty little passport here. But up there you're just another stinkin' wetback. What about *tu patria*? The land of your fathers and the one that gave you life. Do you not love it?" "To tell the truth," I said, "I don't even know it." He brought his face close to mine. His breath was minty and hot. "That will be remedied," he said. "We will make sure you get to know it.

You'll wear out the soles of two or three pairs of Gringo boots in the process. And more importantly, we'll teach you to cherish it, to want more than anything to help save it from those who would hand it over to international communism." That was pretty much that. I'd had my say. Everybody else did, too. But the only guy who was gone after two days was the one who said he'd already done his stint. I guess he had. I couldn't have been expected to not play the U.S. card. As I said, I was confident it was going to get me out. But in the end, it only made things worse. See, the Salvadoran army depended on the United States. On men in Washington who wear suits and sign things with expensive pens. It was the U.S. Congress that provided their guns and bullets and uniforms and helicopters and A-37 fighter-bombers. If you read some of the better books about the civil war, you lean toward the conclusion that if it hadn't been for the massive infusion of U.S. money and materiel beginning in 1983, *los muchachos* probably would have routed the army by '85 or '86. It was Reagan's Central American domino theory. After Nicaragua, the line had to be held in El Salvador. But the fact that Tio Sam had pulled their nuts out of the fire by sending them a lot of hardware and money didn't serve to foster what you would call gratitude in the hearts of most Salvadoran officers. Many of them went for three or four months up to U.S. bases, Bragg and Benning and others, for specialization courses. A lot of them were instructed in the use of weapons systems and counter-insurgency tactics and, from the Carter presidency on, the concept of minimal respect for what were termed the "human rights" of every person, even if he's your enemy. They were told up north by pink and brown and black U.S. officers that torture was a no-no. And that it's not acceptable modern warfare procedure to summarily execute your prisoner, much less cut off his dick and stick it in his mouth to scare his buddies when they find him. Nearly every brigade and battalion around the country had three or four U.S. advisers, most of them army Special Forces officers and non-coms. A lot of them were Hispanic; Chicano or Puerto Rican. But they were still Gringos. From what little I saw they didn't go around demanding deference. In fact where I was, at least, the few weeks I was there and saw them in action, they tried to kind of blend in and make friends. But there seemed to be among the Guanaco officer corps a pervasive conviction that if you wanted to progress through the ranks, you'd better suck up and kiss Yanqui ass. So almost all of them did. Then when they were in the rack at night I guess they felt bad about being a brown-nose and for laughing at that stupid chele l-t's or that dumb nigger captain's shitty jokes and saying "Yessir, yessir," to everything the big sunburned master sergeant–*un pinche sargento para colmo*–suggested about increasing night patrols and morale-building among the troops. You see. These guys, the Salvadoran officers, they'd never had a Gringo grunt before. So I was kind of in for it, right from the beginning. And that's one of the main reasons I didn't stick around for long in that outfit.

CHAPTER 39: THE CHAJUL TIGER

At first, the marimba may appear to be a primitive and even dull instrument, a rudimentary one lacking grace. It's not as sophisticated or versatile as a piano, with which it has much in common. A simple thing, made of aligned slabs of hard wood with sounding boxes beneath them. Until the middle part of the last century, the *cajas de resonancia* of a traditional marimba were hollow dried gourds suspended under the keys in a progression of longer (those beneath the lower register) to shorter (the ones under the higher notes). Some antique instruments suggest an Impressionistic sculpture of a spindly she-goat or bitch after a sixth litter, stretched teats dangling. But since the 1940s or so, the sounding boxes have been constructed by the marimba-maker of wood and are chambers ending in a downward-pointing pyramid, giving the instrument a more refined aspect.

Despite its simplicity, when played by a musician of the caliber of Francisco Pop Yat, the marimba is capable of moving a listener like no other instrument.

About four months after he'd met his mother's employer, the wealthy and mostly idle man he knew as Miguel, Ximena Yat's son gave his new friend three tickets to a concert to be held at the Miguel Angel Asturias Cultural Center in the capital. The program comprised 17th-century American Baroque chamber music in which Francisco and a Mexican cellist were to be the featured soloists.

He also asked a favor of Miguel. He wondered if he and his *novia, la chinita Abril,* would escort his mother to the function.

"She doesn't like the city. She won't go unless you take her, and she'll probably have to be cajoled even so. But I would love for her to be there. It's beautiful music. And I think *la raza nuestra* ought to be represented among all the society types in attendance. The idea of her in the audience, showing off her best *huipil,* will be an inspiration.

"I'll be glad that you and Abril are there too, *por supuesto.* I am not inviting you just so you can be my mother's chauffeur."

Juan felt something that until that moment he did not even know he'd been missing. Something that had to do with his mother, with his compañeros from the Salvadoran hills, and the recent couple years of loneliness that of late were being marvelously assuaged by April.

"Sure, man. It will be an honor and a pleasure."

***

Francisco' s pick-up was running badly. A 1988 Nissan four-cylinder job, it never had much passing power or vigor. Even so, he had never before been obliged to climb the seven kilometer hill from Antigua to San Lucas in first gear.

With Miguel in the passenger seat and the marimba Francisco had built for Efraín Menendez in the bed, the truck began to cough and struggle on the initial slight grade just past the Colegio Bilingue. He had always been able to take this stretch easily in third. But even after downshifting into second the truck waffled and strained.

"Come on. Come on," Paco coaxed. "Just get up this hill and we can practically coast to Guate."

He and Miguel had met Efraín at the Hotel Santo Domingo an hour earlier. They'd lifted the instrument onto the truck and covered it with a tarp and tied it down. Efraín led the conjunto that entertained in the patio bar of the former Dominican monastery that had been converted into the city's premier luxury hotel. He and his *muchachos* had a month off due to renovations underway at the hotel, and Francisco had asked him, a former band mate, for the loan of the marimba for the Asturias Center concert. That would save Paco a lot of bother. It was much easier for him to transport this one the 40 kilometers to the capital than to have to return the 200 kilometers to Xela for his own, make the long haul to the city, then return with it all the way back home. Especially with his truck running like shit.

Maybe it was the dust, thought Paco, churning at full whine up the curvy road. The air filter must be packed. Or maybe the fuel-line's partially clogged, or maybe the timing's way off. *O que putas.*

"Too bad it wouldn't fit in my truck," said Miguel, whose 4 Runner glided up this hill.

"*Lastima,*" said Francisco. But he was in no hurry. He resolved to go slow and hope it didn't overheat. It took 15 minutes just to climb the hill. A few minutes later they were in San Lucas, on the level, and the truck did all right there. The second half of the trip was on a slight downhill grade to *el periférico,* where he got off CA-1 and headed into the city.

Neither Francisco nor Juan was familiar with downtown. Paco lost his bearings in Zone 2 and made a couple wrong turns before he came upon Sixth Avenue and got headed toward *el Centro Civico.* As he went by the produce market he saw ahead of him a mid-city hill capped with the modernistic blue and white Asturias Theater. The building looked like the prow of a huge vessel serenely traversing the chaotic capital.

He turned right onto 22nd Street, following a sign indicating the way to the cultural complex. It was a one-way street going west. Cars were parked in nearly unbroken file on both sides of the street, home to a stretch of *tienditas* and yard-goods bazaars and a couple cheap restaurants. An hourly parking lot was on the left at mid-block.

Francisco's truck was about 15 meters from the next intersection and he was looking for another sign indicating access to the theater when a Chevrolet Suburban with dark-tinted windows turned left onto 22nd heading the wrong way. Paco was obliged to brake harder than he would have liked. He and his friend felt the marimba shift behind them, though not enough to strike the back of the cab.

Being himself unaccustomed to driving in the clogged capital, Paco felt immediately indulgent toward the mistaken driver invisible behind the black windshield before him. The noses of the little pick-up and the high, wide, tank-like wagon were separated by barely a meter. The Suburban's stock bumper had been replaced by a broad wooden plank three inches thick bolted to an iron plate almost as long as the vehicle was wide.

Francisco, smiling amicably, indicated with a finger the sign directing the flow of traffic in the direction he was headed. He mouthed the words, *"Es vía para allá,"* making a sort of chopping motion with his hand to emphasize, in a friendly fashion, that it was he who was going the right way.

What he expected, during these seconds, was that the driver of the Suburban would put it in reverse and back carefully the short distance to the intersection in order to rejoin the correct flow of traffic.

But a compact man–he looked to be about 50–in a green Lacoste polo shirt and beige trousers opened the massive vehicle's driver's side door and jumped more than stepped into the street. He wore a black baseball cap with the word TIGRE embroidered in yellow letters above the visor and yellow-tinged aviator sunglasses. As he approached the few steps toward the passenger window of the pick-up, Francisco saw he carried a large pistol stuck in the waist of his pants right where his sunglasses case was attached to his belt.

The man stuck his face through the open window.

"Move this piece of shit or I'll run it over," he said.

"Hold on," answered Francisco. "This street is one-way that way." He again made the directional gesture with his hand.

"Don't argue with me. *Soy coronel del Ejército de la Patria.*"

"Even so, that doesn't permit you to go the wrong way down a one-way street."

Another man got down from the passenger side of the Suburban. He was much larger than the man who had been driving. He too wore aviator Ray-Bans and carried a weapon, though his was a machine-pistol hanging from a strap over his shoulder.

"*Que ondas, Tigre?* You want me to back it up?" he called to the shorter man.

"Stay put and shut the fuck up," the coronel barked. "That vehicle is going in no direction but forward."

Turning his attention again to Francisco, he asked: "So, *orejón*, what will it be?"

"I'm the one going the right way," insisted Paco, whose brown face took on a reddish hue from a rush of blood. As if to emphasize his point, he stepped on the parking brake.

The other man said nothing more. He walked back to his truck and climbed in.

"*Dele Paco,* maybe we should just back up and let them by." But Francisco did not answer. He sat with his arms folded across his chest.

The driver of the Suburban engaged the 4-wheel drive and shoved the stick into first. He revved the engine and lurched forward.

The Suburban, which had been armored at the same shop the Gringo and European embassies used for the ambassadors' Cadillacs and Mercedes, smashed into the front of Francisco's truck. It surged forward, pushing the skidding pick-up as if it were an oversized packing crate. Francisco, clutching the wheel with both hands, began shouting. Juan reflexively grabbed the door-handle to be ready to open it and leap out. Paco's cries were barely audible above the plaint of tires and metal as the pick-up scraped one after another of the cars parked on his left. Finally the tailgate caught on something and the vehicle swung perpendicular to the Suburban. A second later it was tipped over onto the passenger side and Juan, scrambling to keep himself in an understandable relationship to gravity and the ground, had his back braced against the roof and one foot on the dashboard and one on the seat, for the most part upright in the new configuration of the world but with Francisco inadvertently kicking him as he too sought a foothold while the pickup was pushed, screeching, along the blacktop. The marimba spilled out with a mighty clang and splintering racket.

The driver of the Suburban rammed the flipped truck to the middle of the block and up onto the entrance of the parking lot. The larger vehicle now had the way clear to continue. But the driver did not proceed. He looked first in the side view mirror then over his shoulder through the rear window at what had fallen into the street 15 or so meters back.

"What the fuck is that?" he asked the bodyguard.

"Looks like a marimba."

"Fuck me," said the colonel. He shifted into reverse and laid another patch of rubber. He crushed the instrument beneath his big tires.

"I never ran over a marimba before."

He pulled forward again to the capsized pick-up. Francisco, wincing against a pain in his shoulder, had pulled himself up and out through the driver-side window. Juan was standing spread-eagle in the tipped cab, both hands and both feet planted. Through the windshield he could see the cars parked in the lot and the attendant who had come running to the curb.

Paco stood there in a state of shock behind the front left tire, now incongruously parallel to the ground at the level of his chin. The parking-lot attendant, a young man, stood by his side.

The passenger-side window of the Suburban went down electronically, revealing the big man. He leaned back. The driver removed his sunglasses and fixed Francisco with an amused look.

"I'm accustomed to having my orders carried out, *entendés?* You stupid Indian dirty-ass. See what you could have saved yourself?"

With that he put the vehicle in gear and pulled away.

CHAPTER 40: THE SPEED 6

(**T**he Gardener, take 10)

I spent seven and a half years as a *guerrillero*. Was a combatant from mid-1985 until the end of 1992, when we handed our rifles to the U.N. guys and watched them cut them in half with blow torches. I killed at least three people, and maybe five or six. All of them soldiers, I'm pretty sure. You might be surprised to hear that most of the fighting was in towns, and a lot of the time you were blasting away on *ráfaga* over a wall or around a corner, shooting at where you last saw a *chafa*, and you can never be sure a round from your weapon didn't go through a window or mud wall and kill some kid or *anciano*, heaven forbid. But what I'm saying is that in all that time, on only a few occasions, in maybe 40 engagements–I mean all kinds of combat, from attacks we staged on bases or outposts or prisons, to attacks we were the object of at our own camps, to chance encounters between patrols–did I see the soldier I was shooting at get hit and fall. And who knows if even those guys died, or survived the wound? So all through the war, I never repeated the experience I had at the age of 18 when I killed Sudek: the experience of shooting a person two steps away from me, while he was looking at me. Killing that cop wasn't hard, though, and I don't regret it. I don't regret killing soldiers either, during the war. Not much use in that, going over those years and deeds in a repentant frame of mind. You could get deeply bogged down in that shit. But I tell you, if I could give back life, I'd give it back to every single *milico* I killed, officer or grunt or whatever, before I'd give it back to Sudek. I'd leave that fucker stone cold dead forever. There were a couple newspaper stories about what happened to my Mom. There was an inquiry. Sudek got suspended, with pay, and put on desk duty. But there were no charges brought against him, and all four of the pigs had their version of events down pat and stuck to it. Their story was that Sudek was defending himself, that my mother had attacked him with a baseball bat and in the struggle he wrenched the bat from her and was using it to subdue her, and her esophagus got crushed. His defense was that if you pressed a club like that against the throat of a normal person, that person would just lose the power to resist and go limp. But not die. So she must have had some condition that made her susceptible in a particular way, was what his lawyers and the cop investigators said. My grandmother Chayito, bawling, told me how it really happened. She told me and later she told a reporter from the L.A. Times and she told the police Internal Affairs investigators. I think the Times reporter, a woman, wanted to do more with it. But the gist of her article was the fact that the family disputed what the cops were saying. And it was the word of four cops against the word of abuelita, an old-lady Salvadoran immigrant. Figure out for yourself if we ever had a chance. I shot him two weeks to the day after he killed her. Pedro gave me the Ruger Speed 6 from the confrontation in the 7-11. I had never fired a gun in my life, except an air pistol at some carnival stand, to win a stuffed animal or something like that. But there's no big trick to using a revolver. I found out where he lived, over by Venice in Playa del Rey, and hung around over there, walking up and down the street and at an Einstein Brothers bagel and coffee place across the street from his condo complex. His picture had been in the paper and his address was in the *pinche* telephone book and it was easy to find him. He kept odd hours, not any kind of schedule. But I was able see him going into the complex once and another time coming out through a locked gate at the sidewalk. He had a beige Beemer, not a new one, that he parked in the street. I was working out in my head how I was going to do it, like where, exactly–whether on the sidewalk or try to jump the fence and wait for him inside the gate, or what. But I don't want to give the impression, either, that this was all well-planned or professional. I was winging it. Improvising and working on rage and hate that was a seething slow burn, and I didn't much give a shit what happened to me in the process of doing what I was going to do. Which translates into a huge advantage in a situation like that. It was just after 2 a.m. on the night of June 23, 1985. I was across the street from the entrance to his place. There was a basement joint, a dry cleaners, with a stairwell, and I waited there, half hidden, for a couple hours. I had an empty pizza box, my only real prop, something it had occurred to me would make me unremarkable, like I had a reason to be there, in case anybody noticed me. I was getting tired. At last I hear a motor and peek out and there's the BMW, pulling to the curb about 30 yards past the gate. My heart took off, pounding. I could feel the blood beating in my nostrils. I put the pizza box under my arm, keeping it horizontal like it really had a pizza in it, and put my right hand in my jacket pocket, gripping the gun, and walked across the street toward the gate, timing myself to be approaching it along with him. I walked at a normal pace but felt like a galloping horse with blinders on. I heard his footsteps more than my own, and I didn't look right at him, into his face, until he was 10 feet away and right as I did, as our eyes met I said, "I'm Soledad Cano's son." I dropped the box and pulled out the gun and his face twitched and went split-second scared and he went for his gun, his hand inside his half-zipped sweatshirt to his shoulder-holster and he almost got his gun before I shot him twice in the chest. Two explosions. There in Playa del Rey, California, three blocks from the ocean, on a night that didn't feel like summer, I stood over Chris Sudek for a few seconds watching his back heave. He was face down and his hands were under his chest, like he was trying to reach inside and get the two small hard things in there. He coughed and turned his head. Blood came out of his mouth. Then he was still. To the extent I had imagined this scene, I'd supposed I would fire a bullet into his head. But I didn't. I put the gun in the pocket of my windbreaker, put up the hood and began walking away. I didn't want to hold the weapon anymore, and when I took my hand out of the pocket, the gun felt very heavy hanging there. I walked to the near corner and turned left, heading inland. I wasn't really scared, but my legs felt heavy. I knew I wasn't going to use the gun anymore, even if somebody tried to stop me. It was like: *I don't care.* Cars were parked along the street but there was no traffic. No people around, either. At the middle of that block I picked up my pace, then broke into a jog, across the road, to the next corner, where I turned right. I slowed again to a walk. No one was on this street either, though at the end of the block, at a busier avenue, a pedestrian crossed and disappeared. A couple cars flashed through the traffic light up ahead, near where I'd left Mom's car. I had an almost irresistible urge to get rid of the revolver, to drop it in the dumpster coming up on my right or toss it down a storm drain or heave it as far as I could down the service alley on the other side of the street. I remember repeating to myself, whispering under my breath: *No, No, No.* Don't be stupid. Don't be an idiot. Another 30 or 40 seconds. Hang on. Don't be stupid. I reached the avenue and stopped. I looked to the left. No car was coming and I stepped into the street. I looked to the right and did not see any car in that direction either and broke into a lope because the opposite curb loomed like a vision of the shore to a struggling swimmer. A stride past the middle of the street and there came a screeched shout of "Eeeyyy!" I saw the bicycle swerve, its rider, with one of those tear-drop helmets, hunched over the handlebars. I was flooded in an instant with an adrenaline charge that transformed me into a cat and I jumped forward and to my left and landed on the sidewalk and saw the bike, a road-racer, slipping away fast, the rider's Lycra-sheathed butt raised and back curved. He looked back under his arm at the upside-down jerk behind him to yell: "Idiot!" I was so light now. Almost disembodied. My arms and legs were tingling but weighed nothing and if it weren't for the chunk of steel in my pocket and the lead case around my thumping heart I was gonna levitate and hover there at the level of the streetlamp. I turned and walked, like I was on the moon, to my parked car. I got in and started the engine and put it in gear and pulled away from the curb. Glancing to my left without coming to a stop, I turned right on the red light onto the empty avenue.

The house of Mrs. Sanchez, a widow friend of my grandmother, was two-and-a-half blocks from our own in Lynwood. Until a year earlier, before I'd taken a weekend and summer-evenings job at the movie house, I used to cut her small lawn every ten days or so, depending on how much it had rained or whether Mrs. Sanchez had felt up to watering it. Her lot was enclosed by a waist-high chain-link fence bordered on one side by a gravel pathway that cut from street to street at the middle of the block. I parked across from Mrs. Sanchez' house and reached under the seat for the trowel I'd put there. I got out and crossed the street and walked down the path. Bone-colored gravel crunched under my feet. I grabbed the top-bar of the fence with my right hand and vaulted it with a scissor kick. I looked up. At this midpoint between the streets, away from the lamp-posts, the stars were bright. There was a crescent moon. A silver sickle. I covered the few steps on soft grass to the edge of a shed where Mrs. Sanchez kept gardening tools and some plastic outdoor furniture. The lawn, lush for this neighborhood, did not come right up against the base of the shed. That's where I knelt and began to dig. The top layer of earth was moist and unpacked and the tool went in easily, shearing away chunks. Six inches down the soil was drier and more dense and I had to chop and poke to loosen it inch by inch. But in three minutes I was reaching down almost to my elbow and a mound of dirt was piled beside me. I straightened up and took the gun from my pocket. I reached down to place it at the bottom of the hole and wondered what else it'd been used for since, across the nation in Connecticut, it was lathed or cast or however the hell it was they made these goddamn things. It was like I was performing with it some kind of magic. Because I was certain I was making it disappear as absolutely as if I'd tossed it from a ship in the middle of the Pacific. I refilled the hole, compacting the earth as I scooped in handfuls, careful to leave some of the lighter topsoil to touch up the surface. I stood up and scuffed the spot with the sole of my sneaker.

No one could tell a hole had been dug there.

I picked up the trowel and jumped the fence again and walked back down the path, beginning what turned out to be a long journey away from the place where I'd been raised, a land that, though not my birthright, was a hundred percent mine. As I increased the distance between myself and the base of the southern wall of Mrs. Sanchez' tool shed, the connection I felt with that square foot of earth diminished only slightly. There, unknown to any person in the world except myself, unmarked on any map or grid of that part of the city of angels, lay in eternal repose beneath a foot of earth a hefty chunk of metal like an anchor. And though the line that tied me to it was infinitely elastic, it would never break as long as I lived.

CHAPTER 41: DIVING FOR SAND

Francisco played another marimba, also borrowed, at the Asturias Center concert. Despite a stiff arm, he played masterfully to an appreciative crowd that included his mother and Juan and April.

Ten days later, Paco showed up at the house in Antigua looking for Juan. He found him on the patio, reading Vargas Llosa's *La Guerra del Fin del Mundo*.

"I've got something else for you to read," said Paco, approaching the table where Juan sat, an empty demitasse beside the open book. Paco placed in front of his friend the current issue of *Crónica*, the country's main newsweekly. On the cover was a montage of three photographs, all of the same man. In one he was in muddy fatigues, with grease-paint on his face. The other showed him on an athletic track breaking the tape in a footrace and the third, more of a portrait, exhibited a tanned and smiling visage beneath a black baseball cap embroidered in bright yellow thread with the word TIGRE.

"Recognize this guy?" Francisco asked.

"Of course. The asshole in the Suburban."

"The main article is about him. Col. Abelardo Alvarez. Hero of the counter-insurgency. World class marathoner in his age-group. He's been named co-chairman of the National Olympic Committee."

"What's with this *'Tigre'* shit?"

"That's what everybody calls him. His *pinche* nom de guerre from his glory days against *los guerrilleros*. *'El Tigre de Chajul.'* It's a town up in the boonies, a whole region, really, that he supposedly rid of the communist menace."

Chajul. Juan had heard that place name before. He'd heard the whole phrase before. A story about a kid, a long time ago, while digging a ditch on a hill. He hadn't heard it since, but that didn't matter.

"La puta que lo parió," he whispered softly.

"The article says international human rights organizations have objected to his Olympic designation," Paco went on. "But apparently their opinion has not been taken into account."

Two days later Juan rose early and dressed in poor man's clothes and old boots and put eight tortillas and a packet of salt in a paper bag. He put the bag in a canvas satchel with a poncho and a blanket.

"I'll be gone four or five days, Ximena. April's going to Panajachel. So you take it easy. You might even go to Xela to see Francisco, if you want."

"Gracias, don Miguel. Con cuidado y que le vaya bien."

It didn't matter that he was destitute looking. She still called him "Don." She did not ask him where he was going, or why he had made himself look like a peasant.

He walked south in the cool new day's light along Fourth Avenue, past the Cathedral, to Seventh Street. As he stood on the corner waiting for the next bus bound for the capital, the old man with the Stetson and two canes came hobbling in slow motion down the opposite sidewalk. His hat was perched higher than usual because it sat atop a red woolen watch cap.

He walked very slowly. He wore a clean shirt with a collar and a suit jacket too big for him, even though by local standards he would have been considered a large man. His trousers were pressed and his black oxford shoes clean and polished. Juan never saw him accompanied. Neither did he ever see him carrying a *bolsa* with something from the market, or anything at all. So he assumed the man did not live by himself, that he was someone's father and grandfather and great-grandfather, probably, and that he lived with his family and someone else did the shopping and looked after him. He appeared to have no destination. At his age, he did not have any task or responsibility. This fostered in Juan a feeling of affinity, and he would have liked to approach the old man and invite him to sit with him on one of the stone benches in the small plaza in front of the Belen convent, and talk for a while. About anything. About how things go in a man's life. But Juan couldn't find a pretext to approach him. The most he could manage was a *"Buenos Dias,"* if they happened to pass in opposite directions on the same sidewalk. The old man's *Buenos Dias* in response was a hoarse whisper, and though Juan had greeted him a few times over the previous months, the man never showed a trace of recognition.

The Guate-bound bus was full. Juan had to stand in the aisle during the first half of the trip, up to San Lucas, where several people got off. Four hours later, after a change of buses in the capital's Zone 7, Juan and a nearly full complement of other Salvador-bound passengers were descending a winding road into Valle Nuevo and the border crossing of Las Chinamas. Every few hundred meters the air seemed to heat a degree. By the time they stopped at *Migración* the bus was a sheet metal oven. Juan's back was wet, his forehead beaded. Everyone got off. The Guatemalan vehicle's run ended here. The passengers would continue their trip in a Salvadoran bus on the other side of the river. They filed through a perfunctory check of *cedulas*–travel between Central American nations requires no passport for Central American citizens–and walked across the high bridge. Juan stopped at the span's mid-point and leaned on the railing to let the breeze cool his back.

Downstream, several boys and young men were working in the water. The high sun beat quicksilver stripes on the broad brown ribbon. Four small barges, about twice the size of a bathtub and made of tar-caulked wood, were anchored against the current in a segment of mid-river about five feet deep. In each of the vessels stood an adolescent or young man in his underwear or gym shorts. The tubs and the figures spread-legged on them were not much more than silhouettes against the rippled glare. Alongside each of the craft, one or two boys or young men broke the surface at regular intervals bearing a five-gallon can filled with sand. The can was handed up to the worker in the barge. He dumped it and handed it back to the diver, who took a breath and went back under.

Some of the younger boys were barely tall enough to touch bottom on tip-toe and, head craned and mouth pursed an inch above the water, press the full can toward the bargeman's grasp. When the tub was filled so that the gunwale cleared the surface by the breadth of a few fingers, the worker up top lifted a stowed pole and propelled the vessel to the bank without untying the long tether. There he looped a stern line over a post sunk in the sloping shore and off-loaded the sand with a shovel. That barge's swimmers paddled to the edge and sat and rested for four or five minutes on their upturned buckets.

They did not all dive in the same fashion. About half of them let the can fill with water then jack-knifed to descend head first, their lean and glistening legs stirring the surface with a lethargic kick. Others sucked a gulp of air and went down feet first. Juan tried to picture them beneath the muddy water. Several kids, shades to one another, hovering or crouching, weightless in the cool dim silence to scoop the fine sand into their buckets. But he was unable to conjure a good image. The shimmering surface was too much of a barrier. The boys themselves were the only ones worthy of knowing what it was like.

That seemed right to Juan. He pushed off the rail and walked to the far side of the bridge, back once again into the country where he was born.

CHAPTER 42: SOMETHING OTHER THAN GAS

April was labeling Betacam cassettes, sitting on the cool tiles of the veranda next to a stack of black plastic rectangles, when the doorbell rang. She got up and went to answer it.

A woman stood on the sidewalk with a crying baby. The baby was slung across the woman's torso in a yellow and green shawl. A wet brown nipple pressed against the cheek of the infant, who'd left off suckling to wail. It was a girl, judging from the gold bead in the lobe of the visible ear. The child's face was contorted and her scream was terrible.

"Excuse me," said the mother, a lean *ladina* in a sky-blue polyester dress with puffed short sleeves. "Is 'Ña Ximena in?"

"*Sí,*" said April. "*Pase usted.*"

"*Con permiso,*" said the woman. She stepped into the cool entrance-way. There was a wooden bench with a carved back, eagles and monkeys and lions, against the wall at the foot of three broad steps leading to the veranda.

"Have a seat, please. I'll get Ximena," said April.

The baby's shrieking stabbed in April's ears. She found Ximena at the *pila*.

"'Ña Ximena," said April, "There's a woman here to see you. With a baby."

"*Ya vengo,*" said the old woman. She ladled clear water with an orange plastic bowl onto a pair of Juan's jeans to rinse away the suds. She did this three times, pressing and rubbing the heavy fabric against the corrugated cement bottom of the basin. Then she wrung them with a fold and twist, shook them once and tossed them dripping over a line.

When Ximena and April arrived back at the foyer, the baby had quieted and was suckling again.

"*Buenos dias, 'Ña Ximena,*" said the young mother, standing.

"*Buenos dias, hija,*" answered Ximena. She recognized the woman, whose little girl she had delivered about six months earlier. But she did not recall her name. "How can I serve you?"

"*Es la niña,*" said the woman. "She cries and cries and cries. Doesn't sleep more than two hours at a time. My first one, the boy, by the time he was this age he was sleeping through the night. And nothing of a wailer like this one. *Temo que le haigan echado el ojo.*" I fear someone has put the evil eye on her.

"We shall try to find out," said Ximena, stepping to the woman with her arms out, accepting the child. "Maybe it's just that her tummy hurts. *Que se le estén atravesando los peditos.*" (That she's got gas, or literally, "That her little farts are getting stuck.")

"I don't know. All she has had is the breast. And I've taken care not to eat cabbage or cauliflower and very few onions. Which is a sacrifice for me, the way I love onions."

"*Bueno,* we'll see," said Ximena. "Come inside," she said to the woman, and turned. "You come, too, if you like, *Seño Abril,*" she added without looking back.

The three women made their way down the veranda to the kitchen. Ximena, carrying the baby, took a folded tablecloth from a drawer and placed it on the kitchen table. With her free hand she flipped open one fold, then another, so the cloth covered half the surface but still served as a comfortable pad for the child. She lay her there, face up.

Ximena leaned over the girl and studied her face. She used thumb and forefinger to open wide first one eye then the other. She placed her hands on the baby's shoulders and ran them down the length of the small body, straightening the bent legs. With the baby stretched like that, Ximena's hands grasping the ankles, she pushed the legs, bent at the knee, back up against the midriff. She did this several times.

"Looks like it's not gas," she said.

She unbuttoned the child's red wool sweater and lifted the polyester jersey and folded up toward the child's neck the bottom-layer cotton t-shirt. The taut belly rose and fell. The mother bent over the child's head and cooed. April stood at Ximena's shoulder, craning to see.

Ximena pressed gently on the baby's right side just below the rib cage. Then she slid her hands, one atop the other, to the left side and pressed, then moved her fingers down to just above the pelvis and repeated the pressure on both sides at that level, all the while watching the infant's expression. She lowered her head and rested her ear against the child's abdomen.

After a moment she said: *"No tiene gas."* She left the baby there and walked to the counter were there was a basket of eggs. She lifted one.

"Fresh," she said to the mother, exhibiting a beige egg. "Not carton eggs. These are from yard hens. A friend in Santa Ana brings them twice a week. Never seen the inside of a refri."

She brought the egg to the table.

"Take off her clothes except the undershirt and the diaper," she instructed the mother. The woman undressed the baby, who started to cry. It began as a lethargic plaint but grew quickly to a shriek interrupted only by sucks of air.

"Ay," whispered the mother. It was nearly a sob. "It's been two weeks straight of this, almost all the time she's awake. Sometimes I feel like another person altogether, someone I don't recognize as myself. An evil woman's hands want to reach down and clamp the baby's mouth and hold it shut until the crying stops. *Que Dios me perdone.* On occasion I've had to put her in a basket on the floor and leave the house, leave her alone Gand take the boy and walk around outside for a time, because I was afraid of what I might do."

"No se aflija," said Ximena. Don't afflict yourself. "We're going to find out what's wrong and recover for this child her measure of peace."

Ximena took the egg, curled in the palm of her right hand, and began passing it over the baby's heaving torso. The motion was a light caress of shell-to-skin, up under the t-shirt to the throat and breast and neck and down again lightly, inside the swaddling cloth. Then along the thighs, and shins and the tops and the soles of the feet.

The touch of the egg seemed to calm the baby. Her face relaxed as Ximena passed it over her forehead and down her nose and over her eyelids, down each side of the face to the point of the chin. She asked the mother to turn her over, and passed the egg over the entire back of the body. By the time she finished, the baby was asleep.

The mother dressed the child and replaced her in the shawl-sling.

Ximena brought a terracotta bowl from the sideboard and put it on the table. She rapped the egg lightly on the edge, broke it open and dropped its content into the bowl. She and the woman leaned over to look. April, though she had no idea what she was looking for, leaned in with them.

The egg was partially poached. Chalky striations ran through the white and the yolk had turned dense and a deep shade of orange.

"Someone has cast an envious eye on this creature," said Ximena. "But I would venture that it's a weak spell. It should not prove difficult to counter." She said to the woman: "Come with me."

The mother, with the sleeping baby affixed to her belly, and April followed Ximena out into the rear yard. Two tall *encino* oaks flanked a Tibetan pine in the center. A stand of citrus trees–tangerine, orange and lemon–took up most of the left half of the yard. Ximena led them to one of the three lemon trees. The branches were laden with green fruit a few weeks short of ripeness.

Ximena reached up and touched a few before pulling off one. She chose two more and plucked them. She held the three green lemons in her cupped hands and proffered them to the baby's mother.

"Tonight put one of these against her skin beneath the bottom layer of her clothing while she sleeps. High on her breast, near the shoulder. She'll not be bothered. Do the same tomorrow and the next night, each night a fresh lemon. At dawn of the final night, cut the lemons in quarters and burn them on pine needles with copal. Come by next week to tell me how she's doing."

Ximena and April accompanied the woman and her child back through the house to the front door. Stepping into the street the woman said: *"Usted es buena, 'Ña Ximena. May it work, primero Dios."*

"God willing," said Ximena.

CHAPTER 43: THE PRODIGAL SON, OR WHAT THE DEVIL

The bridge had been washed away the previous week by the river swollen with the season's last rain. It was still too deep to ford. Not even the trucks with chest-high wheels double on the rear axle could make it across, and several of them were parked on the promontory that had been the bridgehead.

Now the only means of crossing was an iron gondola dangling from a rusty cable stretched 40 feet above the brown water. The cable was made fast with old come-alongs anchored to rusty girders, the remains of what had been an unpretentious span. Swirls of froth, a procession of lacy eddies, adorned the river. The current occupied the attention of a few dozen campesinos; men, women and children waiting to climb three or four at a time aboard the iron basket to be transported to the other side. Juan Cano stood among them, just another common Central American man in worn clothes with a battered canvas rucksack on his back.

A campesino about 50 years old sat on a board across the middle of the gondola. He was the vehicle's engine. He wore leather gloves, the palms of which were black and shiny from friction with the cable. His arms were lean with skin like chapped leather. The arms did not look especially muscular but were as strong as those of a mythical hero. Hand over hand across the river, back and forth he hauled the cable-car and its passengers and sacks of rice and beans and sixty-pound bundles of avocadoes in big net purses.

"Once across, is there transport to Arcatao?" Juan asked a woman next to him on the bank.

"Yes," she said. "There is a truck on the other side."

Though he had spent seven years in the hills on the other side of the this river, in and out of the towns and constantly traversing the hamlets, Juan recognized no one in the small crowd. He waited his turn and climbed aboard the rig with a young couple, both of whom wore straw hats. The hats were of genuine straw, not the narrow plastic strips that in recent years had prevailed in the manufacture of woven hats, except in remote pueblos, where most men still used a cowboy-type felt sombrero rather than the billed cap that had become headwear of choice in cities and towns and much of the countryside. The man's hat was older and more ragged than hers but crafted with more skill and detail, with brown straw woven among the pale yellow in patterned bands. Their clothing was clean and patched, worn out from wear and from hundreds of scrubbings against river rocks. Both wore army-style black boots. A canteen made from a gourd hung from his shoulder on loop of hemp twine. The receptacle nestled in a cradle of wire and was plugged at its mouth with a piece of corncob.

The pulley wheel atop the cable creaked with every turn.

On the other side, Juan learned that the truck that made a daily run to Las Vueltas and Ojos de Agua and Arcatao had broken down. He decided to hike. He hooked his thumbs under the canvas straps of his pack and struck out on the trail, which took a more direct route than the rutted road. The straps of his pack tugged at his shoulders and he knew and savored the knowledge that there are many kinds of life and many ways to live. He felt confident that he was a match for whatever might come his way.

A hundred yards up the path he spooked a bird at rest on a low branch. The sudden beat of the black creature's wings was loud and Juan froze, jolted by a surge of the hormonal quintessence of fear that hollows the limbs.

"Holy shit," he whispered.

In an hour he reached another river, a tributary of the Sumpul. Here the campesinos had used split logs, doors, sheets of corrugated zinc and cables to rig a footpath spanning rock and cement pillars they had raised the previous dry season. The water coursed below in clay-colored swirls. After the footbridge came a three hour ascent, slow but steady. By 11 a.m. Juan was soaked with sweat. From the south, behind him, came the drone of an engine and he stopped beneath a tree with fire-red flowers. Out of habit, unnecessary now, he remained hidden beneath the branches to observe the plane's flight. But this was no O-2 spotter or A-37 like those that had menaced him and his comrades during the years of conflict, just a Cessna with businessmen or tourists heading for Tegucigalpa or Copan.

He rested beneath the tree. During the break, Juan thought about the time of *las guindas*, the mass flights of peasants during the war's early years. They had told him, then a green rebel, about how entire uprooted towns had escaped on foot through these northern highlands. The treks lasted weeks. They all went northward, toward the border and what they thought would be safety. The border was not far away, only 20 miles in a straight line from where Juan now sat, but the elderly and children slowed the progress of the harried pilgrims who had to avoid dispersed battalions of soldiers likewise roaming the hills in search of guerrillas and those who sympathized with them. In this part of the country, that meant almost everyone. The peripatetic colonies traveled mostly at night, when they would not be bombed and strafed and rocketed by the old U.S.-made jet-fighters and C-47s and the Huey helicopter gunships.

By the time Juan arrived in 1985, the region had been depopulated by half. Toward the end of the decade, when the war had acquired the characteristics of a stalemate, displaced people and their sons and daughters born in camps on the Honduran side began returning to their ruined towns and villages. With aid from the Catholic archdiocese and international non-governmental organizations, they rebuilt their homes and cleared the brush-covered lands and sowed and harvested. Some of the towns got almost completely back on their feet a few years before the war ended. But they continued to bear the stigma of guerrilla collaborators and were treated as such by the government. Such treatment produced the logical result. In Juan's time in these parts, the army, when it ventured in here, was referred to by most people as *el enemigo*.

Juan resumed his hike. In the hours he'd been on the trail, he had seen only six other people, two groups of two women and a child. They had stopped to chat briefly. The women all wore sandals with thin sponge rubber or plastic soles. One of them had a baby on her back, tied to her with a swatch of cloth. In the second party, one of the woman was five or six months pregnant and carrying a 40-pound child on her shoulders.

By mid-afternoon, the path leveled some and had fewer and rounder rocks. Juan found himself raising his head to look out over verdant valleys and yellow and purple wildflowers instead of at his own muddy boots and what they were treading. He finally reached Arcatao in late afternoon, and tramped dog-tired into the cobblestone plaza.

Ignacio–*Padre Nacho*–was sitting on the steps of the church, so white it smarted the eyes, between a young woman cradling a baby and a young man with a hoe over his shoulder. They interrupted their conversation, which had them all smiling, as if something comical had just been said, to regard the stranger's approach.

"*Buenas tardes, Padre*," said Juan, removing his hat. The priest regarded him for a moment, then he stretched out his arms.

"*?Pero sos el hijo pródigo, o que carajo?*" he asked, embracing Juan. "Are you the prodigal son, or what the devil?"

Ignacio looked younger than his 60 years. He was lean and bushy haired with a gray moustache and salt-and-pepper stubble on the jaw of a tanned face that, for his age and for the fierceness of the sun that had been beating on it for more than three decades, was amazingly unwrinkled. Nothing in his attire indicated he was a priest. He wore blue jeans patched at both knees with black fabric, battered army boots just like those of the father of the baby and a white Texaco t-shirt emblazoned with a red circle around a white star. But even out of vestments, naked even, the priest wore a sort of collar that conferred on him great moral authority. The scar stood out against the suntanned skin as a thin white arc.

Turning to the couple with whom he had been talking: "You'll excuse me, won't you, *compañeros?* We'll baptize the boy Sunday, then."

"*Está bien, padre. Gracias,*" said the mother.

The priest and Juan walked across the square to the rectory where Ignacio lived. It was a large house of adobe block sheathed in stucco and painted the light blue of cornflowers. Inside, the moss-splotched tile roof extended over a stone-paved passage that circumscribed a courtyard. In the courtyard was a well. Beneath the overhang, in the corridor, hung two hammocks. Laundry hung on lines across the bright open center of the house. The rectory, in addition to being Ignacio's abode, was a meeting place for the town council and hostel for the infrequent visitors who sojourned here.

Juan dropped his pack and sat at a wooden table in the shaded broad corridor. Nacho went to the kitchen and returned with a pitcher of cool water and two glasses and poured them both a drink.

"*Mi viejo Clemente,*" said Nacho, looking at the traveler.

Juan almost said, My real name is Juan, but decided against it. Here, he was Clemente.

"They told us that after demobilization you'd gone down to Colombia and joined up with *los muchachos* down there. I know there were a few here who went over to Guate to keep fighting, but I didn't see you as that kind, one who could only be content in the hills, with a rifle."

"Yeah, I went down there," said Juan. "There were always connections between el Frente and *los compas* down there, both the FARC and the ELN. But I didn't go there to live in the bush and fight. It had to do with money we'd paid to the FARC, for some missiles that never were delivered because the war ended. And *el Frente* wanted the money back, for political activity. A long story. Anyway, I got the refund, and got it sent back to our gang. One thing those *compañeros Colombianos* have is money. Lots of it. I ended up staying down there. That's where I've been most of the past three years. There and Panama and Guate."

"Doing what?"

Juan didn't look away from Nacho.

"*Negocios*. Business. But I've quit that now."

CHAPTER 44: RECKLESS *CATRACHOS*

After lunch on the verandah one day, April asked Joe to sit for a session on videotape.

"What do you want me to talk about?"

"About yourself. I mean, the film's about Juan, so somehow it will relate to him. If your part stays in the final cut, there'll be a caption. Like, 'Friend and former comrade.'"

She set up her camera and sat him down in the same chair sometimes occupied by Juan when he was being filmed. She turned it on and left him there.

Joe launched into it. Slowly at first.

"It turned out I wasn't cut out to be a guerrilla fighter in the mountains of Central America. That's not to say you can tell, beforehand, just who is. There were all kinds. The most fertile recruiting grounds were the rural parts of northern and eastern El Salvador, campesino kids, and they made up the bulk of the combatants. *Los milicos*, who acted pretty much as the enforcement arm of the landowners, had been screwing over their parents and grandparents for decades. But there were a lot of former university students, too. Along with kids from towns and small cities. You couldn't really say that just because I was a foreigner, or even a Northern foreigner, that I was too far out of my element to find a niche and a way to embrace the idea of revolution and make it mine. I didn't end up doing that, but it wasn't out of the question, is what I'm saying. There were a dozen *extranjeros* on our front; a couple Chapines, a Mexican couple, both of them doctors, and a few Argentines and *Uruguayos* who'd seen their efforts go very badly down south, but still believed they were the inheritors of El Che. There were three Europeans, too; a German technician on Radio Farabundo Martí. He'd been there for years. And two Basques, ETA guys who made mines and bombs. I liked it while I was doing it. For the first six months, at least. There's a kind of exhilaration in

making a radical change in the way you live, a drastic
overhaul of your daily habits. You see other guys and
women doing it, and you think, I can do that, too. Get
myself on the side of right, fight the good fight against the
bullies who've been taking advantage, making their flags
out of cruelty. So I joined up. Went through basic training,
became comfortable with an assault rifle. I could take it
apart and put it back together in the dark. They're very
captivating pieces of equipment. Solid and finely wrought
and deadly. You become very attached to your gun. And
the camaraderie is like no other you've experienced, even if
you were an athlete and spent a lot of time with teammates.
As I was from age five to 22. It's a tough life, and that's
maybe even part of its... spell, I guess you'd call it. For
weeks on end you get rained on when you're sleeping. You
learn to make a good tent from a tarp or piece of plastic
sheeting, or a lean-to with fronds or banana leaves if you're
gonna be in one place for a week or so. But you're sleeping
on the ground most of the time, on a thin rubber mat, or in
a net hammock. And basically you eat tortillas and beans
every day. And the army, which is bigger than the gang
you're with, wants to kill you, from the ground or from the
sky, with bullets or artillery shells or bombs, they don't
care. But I'll tell you one thing. I sure ain't Juan. Not by a
long shot. I had lunch, *pupusas* and a few beers, at a joint
over by the cemetery with him last week. And he was
talking about why he was going to shoot Alvarez. He was
talking about Camus and the main character in L'Etranger
and ennui and other stuff, and I had to make a fairly
wholesale revision of a sort of scheme of things I thought

I'd worked out, in which Juan was the Man of Action and I guess I was–to some not-very-well-defined extent–the Man of Thought; the academic, the doctor of philosophy, the brusher-away of layers of dirt in a search for meaning. The ponderer. And somehow in that big picture, it had seemed that reflection was the antithesis of action. That seemed to be a natural dichotomy. But he pretty much blew that away for me, because it became clear that Juan, as a man now more mature than the young one I'd known in El Salvador, was as much a thinker as he was a protagonist, that his dynamic was one that led from thought to action and married the two, made an alloy of them stronger than either would be on its own. I tussled with *el Mayor*, and all, yeah. My big claim to fame. But that was pure desperate self-defense. Then I got shot at a few times and shelled by artillery twice while I was with *los muchachos*. Before I actually did get shot, I mean. I was in three operations involving combat, but I never fired my weapon in those skirmishes, was never called on to. Once I was on a patrol and we were ambushed by an army squad west of San Jose las Flores, and we just high-tailed it, though really it was low-tailing, because our escape involved sliding and rolling and half-falling down a steep ravine to get away, the *chafas'* fire coming through the trees from above, bullets going by real close, when you hear this "fffftttt" sound, a sound made of air, like it couldn't hurt you. Until that zipping sound runs smack into a *compa* near you, and kills him. So, it's true, I became a *guerrillero*. I was always going to be distinct, because I was a Gringo and white and older and a university professor and also because I was the one guy in the whole world who had actually clamped my hands on the throat of Ricardo Paniagua and battered his head against the ground. But even so, I did pretty much the same things as everybody else, lived the same life. I got the foot-rot fungus they all say makes you a bona fide insurgent, a fucking torment of redness with white spots between your toes and on the top of the foot that itches like a sonofabitch, and we were out of fungicide on our front when I got it so I had to use a folk-remedy of footbaths in a solution made from bark. And I got into what was probably the best physical shape of my life, if you measure that by proportion of fat to muscle, the kind of stringy muscle guerrillas are made of, and had great stamina. Because being a member of an irregular army means a lot of walking up and down hills for hours with a pack on your back. And not eating a hell of a lot. But I'm coming to this watershed thing, the reason I decided to quit. It came near the end of a medical resupply detail up to the Honduran border. We had *compañeros* in Honduras who would buy stuff–antibiotics, analgesics, quinine, fungicide, gauze, syringes and de-worming medicine–for us in Tegucigalpa or San Pedro Sula and transport it down to the border, to a rendezvous point in the boonies along the Sumpul away from any Honduran customs or immigration post. And we'd pick up maybe 200 pounds of this stuff at a time, four or five guys, and bring it back to our front, which was commanded by Raúl, the same guy who had sent me over to Morazán for the month after I'd first shown up. He was my *comanche* the whole time I was there. And was Juan's too, until Juan took command of a group of his own on a stretch over near Cabañas. One day

Raúl says to me, 'Hey Joe, you up for some heavy humping?' And I said sure. 'I want you to go with Lalo up to the border to pick up some medicine and shit. You'll be back in a few days.' So the next day I and two young guys and Lalo, a veteran, struck out at dawn. We carried only rifles and packs holding a poncho, a sweater, eight tortillas each, a packet of salt and two sandwich-sized plastic bags, one of powdered milk and one of sugar, which mixed together in small doses provided energy and curbed appetite. We walked fast, almost due north, and I kept up fine. We climbed for four or five hours then traversed a long stretch of high plateau with dense stands of tall pine. We stopped at midday the first day to rest and eat in a pine forest where two men were sawing planks from a huge trunk. The men stopped work to sit on the stack of boards they'd already sawed to shoot the breeze with us. Before we continued on our way, one of the sawyers climbed back onto the log scaffold supporting the trunk. He took hold with both hands of the handle of a six-foot-long big-toothed saw they'd left stuck in its furrow. The other man took hold of the handle below. Both were bare-chested. The man up top, standing on the same log he was sawing, pulled up until the handle was higher than his head, then the man below pulled down so that about five feet of saw bit into the wood. Up again, then down. Coarse sawdust fell like snow from the slice in the tree. I watched the stringy muscles ripple in the men's arms and shoulders and their backs and I remember thinking, They'll do that for an hour straight without pause and I know for a fact that after three minutes of it I'd have a knot in my back so painful it would be impossible to continue. That night we got rained on. It was cold. I hardly slept. I stood a *posta* like the other three. From 2 to 4 a.m. I sat on a rock about 15 yards from where the others were curled up on the ground in their ponchos. My teeth chattered as I looked out from beneath my poncho hood through the drizzle and the branches dripping in the dark. Not that an army patrol was likely to be walking around this far north at this hour in the rain. But what would I do if I heard something? I told myself I would cover the short distance between me and my comrades as quietly as possible and rouse them. Then I'd do whatever Lalo told me to do, or just follow his lead. If that meant shooting at the other guys, well, fuck it; they would be shooting at me. If it came to that, I figured I could do it. But no patrol came. We walked into Arcatao at mid-afternoon. Lalo hooked up with the local jefe, an old buddy of his who took us to a partially bombed out house on the edge of town where the supplies were stored. We separated what was going to go back with us, Lalo cajoling his friend and managing to wrangle more for our front than the local commander had planned on parting with. We had a big meal of tortillas and beans and fried eggs that evening and spent a dry night under a roof. At some point, Lalo swings out of his sack in the half light. 'Tweak your hard-ons, boys. We've got a long march ahead of us,' he says. We ate some tortillas, drank some coffee and shouldered the heavy packs, about 30 kilos apiece. We had to climb out of the valley and back over the highest ridges before beginning the descent. By midday we were on a rocky path making a long gradual descent of one side of Cerro Buitre toward the

Rio Sucio. Way up ahead a firefight had broken out, an exchange of M-16 and AK fire that made us stop and listen. It was probably three or four kilometers away but sounded nearer because the reports were being funneled back to us by the hillsides above the river. 'Fuck that,' said Lalo. 'Break time.' He left the path and went uphill. The three of us followed him to a stand of *quebracho* about 20 yards above the path. We all dumped our packs and sat on the ground. 'We're not going anywhere until we're sure it's all clear up ahead,' says Lalo. We'd been sitting there for about 15 minutes. Sporadic fire was still being exchanged to the west, but it was diminishing and seemed to be getting farther away. Then from the east came a faint rumble. Lalo and the two young guerrillas jumped up and looked in the direction of the noise. It grew louder with each second. I got up too. Lalo pushed the safety of his AK down one notch and pulled back the crescent on the bolt to chamber a round. The other two did the same. The slaps of metal against metal sent a charge through me and I felt a numbness and a tingling as I locked and loaded my G-3. 'Everybody on automatic,' says Lalo. 'If that fucker comes within range we're going to blast hell out of it. Spread out and get as clear a line as you can through the trees. Don't fucking shoot each other.' The growl of the chopper fattened to a roar. We were all pointing our rifles at about 30 degrees, more toward the opposite mountainside than toward the sky, sighting through gaps in the trees. The noise in the next several seconds became deafening, like a flash flood in the instant before it knocks you over, and we saw to our left the big dark open-sided thing only a hundred meters away, huge and zooming along the river between the hillsides as if there was no war going on down on the ground. Lalo opened up. We all did, in an acrid smoky riot of explosions. The four muzzles spewed flash in a synchronized pan. The chopper went by only a little higher than where we stood–our gun barrels were only slightly above level–and we saw the bullets strike the cockpit plexiglass and spark where they hit the rotor and we saw them go through the open doorway and pierce the fuselage. Not a couple lucky shots but dozens of bullets riddling the thing. Tatters of leaves and twigs rained down in front of us and we stopped firing and ran through the brush to keep the thing in sight and we saw it rock crazily then veer left and, about 300 yards ahead, crash through the trees, a super-loud crunch of splintering timbers and compacting metal. The other three guys loosed a banshee howl. Lalo, his fist around the stock, pumped his rifle over his head, screaming. He jumped into the air but fell when he landed on the slippery grade and tumbled several feet down. He scrambled to his feet like an ocelot and the two other rebels and I followed him down to the path, heedless of branches switching our chest and face. There was no fire or smoke coming from the crash. Only a rip in the thick foliage. All four of us stood there panting. Lalo says: 'Chino, you come with me. You two'–addressing me and the other guy, I forget his name–'get the packs and bring them down to right across from where it went in. But stay on this side of the river.' They ran off. Fifteen minutes later the kid and I were sitting in the riverside brush with the four packs when Chino appeared high on the opposite bank. 'Joe!' I stood up. 'Lalo says to bring a pack with bandages and morphine.' I knew some of each had been put in my pack so I hoisted it and sloshed across the river, then scrambled up the hill behind Chino. In five minutes we reached the crash site. The tail had broken off and was 30 yards from the crumpled and torn fuselage. Several trees were snapped in half like pencils. I went to Lalo, who was standing over a row of four bodies he and Chino had dragged from the wreck. One was a machine-gunner. He wore a green zippered overall and his body was intact, only the chest was soaked maroon. One of the others was in fatigues. Part of the side of his head was missing and his red-streaked pearl-gray brain spilled out on the ground. The other two bodies were wrecked. They weren't particularly bloody. Though they'd been laid out in an approximate configuration of a person, their segments were connected at impossible angles, like they were made of pipe-cleaners. But that was not the strangest thing. It was their uniforms. They wore dress tunics with brass buttons and ribbons over the breast pocket and creased pants and polished black shoes instead of boots. One was a colonel, with three stars on his epaulet. The other was a major, with one.

Lalo stood over them. 'I don't fucking believe it,' he said softly. 'I don't fucking believe it.'

'What?' I asked. '*Son Catrachos.* Stupid motherfucking Catrachos.' I didn't know the meaning of the word. '*Catrachos?*' '*Hondureños,*' Lalo said. We tried to save the life of a lieutenant colonel, the only one of the eight aboard not killed by either rifle fire or the crash. The bodies of the pilot and co-pilot and other *artillero* were an integral part of the crushed metal and impossible to extract. It looked for a while like Lt. Col. Arias–we could see the nametag on his chest–was going to die of his injuries right where he remained trapped. His shattered legs were jammed under the pilot's seat. The barrel of an M-16 had punctured his thorax and the rifle was sticking out of him like a spear. He was half conscious though deep in shock. Quiet most of the time, every once in a while he moaned and pleaded. A stream of fuel was leaking onto his back from a ruptured tank. Lalo had tried to stanch the flow with a wadded bandanna, but that had not worked. '*Venite*, Joe,' he said. We leaned into the strange new configuration of what had been the inside of the aircraft. The floor was buckled in steep waves. The fumes made us woozy. 'Think it will blow up?' I asked. 'I don't think so. But there must be a big fucking battery or something for the electrical system and I don't want to be around if there's a spark. So fuck it, man. Let's make one good try. And if we can't, well, we can't. He doesn't look like he's going to make it anyway.' Lalo squeezed behind the wounded man into the only space that afforded any maneuverability. He could squat and get his hands under Arias' arms, though that meant Lalo was now taking the piss of fuel down his own collar. Some of the weight of the dead pilot and the wreckage pressing on him would have to be lifted at least a little if Lalo was going to pull him out. So I went around to what was left of the front of the cockpit. I managed to get a grip on one of the bars supporting the pilot's seat and plant my feet, a position that would allow me to get some back into the lifting. The seatback had been flattened forward and the dead pilot was folded so his head was on his knees. His helmeted head was turned sideways, outward, so that to lift, I had to put my face against the dead man's cool face. 'On three,' I said to Lalo. 'You count.' Lalo counted and on three I strained my legs and back and arms. The seat rose slightly and Lalo got Arias' legs halfway out. 'Once more,' said Lalo. I'd felt something give in my back. But when Lalo said '*tres*'' again, I pulled up and Lalo hauled Arias free. We dragged him to a spot beneath a *balsamo* tree. Arias, his head propped against a root, groaned and took hold of the rifle and made a weak effort to pull it out. But the high-rising sight was like a barb on an arrowhead. It didn't budge. Lalo injected him with morphine. Since the Honduran was conscious, Lalo asked him his unit and his mission. 'Don't know. Don't know,' said Arias. '*Ayudenme, por favor. Tengo dos hijas pequeñas.*' He knew he wasn't gonna get an answer, but Lalo asked him what the fuck they were doing flying through Salvadoran air space, especially this part of the country, which they knew was a fucking war zone. '*No sé,*' the poor guy whispered. Those were his last words. He lost consciousness. A couple minutes later he died. The four of us spent that night on a mountaintop three hours' walk from the crash site. Lalo was finally able to make radio contact from there with our camp near Las Flores using the compact Yaesu wrapped in plastic and attached to the strap of his pack. In code, he reported the downing of the helicopter to Raúl. After a few minutes, when the message had been deciphered, the zone commander, foregoing code, says, '*Putisima madre, 'mano.*' Airwave security was a moot point by then. News of the downing was being broadcast throughout the region and the Salvadoran air force was at the crash site with another helicopter. 'That was you guys?' 'How the hell were we supposed to know?' Lalo says.

'*Tranquilo, hombre.* Nobody's blaming you. Any Huey with guns is fair game around here. They were on their way home from a conference of Central American brass in San Salvador. Should never have taken that route. *Por pendejos murieron los Catrachos.*'

'The Catrachos died of stupidity.'

That was what he said."

Joe stopped talking. He'd been looking away half the time during this monologue, at the walls or out the window, directing his eyes only intermittently back to the lens. Now he stood up and stretched.

"April!" he hollered. "I'm done!" He stepped over and turned the thing off.

CHAPTER 45: ON THE STREET OF REFUSE DISPOSAL

Juan perched 30 feet up on an old broken church wall.

Dark wooded hills rose to the west and north and east. The strip of them against the violet-tinged sky connected Acatenango to Fuego and from there ran behind him southward to Agua, green on massive dark green becoming black. The nearly complete circle of hills conspired with the jagged pieces of temple and parts of arch and span strewn below him to make this place, this Valley of Panchoy, an isolated puzzle piece of the world.

The great blocks of brick and mortar had gouged the earth when tumbled by the planet's bucking crust. But the passage of two centuries is a balm, and the wounds were now grassy beds, places of repose for truck-sized chunks of edifice resting at haphazard angles.

Juan was not the sole surveyor of the expanse behind the market on the southwestern edge of Antigua. About 250 meters opposite him, slightly to his right, across the road beyond the two bald unlined unfenced soccer fields, on the wall of the station-house of the *Bomberos Voluntarios*, was an advertisement for the big Salvadoran snack company Diana, whose products and their empty dusty cellophane packages were ubiquitous along roadsides and in market squares throughout Central America. The painted ad was composed simply of large yellow letters spelling DIANA on a rectangular red background and a portrait of a smiling girl who had either just enjoyed or was savoring the prospect of enjoying some corn chips or cheese puffs.

This rosy-cheeked girl, the only other steady unperturbed observer of the scene, was Juan's compatriot. (A Diana billboard girl could not but be Salvadoran.) He enjoyed the idea that she, along with April and Joe, would be a witness.

The roof of the collapsed temple was the sky, against which Juan crouched atop a jagged segment of the ruined building's southern wall.

The crumbled church's formal name was *El Colegio de Cristo Crucificado de Misiones Apostólicas de Propaganda Fide.*

It was known by the townspeople, 280 years ago and now, as *La Recolección* because it had sat, during the few months of 1717 when it existed intact, on the street from which wagons that collected the town's trash departed each morning and to which they returned when full.

The Apostolic Missions had begun its construction in 1701, under the direction of *el criollo* José de Porres. His son Diego took over during the second decade of work and saw it through to consecration. Ten weeks after the first Mass, the earth shook. The temple cracked and yawed and tilted and rained shards of plaster on altar and pews. Though still standing, it was declared unfit for worship and beyond repair. Fifty-six years passed before the ground heaved and shifted again, more violently than before. The roof and most of the facade and the upper portions of the rear and side walls crashed down.

The arch over the main entrance remained standing. Visitors to the ruin passed beneath it, then up a stairway into what had been the atrium. With its high octagonal windows, elaborately ridged and ribbed through the breadth of cracked walls, and half of its scrolled high white molding undisturbed, the ruin was as beautiful as it must have been when unscathed. A huge spreading *jaboncillo* tree stood in front of the eastern half of the facade, shading the grassy grounds.

The Sacatepaquez provincial government had decided to build a new stadium on the open few hectares behind the market across *la calle de los Recolectos*. It was to be a showcase facility, and would host the qualifying trials for the national Olympic track-and-field team for the 2000

Olympic Games in Sydney. A cornerstone ceremony was scheduled for a week from this sunny Saturday on which Juan had vaulted the adobe wall on the San Antonio road and come through the 150 meters of wood and brush to the base of the ruin at its rear.

Col. Abelardo Alvarez, the recently retired Kaibil commander and, even at the age of 51, one of the nation's top ten marathoners, was to take part in the groundbreaking in his capacity as National Olympic Committee co-chairman.

Juan had come across this bit of information while reading *La Prensa Grafica*. He'd sat for some minutes studying the photograph of Col. Alvarez, a reprint of the portrait that had been on the cover of *Crónica*. He got up from his chair on the veranda and went to the hammock in the rear garden where April was resting. He found her awake, hands behind her head, staring up into the branches of a live oak.

He put his hand on her knee. "You know, if you changed your mind it wouldn't change what we've got going. I wouldn't think less of you, is what I'm trying to say."

"But you'd still do it." It wasn't quite a question. "I mean, even if I pulled out."

"Yeah. The film is your trip. I'm not doing it for you."

Joe had been there, ten days ago, at dinner with them when Juan revealed his intention to kill this man.

"But the war's over," Joe had said.

"In El Salvador, yeah. It's just off the world's radar here," was Juan's response. "These fuckers wiped everyone out. Napalm and scorched earth and concentration camps. They killed a hundred thousand civilians, ten times the number of *desaparecidos* in Argentina, and this country has a fifth of Argentina's population. But because those kids down there were white and looked like Europeans or Americans on the photographs their mothers carried around the Plaza de Mayo, that got them lots of space in U.S. and European newspapers, and the world made an outcry about it. Here, because the people being massacred were Indians, the world barely gave a shit. This country is the goddamn Rwanda of the Americas."

Juan now settled his butt into the hammock but remained sitting. He pushed the floor with his toes and the couple swung slightly. "Look, *corazón*, for almost five months I've spent my days gardening and reading and watching movies and listening to music. *Ya basta de eso.* I like the idea of a mission. And if it involves some risk, then I can't deny that increases its appeal. It was like that in the war, and it was like that in Colombia and Panama and Mexico these last couple years in the drug game. This guy who ran over Paco and me thinks he's a god. And once I realized who he was, the massacres he committed, well, he's such a piece of scum that his continued breathing disgusts me. What kind of man, *que clase de cerote*, goes out of his way to smash a fine musical instrument that it took somebody a lot of time and effort to make?" He eased down so that they were pressed against each other their entire lengths. "But that doesn't mean you have to be a part of it."

She shifted so that they were face to face. She caressed his cheek. "I want to be a part of it. Even if it's just as a kind of reporter. And a witness."

"Well," he said, bringing up from his side the folded newspaper he'd had in his hand throughout their talk. "It looks like it's gonna be sooner rather than later. And you'll get on film more than you thought. Not just planning and preparations. The whole *tamal*. As it happens."

"What do you mean? Tape you killing him?"

He showed her the article about the cornerstone ceremony.

"It's gonna be right out in the open, behind the market. He's supposed to give a little speech. A stage and a band, everything. Like a film set, arranged just for you."

High now on the wall of a wrecked temple, Juan felt like something of an Olympian himself, a Greek one poised with a javelin, or a thunderbolt, looking out over the panorama he intended to disturb. He thought of April, and recalled how he used to evaluate some of the new recruits, those untested by battle, on the eve of an operation.

"She's ready," he said out loud, to no one.

And now that he'd found an excellent spot, he was close to being ready, too.

CHAPTER 46: BOVINE ZPG

(The Gardener, take 12)

I know this is supposed to be about me. But I don't want to talk about me today. I want to talk about Nacho. Now there would be a guy worth making a film about, or writing a book about.

I was over there with him for a few days last week, and I've been thinking about him a lot. Right off the bat, he asked me what brought me back up there. And I started to give him some bullshit about wanting to see how things were going, revisit the old stomping grounds. But it sounded so phony it was making me sick as soon as I started, so I just told him, "I've got to dig up *el Dragón*, because there's a *cerote* over in Guate I'm going to shoot." He eventually would have something to say about that. But he didn't get much of a chance to let it sink in, right then, because as we were sitting there drinking water–I'd only been there about 15 minutes–the door that gave onto the plaza slammed and a boy came running across el patio. He stops and, all out of breath, says, "Padre, the calf is breeched. My father asks that you come." Well, besides being a priest, Ignacio is a doctor. That's the main reason the Jesuits sent him up there 30 years ago, an all-purpose tender to both body and soul. And that makes him a veterinarian too, for the rare times when campesinos, who generally know what to do with their animals, need one. So Ignacio says to me, "Come on," and I followed him and the boy out. We walked, stepping lively, the four blocks to where the town ended. Beyond that was hillside farmland and pasture. We followed the boy to where his father and uncle were standing over a black cow lying on her side in the grass. The uncle was an ex-*compa* and recognized me and said something like, *"Puta,* Clem, *q'hubo"* but didn't offer me his hand which had blood on it almost up to the elbow, and he and everybody, us too, was so intent on the cow on the ground and the problem that was maybe going to kill both her and the calf. The father's hands were on his hips, his sleeves rolled up to his biceps and both of his forearms were covered with blood-streaked slime. The uncle held a rope that was tied around the two hooves the men had managed to wrestle from the cow's womb. They were both breathing hard, staring, perplexed. "Totally stuck," said the father. "We tried to get it turned right and finally said Fuck it and were willing to lose the calf, break her if we had to by just pulling her out, but we can't even do that. If you can't get it out, we'll have to bring a mule over to pull it out. I don't want to lose the cow. She gives 15 bottles a day." Ignacio kneeled beside the cow, positioned himself and reached inside. His arm went in past the elbow and he had to lean forward with his face pressed against her flank. He shifted his jaw and twisted his mouth and stuck out his tongue like maybe the correct contortion of his face would help line up the baby right. After a minute or two he exhaled loudly and slumped. His head rested on the cow's hide. He closed his eyes for a couple seconds, then opened them. "I've got the head but can't get a good grip," he said. Then he grunted and heaved and his arm went from the bottom of the cow's vagina to the top and began to withdraw, followed by the calf's head. The boy's father knelt next to Ignacio and the two grabbed the animal by the ears and pulled it from its mother. The pearly red-streaked sack was still around most of the calf, which kind of coughed and started breathing. The uncle, who in the hills had been called Hugo, I don't know his real name, untied the rope from around the hooves, and the cow, without getting up, shifted to where she could nuzzle the panting wet bundle of hide and bones. She licked it clean in a couple minutes. Hugo lifted the shiny calf's leg. *"Es hembra,"* he said, and smiled. So did his brother. After a few minutes, both the calf and the mother struggled to their feet. The newborn found the teat and began suckling. "I could use a drink of something too," says Hugo, and we all went back to his brother's house and everybody who'd had his hand inside the cow washed up and we all had a swig of *guaro*. They invited us to stay to eat, but Nacho tells them, 'Some other time. Bernardo Calderón is barbecuing a *novillo* to celebrate the birth of his first male grandson after two girls. I told him I'd do the slaughtering and since I've got blood on my shirt today anyway, I might as well do it now." So off we go, he and I. We go back across town, which is only about eight blocks, to where the Calderóns lived. I didn't know any of them, because they'd left Arcatao when the war started, gone to Cabañas which wasn't much better but a little, then they'd come back after the war to fix up the old house and work their land around here. The proud grandfather, who was only a few years older than me, around 35, was standing on the porch with the baby, which was wrapped tight like a cocoon in a white cotton blanket.

The baby was stretched out on Calderón's forearm and he was fanning it with his straw hat. "Padre! Check out the apparatus on this little guy," he shouts when he sees Ignacio, and lays the baby down on a table and unwraps the swaddling. The grandfather was a little drunk. With his thick fingers he separated the baby's pink thighs. "There's a righteous pair of balls for you," he says, all proud. Ignacio gives him the once over and says he looks to be in good shape and promises to bring his bag over the next day and check him out thoroughly. The old man offers us *guaro*, and Nacho says, "Well, seeing how there's a new human being to welcome into this vale of tribulation, we'd probably be remiss if we didn't have a belt." We passed around a bottle of *chaparro* and each took a slug. Then we followed Calderon around the corner of the house to where he had the young bull tied to a tree. He was a very good looking hefty cream-colored animal, standing there on the cobblestones, eating some carrot tops. I thought, He doesn't know that's his last meal. And I realized that although I'd seen men, several of them, take their last breath and stop being alive, I had never observed the practiced and purposeful killing of an animal. We didn't eat all that much meat in the hills, but it wasn't like we never had it, either. Every once in a while an animal, a goat or a cow if there were a lot of us or it was a fiesta or something, would be killed and we'd make a huge stew or have *un asado*. But I'd never seen the killing. There were still lots of guns in Arcatao, but no bullet was spent. Ignacio took the same rope that tethered the bull to the tree and looped it around his front hooves then around his rear hooves, then pulled the front and rear feet together with a tug so that the animal fell on its side on the street. The bull, in his eyes, showed the first sign of wondering what the fuck was going on. More like confusion than fear. But his eyes widened when Calderon wrapped the rope, the same one binding the feet, around the horns then under the jaw and pulled back on it and worked it around the tree trunk. He pulled with all his might and the bull's head arched back. He snorted and tried to kick and shift but was immobilized. The angle of his head meant he couldn't see Ignacio, who'd picked up a medium-sized knife that seemed to Juan small for the task at hand. He walked around and squatted at the bull's throat. He patted the loose skin of the neck, searching for the main artery and when he found it he touched the tip of the knife to it and just slid it in. A little girl ran over with a blue plastic basin to catch the thick stream of blood. The bull's sounds had drawn children out of Calderon's house and the nearby houses. About a dozen kids, from toddlers to adolescents, stood around watching, fascinated. Like me. The ribcage heaved and the mouth lathered and the wide honey-colored eye, the one we could see, gleamed. When the basin was about half full, the light in the eye started to go out. Over the next minute, the eye grew duller and the stream thinned to a trickle, then to drops. The eye looked like it was covered with plastic film. It was obvious it couldn't see anything anymore. A child whispered: " *Está muerto.*" Other kids standing around said, in hushed voices, "*Está muerto.*" Calderon put an edge on his machete with a stone from his pocket. He cut off the bull's head, then its hooves with about eight inches of leg above them, for *sopa de patas.* Ignacio did the rest. He sliced the skin down each leg and cut along the belly and peeled the hide off the carcass, tugging it and cutting it loose from the subcutaneous fat, shifting the dead animal until he had in his hands the entire hide. He set it aside in a wet bundle. With the same knife he'd used to puncture the artery, the only one he would use in the whole process, he cut through a thick membrane to open the cavity containing the organs. The bluish intestines spilled out in a pool of blood that hadn't drained, and Ignacio cut them from the stomachs, which would be simmered in a *mondongo* stew or go into the *sopa de patas.* Then he cut out the liver, the kidneys and the heart, which he set on the hide. He removed the lungs and tossed them with the intestines to the skinny dogs that had been trying to approach to lick up the blood but were kept away by the children's well-aimed stones. The removal of the penis, a long and sinewy thing that would be dried and cured and used as a whip, and testicles, which would be grilled and eaten by the men, brought grimaces and laughter from the kids. Then Ignacio cut up the carcass, severing the legs at the top joint, cutting out the long loin along the spine and slicing off hunks of meat from the flank and shoulder and rump. He handed big pieces, with and without vertebrae and ribs, to a woman in a flowered shift, Mrs. Calderón, I guess it was, who carried them in a plastic basin to the cooking area beneath the overhang at the side of the house, where she hung it on hooks dangling from the rafters.

Forty minutes after he'd pushed the knife into the taut throat, Ignacio stood over a dark spot on the cobbled street and a wet velvety hide wrapped around the liver, kidneys and heart, all that remained there of the cream-colored baby bull.

CHAPTER 47: THE PUMPKIN-SMASHING DRAGON

Juan shut off the 4-Runner's motor.

"That day we met? At Tony's place?" he said. He had pulled off the dirt track onto a level patch on the lower slopes of Agua, the biggest of the three volcanoes surrounding Antigua. He and April sat there in the car, a couple kilometers beyond San Juan del Obispo. The Panchoy Valley spread below them. The San Francisco Church and the dome of Capuchinas were recognizable in the grid of Antigua seven kilometers away.

"Yeah?" said April.

"You didn't have your camera with you, when the bank guard shot that guy."

"Nope."

"And that was unusual, wasn't it? Most of the time you carry it around with you."

"So?"

"Do you regret that? I mean, do you wish you would've had it? To film, however coincidentally, the killing of that man?"

April reached over and turned the key, which remained dangling in the ignition, a half turn. She pressed the button that lowered her window. She reached again and flipped the key back. A little haphazard orchard of *nisperos* stood across the track. There was no fruit on the trees. The broad leaves in the breeze made a sound like running water.

"I probably would have shot it, the argument. And I guess the aftermath, too," she finally answered. "It's kind of a fucked-up thing to do. But I probably would have done it." She took a pack of cigarettes from the dash and lit one, blowing smoke in a stream out the window. "I'm kind of fucked-up that way, I think."

"And if you'd filmed that scene, and the guy's last breath, you might not be all that into this Alvarez thing. Don't you think?"

"Maybe. Who knows? I'm better at posing questions than answering them. I guess I won't know until I see Alvarez go down. Then watch the playback a few times and see how it makes me feel."

She opened her door and got out and opened the rear door on her side and took her camera from the seat.

"They're very different, though," she said. "The sidewalk thing was happenstance. Random violence. This is planned and pre-meditated."

"Does that make you an accomplice?"

"Of course."

"OK," said Juan, getting out of the truck. He went to the rear and opened the door and unrolled the blanket wrapped around the Dragunov.

It was impossible to confuse it with another sort of weapon. Not like Oswald's Mannlicher, which would not have been incongruous over the shoulder of some old

Czech farmer in the hills after deer or boar. This piece of craftsmanship had been designed and fashioned exclusively for one group of men's deadly struggle with another group of men.

It had been made by the Soviet State Arsenal at Izhevsk in the days when there still was a Soviet State and that state was supplying the Nicaraguan armed forces. In the mid-80s los compañeros Sandinistas had given 200 "Dragons" to the ERP in Morazán, and within several months *los Erpios* spread them around to the other organizations in the FMLN. Almost every front in the country counted a few in its arsenal.

They had proved especially effective against helicopters. Or rather, against the pilots of choppers, who, during landings and take-offs, were susceptible to having a bead drawn on their chest by a steady-handed skinny campesino kid behind a rock or a roof-top water tank a quarter-mile away.

The thing was a stretched AK, basically. The pistol-type grip was the same as the Kalashnikov' s. But the barrel was much longer, 25 inches, and the magazine smaller, as fire was to be delivered only in single shots. The clip held ten long cartridges, each with enough powder to send the 7.62mm x 54rim bullet rocketing out of the muzzle at 830 meters per second.

The manuals listed its effective range at 1,000 meters with the open sight, and 1,300 meters with a scope like the one screwed onto this gun that Juan had brought back from El Salvador. That was something of a hypothetical limit, attainable perhaps with an exceptional shooter accompanied by perfect conditions and a little luck. Even so, someone with a certain aptitude and practice could use it on a still day to put a bullet in the chest of a man four soccer fields away.

It was three-and-a-half feet long. One dry season in Chalatenango, Juan had fired four or five rounds–not at anyone, just messing around–with another model of the same gun with a folding butt. But this one had *la culata esqueleto,* a frame-like "skeleton" stock of dark smooth wood. With the sight and the strap it weighed a little over 10 pounds.

Juan lifted the gun and cradled it in his left arm then grabbed the short curved stem of a pumpkin sitting against the wheel-well. "Let's see if this thing still works," he said, and walked off on a path through the scrub.

April, who'd been filming since he opened the back door, panned slowly to follow him for a few seconds, then panned further and zoomed to her widest angle for a panoramic shot of the valley.

She cut and caught up to him and they walked a couple hundred meters to the edge of a *milpa.* Last season's cornstalks, dried beige, had been broken and bent double like rows of praying pilgrims. Juan stopped and looked up to his left toward the summit of Agua draped in three layers of gauze. The rest of the sky was the most limpid blue. Oddly, it had rained for an hour the previous day, the effect of the tail of an unseasonal tropical storm in Oaxaca. This day had dawned so brilliantly clear that Acatenango and Fuego seemed within a few long leaps.

A dozen pines stood another 300 or so meters further up the gentle slope. Juan looked around for a good place to put the pumpkin. A young avocado tree 20 meters down the path bordering the cornfield had a fork about chest high. He walked down to it and wedged the pumpkin there.

He and April walked together up the hill toward the pines. About halfway there, beside a large boulder, Juan stopped.

"Let's try a couple from here," he said. "See if I've still got an eye."

He had filled the magazine, though he hoped to use only a few of the ten rounds to get the sight adjusted. He clicked off the safety and pulled back the hook of the bolt and released it to push the first shell into the firing chamber. His heart beat faster, though his breathing remained steady. April had stepped back a few meters and was filming.

Juan leaned forward against the boulder. He shifted until he found a comfortable position, left forearm against the stone, the hand that gripped the stock brushing the rock. His right cheek pressed against the butt. He smelled the oil he'd used to clean the gun. He tried to remember, from the rounds he'd fired years ago, how much kick this thing had. The telescope was long, the opening of the eyepiece an inch from Juan's eye.

The pumpkin sat in the center of the bright circle. He trained the crosshairs on it. It seemed hard to miss. He inhaled. He let the air out slowly and at the end of the breath, in the stillness before he would breathe again, he squeezed the trigger.

The crack stung his ears and expanded and deepened as it rolled down the mountainside. Juan had known it was going to be loud and had prepared himself for it. But still, it was fucking loud.

The pumpkin sat there. Not perforated. Not grazed.

April pressed the Stop button and lowered the camera. "Holy shit," she said. "Somebody's gonna hear that."

"Yeah," said Juan, looking over the rifle down the hill at the tiny orange target. "But nobody will care. They'll think they're cherry bombs, for somebody's saint's day or birthday."

April looked downhill. "Did you hit it?"

"Fuck no. Not it, or the *pinche* tree either." Still peering down toward the tree, he said, "Could you leave off filming? You're gonna have to spot for me."

"OK. But I can't see much from here."

"Go down a little more than halfway and stand off to the right."

She went back down 100 meters, her camera slung across her back.

Juan sighted again and fired.

"It hit the ground behind the tree. Quite a ways. Twenty or 30 yards," shouted April.

Juan turned the elevation knob on the sight. "OK," he called down.

"Ready," she cried.

Before the next report stopped ringing she was shouting, "It hit the tree! The side of the tree! A chunk flew off!"

Juan had seen the impact through the sight. Below the pumpkin, low and to the left.

"Yeah. Come back up if you want, it's pretty close now." He made a fine adjustment of the drop compensation mechanism. When he looked up, instead of seeing April trudging nearer, he saw her farther off, nearly down to the avocado tree.

"Tell me when you're ready again," she shouted.

"Ya!" he yelled. He watched her position herself 10 meters this side of the tree, several steps to the right of the line of fire. A few seconds after she'd shouldered her camera, Juan again took aim.

The next bullet blew the top third, stem and all, off the squash.

April walked back up to Juan. They picked up the ejected shells, then went together up to the pines, another 150 yards. Juan fired two more rounds from there, fine-tuning the sight. Only a few chunks of rind and a stringy orange mess remained in the tree.

Afterward they sat on a bed of rust-colored pine needles. They were high enough above the valley floor to be on a plane with a dozen distant buzzards soaring above something far off dead or dying.

"Are you upset by the sight of your own blood?"

"No," said Juan.

"I thought so," she said. "Me neither."

"And?"

"*No es nada.* Some people are. Then there are others who are no more bothered by seeing their blood than they are by seeing their urine or spit. And I was just thinking, it must be something in a person's constitution. Like whether or not they can carry a tune." She went on. "And there must be people who can never get over the act of killing a person, even if it was in wartime, officially approved and everything. That it becomes a great burden. Something that makes them wake up jittery at three in the morning."

"And you're wondering where I fit into that scheme."

"I'm pretty sure I know."

Juan stuck a pine needle between his bottom front teeth. He worked it back and forth a bit, then took it out and said: "I don't suffer pangs of conscience. Not that I didn't think about it, or that it meant nothing. I'm not a psychopath. But I knew what I was doing when I killed that cop. I don't consider myself a murderer.

"But maybe it is like you say. Somehow part of the hard wiring. It wasn't that difficult for me. Even though I was taken over by a desire for revenge, there was something detached, too, through all of it.

"I never feared death. Not as a kid and not as a combatant. That does not mean I'm brave. But when you're built like that, it makes it easier, I guess, to take someone else's life. And not dream about it. I read something once, I don't even remember who it was who said it; a general, who became a statesman. In the 1800s I think. Anyway this guy said death was no more and no less than passing from one room to another in his father's house. And even though

I never had a father, and am not quite convinced there's a God, that's how I feel about it, too.

"It's not like I killed someone who if it weren't for me was never gonna die. It's something he owed, like everyone owes, including you and me. I just called in Sudek's chit sooner. Jumped him to the front of the line. Like I'm gonna do with Alvarez. Move up his passage from room to room."

CHAPTER 48: A COMFORT JUST KNOWING

(The Gardener, take 15)

For some reason I'm more comfortable doing this now; being taped as I talk. It's not too far off now. This thing that will be the climax of April's film.

Fuck me. If that doesn't sound weird. I mean, you catch yourself saying some strange shit. Here I'm gonna kill this fucker, and it sounds like I'm looking at it as a movie. I don't plan on dying in the course of doing this. I've gone over everything, all the tactical aspects, and they're in line. I did this kind of thing for several years, remember. Helped plan missions that involved people getting killed. And you definitely develop a sort of intuition in the days before as to how well things have been thought through. I mean, even if they were well planned, sometimes you have a gut feeling about the prospects. Sometimes you suspect things are going to get all fucked up and go haywire and people will die needlessly. That happens. It happened a couple times over the years, in operations that were my responsibility.

The only thing is, even when you have that feeling, if you've done everything you can in terms of preparation, you have to just go ahead and try to carry out the mission. Because you can't go to your superiors and say: "I've got a bad feeling about this." It's not a valid argument. In a military sense. Here I've got no superiors. This is my deal. And I've got close to zero apprehension about things going wrong. I'm confident it's going to come off pretty smoothly. But, shit. A lot of guys have thought that. Then a day later they're lying on the ground staring at the sun, swelling up and not blinking. So, you know, I could get killed. I'm aware of that. And not to sound courageous or bombastic or anything, but that's not a huge deal. It's part of the bag. So, on the off chance that this film becomes a kind of postmortem, I'd like to take advantage of the chance to talk about things, and what I'd most like to talk about today is the same guy I was talking about in a previous session, namely Nacho. Padre Ignacio. Because if I had to name someone I really admire, a great man, it would be him. And I was thinking last night in bed about that day a couple weeks ago over in Guanaxia, before I came back with *el Dragón,* and I was thinking about how that day he was a veterinarian, which like, a thousand years ago, is what I wanted to be, and a killer, an executioner, which is one of the things I am, or have been in the past and am about to become again. Now I know it may sound absurd comparing the butchering of a young bull to the assassination of a man. But this guy Alvarez deserves to die more than that *novillo* did. That's what I believe. Anyway, what I want to say in talking about Nacho, is that I find myself lacking. Can you imagine what goes through his mind when he cuts an animal's throat? A guy who had his own throat slashed down to the cartilage of his esophagus? An army officer, a guy probably a lot like Alvarez, stepped over him and grabbed his hair and drew his blade across his neck and left him on the ground to die. Right next to a few others who did die. This is a story that Nacho himself told me. Not this last time, but years ago. And I want to tell you it so you'll know there are people like him out there. Which can be a comfort, just knowing, sometimes. He became a priest and a physician because he killed his own younger brother. That's right, when Ignacio Arostegui, who later joined the Society of Jesus and became a doctor of medicine, was 11 years old, he killed his brother, whose name was Mario and who was seven. He killed him with a field-hockey stick. Of course he was called Nachito by his family and friends in the Basque town where he grew up. And he was celebrating his birthday with a piñata in the backyard of his family's apartment building. Now, the breaking of a piñata on a child's birthday is not a Basque custom, but it was practiced in the Arostegui household because Nacho's mother was Mexican. The elder Ignacio Arostegui, Nacho's father, had been a young tenor of some renown during the 1920s, when he spent five years in the New World as a member of the *Opera Nacional de México*. Nacho's mother worked in the wardrobe department. As Nacho tells it, she and his father fell in love in a grand and operatic fashion during post-performance midnight strolls along *Avenida de la Reforma*. They married and she got pregnant. She went with her husband to Spain, where Ignacio, *padre*, continued to sing and where the couple had four children–two boys and two girls. None of the children's birthday passed without a piñata, a tradition that so delighted the cousins and playmates of the Arostegui children that the birthdays of the four were known by all the neighborhood kids and eagerly anticipated. La piñata, observation of the Day of the Dead and cornmeal tortillas; those were Dolores' New World contributions to her household, an outpost of *mestizaje* in Euskadi, land of rock-lifters and players of *frontón* and anti-Franquistas. The maternal heritage took root in the children. All four preferred tortillas over bread. He said that if one of them went to spend the night at the house of a friend, he or she would take along a paper-wrapped ration. So on Nachito's 11th birthday, a papier mache burro stuffed with candies dangled from a tree on a rope manipulated by the barrel-chested and bearded Ignacio Sr. He tugged and gave slack so that the animal danced in and out of reach of whichever blindfolded child's turn it was to flail at it with the old hockey stick. A dozen happy kids formed a circle around the dancing donkey. They cried encouragement in a chorus of squeals. The paper and wire burro had taken a beating from the first few. It was on the verge of coming apart. And just as the matador is given the culminating task after the bull has been weakened by the *picadores* and *banderilleros,* so Nachito was blindfolded and handed the stick and cheered to finish the job. He took the stick and started swinging. He missed with the first few but with the third struck solidly. The burro's foreleg remained connected to the body by a strip and his belly bulged, a single blow away from bursting. The children's shouts rose in volume and Nachito swung the club hard right into the burro's midsection. *Dulces* fell out on the grass. The children cheered and rushed in. But blind Nachito was charged with his mission and the cries of delight. He attacked the invisible beast with a final wild and mighty swing that at the peak of its acceleration crashed across the side of Marito's head. Nacho said it sounded like a gunshot. And he said that, mere child that he was, he knew in a flash that the crack would never cease to ring in his ears. He entered the seminary directly out of high school. He wanted nothing for himself out of life. He became a priest and a medical doctor. Nacho Arostegui believed that in a sense, he, as an individual with ambition or rights or purpose beyond that of atonement, had died along with his brother. What allowed him to continue living was the conviction, attained through renunciation and prayer, that atonement might be possible if he spent every day of his life trying to ease the suffering of others. He was ordained, then went to medical school in Vitoria. After that, his only intention was to live a simple life serving the mysterious God who had placed Marito within the radius of his swing, and serving his fellow man in whatever backwater of America his superiors deemed fit. The young Padre Nacho arrived in El Salvador in 1955. By the time I deserted from the shitty fucking Salvadoran army and made my way to Chalate, he'd spent 30 years making good on his vows, providing succor to soul and body in and around the towns of Las Vueltas, San Jose las Flores and Arcatao. In the 1980s, most of Chalatenango was guerrilla territory. Around Las Vueltas, most people sympathized with *los muchachos* and their cause–our cause–and almost all the area's families had fighters in the ranks. It was our rearguard. *Los compas* moved around openly and freely most of the time. We trained there, rested, replenished supplies and planned operations. The war's over now. The people who died in it have turned to dirt. And Nacho is still there, trying to get parasites out of kids and sitting through wakes with their parents when he fails. Stitching cuts, marrying young couples, baptizing their babies. Sleeping in an old hammock, eating beans. At peace with himself.

More than I am, anyway.

CHAPTER 49: MAY GOD HEAR YOU, ÑA GUICHA

Juan and Joe Guinness sat in a *pupuseria* across from the Belen convent on the eastern edge of Antigua.

The three members of their little gang of musketeers had decided that Joe would accompany April to the stadium cornerstone ceremony to augment her cover, in case she might eventually be questioned about what happened. A pair of Gringo friends, both professionals, with matching stories of a stroll around town before becoming chance witnesses to sudden violence. That April had her camera with her and was filming was explicable, normal even. The cops had seen her often during the previous months lugging it around, setting it up on the tripod or standing on some corner with it propped on her shoulder, filming this and that along with the addled or loquacious *bolos* she liked to interview.

The woman making the *pupusas* was about ten years older than Juan and good looking, strong of build with a small black mole on her upper lip. The only words he'd ever exchanged with her, during the several meals he'd taken here, had to do with *pupusas*. Juan had picked up from her talk with other customers that she was a Guatemalteca who'd lived for several years in El Salvador. That's where she had learned to make such good *pupusas*.

He and Joe ordered *dos de chicharrón, dos de queso and dos de frijol.* Miriam was at the grill tending the sizzling stuffed patties of *masa*.

"Now there's a fine actress," said Juan, gesturing toward the television at the end of the counter opposite the grill. Juan had always liked Jessica Lange. "Frances" and "Blue Sky," but also the one about her finding out her father was a Nazi war criminal, and just about everything else she'd done.

"Oh, yeah. She's great," said Joe, turning to get a better take on the screen. "Her men are high-quality, too. I think she had a baby with Baryshnikov, and spent years with Sam Shepard. They did a movie together, too, of one of his plays. It takes place in a rundown motel room out West."

"I missed that one."

"Musta come out while you were at war."

"Maybe," said Juan, looking at the TV. He couldn't figure out right away what this drama was. Usually, when he'd been in here before, Miriam had on a soap-opera, a Venezuelan or Mexican production with pouting or frowning girls and pissed-off men. But now a movie was playing on the cable channel, and Jessica Lange was there in a ruffled pink dress talking with another, younger woman. Then Juan heard the younger one call Jessica Lange "Blanche."

"I think it's fucking Streetcar," he said. "A remake. Have you seen this?"

"No. But why on earth would anybody want to remake that?"

Jessica Lange called the other one "Stella." So there was no doubt.

The two men watched.

Miriam brought over the platter of *pupusas* and two Gallos and set them down.

The young guy who worked there was watching the movie too, leaning forward from his seat on the beverage cooler to read the subtitles.

The electricity went off, and the images on the screen were sucked into a tiny white hole that disappeared into blackness. *"Puta,"* muttered the kid. Miriam looked over her shoulder at the television, then at Juan. "That happens," she said.

Joe looked around the place. Two of the walls were made of horizontal reeds that allowed chrome sunlight through in fine planes. The only decorations were posters for Gallo beer. In one of them a well-dressed woman sat on a barstool. She was the only person in the poster, and it looked like she was waiting for someone, for some guy to come in and buy her and himself a Gallo, then take her out of the bar, either to his house or to an hourly motel, for a round of supine *cumbia*. The other poster was aimed at the youthful consumer of beer. It featured a couple who looked to be sophmores in high-school. The amply curved girl was wearing a halter top and cutoff blue jeans so short that the point where the back of the thigh becomes butt cheek was on view, and she was leaning up against the boy, pressing her sheathed breasts against his torso, looking like she knew how to do some animal-type stuff in the dark too, kind of like a female version of Stanley Kowalski. Joe supposed that was part of the reason they called their beer Gallo, to suggest to guys that if they drink a lot of it, they'll be able to fuck all the hens.

"So," said Joe. "You getting antsy?"

"A little. You know, you think about it. Like back in high-school before the big game. It's like the big game."

"Except somebody dies in this."

"Yeah."

Juan spooned a dollop of the mild red sauce then a daub of the hot green sauce onto his final pupusa, one of cheese, then topped that with the vinegar-soaked shredded cabbage-and-carrot *curtido*. He cut off a piece and lifted it to his mouth and chewed and savored.

"You know, a couple weeks ago it crossed my mind that I might be doing this because I was getting bored. So then you ask yourself, Is boredom enough reason to kill a man? And of course the answer is that, in and of itself, No. But then too, it depends on the man. The men, really. The one doing the killing, mostly. But the other one, too."

He cut another piece off his pupusa and ate it and took a long sip of his beer. He looked out the doorway into the street where a boy led a clopping horse by on a halter.

An old Indian *tortillera* came in.

"Buenas tardes, 'Ña Guicha," said Miriam.

"Buenas, 'Ña Guicha," said the young man.

'Ña Guicha returned their greeting and lifted the heavy straw basket full of tortillas from the top of her head and set it down on one of the tables just inside the door. She sat down on the bench beside the table and raised a loose-skinned wrinkled dark brown arm to remove from her crown a striped dishtowel wound into a circular pad.

Guicha had thick braided gray hair and wore simple silver earrings of a thin hammered circle inside a hoop. She was not in *corte y huipil,* but wore a peach-colored blouse with a broad floral patterned collar and a red-and-white checked apron over a dark blue skirt. She was barefoot, and about 70 years old.

The young man went over to where she sat and asked for three quetzales' worth. Guicha peeled back the towels covering the stacks of tortillas to keep them hot and to keep the dust off. She ripped a square of brown paper from a broad sheet tucked among the tortillas and counted out 30 and handed the stack on the brown paper to the young man.

"Gracias, 'Ña Guicha," he said.

"No hay de que," she said, covering her bundle again.

The old woman looked tired. She probably had another mile or so to walk, making the rounds of her regular customers. She sat on the bench, resting. Then she said,

"Miriam, did you know that four days ago I sold a rooster and a hen to a friend of my nephew. He told me he was going to give me *el pisto* the next day, but I have not seen his face since then.

"Don't they know that if one sells an animal, it is not for the pleasure of selling it or to put the money in one's pocket and be able to say, 'I sold my animal,' but rather out of necessity? That is the simple truth. But there are people who don't understand."

"May God hear you, 'Ña Guicha," said Miriam. "Some people cannot be trusted even a little."

'Ña Guicha rewound the towel-pad and placed it on her head. She was preparing to continue on her way. But she sat there another few minutes in her simple chapeau, hand at her chin. Then she asked the young man to help her raise the heavy basket of tortillas. He said, "Surely, with pleasure," and went to her. She bent over and grabbed one side with her two bony hands and he the other side with his two paler and thicker hands and they hefted together in one motion and set the basket on the ring of towel on her head.

"*Gracias, joven,*" said the old woman.

"*No hay de que,*" he said.

Miriam and 'Ña Guicha and the young man all bid each other Adios. The *tortillera* then looked at Juan and Joe for the first time.

Just before turning to leave she said to them, "*Buen provecho.*"

"*Gracias,*" the two men said in unison.

Buen Provecho means something akin to Bon Apetit but also means more than that, in that it is a wish that your meal not only be tasty, but that it serve you, as nourishment and sustenance in carrying on, after you eat it, with whatever it is you have to do.

CHAPTER 50: A TIGER TAMED

The brass band of *la Policía de Finanzas* was seated on folding chairs to the right of the stage made of pipe scaffolding and broad planks. The ensemble comprised about 20 men and their instruments; tubas and drums to the rear, a row of trombones and English horns, trumpets and clarinets up front. The musicians wore navy blue peaked caps and light brown shirts with red trim, or trim that once had been red. Each had had his shirt tailor-made. Most were old, and the uniforms fanned out in a dozen shades of beige, some with sleeve-stripes scarlet, some cerise, some pink.

The musicians, the majority of them, were either fat or mantis-thin. One of the trumpet players in the first row had gained considerable weight and the bulge of his belly produced white ellipses of undershirt between strained buttons. He dozed peacefully, chin on his chest and horn across his lap. Technicians were busy setting up the microphone and speakers. Organizers of the ceremony conversed in small groups. Passers-by and afternoon market-goers stopped to observe.

At the fire station, an Asian woman with a professional video camera was taking some footage of a vintage hook-

and-ladder parked in front of the building. Then she and a man accompanying her, a man who looked to be a foreigner, came around to the near side of the stationhouse and the woman filmed a large advertisement for Diana snacks featuring a smiling girl painted on the cinderblock wall. They sat down on a cement bench in the shade of the wall.

"It's funny," said the woman to the man. "Juan was in the hills for seven years, in all kinds of combat, and was never wounded. You were up there six months, and got shot, in the head no less, and lived to tell about it."

"It's funny in a way. And not so funny in other ways. Like in the way of dental reconstruction. That took two months, and was painful."

She reached out and touched the small round scar on his left cheek. "An inch up or an inch back, and you would have been killed instantly."

"Don't think I haven't thought about that."

Joe used his thumbnail to scrape a Pokémon sticker off the bench. He crumpled it into a ball and shot it with his thumb into the sparse grass. "It's my Richard Burton wound."

"The actor?"

"No, the explorer. British Victorian hero. He and a guy named Speke discovered the source of the Blue Nile and spent years looking for the source of the main river."

"And he got shot through the mouth?"

"Actually he got a spear through the mouth, which is even worse, I suppose. In one cheek out the other, like mine. I don't know what kind of charm he had working on him. But you know, the bullet that hit me, well, it hit me right where a dog, if that's what it was, had licked me about an hour earlier. The exact spot."

"What are you talking about?"

"The day I left El Salvador. Left the Gs. I slept on the ground and got woken up by this canine-type animal licking my face."

"What's that mean? 'Canine-type animal'?"

"That's the thing. I don't know what it was. He was gray, good sized. Kind of like a German Shepherd but not quite. I never saw his master or anyone he might have belonged to, and that part of the country is sparsely inhabited. Anyway he was licking my face. My left cheek." Joe tapped himself with his index finger on the scar.

"I was face-up, but he didn't lick my mouth or my nose or my right cheek. I jumped up and was scared, partly because I'd just had a weird dream. But the dog was calm and walked off and I swear it seemed like he was trying to lead me. Like he was saying, 'Follow me.' In a benevolent way, like a guide. So I followed him. I followed him for an hour then he took off down a hill and I lost him. But at the bottom of that hill was the Sumpul River. I stood there on the Salvadoran side and was thinking, Thank you, dog. Then I waded across. Just as I was stepping out on the Honduran side, I got shot. By somebody I never saw, but who I presume was a soldier."

"What does it feel like? Getting shot?"

"It feels like getting hit with a hammer. But what I remember most was the sound. Not the sound of the gun, though I heard that too, a split second later, and not close.

The sound of my teeth breaking. Like walnuts being crushed, but amplified because it's inside your head. Then it just hurts like hell, 'cause the nerves of your teeth are exposed and every breath stings. But, you know, you can't stop breathing, even if at the moment you think you might want to."

April shifted her camera across her lap and looked out over the pre-speech activity and around at the people coming out from or going into the covered marketplace.

"Anyway, I got new teeth and they work fine. Cornell has a great health plan," said Joe. "But that dog, I still think about him sometimes. It seems strange to me that he licked me right there. You know, I heard a lot of campesino folklore during those months in the hills. *La Siguanaba, El Cipitillo.* And they talk about an animal called *El Cadejo,* which is a ghost dog, an ambivalent creature. One capable of both altruism and treachery."

"Don't spook me right now, please."

Just then they saw Juan as he paused near the middle of the northernmost of the two athletic fields, some 60 meters from the platform where the dignitaries would speak before stepping down to take turns with a new shovel to break the dusty ground. He was dressed in poor man's garb. The neck of his faded gray t-shirt was frayed and stretched in a wide oval that exposed his collar bones. The legend "World's Greatest Grand-dad," in English in white letters, was barely legible on the chest. Baggy khakis patched at the buttocks and torn in the knees were cinched around his waist with a length of hemp rope. A battered pair of black canvas Converse All-Stars with dusty purple laces shod sockless feet. The brim of a Houston Astros baseball cap was pulled low on his brow. Grime covered most of the star on the crown.

Resting on Juan 's right shoulder was a bundle of three visible tools: a hoe, a shovel and an iron-tipped wooden pike used for extracting rocks from the cornfield. The fascia was partially sheathed in a cotton blanket, old and dirty. At the heart of the bundle, nestled within the three staves, was a Russian-made sniper rifle wrapped in a burlap coffee sack.

He turned and walked across the playing field, toward the ruin of La Recolección. He passed along the wall at the front of the church grounds until he reached the San Antonio road, where he turned left. He walked another 150 meters beside the pocked and crumbling old adobe wall until he reached a section just over waist high. He slowed his pace while a barreling bus, its roof piled with big wicker baskets of avocados and mangoes, whipped past. When it had turned the corner and no other vehicle was visible up or down the road, Juan climbed over the wall. He moved deliberately, careful not to jostle the weapon.

It was a few minutes after 4 P.M. but still hot, especially along the edge of the asphalt road. Juan felt an eddy of relief upon passing into the shade of the forest canopy. It was the simplest delight, the stepping into a cooler quadrant, but Juan felt it to be magnified, something akin to joy. The sensation was enhanced, or perhaps had been prompted, by the sight of dozens of violet and white bell-shaped flowers drooping knee-high over the floor of the wood. They had not been there during the previous week's reconnaissance. As he made his way among them toward the base of the back of the ruin, a black grackle in the boughs of a *gravilea* tree chirped a skein of notes, to which Juan responded with a whistled cadence, eliciting in turn an answer from the bird.

When he reached the foot of the western wall, Juan knelt and untied his kit. He unwrapped the rifle and raised it to his shoulder and sighted through the scope back into the woods. He slung it across his back, then spread the burlap sack on top of the tools aligned on the blanket so that, when he came down, he would be able to re-roll the bundle and tie it tight in a matter of seconds.

Getting up the wall was easy. It was sheer and solid to a height of ten or twelve feet. The lowest portion was made of uncut stone and brick from which the stucco had come away to expose niches for his feet and handholds. Past the point at which the wall had broken and collapsed inward, the climb was something any 10-year-old could manage. A huge wedge had fallen from it, and the four-foot-wide wall rose in a jagged ascent of irregular steps, none more than waist-high. In 30 seconds, Juan reached his perch.

He spotted April and Joe. They stood about 15 meters from the far goal of the near field. She had her camera on her shoulder, either filming or pretending to film a half-dozen boys taking turns booting a ball at a lanky goaltender. A new four-door Mitsubishi Montero with government plates was parked beside a late-model Toyota Land Cruiser, also an official vehicle, just beyond the goal.

A line of chairs had been set up on the stage behind a standing microphone. Juan raised the rifle to study the scene through the scope. He recognized the mayor, a handsome young man in a suit who stood to one side talking with three other men, one in jacket-and-tie and the others in the sky-blue and white nylon sweats of the '96 Olympic Team, GUATEMALA emblazoned across their backs. He panned the other knots of likely looking officials, but did not see Alvarez. Juan lowered the rifle. Only the slightest of breezes stirred the leaves of the trees behind him and to his left. The sun was at his back, but high enough still to illuminate his target, who, when standing on the platform, would be directly opposite, facing Juan full-on.

The spot was perfect. He was secluded, out of the way of commerce and transit. He was sighting over the top of the wall, poised against brick and mortar and invisible to anyone looking from the direction of the market and soccer fields. Even visitors to the crumbling ruin, of which there were none, would be unable to see him.

He raised the gun again and drew a bead on the microphone, this time with his finger light against the trigger. He was calm. He thought: If he comes, I'll kill him. If he doesn't come, that's OK, too.

"Dios sabe lo que hace," he said out loud. It was an expression common among Chapines, especially the humble and resigned, but not anything he remembered hearing much as a kid, or similar to anything he'd ever said before. It sounded like Ximena talking. He smiled.

He lifted the rifle strap over his head and propped the weapon against the wall. He leaned forward, chin resting on his folded hands. He watched April. She was looking at melons and papayas displayed on the ground by outside-the-market vendors. Juan wondered if he and she would make love tonight. Then his eyes went to the Diana billboard girl, and he saw in the portrait something that previously had escaped him.

The girl reminded him of Juana, his *tocaya* from the second year of high-school. His first love. And he wondered what might have become of her, whether she'd stayed in California, or gone back to the Texas she so missed, whether she'd continued to write poetry, what kind of work she might be doing. If she were married, with kids.

Juan's attention, along with that of the entire assembly, was drawn suddenly to a white tank of a vehicle, a Chevrolet Suburban approaching along Calle de los Recolectos from the south at reckless speed, its billowing trail of dust obliging pedestrians to cover their mouth and turn away. The wagon braked hard at the entrance to the dirt access road to the fire station and, churning up an orange cloud, cut across the corner of the soccer field. It pulled to a stop beside the Land Cruiser.

The door swung open and out stepped a compact man in blue jeans, a long-sleeved orange-and-black striped polo shirt, a billed cap and aviator sunglasses. Juan took up the rifle and raised it and fixed him in the sight as he walked toward the mayor's group. He stayed on him as hands were shaken all around and shoulders clapped. The glasses and cap concealed most of the face. Even so, Juan could see it was the same man who had attacked Francisco and him on the street in Guate. And there was the cap. Across the black crown, embroidered in bold letters of gold thread was the single word: TIGRE.

Juan lowered his weapon. He watched and waited.

April moved nearer the platform and stood among those who had paused, curious, in their errands. Her little knot of people was a satellite to the group of 50 or so that had gathered in front of the stage. Then she and Joe made their way to a place among the foremost of the standing spectators. She lifted the camera to her shoulder.

The band conductor strode to his place on the soccer-field dirt and faced the arrayed musicians. A baton in his right hand, he raised his arms. Juan saw them sweep down a half-second before he heard the brassy herald of the anthem's commencement, a sight-sound lapse like the one he'd been thrilled by hundreds, thousands of times so long ago when the crack of the bat reached him a split-second after he'd bolted from his half-crouch in centerfield into a full-tilt gallop toward where the stitched sphere's arc would end, in the webbing of his A-2000. He heard the singing voices, fainter than the music but, because he and April had memorized the lyric together, could make out the words.

He'd told her the shot would come at either "tyrants" at the end of the first verse or during the phrase "to vanquish or die" at the end of the second.

"Guatemala feliz! Que tus aras
"No profane jamás el verdugo;
"Ni haya esclavos que laman el yugo
"Ni tiranos que escupan tu faz," sang the assembly.

Alvarez, too, sang with his companions on the dais. When the music began his hand had snapped automatically to a military salute at the brim of his cap. But, perhaps conscious of the oddness of this pose among the civilians flanking him, in the next second he had dropped it to his breast.

The crosshairs of the sight fixed Juan's concentration like an auger on the center of Alvarez's chest and in those seconds he suffered a breeze of panic that tingled his gut. Because that spot, that thoracic center, was covered by a hand and wrist. Could wrist bones deflect a bullet? Juan raised the weapon a fraction of an inch and sighted on the head. He was about to begin to squeeze the trigger when he was deterred by portions of two faces, those of an elderly man and a middle-aged woman standing in the row behind Alvarez. What if he missed even slightly, only inches wide or high of the yellow "G" where the filaments met?

"Si mañana tu suelo sagrado,"

Juan watched Alvarez's mouth.

"Lo amenaza invasion extranjera,"

He moved the sight back down to the back of the right hand, just off chest-center, directly over the heart. Then he knew, with calm assuredness upon him now as suddenly as had been the doubt, that the bullet would pierce the hand easily, slip between metacarpals or shatter them like toothpicks on its way to cleaving the heart.

In that instant he decided not to end Alvarez's life.

"Libre al viento tu hermosa bandera,"

Juan lowered the rifle ever so slightly, so that the sight was fixed on the bulge of stone-washed denim five inches below the silver buckle of the black leather belt. He took a breath and exhaled slowly. At the end of the breath he paused in his breathing.

"A vencer o a morir ..."

He squeezed the trigger. The crack resounded through the roofless church and expanded to fill the valley. Juan saw the impact through the sight, saw his target buckle violently. But that was all. Before Alvarez completed his fall, Juan had ducked with the rifle behind his bulwark. In the next seconds he slung it across his back and hastily descended the wall.

CHAPTER 51: ENFALAC WITHOUT IRON

April awoke just as the objects of the room and the trappings of the world beyond the window were taking form and color from weak light. She tried to recall the setting of her last dream. In it a baby had been crying. Stretched out face-up, she put her hands behind her head. She was listening to Juan's deep slow breathing when she started at the sound of a baby crying.

"What on earth?" she murmured.

She eased out of bed and slipped her feet into a pair of Juan's old Black Knight suede sneakers. She was not annoyed in the slightest at being roused. On the contrary, she was happy to get up. In the days since the shooting time seemed to be going by slowly. She couldn't find a book she liked in the library. It was unseasonably hot.

The local tumult ensuing from the sniper attack had died down. Alvarez had not been killed. All that had emerged in the national, and briefly in the international, news was that he'd been seriously wounded. Details on his condition apparently were something of a state secret.

At the kitchen end of the veranda April found Ximena sitting on one of the benches. In her arms was a tiny baby with an embroidered red cotton cap pulled down over its forehead and ears. The infant, only several weeks old, was wrapped in a cream-colored wool blanket. The whining child was out of sorts, its features scrunched. Ximena was trying to console it by dipping a piece of cotton cloth into a cup of sugared chamomile tea and letting the baby suck it. She was having only partial success.

"*La pobrecita tiene hambre,*" she said, looking up at April. "I've got cow's milk in the 'fridge, but she's too young for that." She dipped again and looked down at the baby mouthing the bunched cloth. "Why don't you run over to the Farmacia Fenix on the plaza and ring the bell. They're on off-hours call. Buy a can of Enfalac formula. Without iron."

"*Como no,*" said April, leaning over the baby for a good look. It was fat-cheeked, of almost exactly the same hue as the cedar of the bench. The eyes were black and displeased. "Where did it come from?"

"About a half hour ago, it was still dark, there was a rap on the front door, two hard blows with the knocker. I'm surprised it didn't wake you and Don Miguel. I went and opened the grate to see who could be bothering people at such an hour, but there was no one. I was about to return to bed, when I heard a sound like a puppy's lament. I opened the door and there in a basket was this creature. There's a note, too, which you can read later. But first, if you don't mind, go get the milk. *Y tambien una pacha.*"

"*Una pacha?*"

"*Un biberón.*"

April still did not understand.

"From what a baby drinks milk."

"Oh. Yes,," said April, and turned to go get dressed.

Twenty minutes later, April was standing in the kitchen cradling the wailing child while Ximena tipped one, two, measures of fine powder from a white can into a plastic bottle decorated with a bunny. She poured in two ounces of warm *agua pura Salvavidas*, screwed on the nipple and shook it. She took the baby from April and sat down at the table and plugged the rubber teat into the eager mouth. The baby sighed, and set to sucking.

"This child has had a *biberón* before. If they're used only to *la teta*, it can take a while for them to latch on to a bottle."

"Either that or it's starving."

"*Que cosa? No entiendo el inglés.*"

"Oh," said April, absorbed in her study of the child. "*Disculpe. Dije que, o ha ya tomado pacha, o se está muriendo de hambre.*"

"She's in no danger of that. I unwrapped her and had a look. Because you know, babies with some defect are the ones most frequently abandoned. But no. She's perfect. And fat."

The infant drained the half-pacha in little more than a minute and set again to howling. Ximena passed her to April, mixed two more ounces, and handed her the bottle.

"Here. You try."

Cradling her in the crook of her left arm, feeding her, April saw the change in the baby's face when, about halfway through this measure, she slowed, her craving abated. She continued sucking, but without the previous single-mindedness. Her bright eyes widened and she looked up and off to the left, toward the rafters of the veranda. Then she directed her attention back to the face of the figure enveloping her. She locked on April's eyes and kept her gaze fixed there while she slowly emptied the rest of the bottle. Her lids began to droop. She struggled to lift them once, then surrendered, releasing her tiny mouth's clamp on the nipple, and fell asleep.

CHAPTER 52: IT'S LIKE A RULE

The man in line in front of them was making no progress with the vice-consul, who was not buying the Gringo's story. It was a difficult story to buy. The man wasn't helping his case by becoming indignant.

"I'll tell you right now I don't appreciate having my integrity questioned," the applicant told the functionary. The applicant was very Caucasian; sandy-haired with cobalt blue eyes. He wore jeans, a wide belt, a pressed shirt with metal points on the tips of the collar. A descendant of prospectors or cowpokes or Mormons. He probably was unused to having his integrity questioned. But he was so obviously overflowing with crap regarding the matter at hand that he should have known the interview was not going to proceed smoothly. Perhaps he had known, and peevishness was part of his tactic.

He was turning a deep shade of pink. "You have no right to do that."

"You're mistaken," said the vice-consul. He was an olive-skinned, curly-headed fellow a couple years younger than the petitioner. "I have every right. In fact it's my job. Although I don't consider it a slight to your integrity, by any means. I'm simply asking what evidence you can provide to the effect that this young lady is your daughter."

The guy said: "I give you my word."

The vice-consul bowed his head and shook it and whispered, "Whoa." Then he looked at the man and said: "That's not sufficient."

The man at the window of the American Services section of the U.S. Embassy, on Avenida Reforma in Zone 10, was flanked by an attractive Guatemalan woman of about 35. She was his wife of one month, according to the marriage certificate they'd presented. Beside the woman stood a pretty girl about 11 years old. When Juan and April and the infant in April's arms had entered 20 minutes earlier, they'd taken seats alongside this threesome. The man had struck up a conversation with April. Maybe he'd wanted to run through his story one last time.

If the girl, whose mother was not a *corte*-clad *indígena* but who was obviously Maya, had a single drop of

European blood in her body it was in a blister on her little toe. Yet she was, according to the man's version of things, his long lost daughter. The American explained that she had been conceived during a brief affair with this woman, her mother, in 1983 in Acapulco, where he had gone on vacation and where she, the mother, had been working at his hotel.

The mother had returned to her Guatemalan homeland to have the baby and had told the father nothing over the years. Indeed there had been no contact between them until a few months before this interview, when the man had traveled to Guatemala hoping against hope to find his Acapulco *novia* and, wouldn't you know, mysterious are the ways of fate and the stratagems of love, I did find her and not only that, but unbeknownst to me, my lovely daughter.

"Yeah," said the diplomat. "But in cases like this, without any documentation, the only evidence we can accept as proof of paternity is genetic. There's an embassy-approved lab right here in Zone 10 that will do a DNA test on you and on your wife's daughter. Will you consent to such a test?"

"I don't know," said the American. "I can't give you an answer to that question right now. I can tell you right now, though, that it sounds pretty gol-darn Dr. Mengele to me." His voice had risen.

"Well, you think about it, Mr. Taylor. But step away from the window please and think about it on your own time. Because you are beginning to try my patience." He looked down at a sheet that must have been passed to him from the woman at the reception window. Because when he looked up, he found April and said: "Ms. Tashima?"

April rose, the baby in a yellow cotton blanket in her arms. Juan got up too, and they stepped to the window.

"We'd like to register our daughter as a U.S. citizen and get her a passport," said April. She slid a manila folder of documents to the man.

He opened the folder. It contained April's passport, Juan's Guatemalan passport in the name of Miguel Zelaya, a birth certificate for the girl, two months old, in the name of Keiko Jade Zelaya, *hija de April Tashima (apellido unico) y Miguel Antonio Zelaya Renderos*, and a marriage certificate stating that Srta. April Tashima and Sr. Miguel Zelaya had wed before the Antigua Justice of the Peace seven months previously.

The last two documents, though false in their particulars, were genuine. They had cost 500 dollars apiece. The *Migración* stamp in April's passport attesting to her arrival in the country ten months earlier, instead of the six corresponding to the truth, had been purchased for $300.

"We'd also like to get a U.S. visa for my husband, as we'll be taking our daughter to the States next week," added April as the vice-consul continued his examination of the papers.

He looked up at April.

"You teach at Berkeley?"

"That's right."

"What's your field?"

"Anthropology."

"Down here doing field-work? Ethnography?"

"I'm on sabbatical. But I'm not an ethnographer. I was making a film. I'm a documentary film-maker."

"Were you able to make your film? What with getting married and getting pregnant, all?" The questions, though posed by an authority-wielding inquisitor, carried more a tone of casual banter than one of judgment or suspicion.

"Yeah. Well, you know, I got a lot of tape. The first six months I was able to work normally. By the time I got big I had pretty much what I wanted. The editing I'll do back home."

"What's it about?"

"Bolos. It's about street drunks."

"Sounds oddly fascinating," he said, and turned his attention to Juan.

"Y usted, Sr. Zelaya, a que se dedica?"

Juan answered in English.

"I'm an antiquarian, if you have to put down something. I collect Maya sculpture and ceramics. But I don't really do it as a job, beyond finding a piece now and then for acquaintances or a friend of a friend. Maybe it would be more accurate to put 'Collector.' What I'm saying, in a roundabout way, I guess, is that I don't have a day-to-day occupation. Gainful employ in the usual sense. I'm fortunate enough to not have to work."

"Your English is flawless. But it says here you've never before applied for a U.S. visa. You've never been to the States?"

"I had North American tutors, U.S. or Canadian, from the time I was a little kid. Afternoons were always English-speaking at my house. Then I went to high-school for four years in Toronto. If truth be told, I went to Niagra Falls, the U.S. side, twice with Canadian friends. And Maine once, camping. We just drove across the border. There wasn't even a customs or immigration post, or anything."

"I see. Well," he said, looking down again at the papers, "I appreciate your frankness." Then, raising his eyes again, "What does your father, or your family, do?"

"We grow cane and refine sugar. *Ingenios Zelaya*, of Zacapa. I've enclosed there copies of bank statements, Guatemalan and Bahamian, to establish that I have ample means of support."

"This is your first marriage?"

"Yes."

The vice-consul, a tall man, leaned across the counter and looked closely at the babe in April's arms. She was penny-colored and round-faced, with a touch of *Chinita*, and obviously the fruit of the union of these two good-looking individuals standing before him. A big friendly smile came over the diplomat's face.

"I swear, it's like a rule," he said. "The girls look like Pop and the boys, at least the first one, almost always look like Mom. My wife and I have a son just a few months older than your daughter, and he's the spit and image of Rachel. Which I'm glad for, mind you. In fact I hope that if the next one's a girl, she looks like her mother too. Be a shame if she got my beak."

He looked again at the baby, then at April. "But I see you in her, too, professor. In any case, she's beautiful. My compliments and congratulations."

He passed Juan a form. "Fill this out and leave it with *la señora*, please." He indicated the woman at the reception window. "Keiko's passport and her U.S. Certificate of Birth Abroad will be ready in two days. By the way, Keiko is a Japanese name, am I right?"

"Yes. It's my mother's name."

"Pretty. Mr. Zelaya's visa will take three or four days. Since you're in Antigua, you might want to wait until Friday and make a single trip to pick up all the documents together. Whatever's convenient."

"Thank you very much," April said to the man.

"Thank you," said Juan.

"De nada," said the official. "Best of luck to you in the States, *y que les vaya muy bien con la niña."*

CHAPTER 53: NOT TOO MUCH PICANTE

It was clear to April and Juan that her film about him, once made, could not be shown. What April had to decide was whether it made sense to finish it at all. She'd been editing it in her head during the previous couple months. She could, she told herself, put all the tapes in a big box and slide it into a closet back home or stack it on a shelf in her office at school. Leave it sprawling and raw. Look at the material again in a few years. Or leave it untouched until 2025. Or forever.

But that, ultimately, seemed unsatisfactory. It would have been lazy. She had been carrying around the idea of this film for nearly five months. The two things, the person of Juan and the documentary, were so bound up one with the other it wasn't easy for April, early on, to say precisely where one ended and the other began. She had spent this season with Juan on a subtle and steady high, moving day by day through the growing conviction that this time in her life weighed more than other semesters.

The fact that the documentary was not for an audience meant she could make it as long as she liked. Even so, she resolved to keep it within the limits previously imagined: 80 minutes at most. That would oblige her to craft it with the eye of an *auteur*, rather than that of a lover.

This is what she decided: If it ends up being a fucking home movie, at least it will be an extraordinary one.

Two days before they were to leave Guatemala, Juan and April sat on a bench in Antigua's central plaza. Keiko slept against April's breast in the marsupial sling. The couple passed between them a bag of peanuts purchased from a gnarled old man at the corner. After spooning them from his glass-sided box, he'd sprinkled on a measure of salt, another of chili powder, then doused the contents with a generous squeeze of lemon.

A boy of about 10 came along with his box under his arm.

"*Lustro?*" he asked Juan.

Juan looked down at his dusty black leather basketball shoes.

"*Dale,*" he said. The boy positioned himself and got to work.

After about a minute, he looked up from his buffing at the woman tipping the last of the nuts into her mouth.

"Con chile, son?" he asked.

"Sí. Son más ricos así."

"But you must be careful of too much *picante*. Could give a bad taste to the milk."

It took a moment for April to realize the boy was referring to her breast milk, that which he presumed she was giving to the baby. She was flattered to be taken for a nursing mother, delighted that a stranger so readily presumed the infant to be her natural-born child. At the same time she felt something akin to embarrassment at having to admit that it was not her own milk nourishing the girl.

"Ella toma pacha," she said. "It seems my own was not enough."

"That happens," said the boy, rapping twice on the side of the box. Juan put up the other foot. "But if you've got the money to buy it, they grow perfectly well on formula, too."

When the boy had finished, the couple rose and began strolling, arms linked, around the plaza's perimeter.

"I'm gonna make the film anyway," said April. "Joe says he'll transcribe the tapes. Then I'll go from there."

"Como quieras," said Juan. "I guess it would be a shame not to, at this point. We'll show it to Keiko when she turns 15."

Fifteen years from now, thought April. He said it so naturally. The number had on her an almost dizzying effect, conjuring a vision of this helpless infant as a young woman seated at the kitchen table after dinner doing algebra homework and waiting for a boyfriend's phone call. Though April had not waded unwittingly into this new world of commitment and responsibility, she felt now the momentousness of what she'd undertaken. With this man at her side. A person who until a half-year ago had been a stranger.

What steeled her resolve was no more than a persistent intuition: that Juan was a partner she could trust to persevere and improvise and not get bent out of shape by the small shit. After that, things would take care of themselves.

"You ever been to San Francisco?"

"Just from the airport to the bus station downtown. When I went to Palo Alto for the interview at Stanford. Almost exactly ten years ago."

They paused by the peanut man, who was dozing on a stool, arms folded across his chest.

"From what little I saw, it looked nice."

"Yeah," she said. "It is." She pulled him along. "Chilly and foggy sometimes. But all in all, a good place to live."

CHAPTER 54: THE UNFULFILLED WISH OF HERNÁN CORTÉS

"*Hoy es miércoles?*" Is it Wednesday?

That is the first thing Jerónimo de Aguilar asked his compatriots on the beach at Cozumel in late February of the year of his Lord 1519. The chronicler Bernal Díaz, in *La*

Historia Verdadera de la Conquista de la Nueva España, describes the scene.

Some of the soldiers and sailors accompanying Hernán Cortés stood on the strand and watched a massive Maya canoe as its paddlers propelled it from the mainland toward the island where the Spaniards had made a landfall and their first contact with the inhabitants.

When the vessel touched shore, a long-haired lean swarthy man in a tattered tunic of rough cotton, the garment of a slave, jumped out. He fell to his knees in the sand. Clasping his hands before him, his face turned heavenward, he cried: "Praise be to God and the blessed Virgin of Seville." His Spanish was clumsy and odd sounding.

Then Aguilar rose and embraced Andrés de Tapia, one of Cortés' captains. He asked him if it was Wednesday.

Aguilar was being reunited with his brothers after eight years of captivity among a people so alien to his upbringing as to be perceived by him as only peripherally human. He had been lost and forsaken among barbaric idolatrous heathen, subjected to slavery, abuse and privation during the prime years of his manhood. At the moment of his deliverance, he inquires as to the day of the week.

What could be less important?

Wait.

Díaz describes Aguilar. He says he wore an old sandal on one foot, with the other sandal tied to his belt. Perhaps having one foot bare made paddling more comfortable. We are not told. But also tied up in his cloak is what turned out to be a tattered breviary, the book of Psalms and prayers to be recited daily by the devout, especially by priests and nuns and seminarians.

During eight years of enslavement, penury and tribulation, Aguilar had not lost his prayer book and had complied with a daily communion with his God. He wanted to be assured, before anything else transpired, that he had remained on track throughout his ordeal, that he had not been astray. The daily prayer book was the compass of his soul.

What is known about Aguilar and his castaway companion Gonzalo Guerrero comes mostly from Díaz and from Diego de Landa, a Franciscan friar, later bishop, who spent most of the middle decades of the 16th century in Yucatán administering clerical concerns and taking notes on the region's history and culture. In 1566, he wrote *Relación de las cosas de Yucatán.*

Aguilar was a lay missionary from Ecija who, like hundreds of others, traveled to the New World in the decades following its "discovery" by Europeans to aid in the mission of converting savages to the One True Faith. He was, for his time, a learned man alongside the mostly illiterate soldiers and mariners and ruffians accompanying the captains and hidalgos–younger-sibling noblemen not adequately provided for in Spain–to the lands of wonder and peril across the ocean sea.

Aguilar was a religious scholar. But he also was drawn by the prospect of documenting the fabulous way of life of the dark, feather-robed heathens he had heard about from those who'd returned from the far side of the world.

Guerrero was concerned only with conquest and riches. He did not set out to bestow enlightenment or learn anything, but only to obtain his share of treasure from virgin lands.

What today is Mexico had not yet been set foot upon by Spaniards when both men left Spain in the first years of the 16th century. They would have been bound for either Santo Domingo or Cuba, where the crown had established its bureaucratic and military and commercial beachheads. As it was, they both came to travel from the greater Antillean islands to Panama, to the fledgling settlement at Darien, where they, like all the recent arrivals, got caught up in intrigue between Vasco Nuñez de Balboa and Diego de Nicueza.

In 1511 they set sail for Santo Domingo in a caravel under the command of Captain Francisco Valdivia, who intended to make an accounting of the dissension at Darien and seek authority to resolve the dispute. But the vessel foundered and broke up on the Víboras shoals south of Jamaica.

Twenty men, including Valdivia, and three women who had been passengers on the caravel cast themselves adrift in a boat without sail. They spent 13 days at sea. Half of the company died by the time they washed up on the shores of Yucatán.

Landa says the survivors fell into the hands of "a bad cacique," or chief, and that Valdivia and several others were immediately sacrificed to Maya gods and their bodies partaken of in cannibalistic ceremony.

All but two succumbed in the following months to disease, despair or the shaman's obsidian blade, a broad black dagger as sharp as a scalpel that was pushed through the rib cage just below the left nipple as the victim was held face up over a stone by four priests. The main celebrant pried open the cavity and reached in to rip from its moorings the beating heart and hold it aloft to spew the blood it contained when so abruptly plucked from its niche.

Aguilar and Guerrero escaped the domain of this chief. The former became the property of another cacique, described as more merciful, in the Yucatec city-state of Tulúm. There he spent the next eight years gathering firewood, drawing water, tending bees and cultivating corn, squash and beans for his master.

Guerrero made his way further south, to Chetumal, where he entered the military service of a local autocrat named Nachan Can. The strange bearded pale man proved such a brave and able fighter and tactician that he rose to the rank of commander of Nachan Can's forces.

Landa writes: "He conquered his master's enemies many times. He taught the Indians to fight, showing them how to make barricades and bastions. In this way, and by living as an Indian, he gained a great reputation and married a woman of high quality, by whom he had children...He decorated his body, let his hair grow, pierced his ears to wear rings like the Indians, and is believed to have become an idol-worshipper."

When Cortés landed on Cozumel with his expedition of eleven ships and 500 men, he and his captains were mystified to hear some of the natives greet them with what sounded like the word "Castilian." Through his Maya interpreter, who had been given the name Melchior during his service to captains Francisco Hernandez de Córdoba and Juan de Grijalva during their brief water-drawing landfalls inYucatan in 1517 and 1518, Cortés learned there were two light-skinned hirsute men living to the south.

He dispatched Indian emissaries with a letter and strings of glass beads to ransom the men. Aguilar's freedom was thus purchased. Before joining the Spaniards in Cozumel, he walked south along the broad flat white gravel trade road to Chetumal.

He found Guerrero, barely recognizable, outside his house playing with his children. Guerrero's wife sat on a mat on the ground weaving a basket of reeds.

Díaz reports that, after reading Cortés' letter, Gonzalo said: 'Brother Aguilar, I am married and have three children, and they look on me here as a Cacique, and a captain in time of war. Go, and God's blessing be with you. But my face is tattooed and my ears are pierced. What would the Spaniards say if they saw me like this? And look how handsome these children of mine are! Please give me some of those beads you have brought, and I will tell them that my brothers have sent them from my own country.'

According to the chronicler, "Gonzalo's Indian wife spoke to Aguilar very angrily in her own language: 'Why has this slave come here to call my husband away? Off with you, and let us have no more of your talk.' Then Aguilar spoke to Gonzalo again, reminding him that he was a Christian and should not destroy his soul for the sake of an Indian woman. Besides, if he did not wish to desert his wife and children, he could take them with him. But neither words nor warnings could persuade Gonzalo to come."

So Aguilar returned to the north, disappointed at his failure to bring Guerrero with him but overjoyed at his own rescue. Díaz describes his first interview with Cortés, to whom Aguilar was taken immediately upon his arrival on the Cozumel shore: "Aguilar thanked God for his deliverance, and Cortés promised that he would be well looked after and compensated. He then asked him about the country and the towns. Aguilar answered that, having been a slave, he only knew about hewing wood and drawing water and working in the maize-fields, and that he had only once made a journey of some twelve miles when he was sent with a load, under which he had collapsed, for it was heavier than he could carry. He understood, however, that there were many towns. When questioned about Gonzalo Guerrero, he said that he was married and had three children, that he was tattooed, and that his ears and lower lip were pierced, that he was a native of Palos, and that the Indians considered him very brave. Aguilar also related how a little more than a year earlier, when a captain and three ships arrived at Cape Catoche–this must have been our expedition under Francisco Hernandez de Cordoba–it had been at Guerrero's suggestion that the Indians had attacked them.

"When Cortes heard this he exclaimed: `I wish I could get my hands on him. For it will never do to leave him here.'"

Jeronimo de Aguilar accompanied Cortes and his soldiers throughout the horrific two-and-a-half year campaign that culminated in the capture and murder of Cuautehemoc and the destruction of Tenochtitlán. His skill as translator and interpreter of local culture and custom made him, after Cortés himself, the most indispensable member of the expedition. He eventually returned to Spain, made his way home, and died years later among his own people.

Guerrero spent the next 17 years demonstrating the perspicacity of Cortés' appraisal. With his knowledge of the invaders' tactics and weapons, he helped organize Maya resistance from Chetumal far southward, and was finally killed, on August 13, 1536, in the Gulf of Honduras off modern-day Saraguama, by the blast of a blunderbuss in combat against his estranged kin.

CHAPTER 55: CICADAS CRYING

The day after April, Juan and their baby departed for California, Joe Guinness finally tracked down Professor Mario Barahona, the old man who'd sent Chepe the letter about Gonzalo Guerrero. He called to introduce himself and ask if he might visit. The man's voice on the phone sounded like that of an elderly woman, halting and tremulous. But it took him only a brief pause to recall his letter to Chepe, despite it having been written two years earlier, and to get straight Joe's connection to the Mexican scholar. Barahona told Joe he was not in good health, but that nevertheless he would be delighted to meet him, and they set a mid-morning appointment for the following day.

The historian lived in the capital near the acre-large map of Guatemala in relief. The first time Joe went up to the city to see him, a few dozen schoolchildren were there on a field trip. The kids skipped or meandered along the raised pathways around the representation of their nation, happy black-haired children, the boys in navy blue pants and the girls in maroon-plaid skirts, all of them wearing white shirts. Laughter floated over their miniature country, and they pointed to rural parts, to the west and south and east of the capital, to say that was where their parents were from, or their *abuelitos*.

Barahona's neighborhood was one of the capital's few quarters with trees along the streets. The homes, once fine but most now bordering on ruin, had gardens behind their high walls or iron grate fences. Professor Barahona's house was a three-story manse with a broad balcony across the facade on the second floor. It was about 80 years old–like the professor–and in need of repair, though not decrepit. Joe rang at the gate on the sidewalk and waited a few minutes before he was buzzed through, without any query on the intercom. Just as he was about to tap the heavy brass knocker, the large door opened to reveal a short old man leaning on two canes, one in each hand.

"Pase Usted," he said, taking a step back and switching the cane in his right hand to his left, which now perched atop two, in order to offer the visitor his hand. His fingers were bony and dry and the grasp was firm.

Joe introduced himself again and the elderly man responded, "Very kind of you to come," in English-accented English. The voice was somewhat high-pitched, but less so than it had seemed on the telephone, when he had spoken only Spanish. Now it did not sound feminine, or frail, though the individual from whom it emanated appeared liable to be toppled if a stiff breeze rushed through the doorway. The professor shuffled a step forward to close the door.

The first thing the old man said, continuing in his British English, after they had sat down in two overstuffed chairs placed beside a solid *caoba* coffee table, was, "I'm glad you've come, because in a few months I'll be dead."

He explained that he had been diagnosed with lung cancer and had ruled out both an operation and chemotherapy. Not that, he said, any of the doctors had made much of effort to persuade him that that was the proper route.

"What would be the point?" he asked. "At my age? I'm ready to go. The only thing I told the doctor was not to get stingy with the morphine when the pain gets worse."

The Mestizo thing he had mentioned in the letter to Chepe, about Guerrero being the progenitor of La Raza was something Barahona embodied as a perfect archetype. His face, even at the age of 84, was extraordinarily handsome. It at first seemed mostly Indian, the color of a brick paver, with a large long aquiline nose in the center. The face too was long, with a tapering but still strong chin and a high forehead. The cheekbones were prominent and scored vertically with longer rays of the deep crows' feet. But his eyes were bluish-gray and round–lacking even the slightest epicanthic fold–and his full head of silver hair was wavy rather than straight. On this day of the men's first meeting, the Guatemalan had about a three-day growth of stubble, sparse on the cheeks and along the jaw line, but dense on the upper lip and chin. The moustache was dark, but the chin whiskers were gray.

Joe would find over the course of this and two subsequent visits over the next week that despite his illness, Barahona was remarkably vigorous mentally. His mobility was curtailed, limited to shuffling around with his canes. He appreciated a hand getting out of a chair. Most of the time he was alone at the house, but his unmarried grand-daughter, a teacher at a downtown high-school, lived there too. She was on hand only in the early morning and evening.

He coughed some, and sometimes was caught short of breath while talking. But after a pause he would resume the conversation.

During their first meeting, which lasted about two hours, the two men talked mostly about the dig in Tres Ceibas, and Joe's work years earlier in Mexico and El Salvador, although the American spared him the details of the problems he'd had in that smaller country to the southeast. Joe told him about Chepe, whose article in Raices the elder man recalled in detail. They talked about Barahona's life and work, the eight years he'd spent at Cambridge in the 1950s, and only got around to mentioning Gonzalo Guerrero and Jeronimo de Aguilar shortly before Joe took his leave.

When leaving that first time, Joe reverted momentarily to Spanish and used the words *"ligeramente obsesionado"* to describe the years-long fascination he had regarding the two shipwrecked Spaniards.

"I don't like light beer or light cream cheese or any of *las mierdas* light they've come out with these days," Barahona had responded.. "But I suppose if you're going to have an obsession, it might be better that it be light."

The second time Joe went to Guate to see him it was late afternoon. The first thing they did was have an espresso the professor made with an Italian machine on the kitchen counter. When he'd prepared the coffee and served it in gray and blue demitasses at the kitchen table, he shuffled back to a cabinet beside the refrigerator and took from it a leather pouch. He brought that over to the table and extracted from it a round bottle of Guatemala's finest rum, a brown *añejo* from Zacapa, and poured some into both of the cups. The two men sat and sipped.

When they finished, Barahona moved the cups and saucers and rum bottle to the end of the table to make room and rose, pressing himself up with the aid of the tabletop.

"I've got something you'll want to see," he said.

He came back with a leather briefcase and set it on the table.

"They seem such a perfect dichotomy," he said. "One intrepid, audacious, violent. Unbound by the conventions that up to a certain point had ruled his life. Guerrero is the personification of the idea that life is nothing if it is not change. And adaptation. And daring. At the other extreme is Aguilar; an incarnation of the will to conserve, to cling to the familiar idea of one's self. To accept one's lot more or less complacently. Perhaps with faith or resignation or hope, I don't know, but to accept it without really challenging fate.

"I don't know," he said again. He'd been looking at the briefcase as he spoke, unfastening the straps from the buckles. Then he looked at Joe.

"One could be tempted to believe these two men personify two ways of being. Two ways of living life."

Joe felt strange. Like he was listening to himself.

"Mutually exclusive ways of living?" the American asked.

Barahona's hands rested on the briefcase, now lying flat and open, its flap with the straps extended. "You may be surprised by this," he said. He reached into the case and took out a sort of book much like the codices Joe had seen and pored over at the *Museo de Antropología* in Mexico. This one was of a fine deerskin parchment cut in a seven-inch wide strip and folded back upon itself several times. It gave off a musty but pleasant smell.

"The parchment is delicate and should be handled as little as possible," the Guatemalan said. "I have the transcriptions here on paper, and that is what you will want to copy and read and work from. But I want you to at least see the original writing."

The pages folded open and Joe rose from his chair as his host extended the strip to its full length of about four feet. Barely breathing, the visitor leaned over to examine it. It was covered with lines of a scratchy but legible script.

The writing was divided into blocks. Joe's eyes fell first on the middle portion of the second block and he began to read out loud, slowly, like a child sounding out syllables from a primer:

"Una luna más, el zacate dorado aguanta"
"One moon more moon, the golden grass holds out"

He looked at the professor.

"They are poems," Barahona said. "Poems of love. Four of them. And at the end a few sentences intended as a sort of testament. But what he was most concerned about writing down was the poetic expression of romantic love for Sky, his wife and the mother of the three children he left behind in Chetumal when he led an expedition to the south to fight the Spaniards. The campaign in which he perished."

Barahona reached into the case again and pulled out a manila folder. He handed it to Joe.

"Here you can read them much more easily. I'm quite sure I have them transcribed precisely. I reproduced the texts letter for letter, with errors of spelling intact. I find them lovely. Simple and astonishingly modern-seeming, which I suppose goes to prove that the heart's longing has a language with little regard for time."

Joe set the folder aside and bent again over the parchment and read the three lines at the top of the document. "These verses are dedicated to my beloved wife Lady Ichin, which in Castilian is the Firmament, and who is aptly named because she, for me, is Heaven."

Joe sat back down and opened the folder.

What he had just read on the parchment was written in typescript on the first page. He set that aside and began to read the words on the second page.

April and the Gardener

Días de calor y florez
Días de chicharras
Pronto muere Cristo de nuevo
Dudo que resucite esta vez
Salvo que
Salvo que le amamantes tu
Que le des de beber
De tu seno perfecto

Los palos se tapan con mantillas
De encaje rosado y blanco
Delicado encaje morado
Porque no se callan
Estos vichos chillones
El coro constante, "Eechiiin, eechiin."
Que aprendan, al menos,
Tu nombre cabal.

Ya vendrá el agua
Una luna más
El zacate dorado aguanta
Resisten los amates, las palmeras
El sol despiadado
El polvo revuelto, el viento seco.
Aguanta mi alma también
Hasta que sueltes la lluvia

(Days of heat and flowers
Days of cicadas
Soon Christ dies again

I doubt he will resurrect this time.
Unless
Unless you suckle him
Give him to drink
From your perfect breast

The trees put on shawls
Of pink and white lace
Delicate purple lace
Will they not be still
These wailing bugs
The constant chorus, "Eechiiin, eechiiin."
Let them at least learn
Your name as it is.

The water will come soon
One moon more
The golden grass holds out
The amate trees and palms resist
The pitiless sun
Whirling dust, the dry wind
Like them, my soul holds on
Until you let loose the rain.)

Joe was in a state of agitation. He was moved by the poem, obviously composed at the end of the dry season during the dusty hot weeks prior to the Christian calendar's Easter, when jacarandas and *siemprevivas* and bride's bouquet and *paloblancos* burst with flower and the trill of cicadas fills the air. Or by the combination of the poem itself, its sentiment, and the knowledge that it had been written 450 years earlier by a man he'd spent so much time imagining. A man he'd never thought of as a poet.

The next poem described a rainbow after an out-of-season shower, and how he, Gonzalo Guerrero, had been stunned by the sight of it and how he imagined its point of origin, where it touched the earth and how, without her knowing it, the rainbow he was seeing was issuing from her head of black hair, "all the trapped colors of earth's blackness escaping to paint a bridge of light."

The third one Guerrero had provided a title for: *Arrullo* (Lullaby). In it he said he would be his wife's lullaby, that his hand resting on her belly–he used the word *vientre* (womb)–would put her soul at peace, calm her breathing and permit her deep sleep.

> *Te cantaré en vos bajisima*
> *Que ni sabrás si me oyes o no*
> *La canción susurrada.*

> I will sing to you in such a quiet voice
> That you'll not even know if you hear or not
> The whispered song.

He urges her to sleep and "to dream of flying, of losing yourself in a cascade of wind beyond the heights of nothingness." He will allow nothing to wake her, "neither lightning nor earthquake."

After a while, the two scholars drank another coffee with rum.

They met once more, the following week.

Joe Guinness was Professor Barahona's last new acquaintance. One evening a month after he returned to Ithaca, the American called his home in Guatemala City and Sarita, the grand-daughter, answered. She told him the professor had passed away that morning.

CHAPTER 56: THE BREATH TO PROCLAIM HIS GOODNESS

Juan was with Keiko in the kitchen of April's Fillmore District apartment, a two-bedroom third floor walkup. The baby, whose age they figured at about five months, sat partially propped in a high-chair and was playing with water from a lidded plastic cup. The game was to pour some out and spread it over the tray with her hand, slapping occasionally to splash herself.

It was a Sunday afternoon. Juan was listening to the broadcast of a Giants game while he prepared a snack for himself and April and a puree of boiled carrots and squash for their daughter. He took a jar of anchovy filets in olive oil from the cupboard and set it on the table. He put two slices of pumpernickel in the toaster and took the butter from the refrigerator and cut thin slices from the stick. While the bread toasted he blended the vegetables and a little butter in the compact German machine. It was an inter-league game. The Mariners were murdering the home team, seven to zip in the fourth inning. Ken Griffey, Jr. had hit a homer and a 3-ribbie triple.

Juan buttered the toast and cut it into strips and placed a filet on each butter-soaked dark strip. He'd given Keiko four or five spoonfuls of mustard-colored mush when April called from the living room: "Juan! Quick! Come here!"

He bolted. Keiko started to cry before he reached the kitchen door. Juan found April on her exercise mat before the TV. She'd been doing her stretching while listening to, half-watching the Univision news program.

April had adopted the habit of watching the news in Spanish. She'd asked Juan to speak at least some Spanish with her around the house, to help her maintain the fluency she'd achieved in Antigua. But he hardly ever did. He said he was enjoying speaking English again. Even so, he spoke Spanish to Keiko most of the time.

April sometimes wondered if this child would end up confused, linguistically. The baby's namesake grandmother took care of her three mornings a week and spoke to her in Japanese. Upon hearing this, April had reminded the elder Keiko, who was aware of the child's provenance, that the girl had no Japanese blood.

"So? She's still my grand-daughter. And who knows? Japanese might come in handy some day."

April was sitting on the mat hugging her knees, her attention fixed on the tube. The woman newscaster was talking about a meeting in Italy between Bob Dylan and the Pope. April turned to him and, speaking very fast, said: "She said the special report–in the closing segment–is on a Guatemalan soldier from nearly 20 years ago. And that he talks about a massacre he took part in that was directed by, I swear this is what she said, 'The Gelded Tiger of Chajul.' That's what *'capado'* means, right? That's the expression she used, *'El Tigre Capado de Chajul.'"*

Juan heard what April said but was more concerned with Keiko's protest at having been so abruptly deserted in the middle of eating. He went back to the kitchen, lifted her from the chair and carried her, cooing and kissing her smooth chubby wet salty cheek, into the living room.

April was shuffling through a stack of videotapes. "What can I tape over here?" she asked out loud. "Here's Godfather Part Two off HBO. We didn't even get it all. We'll just rent it."

She inserted the cartridge and hit the record button. The commercial, for a European brand of automobile tire, showed a creamy pink robust tranquil baby only a bit older than Keiko sitting naked in the middle of a tire as if it were a sort of life preserver. The soundtrack provided revving engine noise and shifting gears suggesting a spin along a winding mountain road. The infant was unperturbed. He didn't blink once.

Then the anchorwoman, a chestnut-haired beauty with a generic New World accent, introduced the in-depth piece.

"Horacio Mam Menendez says he was born again five years ago in the misty heights of his native mountains of western Guatemala. With a Bible in his hand and a canvas pack on his back, he has spent the past half-decade as an itinerant preacher spreading what he calls the Good News about Jesus Christ to his highland Maya compatriots. He lives the life of an ascetic, inspired, he says, by John the

Baptist and motivated by the hope that the deprivations he endures, with only a wool poncho to cloak him night and day, will serve in God's eyes as penance for past sins."

The scene switched to Guatemala City, the *plaza mayor* in the heart of downtown, bordered on one side by the verdigris Presidential Palace and another by the 18th-century Cathedral. The camera panned the facade of the palace, then closed in on a pair of traditionally garbed Maya women walking across the square. It came to rest on the reporter, a lean young dark-haired man in a suit jacket the sleeves of which were too short standing before the large circular fountain in the plaza's center.

"Three months ago, retired Army colonel Abelardo Alvarez was gravely wounded–hospital sources only recently confirmed he was castrated by a sniper's bullet–in an assassination attempt. The attack, coming amid the final stage of negotiations to end a civil war that soaked the Maya highlands in blood for decades, raised concern about prospects for reconciliation in a society still grievously divided by issues of class and race.

"No group claimed responsibility for the shooting. But new testimony, a first-person account by a participant in an atrocity directed by Alvarez while a lieutenant 17 years ago, makes clear that the officer, known as *El Tigre de Chajul,* was not lacking in enemies.

"Here with me is Horacio Mam, former private in the Guatemalan army, currently an Evangelical preacher. Last week he presented himself before the Truth Commission established by the Peace Accords. To these five people assigned the task of clarifying at least some of the many crimes committed in the war, he told his story. It is a story of Alvarez, his soldiers and a small Ixil Maya village one early morning in February 1979."

The camera widened its angle to take in Mam, who was standing beside the low basin wall around *la fuente.*

The preacher's face was gaunt and deeply creased, topped by a hand-made coarse wool cap with dangling earflaps. Sparse black whiskers on his upper lip and the point of his chin had grown into a wispy goatee that shifted in the breeze. He grasped in his left hand a crude knobby stave.

For the next two minutes he told the story of what happened in the nameless hamlet half his life ago. He told it calmly with great detail.

At the end he said: "I myself raped two women. I did not kill them. They were killed by others. But that does not mitigate my crime. I am guilty and shall forever be so. If there is to be a trial for this abomination we visited on our brothers and sisters, I place myself at the disposition of the judiciary. Any sentence issued against me, however harsh, is justified.

"In any case, I intend to live the rest of my days, whether in prison or out, in poverty and in the same celibacy with which Lieutenant Alvarez has been chastised, asking the Lord for nothing more than the breath I will use to proclaim his goodness and glory."

When he finished and the program ended, April hit the Stop button on the VCR and turned off the television.

"Sorry, *corazón*," she said to Juan as she sat back down on her pad. "I have to cut out part of your rap to make room for this. There's nothing like having been there."

CHAPTER 57: UNFORGETTABLE

Rosario "Chayo" Zelaya, *viuda* de Cano, didn't know what to do about the matter of where she should sleep.

For the previous eight years, since moving to Seattle and into the home of her younger daughter, Marta, she had shared a bedroom with her grand-daughter Mari. Chayo loved that arrangement. She thanked God every night for Marta and Mari and for her bald *yerno* Willie, who grumbled occasionally when he thought she was out of earshot, but who for the most part was the embodiment of patience and respect for his mother-in-law.

Mari always had seemed happy to have her grandmother rooming with her. To listen, at night before going to sleep, to *abuelita's* stories like the one about the little *zoplilote* vulture who stuck flower petals to himself with honey to make himself beautiful as a quetzal, and who almost drowned because of it. And of *el cipitillo*, the mischievous man-child with his bottom half on backwards, so that when he dropped his pants his *culito* was there below his belly. *Abuela* would sing songs in Spanish that would make Mari feel sleepy. Until she was ten, the girl had the habit of slipping from her own bed in the hour before dawn to pad dreamily across the rug. She would nudge her grandmother and crawl in. For years, the two woke up together almost every day.

But Mari had turned 13. Her breasts now bulged, her hips were no longer those of a child. She suddenly had turned awkward and un-pretty–though Chayo knew that would not last–grace having deserted the new body like an unfaithful friend. Chayo wanted Mari to have her own room, like her brother Robi down the hall. The grandmother had raised the subject the previous evening.

"Dearest, you need this room to yourself now that you're a young woman. I'm in the way."

"That's not true, *abuela*." Mari had looked up from where, busy with homework, she sat at a desk beneath the window separating the two single beds.

But the poor thing, *tan dulce*. You could see it in her eyes, thought Chayo as she went about her morning routine. She was home alone–in the bigger and nicer house they'd moved into a year ago–as she was for an hour every morning after the kids left for school, Marta to her job at the Post Office and William to the auto body shop.

She relished this time. She used it to have a second cup of coffee and read the newspaper, clear the table and wash the breakfast dishes, straighten up the bedrooms and make the beds, so that when first Marta, then Mari arrived in the afternoon (Robi, an athlete, didn't get home until right before dinner), they would find the house neat and clean. Going about her chores, Chayo would hum or sing.

This morning she'd put on Luis Miguel's bolero CD. Since learning to read–in evening literacy classes 20 years earlier in L.A.–Chayo had been a fan of *Gente,* a weekly published in Mexico and for sale at even the gringo newsstands. She knew all about Luismi. What a beautiful voice he had, and what a fine man he had become. Whoever would have thought a Caribbean teen-idol, *tan menudito y baboso*, would have turned out so handsome and strong?

These ruminations on Luis Miguel, or the words of the love songs he was singing, turned into a reverie this May morning as she made first her own then her granddaughter's bed.   The death of her elder daughter had been a harsh blow, that was true. So much more painful than the loss of her husband. For several months after Soledad was killed and Juan disappeared, Chayo had lost the desire to go on living. But she had been lifted up by the daughter who remained. Marta and Willie had carried her away from that dry smoggy city, unbearable in its reminders of how things had been, to this green and flowery place.

Mari's flannel pajamas, beige lions and giraffes on a red background, lay at the foot of her bed. The top was inside out, as it was every day, from the way she peeled it off over her head. Chayo picked up the jersey. She reached her right hand into a sleeve and pulled it back out, then did the same with the other sleeve. She spread the soft shirt, which seemed still warm from Mari's body, on the bed. She folded it. Every morning without fail this reaching into the empty space that the girl's form had filled during the night summed up for Chayo the beauty of what it was she'd lost and at the same time the beauty of what she had still.

Though the sky was blue when she opened the front door to leave, she withdrew a yellow umbrella from the stand on the porch and stepped out with it hooked over her arm, heading off for the house of Mr. Singer, the widowed retired physician for whom she cooked and kept house. The disc's final bolero remained stuck in her head. She walked along, singing the verses she knew and humming through the rest.

"He besado otras bocas buscando nuevas ansiedades," she sang.

"Otros brazos extraños me estrechan llenos de ilusión
"Pero solo consiguen hacerme recordar los tuyos
"Que inolvidablemente vivirán en mí ..."

Her steps marked the tempo, to which she provided both the lead and the female chorus, cooing, *"In-ol-vi-da-ble."* After a couple minutes of this, she stopped and leaned forward to rest her hands just above her knees and laugh, mostly at herself.

She didn't notice the man walking behind her as he drew nearer.

He'd been waiting in a rented car across the street and a bit down from the house. When he saw her leave, he got out, lifting the infant who'd been sitting in his lap to the crook of his left arm. He closed the door softly and crossed the street and walked about 20 yards behind the singing woman. He kept that distance for the first block, then began closing it.

He still didn't know what he was going to say.

The baby began to cry.

Chayo stopped and turned around and said reflexively, "*Pobrecita.*" She was looking at the whimpering child and not at the man. She took a step in the direction from which she'd come, toward them both and said in her own language, her eyes still fixed on the baby, "*Que es lo que tiene esta hermosa criatura que la hace llorar?*"

"It's just that she wants to meet her *bisabuela,* is all," said the man.

The voice, though long unheard, was one Chayo knew as well as her own, and she shifted her sight to regard the man.

About the author

Douglas Grant Mine is a former foreign correspondent (Argentina, Central America) and current raconteur of stories that are true, made up or commingled. Dogwalker, potwasher and gleaner in the chaff, he is a longtime non-matriculating student of life and table fare in *centroitalia*.

Also by DGM

Champions of the World, Simon&Schuster, NY, NY 1988

Praise for Champions of the World:

"*Champions of the World* is history breathed to life with chilling precision and insight." Bill Montalbano, Los Angeles Times

"A powerful contribution to the literature of political experience." Bob Shacochis, finalist National Book Award

"A moving novel that any person concerned with recent history in Latin America should read." Hiber Conteris, winner of the Premio Casa de las Americas.

ACKNOWLEDGMENTS

My heartfelt thanks to Charles Simpson and Stephen Philp for their decades of encouragement as readers of my work and as *amigos de alma*. In the same vein, to Mark DeBrito, José Gelabert and Fernando Lugo. I'm grateful for Irene Vilar's early enthusiasm and red pencil. Thank you to TWBS for good advice and for helping to push the manuscript across the finish line. I also want to acknowledge the anonymous editor at McSweeney's who told me: "So many of us here read and loved this book," because those kind words proved I was not deluded in believing it was indeed quite good.

Of course the most abundant share of my gratitude goes to Nicoletta, without whom this book, like many other things I hold dear, would not exist.